MY BEBRIS
Bebris, Carrie.
The intrigue at Highbury, or,
Emma's match /

MAR   2010

w2/11 w1/14 w5/17

The
Intrigue at Highbury

Other Mr. & Mrs. Darcy Mysteries by Carrie Bebris

The
Intrigue at Highbury

OR, EMMA'S MATCH

A Mr. & Mrs. Darcy Mystery

Carrie Bebris

A TOM DOHERTY ASSOCIATES BOOK

NEW YORK

THE INTRIGUE AT HIGHBURY

Copyright © 2010 by Carrie Bebris

A Tor Book
Published by Tom Doherty Associates, LLC
175 Fifth Avenue
New York, NY 10010

www.tor-forge.com

Tor® is a registered trademark of Tom Doherty Associates, LLC.

Library of Congress Cataloging-in-Publication Data

Bebris, Carrie.
    The intrigue at Highbury, or, Emma's match : [a Mr. & Mrs. Darcy Mystery] / Carrie Bebris. — 1st ed.
        p. cm.
    "A Tom Doherty Associates book."
    ISBN 978-0-7653-1848-0
  1. Bennet, Elizabeth (Fictitious character)—Fiction.   2. Darcy, Fitzwilliam (Fictitious character)—Fiction.   3. Married people—Fiction.   4. Murder—Investigation—Fiction.   5. England—Fiction.   I. Title.   II. Title: Intrigue at Highbury. III. Title: Emma's match.
    PS3602.E267I48 2010
    813'.6—dc22

                                                                2009040697

First Edition: March 2010

Printed in the United States of America

0   9   8   7   6   5   4   3   2   1

To Anne Klemm
and
Brian M. Thomsen

Acknowledgments

A book is seldom the product of a single individual. And while all books present challenges during the gestational process, this one had more than the usual number, and I am grateful to the many individuals who supported me in ways large and small during its creation.

First, I thank my family. Living with a writer is no easy thing, and I appreciate their patience, understanding, and sacrifices that granted me the time and space to write. My father, especially, took on several responsibilities at various points that further freed me to withdraw to the world of Highbury.

The value of a good editor cannot be overstated, and I have been blessed with more than one. Brian M. Thomsen believed in the Mr. & Mrs. Darcy series from the start, and helped me shape it as the Darcys' adventures continued in successive books. His favorite Jane Austen novel was *Emma,* the story on which *The Intrigue at Highbury* is based, and he very much looked forward to this novel. Unfortunately, while I was writing the manuscript, Brian passed away. I miss not only his editorial guidance but also his friendship. Farewell, Brian, and thank you.

Acknowledgments

The Darcys and I are now under the editorial direction of Kristin Sevick, who is a joy to work with and whose fresh perspective is a boon. Kristin's skill, enthusiasm, and humor helped make the transition as smooth as any such change could be. I am very grateful to have landed in her hands and look forward to continuing our new relationship.

My longtime friend Anne Klemm has provided assistance throughout the life of the series, from helping me refine premises and plots to accompanying me on research trips (adventures of their own!) to offering criticism of early drafts. While I have always appreciated her help, with this book I am particularly grateful for her continued support.

Thanks also to my agent, Irene Goodman, for her wisdom and sound advice; to artist Teresa Fasolino for another beautiful cover painting; to Dot Lin for her enthusiastic promotion of the series; and to fellow writers Mary Holmes, Pamela Johnson, Victoria Hinshaw, and Sharon Short for their creative encouragement and friendship.

Once again, I wish to recognize the Jane Austen Society of North America, particularly those members—friends—who have generously shared their specialized knowledge of Regency life. I am indebted to Martha Caprarotta for her seamstress expertise and to Dr. Cheryl Kinney for information about poison and nineteenth-century postmortem practices.

Finally, I thank you, my readers—for your notes and e-mails, for your interest in the series, and, most of all, for wanting, like me, to enjoy the Darcys' company awhile longer.

"I do believe . . . this is the most troublesome parish that ever was."

—*Mrs. Elton,* Emma

The
Intrigue at Highbury

Prologue

A young lady who faints, must be recovered; questions must be answered, and surprises explained.

—Emma

*T*he woman appeared in the road ahead, seemingly out of nowhere. In the twilight and the distance, her features were indistinct, save for the pale hair that tumbled about her shoulders. Were it not for the white dress that caught the light of the rising moon, the coachman might not have seen her at all. As it was, the crescent struggling for dominance against temperamental autumn clouds barely illuminated the figure, lending her such an ethereal cast that she might have been mistaken for an apparition, one left wandering the woods two nights after All Souls' Day had released her fellow spirits from their suffering.

Her cry, however, was unmistakably human.

It pierced the darkness, overpowered the rattle of harnesses and thud of horses' hooves, penetrated the carriage walls to startle Elizabeth Darcy from the slumber into which she had just drifted.

She opened her eyes and instinctively looked toward her husband. So little light reached the inside of the coach that she could barely distinguish his silhouette. Disoriented from having wakened so abruptly in an unfamiliar place, her next thoughts went to their infant daughter. Her anxiety eased momentarily when she recalled that Lily-Anne was safe in their London townhouse with Darcy's sister, but her heart raced as the coachman, Jeffrey, brought the horses to a stop.

"There's a woman ahead, sir," said Jeffrey. Though the coachman remained seated, the body of the carriage rocked slightly as the groom disembarked to take hold of the lead pair of horses. "Coming towards us," Jeffrey continued. "Looks like she's limping."

"Is she alone?" Mr. Darcy asked.

"Yes, sir."

Darcy pressed his wife's hand. "Remain here."

He quit the carriage. The light that had illuminated their path gradually receded, indicating that Darcy had removed the lantern from the front of the vehicle and carried it with him. The rear lantern remained, so the carriage was not left in total darkness.

"Oh, a gentleman!" Elizabeth heard the stranger exclaim. "Thank goodness! Can you help me, sir?"

"What is the trouble?"

The light diminished further. In the increased darkness, still disoriented by sleep, Elizabeth tried to gain her bearings.

They were traveling to Sussex, she reminded herself, to visit Darcy's cousins Colonel and Anne Fitzwilliam. The newlyweds had recently taken possession of Brierwood, a property Anne's mother had settled upon her following her marriage, and the Darcys were to be the couple's first guests. The letter of invitation from Anne had included a confidential admission that had delighted Elizabeth and inspired them to bring a family heirloom: a set of christening clothes. The priceless garments had been passed down through generations of Darcy's maternal line, and all looked forward to the newest member of the family wearing them within the year. They also brought another gift for Anne, a gold signet ring worn by Darcy's late mother, the beloved aunt for whom Anne had been named.

Elizabeth was starting to doubt, however, whether they would ever arrive to present the gifts. The journey south from Derbyshire to London had been plagued by so many delays that they had left Lily-Anne behind with Darcy's sister, Georgiana, to rest from the rigors of travel before continuing on. It had been a fortuitous decision, as a loose wheel had slowed their progress still more after leaving town. Now, instead of reaching Brierwood today as planned, they found themselves only as far as Surrey. They intended to stop for the night in the next village, Highbury, where they understood a decent inn could be found. When they realized they would be further delayed, the Darcys had sent their personal servants and the heaviest luggage ahead by public coach to meet them at the inn. They traveled with only the small chest containing the ring and baptismal gown.

Elizabeth looked forward to reaching the inn, where she knew her maid would have made their room as comfortable as possible. At present, however, she was decidedly uncomfortable. Though she pulled her mantle about her more tightly, it was not the chill that distressed her, but the darkness. They had thought to be in Highbury well before sunset. It was risky to travel at night—not only could roads hold obstacles difficult for horses and drivers to see, but all manner of disreputable individuals might roam them. Now that she was more awake, this unexpected stop filled her with uneasiness.

She drew aside the curtain covering the window of the carriage door. The rear lantern offered some side illumination but cast the forward part of the vehicle in shadow, and the lantern Darcy carried was now too far distant to provide light to those left behind. Even were it brighter, from this vantage point she could not observe the scene transpiring ahead. Nor could she any longer make out the woman's words, only her distraught tone, as a cold wind stirred dead leaves yet clinging to their branches. One of the horses snorted and tossed its head.

Elizabeth shared the animal's impatience. Anxious to see for herself what was happening, she set aside her lap blanket and muff. Her reticule she wrapped by its drawstring round her wrist, and she called the footman from the rear of the vehicle to help her out of the carriage.

Just as he took her hand to assist her, a dark blur streaked past his head. It so startled them both that she nearly fell, but he caught her. Had his reflexes been the least bit slower, she would certainly have suffered injury, for the flying shape swooped towards the horses, agitating them tremendously. The carriage shifted as the groom struggled to control his team.

After circling thrice, the creature flew toward Jeffrey. He dropped the reins to protect his face, but the defensive instinct proved unnecessary. The great black bird landed on the seat beside him and emitted a throaty *kaugh*.

It was a raven, the most enormous Elizabeth had ever seen. It perched on the seat as if it, not Jeffrey, were in command of the carriage, and cawed at the coachman for presuming to usurp its rightful place.

"Shoo." The unnerved coachman's voice would not have intimidated even Lily-Anne.

The raven cawed again, each cry deeper and louder than the one previous. Poor Jeffrey, who in all his fifty years had never received such abuse, looked almost willing to concede his place if only the sinister bird would leave him be. But then he remembered himself, and seemed about to assert his authority over the mouthy upstart, when the creature took flight once more.

It rose up, then dived and circled the horses again. The animals snorted and shied, jostling the carriage as the bird swept past them and round the back of the jerking vehicle. A moment later, they heard the sound of breaking glass.

And were suddenly enveloped by darkness.

"Devil take that bird—it must have broken the lamp," Ben, the footman, said. "I will try to get it working again."

The raven had flown into the trees. Though it no longer molested them, it continued to heckle their party from above. The groom had all he could do to soothe the horses as Jeffrey escorted Elizabeth to Darcy.

The stranger, all the while, had not ceased her laments, and had carried them on loudly enough that Darcy was unaware of the avian vandal harassing the coach. Just as Elizabeth approached, the young woman swayed. Darcy caught her in one arm, the other still holding the heavy lantern. He looked towards the carriage to signal for assistance, and was clearly surprised to find Elizabeth and his coachman so close. Jeffrey relieved him of the lantern.

"I thought I told you to remain in the coach," Darcy said.

"I thought I could be of more use here," Elizabeth replied. "And a disagreeable bird has just extinguished the other lamp, so I would as soon be with you while Ben repairs it."

"Very well. Allow me to present Miss Jones." His tone was as dry as the leaves.

Miss Jones had not lost consciousness, but had quieted during her swoon. She was quite young—a slip of a thing, barely more than a girl, perhaps sixteen—with delicate features and large blue eyes. Her thin muslin dress had seen better days, but looked to have at one time been fine. It was trimmed with beadwork and pink ribbon. A matching ribbon tied back her long, thick hair.

"Whatever is she doing wandering about the woods alone at night?" Elizabeth asked.

Darcy tried to help Miss Jones stand upright, but the girl continued to lean on him rather more than Elizabeth thought necessary. Darcy himself appeared displeased by the prolonged contact. "She is injured and hysterical. I have been unable to obtain any particulars beyond her name."

Elizabeth started to address Miss Jones but was cut off before she could utter a syllable.

"Oh, what a relief to have another woman present! Not that you, sir, have been anything but a gentleman, but it is so much more in a woman's nature to attend injuries. And I am injured, ma'am—my ankle—how it pains me!" Miss Jones attempted to stand but her leg buckled, requiring Darcy to continue supporting her. "Is there anyone else in your party? A surgeon, perhaps?"

"Only the two of us, I am afraid," Elizabeth said.

"Oh, do not say *only* the two of you—how fortunate I am that you should be traveling this road just when I am in need of assistance. Will you—might I ask you to examine my ankle, ma'am—Mrs.—Mrs.—?"

"Darcy."

"Mrs. Darcy? I would not impose on your kindness, but I am in such extraordinary pain! Perhaps Mr. Darcy could help settle me on the ground, and then, being a gentleman, gaze off into those trees behind me while you look at my ankle?"

"For both modesty's and comfort's sake, would you not rather be examined in the carriage?" Darcy asked.

"Oh, I am sure I cannot walk another step! It would not surprise me at all if the ankle were broken. In fact, it is certainly broken—indeed, I cannot stand here a minute more."

"All the more reason to—"

"No, I must sit down." She began to lower herself. "If you will just help me—yes, just so—there—I shall be fine right here. I am sure I shall be much better able to reach the carriage after relieving my ankle of weight for a few minutes while Mrs. Darcy examines it."

When she was settled, the coachman held the lantern while Elizabeth knelt to examine Miss Jones's ankle. Both Jeffrey and Darcy averted their gazes as Elizabeth lifted the soiled hem of the woman's dress. Pea-sized white beads threatened to slip off several frayed threads. Miss Jones's shoes were worn; bits of damp earth from the road clung to them.

As Elizabeth reached for the injured foot, Jeffrey dutifully scanned the trees behind Miss Jones to preserve her delicacy. Darcy aimed his gaze toward the carriage, of which they could see little. The vehicle was still dark, and beyond the reach of their own light. The horses, from the sound of them, remained excited, though the raven either watched them in silence or had at last flown away, for its ominous *kaugh* had ceased.

Elizabeth palpated the ankle. Miss Jones cried out, momentarily drawing Darcy's attention before he remembered himself and joined Jeffrey in admiring the trees.

"I wonder how Ben is getting on with that lamp," Jeffrey said.

Miss Jones's ankle did not look broken—indeed, it was not even bruised or swollen. Miss Jones, however, exclaimed at each gentle prod as if Elizabeth were branding her. The girl had a low tolerance for pain.

"How did you injure yourself?" Elizabeth asked.

"I tripped over a tree root."

"Was no one with you? You must live very close, then."

"Not at all. I do not even live in this part of the country—I am visiting my cousins. They live on a nearby farm—at least, it was nearby—I was out walking, and lost my way. I was wandering for hours, and the darker it became, the more I feared I would never find my way back to them. In my panic I did not see the tree root."

Darcy could not help but turn his attention on her. "Your cousins allowed you to walk about unescorted in strange country?"

"They were visiting a friend. I had a slight headache and stayed behind. But then it improved, so I decided to meet them coming home. I thought I knew the way. Oh!—That hurts!"

Elizabeth released her foot. "You must have merely turned the ankle, for I detect no break or sprain. Let us get you to the carriage and transport you to your cousins. What are their names?"

"Their names?" She winced. "Jones. Jones—just like mine."

Miss Jones found she could stand unsupported, but still moaned and complained. Elizabeth was sympathetic to her discomfort, but wished the girl were not quite so vocal about it. To hear her grievances, one would think her entire leg had been amputated.

Darcy drew Elizabeth aside. "We have no notion of where to find these relations of hers, and Miss Jones herself will be of no help. We will take her with us to the inn at Highbury. Surely someone there knows the cousins."

Elizabeth had begun to believe they would never reach the inn. She peered towards the carriage. Darkness yet shrouded it; she could barely discern the vehicle and could not make out their servants at all. "Ben must yet be repairing the lantern, but I see no sign of our groom, either."

Darcy frowned. "Perhaps he is assisting Ben behind the carriage." He called the men's names, but received no response. The silence was more disturbing than the raven's cry. Only the horses' snorts penetrated the stillness.

He glanced meaningfully at her reticule. "Have you—"

"Yes. Do you want it?"

He shook his head. "Keep it at hand and stay here with Jeffrey and Miss Jones." From the folds of his greatcoat he produced the small pistol he carried with him when they traveled, and walked towards the carriage.

He left the light with Jeffrey and the women, making it more difficult for Elizabeth to see his figure. Her nerves were taut as she and the coachman watched her husband retreat into the darkness surrounding the vehicle. Miss Jones's continual complaints did not help.

"Oh! Where is he going? Can we not leave this place at once? I have heard there are highwaymen about—"

"Highwaymen!" Elizabeth said. "Why did you not say so before now?"

"Heavens, I did not want to speak of such people!"

With now even greater anxiety, Elizabeth turned her attention back to the carriage. She could just distinguish Darcy moving round its side. "Then kindly hold your tongue so as not to draw them to us."

Behind her, Miss Jones mercifully lapsed into silence. The horses, however, were restless, and created quite enough noise themselves as they hoofed the ground and shook their harnesses. Elizabeth held her breath, unable to release it until she saw her husband safe again.

In a moment, Darcy came back into sight, running towards them. He bore grim news. Their servants lay unconscious.

Their chest was gone.

Elizabeth whirled round. So was Miss Jones.

Volume the First

IN WHICH IS RELATED A SUCCESSION OF CURIOUS
INCIDENTS ORIGINATING A FORTNIGHT PREVIOUS IN
THE VILLAGE OF HIGHBURY

"Ah! my dear, I wish you would not make matches and foretel things, for whatever you say always comes to pass. Pray do not make any more matches."

—Mr. Woodhouse to Emma Woodhouse, *Emma*

One

"When such success has blessed me in this instance, dear papa, you cannot think that I shall leave off match making."

—Emma Woodhouse, *Emma*

*E*mma Woodhouse Knightley, handsome, clever, and rich, with a comfortable home and happy disposition—a happiness recently compounded by her marriage to a gentleman of noble character and steadfast heart—seemed to unite some of the best blessings of existence; and had lived nearly twenty-two years in the world with very little to distress or vex her.

With two notable exceptions: the Reverend and Mrs. Philip Elton.

"I am still appalled by their conversation," Emma said to her husband as they sat in Hartfield's drawing room after dinner. Her father had just retired for the night, leaving the newlyweds to enjoy an hour of peace before retiring themselves. Emma's mind, however, was anything but quiet as she dwelled upon the discussion she had overheard that morning, and neither the familiar comforts of the room—the Chippendale sofa and side chairs, the portrait of her late mother above the great hearth—nor the novelty of her bridegroom's now-permanent presence there, could quell her agitation.

"That is what comes of eavesdropping," Mr. Knightley said.

"I was not eavesdropping," Emma insisted. "I was tying my bootlace."

The lace had come undone as she left the home of Miss Bates, a middle-aged spinster who lived with her elderly mother in reduced circumstances on the upper floor of a modest house. Emma had visited their rooms many times (though perhaps not so often as she ought), but never before had the humble apartment felt so small. The Eltons had called so shortly after Emma's own arrival that it was some time before she could with propriety effect an escape. "I paused at the base of the stairs to fix the lace. Could I help it that the Eltons emerged from the apartment and began their discussion on the landing before I had done?"

Mr. Knightley's expression suggested that she might have secured the half-boot more rapidly had she wanted to. Sixteen years her senior, he had known Emma her whole life, and was as well acquainted with her foibles as he was with her charms. His dark eyes narrowed in doubt, and for a moment she dreaded an admonition delivered in his usual forthright manner. Instead, he rose and stirred the fire. The flickering light shadowed his countenance and silhouetted his tall frame. Though he possessed the maturity and bearing of a man eight-and-thirty, he had maintained the firm figure of younger days, and Emma congratulated herself on having found such a fine-looking husband once she had finally opened her eyes to the gentleman next door.

He returned the poker to its stand and adjusted the screen to shield them from the heat. "It is fortunate that you managed to exit without the Eltons' seeing you in the stairwell." He sat down beside her on the sofa. "To have been caught listening to their conversation, however involuntarily, would not have reflected well on you."

The last position in which Emma would want to find herself was that of giving Augusta Elton any room to expand her already inflated sense of superiority. Mrs. Elton's greatest claim to society was a brother-in-law who owned a barouche-landau and an estate near Bristol. Though the house was named Maple Grove, Mrs. Elton seemed to think it was St. James's Palace. She also took extraordinary pride in her status as the vicar's wife, performing her role with pretensions of elegance and a pronounced air of noblesse oblige. Sadly, Mr. Elton, though a clergyman, was nearly as vain and insufferable as she.

"It is still more fortunate that I *did* overhear them, for now I can rescue poor Miss Bates from their plotting."

"Emma—"

"Honestly, you should have heard them! Talking about how Miss Bates will surely become dependent upon parish charity after her mother dies."

"I doubt that will happen, with her niece marrying Frank Churchill next week. A gentleman who stands to inherit an estate the size of Enscombe will not forsake his wife's aunt."

Emma knew that Mr. Knightley spoke not from conviction of Frank Churchill's reliability, but from his own principles. Because Mr. Knightley would never neglect a needy relation, he expected all gentlemen to demonstrate the same sense of duty. In fact, he had forfeited his own independence to act rightly by Emma's father. Upon their marriage, Mr. Knightley had graciously moved into the house of Emma's birth so that she need not abandon the invalid Mr. Woodhouse or subject the old man to the trauma of leaving his lifelong home to live with them at Mr. Knightley's more sizable estate, Donwell Abbey. Though the distance was slight—Hartfield bordered Mr. Knightley's grounds—Mr. Woodhouse suffered from a nervous disposition and did not bear well change of any sort. The living arrangement left Donwell Abbey without its master in residence, and Emma appreciated the sacrifice her husband had made on behalf of herself and her father.

The vicar and his wife, however, were entirely capable of more selfish conduct, and therefore anticipated it in others. "The Eltons are convinced that once Frank Churchill and Jane Fairfax wed and move so far away as Yorkshire, the Bates ladies will be forgotten," Emma said. "Mrs. Elton is determined to make certain that Miss Bates becomes someone else's responsibility and not the parish's."

To be specific, Mrs. Elton had proposed marrying off Miss Bates to any man—gentleman or not—who would have her. Granted, finding a husband for a woman of forty-odd years would prove a daunting enterprise, and Miss Bates's situation was further challenged by the spinster's propensity for endless chatter. Emma herself found Miss Bates's trivial tidings and cheerful effusions tedious; she could scarcely imagine a husband willing to endure them day and night.

Mrs. Elton, however, had gone so far as to suggest an addlepated local farmer as the ideal candidate, and declared to Mr. Elton her intention of arranging the match. In that, the vicar's wife had gone *too* far.

"She cannot be permitted to proceed," Emma continued. "Not when I have the ability to arrange a superior establishment for Miss Bates."

"You told me, Emma, after Harriet Smith married Robert Martin despite your interference, that you had given up matchmaking."

"This is not matchmaking. It is—" She considered her words carefully, for there was no bluffing her husband. Mr. Knightley knew her better than did any other soul on earth. "It is merely taking advantage of an opportunity."

"An opportunity to meddle."

Now Emma found herself vexed not only at the Eltons, but at her "dear Mr. Knightley." This latest was a slight vexation—a trifle, really. Well, perhaps more than a trifle. But it was her husband's fault for willfully misinterpreting her motives for the scheme she had spent all afternoon contemplating.

"An opportunity to show kindness towards someone to whom you yourself have said I ought to demonstrate greater generosity. You should be pleased that I have taken to heart your reproofs regarding my lack of consideration for Miss Bates, and that I wish to make amends for my previous neglect. Her situation is indeed pitiable. She has sacrificed half her life to the care of her near-deaf mother. Is she to spend her old age either alone in poverty, or with some half-wit imposed upon her by Mrs. Elton?"

"We can guard Miss Bates from any maneuverings Mrs. Elton might undertake without your trying to orchestrate a match of your own."

"Can we? Miss Bates is so appreciative of any attention or kindness shown her that even if she had reservations about the groom, she would wed him simply out of gratitude, or in deference to Mrs. Elton for arranging the marriage. If Miss Bates ever possessed enough quickness of mind to recognize an unfavorable situation when presented with one, years of deprivation have surely worn down her ability to resist it."

Mr. Knightley could remember Miss Bates at a more carefree period of her life—before her father, a former vicar of Highbury, had died. As a clergyman's benefice made no provisions for surviving dependents, Mr. Bates's widow and daughter had been left to shift as best they could on an income insufficient to support even one of them, let alone two, in moderate comfort. The pair, however, being of naturally content temperaments and possessing enough sense to live within their means, accepted their situation with grace, and made the best of it.

"Miss Bates never exhibited your cleverness, Emma, nor even an intellect as strong as her younger sister's. Yet you will not meet a kinder-hearted soul in all Surrey. Leave her in peace."

"Her good heart is precisely why I wish to perform a kindness for her in turn. You would merely save her from the evils of Mrs. Elton, whereas I hope to secure her a future happier than her present. Somewhere in England there must be a gentleman—a good, decent gentleman, not merely the first unmarried farmer Mrs. Elton can manipulate—who can appreciate Miss Bates."

"It would not be a kindness to introduce hopes that Miss Bates must have set aside long ago, only to have them once more disappointed."

"Why do you assume they will be disappointed? She need not captivate the entire Polite World, merely a single man." Ideally, one in possession of a good fortune. "And the celebration of her niece's marriage to Frank Churchill will bring more new gentlemen to Highbury than I daresay this village has ever seen at once."

Though the wedding would take place in London, where the bride had been raised, Frank and Jane would visit the village before removing to the Churchill estate in Yorkshire. What had initially been conceived as a small dinner party to receive the postnuptial well-wishes of their Highbury friends had burgeoned into an elaborate affair once Mr. Weston, Frank's father, began issuing invitations. Not only was every respectable family in the neighborhood to attend, but auld acquaintance must not be forgot. Because Randalls, the Westons' home, had but two spare bedrooms and the Crown Inn could not accommodate everybody, Donwell Abbey would host the affair and lodge many of the out-of-town guests.

The venue had been Emma's idea, motivated by her friendship with Mrs. Weston, Frank's stepmother. Though Mr. Knightley acquiesced, he was not without uneasiness over the thought of visitors—many of them strangers—occupying his house in his absence. He and Emma, therefore, would stay at Donwell while Emma's visiting sister and her family stayed with Mr. Woodhouse. Emma credited their newlywed status for her successful application on this point, for under few other circumstances could she imagine Mr. Knightley's being persuaded to go so out of his way regarding an event that honored Frank Churchill. Mr. Knightley thought the young man self-centered and more fortunate in his relationships—especially his betrothal to Jane Fairfax—than he deserved.

His unexpected role as a host did, however, enable Mr. Knightley to perform a service for the Bates ladies. He proposed that Mrs. and Miss Bates also consider themselves sponsors of the gathering. Through his means, they would be able to give Jane a proper send-off.

"This affair has already grown to answer more purposes than anyone originally intended," Mr. Knightley said. "Now it is to serve as a promenade of suitors for your appraisal?"

"Is that not a tacit component of most social events? The difference is that this time, no one—including the lady herself—will know that this gathering is, of sorts, a coming-out ball. I shall be entirely discreet in my evaluations."

"I do not think this wise. Even did I not harbor reservations about the presumption of attempting to find a husband for Miss Bates, one cannot learn much of use about a gentleman at a dinner party."

"I disagree."

"And should a man whom you judge suitable present himself, what course of action do you intend to pursue in consequence?"

Emma had not yet settled her mind as to that part of her plan. For the present, merely finding a worthy object was challenge enough.

Two

She had been a friend and companion such as few possessed: intelligent, well-informed, useful, gentle, knowing all the ways of the family, interested in all its concerns, and peculiarly interested in [Emma], in every pleasure, every scheme of hers.
—description of Mrs. Weston, Emma

oping for a more sympathetic audience—perhaps even a conspirator—in her plan for Miss Bates, Emma visited Randalls the following day. Just over a year ago, Emma's dearest friend had married Mr. Weston, and Emma fancied that she herself had brought about the match between her former governess and the longtime widower. Where Mr. Knightley had responded to Emma's plan with skepticism, surely Mrs. Weston would recognize the merit, the necessity, of the idea, and approve it. Mrs. Weston possessed good principles and sound judgment; if Emma's intentions towards Miss Bates were indeed misguided, Mrs. Weston would advise her—though with a heart prejudiced by a near-mother's affection for the girl, now woman, she had helped raise from age five.

Emma would listen to Mrs. Weston's counsel, then act as she generally did: precisely as Emma wished.

She found Mrs. Weston walking out-of-doors along a path that circled the house. The day was overcast, and a brisk autumn breeze endeavored to dislodge colored leaves from Randalls's trees. It did manage to catch the brim of Mrs. Weston's bonnet, freeing tendrils of dark hair as she spied Emma and came to greet her. Rosy cheeks revealed that she had been walking for some time.

"You are taking your walk early today," Emma said.

"I thought I should do so before the day's tasks overtook me." The breeze swelled, prompting Mrs. Weston to shiver and cross her arms over the front of her spencer. "We go to London soon for Frank and Jane's wedding, and there are still countless details to oversee for the dinner party."

"Donwell Abbey could not be blessed with a more capable housekeeper. Depend upon it, Mrs. Hodges has everything in order."

"I am entirely confident that she does. It is only that . . ."

Such was the accord between them that Emma's friend did not need to complete the sentence for Emma to know her apprehension. Though still rather new to her role as stepmother, Mrs. Weston's affection for Frank equaled his father's. As a young militia officer with no fortune of his own, the newly widowed Mr. Weston had, of necessity, commended his three-year-old son to his late wife's wealthy brother and sister-in-law, Edgar and Agnes Churchill, who had raised him as their own while Mr. Weston earned his place in the world. Now that Frank was grown and heir to the Churchill fortune—he had even taken the name "Churchill" upon reaching his majority—there was nothing of a material nature that he needed from Mr. Weston. Frank's legacy from his father and new mother, therefore, comprised unconditional love: the one asset he had found wanting on the grand estate of Enscombe. Fondness and regard had been shown, but never—particularly on his late aunt's part—unconditionally.

"This party is Mr. Weston's opportunity to act as a father by his son," Emma finished. "And you want all to go off perfectly."

"Yes," Mrs. Weston admitted. "Do thank Mr. Knightley once more for his trouble on our behalf. I hope you already know that *you* have my unending gratitude."

"Mr. Knightley considers it no trouble, and neither do I," Emma said. "He has great respect for all of you, and has always held a high opinion of Jane Fairfax."

Jane, like Frank, had been raised elsewhere; left orphaned and fortuneless as a young girl, she had been taken in by her father's friend

Colonel Campbell and educated along with his own daughter in London. Her frequent visits to her aunt and grandmother, however, had given all Highbury a proprietary interest in her, and she was generally acknowledged to be one of the most pretty and accomplished young ladies the village had ever produced. Emma, however, had never cultivated a close friendship with Jane, despite their being the same age; she had found Jane's reserved nature unamiable.

Their ambling had taken them round the back of the house, where a peddler's cart stood just outside the servants' entrance.

"Now, *there* is an unusual sight," Emma said. "I cannot recall the last time a peddler visited Highbury."

"Oh, how fortunate!" Mrs. Weston said. "I am in need of lace for a handkerchief I am making for Jane to carry with her on her wedding day. I could not find anything at Ford's that quite suited, and thought I would have to obtain some when I arrived in London. Perhaps this peddler has something more to my liking and can spare me the necessity of seeking it in town."

"You would willingly forgo an opportunity to visit a London lace merchant? You so seldom go to town, and have not been at all since Anna was born."

"Only in the interest of expediency—our time in London will be so brief, and most of it commanded by others. And only if the peddler has something that indeed satisfies my purpose."

They went within, where they found a goodly assortment of wares arranged on the kitchen worktables, and nearly every servant at Randalls arranged round their seller. There were cooking utensils and sewing notions, hammered tins and wooden boxes, garden implements and currycombs, baskets and tools. One of the footmen examined a set of fire-irons, while Mr. Weston's valet inspected a razor.

The female servants, however, all devoted their full attention to the peddler.

He was a respectable-looking fellow, a tall, well-built man of years that approximated Mr. Knightley's. His clothing and person were neat and clean. He wore his hair short, but the brown locks would not be tamed, and they curled round his head in a willful fashion that was not unbecoming. Lively, intelligent blue eyes and gentlemanlike features formed a countenance that was altogether pleasant to look upon.

At least, all the maids seemed of that opinion as they listened to him describe the uses of various cordials in a case he balanced on his left arm against his chest. "I obtained these directly from a gypsy herb-woman. They are great healers, the gypsies, and I've a fine stock of remedies for whatever might ail you or anyone in the household."

Emma wondered what the village apothecary might think of the peddler's infringing on his business. Her father would be quite discomposed by the notion of anyone's curative talents exceeding those of his most capable and valued Mr. Perry.

"This," he continued, holding up a small bottle for all to see, "contains elixir of a different sort." A mischievous cast overtook his expression. He looked at one of the youngest maids. She was a pretty, well-mannered girl, the daughter of Hartfield's coachman. "What do you suppose it does?" he asked her.

The housemaid blushed at having the handsome peddler's full attention directed toward herself. "I—I cannot guess."

"A sip before bed, and dream of he you'll wed."

One of the kitchen maids giggled. "Hannah's too young to be thinkin' such thoughts." Despite the scullery maid's appearing not much older than Hannah, her expression suggested that the peddler himself would play a prominent role in her own reveries, with or without the assistance of any draught.

"No one is too young, or too old, to dream." The peddler's voice deepened the flush of Hannah's cheeks. "Here." He offered the philtre to Hannah.

"But I haven't money for such—"

He shook his head. "It is yours." As she timidly accepted the gift, he winked. "But you must promise to tell me one year hence if it worked."

Hannah lowered her eyes, but smiled.

He set the box upon the closest table, and it was only then that Emma made a startling discovery: The peddler had but one hand. His left arm simply ended at the wrist. Whether the appendage had been absent from birth or lost later, she could not determine. It appeared,

however, that he enjoyed full use of the arm, and had learned to compensate for the missing hand so proficiently that he was scarcely im-
paired by its lack. He handled his merchandise with dexterity that
rivaled that of any ten-fingered trader, and handled his audience still
more deftly.

Emma perceived something vaguely familiar about Mr. Deal, but
could not identify precisely what inspired the impression. As the
peddler enumerated the superior attributes of a copper teakettle,
he caught sight of Emma and Mrs. Weston, and offered a silent bow.
The gesture alerted the housekeeper to their presence, and she now
commanded her staff's attention.

"Everybody has been idle long enough," she announced. "Should
you want an item for use in household duties, I will consider it.
If you care to purchase anything for yourself, do so and return to
work."

The subsequent exchange of money and merchandise required
some minutes to complete, particularly as every maid found at least
one trinket without which she could no longer continue to exist, and
must pay for with a bright-eyed smile along with her pennies. The
peddler answered the scullery maid's overeager query about whether
he would return to Randalls before leaving the neighborhood with a
simple, "If your mistress permits me," and refrained altogether from
acknowledging her intimation regarding a private presentation of his
goods.

The housekeeper, overhearing, admonished the scullery maid with
a disapproving look. "Get along with you now, Nellie."

With a last hopeful smile, Nellie purchased a philtre identical to
the one the peddler had given Hannah.

When the room at last cleared, the housekeeper introduced him
to her mistress. "This is Hiram Deal, ma'am. A new trader in these
parts, but my sister up in Richmond mentioned him in a letter this
summer as being an honest seller."

"Deal is a fitting name for a peddler," Emma observed. "Do you
come from a family of merchants?"

His responding smile was easy; he had heard the question before,
likely many times.

"It is indeed an apt name, ma'am. Though whether I was born to it because I was meant to be a trader, or became a trader because I was born to the name, I cannot say, for I never knew my father and inherited naught but my name from him. It has, however, served me well, for it is a name my customers remember, and I take care that the recollection is a favorable one."

"Well, Mr. Deal, you have an opportunity to make another favorable impression if you can assist me this morning," said Mrs. Weston. "I am in need of some fine lace."

"Most certainly, ma'am. White?"

"Yes, for a bride's handkerchief."

"I have several exquisite laces on my cart—including a superior Brussels that might be the very thing you seek. Shall I bring them inside for your inspection?"

Mrs. Weston instructed the housekeeper to conduct Mr. Deal to the sitting room, where she and Emma could evaluate the laces in greater comfort, and retrieved the handkerchief. The peddler soon appeared with half a dozen laces, which he spread upon a table along with other goods of interest to ladies.

The laces were all lovely, and Mrs. Weston had difficulty making a selection. After soliciting Emma's opinion, she narrowed her choice to three, then two. Finality, however, eluded her.

She sighed and looked to Emma once more. "I want the handkerchief to be perfect, something Jane will cherish as a keepsake."

"Jane Fairfax would treasure a rag if it came from you, so appreciative is she for the affection with which you have welcomed her to your family. There is no wrong choice."

"All the same . . ." She fingered the more expensive of the two laces. "This one, do you think? I want her to know how truly happy I am in the connexion."

Emma preferred the other, and from her limited knowledge of Jane Fairfax's taste, thought it the better selection. Jane was not a person to equate the cost of a gift with the amount of sentiment with which it was offered; neither, for that matter, was Mrs. Weston. Emma was about to assure her that neither Jane nor anyone else was likely to judge Mrs. Weston's fondness for her new daughter-in-law by the difference in price between one lace and another—particularly another that nobody would ever know had even been under consideration—when Mr. Deal interjected.

"If I may offer a suggestion, ma'am?" He nodded toward the lace in her hand. "That lace is rather fragile, and therefore might not hold up as well to the emotions of the day. The bride—Miss Fairfax, I believe you called her?—would perhaps be better served by a handkerchief edged in the stronger lace, so that she can use it freely without anxiety over ruining so valued a gift. And the less delicate lace is just as lovely."

Mrs. Weston, ever practical, appreciated his sensible advice, and Emma admired his sincere interest in providing his customer with the item best suited to her needs rather than the one most profitable to him. The matter was decided.

"The pattern complements the style in which you embroidered the monogram," Mr. Deal added as he set aside the other laces. "I think both you and the new 'Mrs. C———' will be well pleased with your choice."

"Mrs. Churchill," Mrs. Weston provided. "In but a few days' time, she shall be Mrs. Frank Churchill."

"Indeed? I once knew a family by the name of Churchill. That was a long time ago, however, and far from here." He drew his brows together. "Forgive me, ma'am, but you said Miss Fairfax was marrying your son, and I understood your name to be Weston. I hope I have not been improperly addressing you all this while?"

"No. Frank has taken his uncle's name, and lives with him."

Mr. Deal asked no more, only wished the couple joy. He then begged leave to show the other items he had brought, and Emma and Mrs. Weston spent a delightful interlude perusing items they had not known they wanted until laid before them. A set of hair combs caught Emma's eye, along with several other treasures. Each had a history—where it had been fashioned, how he had procured it, lore surrounding its use, or perhaps an anecdote about a previous owner. Mr. Deal was a natural storyteller, and Emma found herself quite entertained.

The chime of the case clock announced that she had stayed far longer than she had intended. As she had brought no money with her to Randalls, she invited the peddler to wait upon her at Hartfield the following day with those items that she had determined were indispensible to her continued happiness. Resolved against being too easily persuaded to part with all of her pin money, she left the combs among his wares for purchase by some other lady.

She was nearly home before she realized that the peddler had entirely distracted her from the original purpose of her call. Emma, too, had gone to Randalls with the intent of solicitation—winning Mrs. Weston's approval of her plan for Miss Bates.

Three

[Miss Bates] was a happy woman, and a woman whom no one named without good-will. . . . She loved every body, was interested in every body's happiness, quicksighted to every body's merits; thought herself a most fortunate creature, and surrounded with blessings. . . . The simplicity and cheerfulness of her nature, her contented and grateful spirit, were a recommendation to every body, and a mine of felicity to herself.

—Emma

*E*mma wished Mr. Deal could sell her a physic that would cure her dilemma. The matter of Miss Bates, and how to present her to best advantage at the Donwell party, was proving exceedingly troublesome. Miss Bates looked every one of her more than forty years, and her wardrobe even older. Seeking inspiration, she decided to call upon Miss Bates at home.

In her eagerness to advance her plan, Emma forgot that today was Wednesday. And in the Bates house, Wednesdays marked the arrival of Jane Fairfax's weekly letters, from which no visitor could escape. The letter must be read aloud, in full, with spontaneous explications by Miss Bates in case the listener failed to realize or appreciate the significance of any particulars. And, of course, select passages of the text must be repeated, sometimes twice or thrice at successively higher volumes, for old Mrs. Bates's comprehension.

"Jane says that all is in readiness for the wedding." Miss Bates adjusted her reading spectacles, which fit her loosely about the ears and defiantly slid down her nose every time she glanced at the letter. "By this day week, our Jane will be Mrs. Frank Churchill! Mother and I are so excited to be going to London—we have not been since before my father died. Jane writes that Colonel Campbell is sending his own carriage to collect us, so that we do not have to travel by coach. Did you hear that, Mother? Colonel Campbell is sending his carriage. His *carriage*."

Mrs. Bates, seated by the fire in an upholstered chair that had seen more prosperous years, looked up from her knitting and smiled. From the blank expression of her eyes, Emma doubted she had heard a word. Her head bent back down over her needles, her hair so white that one could barely distinguish the thin strands from the mobcap that covered most of them.

"Only imagine—a year ago we had no notion of a wedding," Miss Bates said. "We of course thought Jane would be working as a governess by now, as with no fortune of her own, those were her expectations. What a surprise it was to us all—was it not a great surprise, Mother?—when we learned she was secretly engaged to Frank Churchill during the whole of her visit here this past spring and summer! And neither of them able to say a word for fear of his being disinherited if his aunt learned of it."

Though Emma pretended to accord Miss Bates her full attention, this was all information she had heard many times before. It was the spinster's appearance, not words, that commandeered her interest. Her faded blue morning dress needed to be taken in, but was so worn as to make the effort futile. Beneath the thin muslin, however, Miss Bates had a pleasing figure—neither too plump nor too thin—and a darker shade of fabric might bring out the amber color of her eyes.

Emma knew that Miss Bates had made a new gown to wear to the wedding ceremony in London. Initially, Emma had attempted to offer guidance on the style and creation of the gown, but then the officious Mrs. Elton had inserted herself in the business and would have her own way about it. She had so commandeered the project that Emma had washed her hands of it rather than subject herself to Mrs. Elton's pretensions as an arbiter of fashion. She now wondered at the result.

Miss Bates at last paused her discourse long enough for Emma to interject. "Have you finished the dress you plan to wear to the wedding?"

"Indeed, yes! Why, just yesterday I stitched on the last bead and Mrs. Elton declared it done. Would you care to see it?" Miss Bates set aside the letter and hurried into the bedroom, talking the whole way. "It was so generous of Frank—a new dress for me, and another for my mother. We are fortunate that Jane found such a fine young man. She says she never imagined when she went to Weymouth with the Campbells last autumn that she would fall in love."

Miss Bates continued to voice her boundless gratitude to Frank Churchill, for not only having accompanied Jane to Layton and Shears to select the silk ("Layton and Shears—one of London's finest linen-drapers!"), but also having paid for it ("Mr. Churchill insisted!"); for having traveled all the way from London to deliver the parcel himself ("and what a parcel it was! Not merely the fabric, but also a selection of trimmings!"); and for having also brought the most recent edition of *Ackermann's Repository* so that she might see plates of the latest fashions.

She returned with the gown. To Emma's dismay, it was far too youthful for a middle-aged spinster. Indeed, Emma herself would not have worn it, even at her coming-out. Double flounces, ells of ribbon, and abundant beadwork competed so vigorously for attention that one wanted to shut one's eyes against the assault. Rather than choosing from the trimmings Frank had sent, she must have used them all.

Even Miss Bates regarded the dress with apprehension. "It is a little . . . fancier . . . than I am used to. But Mrs. Elton insisted this was 'all the thing.' It was so kind of her to help me, for I do not keep up with the styles as she does. Imagine—me, wearing such a fine dress! I think I shall be afraid to sit down in it."

Mrs. Elton's taste in attire appeared ostentatious enough on Mrs. Elton; on Miss Bates, the gown would look ridiculous. But anything was an improvement over the tired dresses that comprised the rest of her wardrobe, and Emma supposed she had no choice but to encourage her to wear it to the Donwell dinner party. Unless . . .

Unless the spinster had a more suitable alternative.

As Miss Bates rattled on about the process of constructing the gown, Emma's mind turned upon hemlines and sleeve lengths for an entirely different garment. She would surprise Miss Bates with a new gown for the Donwell affair. It would have to be simple, for there was little time in which to make it, but a plainer dress would become Miss Bates more. It would certainly be more to the wearer's taste. Indeed, Emma could have the pleasure of presenting to Miss Bates the dress she had wanted all along.

Material could be obtained at Ford's—she had seen a pretty emerald-green sarcenet the last time she was there—and Miss Bates had just uttered her measurements from the dress newly completed. (At last, an advantage to the spinster's repetitive discourse.) There was not enough time for Emma to do the sewing, even if she borrowed Hannah from Randalls, as she often did for needlework. She would have to bring in the London seamstress who had made her own wedding clothes.

But it could be done.

The more Emma contemplated the idea, the more enamored of it she became. Within a quarter hour she thought the enterprise quite brilliant.

She rose to depart. There was no time to waste if the new dress was to be ready in time for the ball. Even Emma was no fairy godmother.

Before she could take her leave, however, sounds of bustle in the street below sent Miss Bates to the window.

"Oh, it is the peddler! Mr. Deal, the one everybody has been talking of." She turned to face the room. "Mother, the peddler is below. The peddler. *PED-ler*. The man of whom Mrs. Elton spoke."

The old woman at last seemed to understand her daughter. At least, she nodded as if she did, her knitting needles never missing a purl.

Since Mr. Deal's arrival in Highbury, the sight of the trader's cart brought most other village activity to a standstill. Nellie, the scullery maid at Randalls, was hardly alone in her patent admiration of Mr. Deal. Parlor maids, chambermaids, dairymaids, still-room maids, laundry maids, nursery maids—in short, all manner of maids, along with a good many farmers' and tradesmen's daughters—suddenly found themselves in dire want of goods that simply could not be procured at Ford's. Matrons regarded the handsome trader wistfully while buying one of his gypsy remedies for their husbands' snoring or digestive ailments. Even Mr. Woodhouse, who as a rule distrusted strangers, had pronounced him "an acceptable fellow," after he had called at Hartfield, but added that he hoped the peddler would not stay in Highbury long, and expressed apprehension as to his traveling about the country so much, particularly without a proper muffler round his neck against the wind.

Miss Bates's attention returned to the street. "Look at all the people stopping to talk to him. There is Miss Cole. Oh— and Miss Nash from the school. He certainly seems to attract a crowd. I wonder what he has for sale today—I cannot quite see into his cart. Mrs. Elton says he sells all manner of things."

"Have you not yet met him yourself?" Emma found it difficult to believe that a villager remained who had not yet encountered Mr. Deal.

"Whenever I hear of him, he is always just gone. He has never stopped this close to our house before."

"Then let us go down." Emma needed nothing for herself, but—in restrained quantities—one of the laces she had seen with Mrs. Weston would be the very thing to enhance the surprise dress she was planning.

Miss Bates was delighted by the proposal. "Not that we are likely to buy anything from him. We have so few needs—is that not right, Mother? Our friends are so kind that we have few needs—but there is no harm in seeing what he has for sale."

Mrs. Bates elected to remain beside the fire with her knitting, but Patty, the Bates's maid-of-all-work, begged leave to go down for a few minutes. Their departure was delayed while Miss Bates saw to it that her mother was comfortably settled, her spectacles adjusted, her workbag within reach, the fire screen positioned at just the proper distance.

In the time it took the three women to reach the street, still more customers had gathered round the peddler's cart. Mr. Deal acknowledged Emma and Miss Bates with a nod as he extolled the workmanship of a locket that Miss Cole admired. When he had done, he greeted Emma and asked after her father's health. The enquiry would please her father very much when she told him, as no topic of conversation delighted him more than discussions of anyone's health, particularly his own.

Emma then introduced her companion. The peddler bowed to Miss Bates, a generous bow worthy of her former condition in life, and was all consideration. What was she in want of this morning, that he might have the privilege of supplying her?

"I—" Self-consciousness overtook her. "I do not know."

It was the shortest reply Emma had ever heard Miss Bates utter.

He smiled. "Well, then, if you will allow me, I have a shawl that came into my mind the moment I saw you."

His warm, genuine manner quite flustered Miss Bates, who, while yet the recipient of gracious conduct from Mr. Knightley, Mr. Woodhouse, and others secure enough in their social stations and in themselves to treat a gentlewoman with courtesy no matter her present circumstances, nevertheless had grown used to a certain amount of patronization from other individuals, particularly those whose own positions had risen as hers had sunk, and who needed to exalt themselves by reminding others of their inferior places. Mrs. Elton was one of these; her husband, though his public conduct was not as overt, in private was little better.

Certainly, the merchants of Highbury, many of them lifelong acquaintances, remained kind to Miss Bates, though her purchases, which had never been extravagant, had dwindled steadily in the years since her father's passing. But Mr. Deal had a way of addressing a woman, any woman—nay, any person—as if the individual to whom he spoke was the only one present. Even in a crowd, each listener felt singled out. It was this ability, even more than his pleasing countenance, that so strongly drew others to him.

And left Miss Bates, for perhaps the first time in her life, tongue-tied.

Mr. Deal produced the shawl and permitted Miss Bates to put it around her shoulders. It indeed flattered her. Not only did it cover the unattractive old dress she wore, but its ivory hue complemented her coloring, lending her face a softer, warmer tone than the starker white of the shawl she normally wore. And the craftsmanship was lovely: someone had spent considerable time on the knotwork of its fringe.

"It becomes you," Emma said.

Miss Bates ran her fingertips over the folds of silk draped over her arm. "I do not believe I have ever worn anything so lovely." She glanced up at Mr. Deal. "How much does it cost?"

Mr. Deal took in her outdated dress, her worn bonnet, and named a price Emma knew to be below what the shawl could have fetched from a more affluent buyer. Yet it was still beyond Miss Bates's means.

It was not, however, beyond Mrs. Knightley's. And Emma resolved that only this shawl could adequately complement the new dress she was planning.

"Oh . . ." Miss Bates stroked the fabric a final time and removed the shawl. "Worth every penny, certainly. Such a lovely garment— every inch of it lovely—I could not possibly—a younger woman ought to have it—yes, a younger woman . . ."

At that moment, Mrs. Elton approached. She was in conversation with a man Emma recognized as one of the local farmers, although she did not know his name. As they walked, Mrs. Elton held one side of her skirt, the side nearest him, close to herself, as if, though he was not dirty, she feared contamination by the proximity.

Emma was determined to intercept the vicar's vain wife before she caught a glimpse of the shawl and decided that *she* was the younger woman who ought to possess it. Emma took the shawl and handed it to Mr. Deal. "I am afraid I cannot tarry, but if you call at Donwell Abbey tomorrow, I shall be there overseeing arrangements for a large party Thursday week, and there are a few items"—she looked pointedly at the shawl—"that I am in want of."

His expression assured her that he had caught her meaning.

After taking a hasty leave of Miss Bates, Emma walked down the street toward Mrs. Elton and her companion. He was a man of perhaps fifty, and moved slowly for one of his apparent age and state of health. Emma recalled that on other occasions when she had seen him, he exhibited an air of vagueness similar to that of old Mrs. Bates when her deafness prevented her from following a conversation.

". . . must be terribly lonely on that farm all by yourself since your brother died," Mrs. Elton was saying.

"Abe, he took—he took—he took good care a' me."

"I am quite sure he did. And the farm is all yours now?"

"It—it is, ma'am. All mine."

He spoke as slowly as he walked, as if he had to stop and remember how to form each word before he could articulate it. Emma realized with a start who he was.

The half-wit to whom Mrs. Elton thought to marry off Miss Bates.

Emma smiled in secret satisfaction. She was well on her way to thwarting Mrs. Elton's plan. Any of the guests at the Donwell party would make a better husband than the village idiot. And armed with Emma's dress and the peddler's shawl, Miss Bates would surely impress one of them. Of this, Emma was certain.

She glanced back at Miss Bates before crossing to waylay Mrs. Elton. A section of the spinster's upswept hair had become loose, allowing grey tendrils to hang down lopsidedly. Emma sighed.

Almost certain.

Four

"Frank Churchill is, indeed, the favourite of fortune. . . .
His aunt is in the way.—His aunt dies."

—Mr. Knightley, *Emma*

*T*he London wedding of Frank Churchill and Jane Fairfax was a quiet, intimate affair limited to immediate family. Such would have been the bride's preference in any case; Miss Fairfax was a lady of reserved nature, who eschewed loud crushes and ostentation. As the groom's aunt had died unexpectedly only a few months before, Frank was equally in favor of demonstrating restraint on their nuptial day. All knew that the proud, temperamental woman who had raised him would have opposed the match between the Churchill heir presumptive and an accomplished but genteelly impoverished orphan; only old Mrs. Churchill's death had enabled their clandestine engagement to be revealed and the marriage to take place. To conduct the event with excessive gaiety, particularly whilst his uncle yet mourned, would have appeared disrespectful and held an air of celebrating Agnes Churchill's untimely demise as in fact fortuitous. So a small company partook of the wedding breakfast following the ceremony, deferring more expansive and convivial recognition of the union until the party at Donwell Abbey.

After a few additional days in London, the bridal party traveled to

Highbury. The newlyweds and Frank's uncle, Mr. Edgar Churchill, would stay at Randalls during the Donwell festivities, then journey north to Yorkshire so that Jane could settle at Enscombe. Though the Churchill estate would not belong to Frank until after his uncle passed away, Jane would serve as mistress of the house and continue in that capacity until it was hers by right, unless Edgar Churchill should remarry in the interim. It was a role all expected she would perform with more graciousness and generosity than had her predecessor— all, that is, except Mr. Edgar Churchill, who, while not insensible of his late wife's faults, had through inaction condoned them during her life, and through the softening effects of memory diminished them since her death.

Edgar Churchill himself seemed amiable enough. All Highbury had eagerly anticipated his coming, for though well known to its residents for five-and-twenty years as Mr. Weston's wealthy brother-in-law and Frank's benefactor, he had not once set foot in the village before now. He was a hale individual, his stout figure a striking contrast to the image everybody had formed of him: a slight man whose constitution approximated that of his indisposed wife, only with a weaker spine. His short stature suggested that Frank must have inherited his more generous height from Mr. Weston rather than his Churchill forebears, but a likeness in facial features and mien marked uncle and nephew as Churchills. While Edgar did exhibit the infamous Churchill pride, he also demonstrated an admirable degree of condescension, and conversed more easily with his inferiors than did many gentlemen of his class.

Emma met Edgar Churchill during a visit to Randalls on the day of his arrival from London. It was a brief, formal call, just long enough to be properly introduced and express pleasure in the acquaintance. She was happy, therefore, to encounter him by chance the following afternoon in a more relaxed context. He and Frank, being on their way to visit the Bates ladies, happened upon Hiram Deal in Broadway Lane. Frank was as delighted by the peddler as was everybody else in Highbury, particularly when he learned that Mr. Deal had among his wares not one, but two tortoiseshell snuff boxes.

Edgar Churchill stood to one side, observing their exchange but not himself engaging in any business with the peddler. As Frank examined the snuff boxes and quizzed Mr. Deal as to their relative merits, Emma approached the elder Mr. Churchill.

"We are glad you came to Highbury," Emma said by way of opening. "Mr. Frank Churchill speaks so well of you whenever he visits that we have all been eager to make your acquaintance. I believe it means a great deal to him to be at once with both his father and the uncle who has been as a father to him these many years."

Edgar Churchill looked not at her, but toward Frank, who was engrossed in conversation with Mr. Deal. "I thought I would never be a father," he said.

His voice held wistfulness. Frank's marriage had no doubt brought on memories of Edgar's own, along with fresh grief for the late wife nobody missed but him. Emma wondered whether the senior Churchills' childless state had been a source of pain to them over the years. She had always thought of them, particularly the haughty and selfish Agnes Churchill, as regretting the lack of a legal heir more than the lack of a child in all of its immature, demanding physicality. Of the many impressions Emma had formed of the Churchills, that of nurturing parents had not been among them. But now, as Edgar gazed at Frank and the peddler, she saw that at least one of the Churchills knew what it meant to experience regret.

"You have a fine son, regardless of how he came to you."

Her remark had been intended to soothe, but instead he turned to her with a startled look. "What prompts you to say such a thing?"

Emma rued her loose tongue. She had insulted him, spoken too freely, too familiarly, about a delicate matter. "I beg your pardon. I meant only that Frank—"

"Frank is not my son; he is Mr. Weston's son." He looked past her shoulder. "Though he is my heir, I have never forgotten that."

Emma turned around. Mr. Weston had approached unheard, and looked as if he wished the conversation between her and Mr. Churchill had also gone unheard, to his ears. Mr. Weston was a man of such buoyant temperament that he deplored awkwardness and conflict, and was happiest when all around him were existing in perfect harmony.

Glancing from Emma to Mr. Churchill, he cleared his throat. "You have been most generous toward Frank, both you and Mrs. Churchill, and for your attentions to him all these years I am more thankful than I can ever express."

At the mention of his late wife, Edgar Churchill stiffened. Clearly, the gentleman still mourned deeply, in more than merely his attire. "Deprived of the opportunity to raise my own son, it was a privilege to raise yours."

His statement was oddly delivered, and made still more so by his bow and abrupt departure. He quit not only their conversation, but also the street itself, disengaging Frank from Mr. Deal to hasten him along to the Bates house. Frank handed payment to Mr. Deal and hurried off with his uncle.

"I am afraid that I offended Mr. Churchill," she said to Mr. Weston. "Though I am not quite certain how. I referred to Frank as his adopted son, but if anyone were to feel that appellation too keenly, I should think it would have been you."

"I doubt his displeasure arises from any words you uttered. He has not been quite himself since his arrival here. I believe Frank's marriage has put him in mind of his own son."

Emma's mind raced to comprehend him. "You cannot mean that Edgar Churchill has a *natural* child?"

"No, no—nothing like that. Mrs. Churchill ruled him so completely that he would not have dared take a mistress."

"Then whatever do you mean?"

Mr. Weston glanced around. Having assured himself that they would not be overheard, he nevertheless lowered his voice. "They had a child, a boy, early in their marriage, years before I met Frank's mother. She—Cecilia, my late wife—was a very young girl at the time, and was not fully aware of all that occurred. But while she was carrying Frank, she told me that her brother's wife had delivered a stillborn son. From the low talk of servants who assumed a child would neither attend nor comprehend their gossip, she formed the impression that it had been a difficult birth. Whatever occurred, Mrs. Churchill never carried another child. Cecilia knew no other details, as the episode was never spoken of at Enscombe, but her

dim memory of it caused her anxiety until our Frank was safely
delivered."

"Do you suppose that is why they offered to raise Frank after your
wife died? To replace their lost son?"

Mr. Weston, ever good-humored, chuckled. "No. They simply did
not think me capable of properly raising a Churchill. And in that respect they were correct, for I would have raised a Weston." His expression grew more sober. "Too, by then they had aged to the point
of relinquishing hope of ever having a child of their own. With no
closer relation than Frank to whom to leave their estate, they wanted
to control the upbringing of their heir. As Frank was growing up, I
sometimes wondered whether I had made the proper choice in allowing them to do so, but I think he turned out a fine young man,
whether despite or because of their influence."

Five

Mr. Churchill, independent of his wife, was feared by nobody; an easy, guidable man, to be persuaded into anything by his nephew.

—Emma

*T*he evening of the Donwell dinner party began promisingly enough. The Westons, Churchills, and Bateses all arrived on schedule to join the Knightleys in receiving their many guests, and Miss Bates looked as handsome as Emma had ever seen her. The seamstress and her assistants had produced just the dress Emma had envisioned, and it became Miss Bates like nothing else she had ever owned. She had, in fact, been so moved by the gift when Emma presented it for a final fitting that she was silent for a full minute as she blinked back tears, before erupting in thankfulness. The shawl complemented the dress perfectly, just as Emma had known it would.

Miss Bates's hair, arranged by Emma's own lady's maid in a simple yet elegant style beneath a bandeau, framed her face becomingly. To Emma's surprise, she wore the very combs Emma had admired among Mr. Deal's wares. She wondered, however, that Miss Bates had indulged in purchasing them at the sacrifice of more pressing wants.

She told Miss Bates that she looked lovely, and meant it. "I was tempted by those combs myself when I saw them among the peddler's goods, but I am glad you bought them, for they look so nice in your hair."

"Oh, I did not buy them! I had been telling Mr. Deal all about Jane's good fortune in marrying Frank, and how Frank had lately had some of his late aunt's jewels reset in a pair of hair ornaments for Jane, when he produced these combs. They were so pretty, and such a story Mr. Deal told!—but he would not name a price. He insisted on giving them to me—positively insisted—said he hoped they would bring *me* good fortune. But I am already so blessed—we have such good friends—kind, dear friends, such as yourself—not to mention a new nephew who will now ensure Jane's happiness— How could I possibly be in want of more good fortune?"

Emma smiled. If only Miss Bates knew what fortune this night might bring.

Emma had identified three gentlemen on tonight's guest list as particularly promising candidates for Miss Bates's hand: the Reverend Mr. Wynnken, Mr. Timothy Nodd, and Major Oliver Barnes-Lincoln. All were unmarried gentlemen between the ages of two score and three. Each had a respectable profession—the church, the law, the army—that would enable him to provide Miss Bates a comfortable establishment suitable for a gentlewoman. These were also professions that would enable the groom to spend time out of the house—away from Miss Bates's chatter—as needed.

The guests began to arrive. Miss Bates greeted local families with the ease of familiarity, and persons less well known to her with delight.

"Mr. and Mrs. Perry! How good of you to come. Jane looks radiant, does she not? It must please you, Mr. Perry, to see Jane in such a fine state of health after your kind ministrations to her earlier this year. Yes, love does work wonders—Mrs. Goddard! Indeed, it is a new gown . . . why, thank you, I am most obliged for the compliment; I do not think I have ever owned anything like it.—Oh, *you* are Major Barnes-Lincoln! Colonel Campbell speaks so highly of you, Major. You are most welcome in Highbury. How do you find it?"

Major Barnes-Lincoln replied that he liked it quite well, and lingered a few moments longer than necessary—at least, in Emma's hopeful perception—before seeking the company of Colonel Campbell.

Mrs. Elton, upon entering with her husband, was astonished to find Miss Bates in a new dress, and her approval of it was all hyperbole and insincerity. She took as a personal slight the notion that Miss Bates should have acquired the garment without her involvement. "My dear Miss Bates, you are such a sly creature! I never guessed you were planning a second gown all the while I toiled to make the first just so. Had I known, I could have advised you on this one as well. I see you chose a plain skirt—I would have suggested beadwork, or perhaps more ribbon."

"It was a surprise from Miss—Mrs. Knightley. Miss Woodhouse, I almost said. Forgive me, Mrs. Knightley, you are so recently married that I nearly forgot myself. But yes, the gown was a surprise—a most delightful surprise."

At this intelligence, Mrs. Elton's countenance hardened. "A surprise from Mrs. Knightley?" She turned to Emma with a smile that did not reach her eyes. "You must be very confident in your judgment, to risk imposing your own preferences on someone else."

Emma was happily spared the necessity of replying by the entrance of Mr. and Mrs. Patrick Dixon. When the butler announced the couple, Mrs. Elton immediately turned around to assess Jane's dearest friend—the former Miss Campbell—and her husband.

Emma averted her gaze, ashamed to recall the unkind speculation in which she had engaged last spring, that Jane Fairfax had developed an improper attachment to Mr. Dixon before his marriage to her friend. Had Emma kept the supposition to herself, she might now meet him without a blush, but she had carelessly shared her suspicions with Frank Churchill, who had encouraged her error so as to divert her notice from his own feelings for Jane. Though she had forgiven Frank his duplicity, she could not yet hear the name "Dixon" without mortification. Fortunately, Mr. Dixon himself remained unaware that he had ever been the object of calumnious conjecture.

A Mr. Thomas Dixon accompanied the Patrick Dixons. Thomas, Emma had been given to understand, was some sort of cousin, one of those adjunct relations that every family has and nobody else is quite sure as to which particular limb of the family tree they occupy.

All she knew was that he was a younger son of some forgotten Irish landowner, and was dependent upon Patrick Dixon for his maintenance. Emma was surprised to learn that he had been among the party at Weymouth that had given rise to her suspicions regarding Jane Fairfax and Mr. Patrick Dixon, for neither Frank Churchill nor Jane—nor Miss Bates, who could be counted upon to blurt out every known particular about her niece at some point—had ever alluded to his presence at the spa town during the period of Frank and Jane's meeting and clandestine courtship.

Having heard that Thomas was a younger son, Emma had formed a picture in her mind of a young man. Upon meeting him in person, however, she was surprised to discover that he was in fact considerably older than Mr. Patrick Dixon. From the grey at his temples and the laughter-lines about his animated blue eyes, she would guess him to be in his middle forties. She also had not been expecting a gentleman of such flamboyant appearance. He was dressed to the nines in a formfitting bright blue double-breasted dress coat and a shirt so ruffled that it erupted from his waistcoat in an avalanche of lace. Snug yellow pantaloons and silk stockings accentuated his trim figure and led the eye to low-heeled patent leather pumps with jeweled buckles. His cravat was so intricately tied that Beau Brummell himself would approve; white gloves and a tall-crowned silk top hat completed the ensemble.

"Mrs. Knightley—it is already a delightful party, and it has barely begun!" Thomas Dixon clasped her hand and raised it to his lips. "May I say, you are wearing the most exquisite gown. And your slippers— they must have come from Willis in London."

When Emma confessed that they had not, Thomas Dixon nevertheless complimented her taste. "It is far superior to *that* lady's," he said in a conspiratorial whisper. "Her shoes are simply all wrong." Emma followed his gaze; he was looking at Mrs. Elton.

She liked him already.

At last, Emma had received all her guests and was free to mingle among them whilst awaiting the call to dinner. Major Barnes-Lincoln remained in conversation with Colonel Campbell, and had been joined by one of Mr. Weston's old militia acquaintances. Mr. Nodd and Mr. Wynnken were engaged in separate conversations of their own; Emma would steer Miss Bates toward one of them as soon as the spinster had done arranging her mother near the fire. Mr. Woodhouse was already seated nearby with Emma's sister, Mrs. Weston, and Mr. Perry, all of whom were assuring him that the soup would not be over-rich, nor the pork over-salted, and that no harm would come of the diners' indulging in syllabub if the portions were kept quite small.

All was proceeding smoothly.

Nearly all, that is. Mr. Edgar Churchill seemed rather out of sorts as he stood off to one side of the crowded drawing room with Frank and Jane. Edgar held in his hand a glass of wine—his third—despite the fact that no one else drank. He had complained of thirst almost immediately upon his arrival, had of course been accommodated, and quickly swallowed two glasses. He now appeared much redder in the face than when Emma had received him. Frank's palm rested on the decanter, though Emma could not tell whether he stood ready to refill Edgar's glass yet again, or to prevent his uncle from doing so himself. She hoped it was the latter. Edgar needed no more wine at present. The hand supporting his wineglass trembled, threatening to spill its contents on the Persian rug; the other fluttered nervously at his side, fingers thrumming against his leg.

The sooner dinner began and Edgar Churchill consumed food to offset the wine, the better.

Emma went to tell them that the formal procession to the dining room would commence presently. As the newest bride and guest of honor, Jane Churchill would enjoy the privilege of leading the way. When Mrs. Knightley reached the trio, however, she found their thoughts far from the imminent meal. Edgar was bitterly vocalizing his discomfort.

"Too hot—intolerably hot . . ." He tugged at his cravat as if it choked him. "Ridiculous to have a fire in a room with so many people. Idiotic notion—What, we are all invited to dinner only to be cooked ourselves?"

"The room *is* close, sir," said Frank, "but hardly intolerable."

"Do not presume to tell me what is intolerable."

"I am sure we will go in to dinner momentarily," said Jane. "Look, here is Mrs. Knightley now, probably come to inform us so."

"Indeed, yes," Emma said. "I anticipate the butler's cue at any—"

"Why can we not go in now? For what are we kept waiting in this inferno?" He downed another half glass. "Nobody tells me anything! A gentleman has a right to know certain matters."

Frank put his hand on Edgar's arm in an attempt to placate him. "Sir, a little patience—"

"Patience? I am out of patience! I spent it all; I have no more. And what did it buy?" He stared at Frank's hand on his arm, then raised his gaze to his face. "Deceit—that is what it bought me. A gentleman ought not be surprised by news of his son."

"I am deeply sorry, sir. I should have told you of my engagement. It was wrong of me to conceal it. Were it not for trepidation over how Jane would be received by my aunt—"

"She was so proud, too proud!" His rant was starting to draw the notice of others.

Emma's perfect evening was rapidly coming undone. Surely Edgar Churchill was not intoxicated before dinner even began? At least, she comforted herself, her scheme for Miss Bates was unaffected by Mr. Churchill's behavior. The spinster was even now smiling broadly as she conversed with Mr. Nodd. From this range, Emma could not hear the subject of their discourse—a good sign, she decided, for it suggested that Miss Bates's chatter was restrained at present, if only in volume.

The butler's welcome news that dinner was at last ready to be served brought Emma immense relief. She paired her guests in order of precedence, attributing to hunger the less than blissful expression that momentarily flashed across Mr. Nodd's countenance as Miss Bates took his arm. Edgar, however, caused her greater distress: he refused to take his place in the promenade. He provided no reason, merely obstinance, despite Frank and Jane's repeated efforts to mollify him.

Emma and Mr. Knightley sent the other guests ahead, hoping that once the drawing room emptied, Mr. Churchill would become more complacent. But his agitation only increased.

"Gone! Shut me out! Shut me out, they did! Who decided? Who decided he should go?" He fairly impaled Emma with an angry glare. "You!"

Emma had witnessed the effects of too much wine before, but never to such a degree. She was too stunned to respond, and was grateful that her husband had also stayed behind to help manage Mr. Churchill.

Mr. Knightley interposed himself between Emma and their agitated guest. "Mr. Churchill, perhaps you had better—"

Mr. Churchill ignored Mr. Knightley altogether, seeming to look right through him as he continued to address Emma. "Always directing everybody around you. Manipulating us all. How could you live with yourself?" He laughed hysterically. "Apparently, you could not."

"Mr. Churchill!" Guest or no, Mr. Knightley had done with politeness. "If you cannot act with civility, I shall be forced to have a servant conduct you back to Randalls. Perhaps a proper night's rest will enable you to regain command of yourself."

Edgar Churchill at last raised his gaze to Mr. Knightley's stern countenance. "You do not know what it is to mourn." He looked then at Emma. "And neither do you, Agnes."

Oh, dear. Edgar Churchill was farther gone than she had realized. His pupils were wide, his face all confusion.

"I am not Mrs. Churchill," Emma said gently.

"Are you not?" He looked about the room. "Where is she? Where did she go?" His voice cracked. "She was just here . . ."

He was still discomposed, but no longer belligerent. Emma pitied him. Mr. Knightley's glower softened.

"Mr. Churchill, if you are feeling indisposed, allow me to call for your carriage."

His unfocused gaze continued to sweep the room. "Where is Frank? Where is my son? I want my son."

Emma and Mr. Knightley exchanged glances. "It would be cruel to send him back to an unfamiliar house alone," she said. "And even if we did, I think he needs to eat something before he leaves."

"Do you believe him collected enough to join the other guests?"

"He is placed near Frank Churchill at the dining table. That should comfort him."

It was settled. Mr. Knightley took Mr. Churchill's wineglass from him and set it on a nearby table, then he and Emma escorted Frank's uncle to the dining room. He moved slowly, his fit of temper apparently having depleted his energy. The continual thrumming of his left hand, however, bespoke a spirit not yet at ease.

When they entered the dining room, the rest of the party was—mercifully—so immersed in conversation that their entrance was scarcely noticed. Frank, however, had been watching the door. He observed his uncle's demeanor and immediately came to them. "Are you well, sir?"

Mr. Churchill attempted to speak, but his voice broke. He tried to force out words but hoarseness had overtaken him. Perhaps it was just as well—he could not cause a further scene.

"Come." Frank led him to his chair. "We have been missing you."

Emma was glad that Mr. Perry happened to be placed across the table from Edgar Churchill. The apothecary was used to dealing with people in all manner of conditions and temperaments, and himself possessed a soothing demeanor. His conversation would help further steady the senior Mr. Churchill.

When all were seated, Emma's gaze took in the whole assembly. The guests of honor, Frank and Jane Churchill, exhibited the proper degree of newlywed felicity. Their friends shared their joy; their families—particularly Miss Bates—fairly radiated it. Miss Bates, in fact, seated (by no accident) between Mr. Nodd and Mr. Wynnken, and across from Major Barnes-Lincoln, wore a look of such happiness that in the candlelight she looked almost pretty, and Emma harbored hopes that the demands of chewing and swallowing would by necessity check the flow of her conversation enough to allow the gentlemen around her to participate in it.

Mrs. Knightley met her husband's gaze and smiled. Their first dinner party, in both its official and tacit objectives, looked to be a success after all.

That was the last peaceful moment of the night.

Though Edgar Churchill had the courtesy to tolerate the soup course, somewhere between the fish and the pheasant the company nearly bore witness to a return of his bisque.

The heaving gentleman was hastily removed from the dining room to an empty bedchamber, where Mr. Perry attended him. Frank rose to accompany them, but upon being assured of Mr. Perry's having the situation well in hand, was persuaded to remain in the dining room with all of the people assembled there for his benefit. Emma and Mr. Knightley, their sense of obligation equally divided between their duty to one ill guest and responsibility to dozens of others, settled it between them that Mr. Knightley, more familiar with the Donwell household, would accompany the apothecary and his patient to oversee any provisions required to make Mr. Churchill more comfortable.

To Emma, meanwhile, fell the unenviable task of presiding over a dining table whose atmosphere had altered considerably. The unseemly intoxication of the groom's uncle, a gentleman of Edgar Churchill's stature, was a subject on everyone's minds but no one's tongues as they awkwardly tried to converse about any other subject in the world. Miss Bates had no trouble filling the uncomfortable silence, and Emma for once was grateful for her steady, cheerful chatter. The more she spoke, however, the more pained Mr. Wynnken appeared, and the major looked as if he very much wished that she, too, would retire from the room pleading indisposition. Mr. Nodd seemed in danger of nodding off altogether. Emma's matchmaking plans were unraveling before her eyes.

Mr. Woodhouse blamed the bisque. Rich food, he had long maintained, was never good for anybody's digestion, but especially for an elderly gentleman such as Edgar Churchill. (At nine-and-fifty, Mr. Woodhouse was yet on the light side of sixty, the year which, in his mind, marked the threshold of old age. In temperament and habits, however, Mr. Woodhouse had been old at thirty.) He passionately attempted to dissuade everyone near him from so much as tasting the syllabub. Only Mrs. Elton complied—not out of doubts regarding the dessert's richness, but out of conviction of its inferiority to the syllabub served at Maple Grove.

When Mr. Knightley returned and reported that Mr. Churchill had fallen into slumber, a sense of ease rippled through the assembly. Edgar Churchill would sleep off his overindulgence. For the present, both he and his embarrassing behavior could be quite guiltlessly forgotten.

Six

Mr. Knightley, who, for some reason best known to himself, had certainly taken an early dislike to Frank Churchill, was only growing to dislike him more.

—Emma

*I*t was most inconsiderate of Edgar Churchill to die during his nephew's marriage celebration.

The women had returned to the drawing room, leaving the men to their port and tobacco, when a footman entered and discreetly informed Emma that she was wanted posthaste by Mr. Perry. She reached Edgar's chamber to discover her husband and Frank Churchill also about to enter.

"Has Mr. Churchill's condition declined?" she asked.

"We were not told." Mr. Knightley opened the door.

Edgar Churchill lay prostrate beneath a sheet. Mr. Perry, his round face and keen eyes bearing an unusually grave expression, stood over him. The apothecary had removed his own coat and rolled up his shirtsleeves, which he now restored to their proper position at his wrists. Two maids gathered soiled linen; despite the chill, a window had been opened.

"My uncle is worse?" Frank asked.

"I am terribly sorry, Mr. Churchill. Your uncle is dead."

Emma gasped.

"How can that be?" Frank exclaimed. "You assured me earlier that he would be fine—that you would see to his care. Mr. Knightley informed us all that he was sleeping."

"He was—so deeply that he did not waken, even when he evacuated his stomach. After the servants tidied him up and put him into a nightshirt, he continued to sleep soundly, though his pulse was quite rapid and his breathing turned shallow. I did not anticipate that he would stop breathing altogether." Mr. Perry ran a hand through his thinning hair. The loss of a patient, even one so little known to him, clearly distressed him. "I could not revive him—it was as if his lungs had simply forgotten their duty."

"He had but three glasses of wine," Frank said. "I have seen him drink more with no ill effect."

"You knew him better than I," Mr. Perry said, "but he did not appear tonight to be a man who can hold his liquor."

"His conduct this evening was most unusual. I cannot account for it, except that he has not been himself since my aunt's death, most particularly this se'nnight past."

"Had he any wine or other spirits before coming here?" Mr. Knightley asked. "He seemed quite agitated about your having entered into your engagement with Jane Fairfax without his knowledge. Perhaps he was not as favorably disposed to the marriage as you believed, and dwelled upon his displeasure over Madeira or brandy before coming to dinner."

"Nay, only tea, which we took with the Westons at half past four." He approached his uncle, touched his hand. "I regret the pain all the secrecy surrounding our betrothal caused. Yet it was necessary at the time. Who could have imagined, when I met Jane, that within a twelvemonth I would have my independence? That I would lose both aunt and uncle in so short a span? I would not have dreamed it, nor wished it, for the world."

Indeed, Emma thought, who *could* have imagined the two deaths occurring so unexpectedly? And with such fortuitous results for one individual?

Frank stepped away from the lifeless body. "I must impart the news to Jane before the rest of the company learns of it. What a somber end to our celebration! And what an odd homecoming it will be when I bring my bride to Enscombe—installing her as mistress and myself as master all at once." He left to find his wife.

Emma felt sorrow for both the misters Churchill. This was a shocking loss to Frank, particularly following so rapidly upon the death of his aunt. She could not help but also realize the unpleasant repercussions of this event to herself. Surely this was the most infamous dinner party in Highbury's history! One of their most prominent guests had died—practically at the dining table. She could envision now how Mrs. Elton would describe the event in her next letter to Maple Grove.

No one would ever dine at Donwell again. Everybody would assume—

Her stomach churned. What if their assumptions proved true? What if, in fact, it was not drink that had killed Mr. Churchill, but spoiled partridge or tainted mussels, or some lethal root mistaken by the cook for horseradish?

"Mr. Perry, might he have died because of something he ate?"

"Unless others were ill when you left them just now, I doubt it was anything you served." He offered a reassuring half-smile. "You need not fear having inadvertently poisoned your guests, Mrs. Knightley. Mr. Churchill's distress seemed to have begun before anybody even entered the dining room. I believe the rest of us are quite safe."

Emma's uneasiness diminished, but Mr. Knightley now frowned.

"Perry, what do you believe caused Edgar Churchill's death?"

"He could have ingested something earlier that did not agree with him, perhaps with his tea. One might expect, were this the case, that Frank Churchill and the Westons would be suffering similar effects if they took tea together. Edgar Churchill, however, was older, and would be more vulnerable to any virulence that he happened to encounter, particularly if he was already suffering melancholy due to the recent loss of his wife."

The apothecary put on his coat, buttoning it across his generous paunch. "I know nothing about Edgar Churchill's state of health before tonight," he added. "It may be that he took medicine for some malady and accidentally used too much."

"What sort of medicine? Laudanum?"

Mr. Perry shook his head. "Several of his symptoms do not correspond with opium overdose. Laudanum contracts the pupils, whereas his were quite dilated, and does not excite but slows the pulse. As I have also not observed among patients taking laudanum the sort of raving in which Mr. Churchill indulged, I would suspect another drug to be the agent of his demise, if it was caused by any drug at all. Perhaps Frank can tell you whether his uncle was taking remedies for any complaints."

"Could more be determined by examining Edgar Churchill's remains?" Mr. Knightley asked.

"I doubt it, but I can make an attempt. I need to retrieve some instruments from my office, however."

Mr. Perry departed, leaving the Knightleys with the uncomfortable business of breaking the news to their guests.

"We should return to the drawing room," Emma stated, "and attempt to control what is said of this matter—if word has not somehow reached everybody's ears already. Doubtless, the servants are talking amongst themselves, and Frank Churchill's disclosure to Jane might have been overheard."

"Frank Churchill is a man capable of great secrecy when it suits him."

"Do you intend to ask him about his uncle's general health?"

Her husband was silent for a minute. "I have several questions for Frank Churchill."

Emma did not like his tone. "Surely you do not believe Edgar Churchill's death to be anything but a most unfortunate accident?"

"As Frank Churchill himself stated only minutes ago, his uncle's death results in his inheriting a handsome estate just as he is taking a wife and starting a family of his own. I would not be a very competent magistrate if I failed to notice the coincidence."

"Frank Churchill is as shocked by this event as we are."

"Not too shocked to immediately realize the benefit of it to himself."

Of course he had realized it—Frank was only human, after all. She herself had even thought almost immediately of the likely gossip and its effect on her own reputation in the village. It was not a reaction of which she was proud, but it was natural.

"You are unjust. From the moment Frank first came to Highbury—nay, before he even visited the village—you did not like him. All Highbury adored him, yet you privately expressed to me criticism of his character that I daresay you continue to harbor. You believed him derelict in his duty toward his father whilst he served the will of his rich aunt and uncle, the very people towards whom you now accuse him of not feeling enough. Could not your prejudice against him be causing your distrust?"

"I neither accuse nor suspect Frank Churchill of anything at present. But even did I not have a responsibility as magistrate, a guest has died in our house, and until the cause is clear, I cannot be easy. Nor, I should think, could you, given that this event will doubtless be the talk of the village for months."

"Highbury will not think ill of Frank, and neither should you. Now, come assist me in disbanding this party and mitigating the inevitable gossip."

"I am afraid no one can leave Donwell quite yet. One of our guests might have observed something regarding Mr. Churchill that we did not, and I want to speak with each person while his memory is untarnished."

Emma regarded him in horror. "You are *not* going to conclude Frank and Jane's marriage fête by interrogating all their friends and family?"

"I will merely ask a few questions of each guest, in as discreet a manner as possible—a brief but personal conversation. I shall give the appearance of breaking the news of Edgar Churchill's death gently and individually."

Emma inwardly cringed. Mr. Knightley's straightforward manner—which she considered one of his most admirable qualities—would doubtless defeat all his intentions of delicacy.

"Will you allow me to assist you?"

"You can aid me best by keeping everyone calm and diverted while I conduct the tête-à-têtes."

"Then perhaps one of the other parish officials? There are so many guests that it will take you all night to question them."

"Whom else can I trust to handle this properly? Mr. Elton? His vanity would turn the process into a witch hunt. Mr. Weston? As much as I esteem him and his friendship, and value his help in other matters, under these circumstances he is entirely the wrong person to further involve in the affair. Not only does his connexion to the Churchills render him biased, but he is of too social a disposition. He would take every person he interviewed into our trust, and there would be the end of any confidentiality."

Though Emma loved the avuncular Mr. Weston, she had to concede Mr. Knightley's assessment of his fitness for this particular duty. The man possessed such an open, honest character that he was constitutionally incapable of keeping a secret.

"What about Mr. Cole or Mr. Cox?" she suggested.

"They have no experience with investigations, and their connexion to the Churchills is slight; their involvement at this stage would appear odd enough to inspire the very speculation and gossip we hope to discourage. The one person I might depend upon is Mr. Perry. Though he serves as our coroner, his interest would most likely be seen as medically, not legally, motivated. But his time at present is better spent examining Mr. Churchill's remains, and I want to conduct the interviews and disperse immaterial witnesses as quickly as possible. No, I am afraid I must do this myself."

As there was no dissuading him, Emma returned to the drawing room to divert her guests' attention from a process which, despite Mr. Knightley's characterizing it as a series of "personal conversations," had to her all the hallmarks of an inquisition.

Fortunately, Edgar Churchill had interacted with only his most intimate acquaintances whilst in the drawing room, and Frank, though he had flitted from group to group, had in his usual style said little of consequence, so most of the guests had observed nothing of import and were released fairly quickly. They all might see their beds before the hour grew unconscionably late. Emma was particularly eager to send her father home, as word of anyone's death was sure to upset him. The Westons took the news of Edgar Churchill's demise particularly hard, and Miss Bates's exclamations, though heartfelt, were enough to inspire a hasty retreat by every member of the company even had propriety not.

Despite her warm defense of Frank, Emma could not dismiss Mr. Knightley's skepticism from her mind as she encouraged their overnight guests to retire to their individual chambers, and saw the rest depart. There would be no more merriment, let alone matchmaking, among this assembly. Guests originally expected to stay a se'nnight were already forming plans to leave on the morrow. So much for her hopes regarding Miss Bates. The only person's prospects that had improved this evening were Frank's.

Yes, it was most inconsiderate of Edgar Churchill to die during his nephew's marriage celebration.

But for his nephew, it was also most convenient.

Volume the Second

IN WHICH MR. AND MRS. DARCY BECOME ACQUAINTED
WITH MR. AND MRS. KNIGHTLEY . . . AND
ALL OF HIGHBURY

"There are secrets in all families, you know."

—Mr. Weston, *Emma*

Seven

"The sooner every party breaks up, the better."
—Mr. Woodhouse, *Emma*

*D*onwell Abbey was an impressive residence, its entire façade alight against the surrounding darkness. Like a number of England's great houses, Donwell had once been home to a religious order before King Henry the Eighth dissolved the monasteries, and its stone walls yet evinced dignity and grace. Though successive generations of private owners had influenced its current architecture, enough carved saints piously embellished its remaining pointed arches to recall the building's hallowed origins.

It was appropriate that a former center of religious life should yet serve parish business—as the home of the magistrate—and on any other occasion Fitzwilliam Darcy would have welcomed the opportunity to become acquainted with the master of such a house. But the purpose of this visit was not pleasure, nor was Darcy in a social mood.

Unfortunately, it appeared that pleasure was foremost on the mind of Mr. George Knightley this evening. Carriages lined the circular drive before the mansion's stately front doors. Half the neighborhood must be within.

"It appears the magistrate is hosting a party," Elizabeth said as their coach joined the queue. "I doubt he will welcome an intrusion from us."

Darcy concurred. Upon reaching Highbury, they had stopped at the first house they saw to enquire where the constable or magistrate might be found, and were directed to Donwell Abbey. Their informant had failed to mention that the present might not be a suitable time to impose on Mr. Knightley's notice. Had Darcy known, he might have postponed this call until morning. He and Elizabeth had wanted, however, to alert the local authorities as soon as possible to the presence of highway robbers in the area, not only in hopes of their own stolen possessions being recovered but also to prevent others from being similarly victimized. Too, while they were nearly certain that "Miss Jones" had conspired with the thieves to create a distraction, the very slight chance that an innocent woman had in fact been abducted along with their chest impelled Darcy and Elizabeth to report the incident posthaste.

"If the highwaymen are still about, his own guests could be at risk when they depart. Let us advise the butler of our reason for calling; he will know whether his master will consider our business urgent enough to warrant an interruption." The competence and dedication of magistrates varied widely from parish to parish; Darcy hoped Mr. Knightley would prove himself to be among England's more conscientious administrators. "If Mr. Knightley does not see us tonight, I shall request that he contact us at the inn."

His valet had by now secured a room at the Crown, which they both looked forward to reaching. Already weary from the long day of travel, anxiety over the health of their groom and footman compounded their desire to dispatch their business quickly so that all could rest. Though upon regaining consciousness the two servants had insisted they were none the worse for the assault, Elizabeth had assessed them with a mother's eye and remained troubled all the way to Highbury.

He stepped out of the carriage and turned to assist her. As he offered his hand, the doors of Donwell Abbey opened and people spilled onto the steps. They chattered, as guests normally do when leaving a large assembly, bidding each other farewell and exchanging promises to call upon each other soon. But there was a muted quality to the burble, an unusual restraint, and repeated murmuring of the words "shocking" and "Churchill."

Darcy and Elizabeth paused to allow the majority of departing guests to clear the stairs. Two ladies and a gentleman escorted an older man in a thick muffler and heavy greatcoat.

"Poor Mr. Churchill!" the old man exclaimed. "I am quite certain it was the bisque. Do not allow the servants to dine on the leftover soup, Emma. Nor the syllabub."

"I shall make sure they are safe, Papa."

Darcy approached the butler. "We have been told that this is the home of Mr. George Knightley, the magistrate?" At the servant's affirmation, Darcy presented his card and lowered his voice. "My wife and I are passing through Highbury. We were just robbed on the road from London and would like to apprise Mr. Knightley of the incident." He gestured towards the departing guests. "If this is not an appropriate time, we can return at his first convenience."

The butler invited them to step into the entry hall, where they were dwarfed by great columns supporting the ribbed vault ceiling. Tapestries adorned the grey stone walls; the one nearest them depicted a medieval hunt. The servant soon returned with a tall, authoritative-looking gentleman.

"I understand you are looking for the magistrate. I am Mr. George Knightley."

Darcy bowed. "Mr. Fitzwilliam Darcy, of Derbyshire, and my wife. Pray excuse us for arriving at such an inopportune moment."

"Our party was just concluding. I do have another pressing matter, so we might have to continue our conversation tomorrow, but I can give you a few minutes now. Let us discuss your business in the library."

They followed him through former cloisters to a large chamber that held at least as many volumes as did Pemberley's library. A passing glance at some of the titles—Darcy could not help himself—revealed a wide range of subjects and authors: philosophy, economics, history, science, law, politics, poetry. He saw, too, that Mr. Knightley shared his commitment to keeping abreast of the latest agricultural theories and practices. On one of the tables lay open a book that Darcy had been reading himself before leaving Pemberley.

Mr. Knightley motioned them toward two armchairs, then took a seat on the opposite side of the table. "I am sorry that your introduction to Highbury was less than cordial. Tell me what occurred."

"We were on the road from London, a mile or two outside of the village, when a young woman hailed our carriage," Darcy said. "We stopped to assist her. Claiming to have injured her ankle, she drew us and our coachman away from the carriage. While we were thus distracted, someone else struck our other two servants unconscious and stole our chest. Then the woman slipped away as well."

"Did you see the assailants?"

"No. The rear carriage lantern broke, and I had brought the forward lantern with me when I approached the woman. Our servants did not see anyone, either. When they regained consciousness, our footman said he had been hit from behind while repairing the lantern. After some minutes, the groom went to check on him, discovered him lying on the ground, and was struck from behind, as well."

"So the robbers never directly confronted you?"

"We saw only the woman."

Mr. Knightley closed the agricultural volume and set it aside, along with a page of notes. From a drawer he withdrew a fresh sheet of paper and reached for his quill. "Kindly describe her. You said she was young?"

"Perhaps sixteen. She had blond hair."

"Light blond," Elizabeth said. "Her face and arms were tanned, considerably browner than her ankle, which she asked me to examine. She had small bones but seemed strong. She wore a white muslin dress. It was somewhat dirty, but not beyond what one would expect for a person who had been wandering lost in the woods for hours, as she claimed to have done."

Mr. Knightley nodded as he took down the details. "What story did she tell?"

"She identified herself as 'Miss Jones,' though I would be astonished if that is indeed her true name," Darcy said. "She said she was visiting cousins, also named Jones, at a nearby farm."

"We have two families named Jones who farm in this parish. I shall enquire after the woman. Did she offer any other information?"

"Nothing about herself," Elizabeth said, "though just before she disappeared, she told me there were highwaymen about."

"This is the first I have heard of any highwaymen in the area. The worst menace we have known recently is a rash of poultry thefts. Have you any reason to think you were targeted on purpose? Was anyone paying particular attention to you or your belongings when you last stopped to water the horses?"

Darcy could recall no such unwanted notice, nor could Elizabeth. "I expect they waited along the road to take advantage of any promising traveler, and we merely happened into their path first."

"You are fortunate that they did not confront you directly and seize the chest by force. Were you armed?"

"Yes."

"Did you lose the weapon with the chest?"

Darcy shook his head. His small traveler's pistol had been concealed in his greatcoat, and the robbers likely never suspected that Elizabeth carried an even smaller one in her reticule—or that she was a surprisingly talented markswoman. "My pistol was not inside it. The chest contained an heirloom set of christening garments and a signet ring that belonged to my late mother."

Mr. Knightley dipped his pen again and looked to them both. "I shall require a description of the items if we are to have any hope of recovering them."

"The christening clothes are a beautiful set," Elizabeth said. "An embroidered gown of cream satin, trimmed with silk braid and silk ribbon ties. There is also a long pinner bib with Hollie point lace, and a lace-edged cap."

"The signet ring is gold, inscribed with the initials *A.F.*," Darcy added. The letters stood for Anne Fitzwilliam, the name Darcy's mother had borne before her marriage. Upon Anne de Bourgh's marriage to Colonel Fitzwilliam, the name had become hers, and Darcy had thought the ring ought to be, as well. Now the cherished baptismal set and ring were in the possession of conscienceless thieves with no value for their history or appreciation of their worth. Both Darcy and Elizabeth were deeply disturbed by the theft.

They provided a few more particulars. When they had done, Mr. Knightley returned the quill to its stand. His countenance, sober since their interview had commenced, grew more grim.

"Until we know more about the highwaymen, I am afraid I cannot be optimistic about your belongings being recovered," he said. "I do, however, pledge to do all I can. In the morning, I would like you to accompany the constable, Mr. Cole, to the area on the London road where you encountered Miss Jones. Perhaps daylight will reveal clues as to the identities of these bandits."

The butler entered. "Mr. Perry has returned, sir."

"Thank you. I shall attend him directly." Mr. Knightley rose. "I will send someone now to the Jones farms to learn what we can, but then I must excuse myself to address another matter before I can discuss this one with you further." He withdrew his watch from the pocket of his waistcoat. "The hour is grown quite late. I hope you do not intend to continue your travels tonight?"

"No, we plan to take a room at the Crown Inn. Our servants and remaining luggage were to meet us there."

"I am afraid they undoubtedly found the Crown full. The assembly that was breaking up as you arrived here included many guests who have taken rooms there."

"Is there another inn?"

"Unfortunately, no. We are a small village." He paused. "But a hospitable one, I like to believe. Allow me to offer you accommodation here."

"We do not wish to intrude on your celebration," Elizabeth said.

"Not at all. I am sorry to say that the celebration reached a premature end. The dinner honored friends who recently wed, and the groom's uncle unexpectedly died not long before your arrival."

Darcy now understood the odd hush that had enveloped the crowd as it departed. "Surely you do not want strangers among you at such a time."

"Half the guests are strangers to me—friends of the bride and groom. Your presence will be no intrusion, and I insist upon extending you a kinder welcome to Highbury than did Miss Jones. Permit me to send for your things at the Crown. In the morning, we can discuss your incident in greater detail and attempt to locate your stolen belongings."

Mr. Knightley summoned a servant and instructed him regarding the arrangements. "And send a man to Hartfield to ensure that Mr. Woodhouse reached home safely," he added.

"Now," he said, leading the Darcys out of the library, "let us find Mrs. Knightley so that she can make your acquaintance."

As they passed through the cloisters once more, Darcy mentioned the agricultural book he had seen on Mr. Knightley's desk. "I have recently been reading Stuart myself, and am not certain I agree with all of his recommendations. Perhaps after more urgent business has been resolved, we can exchange opinions of his theories."

Mr. Knightley appeared pleasantly surprised by the suggestion. "I should like that very much. Few among my acquaintance, save my steward, enjoy discussing such issues as much as I do."

"Mr. Darcy has the same difficulty," Elizabeth said. "Though, while we were in London, he managed to find enough gentlemen of similar interests at Lord Chatfield's dinner party that they spent half the evening discussing husbandry."

"It was not half the evening."

She chuckled. "Tell that to the wives."

Darcy addressed Mr. Knightley. "And none of those gentlemen had read Stuart's book."

Mr. Knightley had followed the marital exchange with interest. "You are acquainted with the Earl of Chatfield?"

"Indeed, I have the honor of calling him a friend," Darcy said.

"As do I, though we missed each other the last several times I was in town. I begin to believe he knows absolutely everybody."

Darcy was inclined to agree. The earl liked nothing better than to collect a group of diverse individuals around his dining room table to see what sort of conversation resulted, and in all of the parties Darcy had attended, he had never dined with the same group of people twice.

His lordship belonged to several learned societies, and counted members of still more among his seemingly endless connexions. Men of arts and letters and science, men of medicine and law, military men and men of God—from artists to zoologists, philanthropists to philosophers, one could never predict whom one might encounter at a gathering hosted by Lord Chatfield. For all his intellectual curiosity, however, the earl was a discriminating judge of character, and the fact that Chatfield included Mr. Knightley among his friends further reassured Darcy of the magistrate's reliability.

When they reached the main hall, they found not Mrs. Knightley, but a gentlemanlike man about Mr. Knightley's age, carrying an apothecary's bag.

"Mr. Perry, I am glad you were able to return so quickly," Mr. Knightley said. "I will join you in a few minutes. First, however, can you visit the servants' hall? Mr. and Mrs. Darcy's coach was robbed, and their groom and footman were struck unconscious. They are awake now, but we should like them examined."

"My goodness! You were not yourselves injured, I hope?"

After the Darcys gave their assurances, Mr. Knightley directed a passing footman to accompany the apothecary to the servants' hall. He then turned back to Mr. Perry. "When you have done downstairs, a servant will escort you to Mr. Churchill's chamber. I will meet you there. Do you require additional assistants?"

"For Mr. Churchill? No. I shall conduct only a preliminary examination here. Should we believe a more thorough autopsy is warranted, the remains can be moved to my office and a surgeon summoned."

The word "autopsy" commanded Darcy's attention. Apparently, the apothecary's patient was the deceased uncle, and there had been something peculiar about his demise.

As Mr. Perry headed for the servants' hall, Mr. Knightley regarded the Darcys apprehensively. "I wish Mr. Perry had exercised more caution in his speech just now," he said. "The circumstances of Mr. Churchill's death were a bit unusual, but not a general cause for concern. If you could refrain from mentioning the autopsy before anyone else, I would be most obliged."

Darcy perfectly comprehended the magistrate's position: Mr. Knightley did not want to create panic or invite rampant speculation whilst he had yet to determine whether there was anything about which to panic or speculate. Nor did he want to compromise the coroner's ability to fully probe questions raised by the postmortem examination.

"Unfortunately, Mrs. Darcy and I have found ourselves called upon to investigate several suspicious deaths, more than one of which proved to be murder." The incidents were not subjects he and Elizabeth were themselves in the habit of discussing with others, particularly someone with whom they were barely acquainted, but he wanted to assure Mr. Knightley that he recognized what was at stake. "We understand the importance of maintaining silence on such matters, and you may depend upon ours regarding Mr. Churchill."

"I appreciate your discretion. Murder is a crime with which we, thankfully, are little acquainted in Highbury, and I trust that remains the case. I expect Mr. Perry's findings to confirm Mr. Churchill's death as accidental. One merely prefers certainty."

Mrs. Knightley, the butler informed their host, was engaged with the Westons and Churchills at present, and Mr. Knightley decided to leave them undisturbed. With apologies for what he perceived as neglect, but which the Darcys did not take as such, he consigned them to the care of the housekeeper.

"I shall introduce you to Mrs. Knightley on the morrow. Meanwhile, do not hesitate to ask for anything you require." Mr. Knightley started to retreat, but then halted and turned to them once more. "By the bye—did you solve them? The murders?"

"We did indeed," Darcy said.

Mr. Knightley did not reply. He merely looked pensive as he headed to meet the apothecary in Mr. Churchill's chamber.

Eight

"As it seems a matter of justice, it shall be done."
—Mr. Knightley, Emma

I believe," Elizabeth said to Darcy as she sat at the dressing table, preparing to go down to breakfast, "that you and I have grown alarmingly accustomed to the presence of death and mayhem in our everyday existence."

Across the bedchamber, he paused over the letter he was writing to Colonel Fitzwilliam. "Why do you say so?"

"One might expect that being set upon by thieves and arriving here in the midst of a fatal fête would disturb one's equanimity, yet I think I fell asleep last night the moment I closed my eyes." Indeed, by the time their servants and luggage were collected from the Crown, little had remained of the night, and Elizabeth had noticed almost nothing about their chamber save the great canopied walnut bed centered on one wall. Upon awakening, she had found herself in a spacious, well-appointed room with sturdy, centuries-old furnishings and a view of Donwell's apple orchard in the distance.

"You were exhausted from the travel and turmoil."

She knew Darcy had been, as well. Despite her fatigue, his restlessness had disturbed her slumber more than once during the night, and this morning his mood remained more serious than usual.

"Even so, if misadventure continues to find us whenever we leave home, people will stop inviting us to visit." She adjusted the lace of her chemisette and pinched her cheeks to add color to them. "I doubt Mr. Knightley has any notion what he took on by encouraging us to stay. It was noble of you to warn him."

"I did nothing of the sort." He added a line to the end of his letter, then signed his name. "In mentioning those previous incidents, I merely sought to assure him of our discretion regarding the Churchill matter."

"Nevertheless, I approve your conscientiousness. Mr. Knightley seems a good sort of man, and I look forward to meeting his wife."

She turned back to the mirror and made the finishing touches to her toilette. Though more inclined to wear a simpler dress to breakfast, Elizabeth wanted to make a good impression upon Mrs. Knightley, and so had chosen her chintz morning gown, with its scalloped front-button closure from bodice to hem. With winter approaching, her maid had attached the long, ribbon-trimmed sleeves just before they left Derbyshire, for which Elizabeth was grateful. Despite the fire in their chamber, the air held a nip that she attributed to the wind rustling the leaves outside.

Darcy, too, had chosen his attire with care. The navy blue coat was among her favorites, for it complemented his dark hair and eyes, and showed to advantage the broad shoulders that never shirked a burden placed upon them.

She smoothed the curls that peeked from under her cap, and rose. "Altogether, I declare this a better experience than the last night we passed in an abbey."

Her lighthearted reference to Northanger Abbey and the intrigue it had held elicited the smile from Darcy that she had hoped to provoke. It was slight and brief, but she was glad to see it flicker across his countenance.

"Here, however, it is *my* mother's jewelry that is missing."

"I rue the ring's disappearance," she said, "but the christening garments distress me most." The set had been worn by three generations of Darcy's family: first, Hugh Fitzwilliam, the Ninth Earl of Southwell, and his two sisters, Lady Catherine and Lady Anne, Darcy's mother. In time, their children had worn it: Hugh's three sons, including James—now Colonel—Fitzwilliam; Darcy and his sister, Georgiana; and Lady Catherine's daughter, Anne de Bourgh. Most recently, Darcy's daughter, Lily-Anne, had been baptized in the set. "We cannot replace a christening gown worn by yourself and your daughter, and so many of your other relations. I had hoped to see more children of ours wear it after Anne and Colonel Fitzwilliam's child is christened."

"I do not intend to leave Highbury until we have exhausted all possible avenues for recovering our belongings. Mr. Knightley might already have learned something about the thieves during the night." He dripped melted wax onto the letter and sealed it. "Though doubtless he is more occupied with Mr. Churchill."

"It would be unnatural if he were not. To have a guest die during dinner—what a dreadful event! And then two strangers arrive in the midst of it to report a robbery. I think it speaks well of Mr. Knightley's character and sense of duty that he gave us any of his time at all."

"If highwaymen indeed threaten the village, their presence requires his attention even while he investigates the Churchill matter." Darcy rose, the letter in one hand. The other he offered to Elizabeth and led her to the door.

"The question he posed to us at parting—do you suppose he suspects Mr. Churchill's death was not accidental?"

"We do not know enough about the circumstances, or our host, to speculate. Nor is it our concern."

"It most certainly is," she replied as they stepped into the corridor. "For if we are still at Donwell for dinner, I hear we should avoid the bisque."

Mrs. Knightley was younger than Elizabeth had expected. Given Mr. Knightley's age, she had thought the magistrate's wife would be closer in years to her husband's, but instead the mistress of Donwell

Abbey appeared to be within a year or two of Elizabeth's own. Elizabeth recognized her as the lady whose father had left Donwell in dread of leftover syllabub the previous night. She was a beautiful young woman with a slender figure, flawless complexion, and intelligent hazel eyes. Her manners were graceful and her demeanor amiable, though the strain of the previous evening's events was apparent in the smile she offered upon introducing herself.

Their hostess had been alone at table when the Darcys entered the breakfast room, the duty of seeing off numerous departing guests having prevented her from breaking her own fast until now. "Pray forgive my not having received you last night," she said. "I did not know of your arrival until after you had retired. I am sorry to learn of the incident that brought you to us. Mr. Knightley assures me that neither of you came to harm?"

"We did not, but two of our servants were rendered unconscious for a time."

"They have been attended to. Mr. Perry determined that they suffered no serious injury, but did advise a day of rest before they resume their duties."

Elizabeth was relieved for the health of their servants, both loyal employees who had served the Darcy family for years. "I daresay we shall not be continuing our journey for at least that long, as your husband wanted to speak with us more today. Is Mr. Knightley about?"

"I have not seen him downstairs yet this morning, which surprises me, as he seldom rises this late." Emma gestured toward the sideboard, where the morning's meal had been set out for the convenience of guests leaving at various times. "After the events of last night, you must be famished. I believe the rolls are still warm, and if you will indulge a bride's boasting of her new husband's strawberry fields, Donwell's jam is the finest in Surrey."

"You are but recently married?"

"Last month." From Mrs. Knightley's smile and the brightness of her eyes, Elizabeth was certain she had married for affection.

The rolls were indeed still warm, the tea hot, and the other offerings so appealing that Elizabeth realized just how hungry she was. She would have utterly failed as the heroine of a sentimental novel—far from being too traumatized to eat after an encounter with highway-men, she was tantalized by the smell of the baked apples alone.

She and Darcy had just brought their plates to the table and taken seats across from Mrs. Knightley when her husband entered. Though he greeted them with cordiality equal to what he had shown the pre-vious evening, his manner had an increased gravity about it. Eliza-beth glanced at Mrs. Knightley, and read concern in her countenance as she, too, studied the magistrate.

"Do sit down," Mrs. Knightley urged her husband. "Allow me to get your breakfast."

He regarded her fondly, like a man unaccustomed but grateful to have a woman looking after him after years as a bachelor. "Do not in-terrupt your own meal." He moved to the sideboard. "Have all of our other guests gone home?"

"All but the Dixons. Mrs. Dixon remains in Highbury to condole with Jane Churchill and be of whatever use she may until Edgar Churchill is laid to rest. However, now that Mr. Churchill no longer requires one of the spare bedchambers at Randalls, she and her hus-band have quit Donwell so that they can be closer at hand. That leaves only Thomas Dixon here."

Despite Mr. Knightley's assertion of competence in the task of obtaining his own breakfast, his wife went to the sideboard anyway. Under the guise of obtaining a second roll for herself, she spoke softly—though not quite low enough for Elizabeth to disregard their conver-sation. Elizabeth did, however, pretend not to hear it.

"Did you sleep at all?"

"Very little. I have just finished with Perry."

"He was not here all night?"

"No. He returned again this morning after consulting some of his books."

"And did he put your suspicions to rest?"

Mr. Knightley's silence was answer enough.

Elizabeth met Darcy's gaze and saw that he, too, had overheard the exchange. He busied himself cutting the cold pork on his plate. Darcy was uncomfortable with even accidental eavesdropping.

Mrs. Knightley cleared her throat and returned to her seat. "I am sure Mr. and Mrs. Darcy are wondering whether you learned anything overnight about the highwaymen."

"I dispatched the parish constable to both of the Jones farms." Mr. Knightley brought his breakfast to the table and sat down at its head, between his wife and Elizabeth. "Neither of the families have relations visiting, or knew anything of the woman you described. I believe we are safe in assuming that 'Miss Jones' was working with the thieves and fled with them after providing the distraction they required."

"What is our next step, then?" Elizabeth asked.

"If your servants are sufficiently recovered, I should like to interview them. Perhaps they can recall something of use. I would also like to return with you and the constable to the location where the incident occurred, to look for evidence that might have been left behind."

"We are at your disposal," Darcy said. "Obviously, we want to resolve this matter as soon as possible."

"So do I. Is there anything else you can tell me? You said the rear carriage lantern broke. How did that happen?"

"When we stopped to assist Miss Jones, a raven swooped down," Elizabeth said. "I cannot imagine what brought it out, particularly after dark. I certainly have never seen one behave so aggressively. It flew behind the coach, we heard glass break, and the light went out."

"The bird broke the glass?" Mrs. Knightley asked.

"Or someone took advantage of the bird's appearance to break the glass at that moment," Mr. Knightley suggested.

"The more I hear about these highwaymen, the more anxious I become." Mrs. Knightley set down her roll, uneaten. "We must keep word of them from my father—he is still unnerved by the gypsies."

"There are gypsies in the vicinity?" Darcy asked.

"A caravan passed through here last spring," Mr. Knightley explained. "On that occasion, they camped along the Richmond road. They frightened a couple of girls, but moved on before they could be apprehended."

"Frightened? They terrorized poor Harriet. If Frank Churchill had not come along at the critical moment, heaven only knows what might have befallen her."

Mr. Knightley regarded his wife in silence for a moment, his expression contemplative. "I had forgotten about that. Yes, Frank Churchill *did* happen to arrive at just the right time, did he not? As I recall, he decided on some whim to send his horses ahead and walk a mile or two up the road?"

"It was not a whim—he said he was inspired by the fineness of the morning."

"He was in too great a hurry that day to take proper leave of you, yet he had time to stroll toward Richmond at a pace so leisurely that no one noticed his approach until he was among them." Mr. Knightley made a sound of disgust. "You are correct: that is not a whim. That is Frank Churchill to the core."

"Mr. Knightley, you will prejudice our visitors against the gentleman before they even meet him." Mrs. Knightley turned to the Darcys. "Frank Churchill is actually a charming fellow. My husband unfairly expects all young men to conform to his own exacting standards of behavior."

"My standards are no more rigorous than what society expects of any well-bred gentleman."

Mrs. Knightley smiled at the Darcys. "I look forward to introducing you should an opportunity present itself."

"I take it that Frank Churchill is not the Mr. Churchill who passed away last night?" Elizabeth asked.

"Oh, dear. You learned of that already? No, it was Edgar Churchill who died. Frank is his nephew—adopted son, actually; Edgar's only heir. It was Frank and his new wife, Jane, whom last night's dinner was meant to honor." She looked at her husband. "Truly, Mr. Knightley, could you not show a hint of compassion for him, just for today? Tomorrow you may return to being critical."

"I feel his loss keenly. How is that?"

"Much better. Now, when do you propose taking the Darcys to the London road?"

Mr. Knightley, having finished his breakfast, swallowed a final sip of coffee. "We can proceed as soon as you are ready," he said to the Darcys.

"Let us go now, then," Darcy replied.

As Elizabeth and Darcy waited in the hall with Mr. Knightley for a servant to retrieve their cloaks, a gentleman arrived whom they recognized as one of the guests from the night before. Mr. Knightley introduced him as Mr. Frank Churchill.

"Mr. Darcy and I heard of your recent marriage and your uncle's death," Elizabeth said. "Please accept our congratulations on the former and condolences on the latter."

"With gratitude. It has been a bewildering four-and-twenty hours, to go from a state of elation to one of grief. I hope by this call, however, to begin to put both my feelings and my uncle's final affairs in order."

He seemed a pleasant young man, her own age or perhaps a year older, with a handsome, clean-shaven countenance and clear blue eyes that looked as if they seldom took the world seriously. Mrs. Knightley had called him "charming," and Elizabeth sensed he was a gentleman who took pains to make himself liked by all he met. Even now, despite his recent bereavement, his manners were calculated to please. His demeanor was warm, and lighter than Mr. Knightley's had been at breakfast while discussing the same death.

Frank turned to Mr. Knightley. "I have written to Mr. Ian MacAllister, my uncle's solicitor in London, to inform him of Mr. Churchill's death. Among other business, I asked him to arrange for an undertaker to come today to collect my uncle's remains and prepare them for transport to Yorkshire. I assume he will engage the same man who handled my aunt's arrangements."

"Before I can release Mr. Churchill, I must confirm that Mr. Perry has done with him."

Frank chuckled. It was a thin sound, as if he realized its inappropriateness. "While I hold Mr. Perry's medical skills in as much esteem as does everybody in Highbury, I think my uncle is beyond the good apothecary's aid. Even the eminent Mr. Flint, my late aunt's physician, could not revive him at this point."

Mr. Knightley did not return the humor. "As you yourself stated last night, Edgar Churchill's death was sudden and unexpected. Mr. Perry only wishes to ascertain, if he can, the nature of your uncle's final illness. We would like to be able to assure the village that no virulent disease threatens Highbury."

Despite the opinion that Mr. Knightley held of Frank, Elizabeth thought he could speak a little more sympathetically toward a young man who just lost his uncle and benefactor. If Donwell Abbey had hosted last night's party in Frank's honor, Mr. Knightley must be on at least somewhat friendly terms with Frank Churchill. Yet now he was comporting himself like—

Like a magistrate.

Elizabeth regarded the two gentlemen more closely, particularly Mr. Knightley. She knew that Mr. Knightley harbored suspicions about the cause of Edgar Churchill's demise.

Suspicions which apparently included Edgar's heir.

Nine

The gipsies did not wait for the operations of justice; they took themselves off in a hurry.

—Emma

*T*he site of the robbery proved easier to find than Darcy had anticipated. The horses had stamped and skittered so much during the episode that their hoof marks—along with plenty of human footprints—covered that section of the road, and shards of glass from the carriage lamp still lay in the dirt.

Darcy wished they had arrived sooner, before other traffic had marred the scene. Returning before any subsequent vehicles had passed through would have been impossible, but he could not help but reflect that some of the fresher wheel marks likely belonged to Mr. Knightley's departing guests. There was no help for it, however—the magistrate had, rightfully so, spent the earlier part of the morning occupied with the matter of Edgar Churchill. In Mr. Knightley's place, Darcy, too, would have fixed a higher priority on investigating a suspicious death in a prominent local family—not to mention one that had occurred in his own home—over the robbery of strangers passing through the village.

Fortunately, the later vehicles and pedestrians had not utterly obliterated two sets of men's boot prints that led out of and back into the trees on one side of the road. Miss Jones's accomplices had apparently hidden in the elms, then approached the carriage from behind once the rear lamp was extinguished. Their trail, however, disappeared once it reentered the woods.

Darcy moved among the elms with Mr. Knightley and Mr. Cole, the parish constable. As he searched for some indication of which direction the thieves had gone, he saw Elizabeth go back to the road. She paused when she reached the spot where their coach had stopped the night before, and stared with a deflated expression at the jumble of prints toward the rear.

He approached. She picked up a glass shard from the ground and lifted her gaze to the treetops.

"There is not even a sign of that troublesome raven."

Darcy, too, felt frustrated by the lack of leads this excursion had produced. "The bird has doubtless found another shiny object to capture its interest."

She released a sigh as Mr. Knightley joined them. "We are not going to recover our belongings, are we?"

"Come, now," Mr. Knightley said. "Surely you can grant me and Mr. Cole at least a day before resigning hope?"

"Of course. Though I do not know how you intend to solve a robbery without any evidence."

"I hardly expected the bandits to leave behind a calling card. We do, however, have another potential source of information. There has been a peddler in the village of late. It is possible that the thieves approached him, trying to sell the stolen goods. If he is still in the neighborhood, we will question him. Even if he has not personally encountered the robbers, his profession brings him into contact with so many people that he might have heard something about highwaymen in the area."

"Perhaps he should also be asked about gypsies," Darcy said. "Might the band your wife spoke of this morning have returned? You did mention a recent series of poultry thefts."

"It is possible—we have not yet caught the poultry thieves. However, filching turkeys from unguarded outbuildings is hardly as bold an enterprise as stopping a private carriage and stealing a gentleman's chest."

"Both crimes employ stealth rather than direct confrontation. Our robbers might not be the same individuals who are raiding Highbury's henhouses, but they could be members of the same caravan."

Mr. Knightley pondered this a moment. "Did Miss Jones appear of gypsy blood?"

"I have never met a gypsy, only seen depictions," Darcy replied, "but Miss Jones looked quite English. However, there are tales of English men and women traveling with gypsy caravans, and the ruse to which we fell victim is just the sort of trickery one would expect from gypsies."

A man on horseback came down the road, headed toward Highbury. The rider slowed as he neared them, and Darcy recognized the livery of Donwell Abbey. The servant hailed Mr. Knightley. "I have a reply for you, sir."

Mr. Knightley turned to the others. "Pray, excuse me a moment." He took the letter from the servant, whom he bade continue to Donwell.

Elizabeth tossed the glass fragment back onto the ground. The shard clinked against a solitary, dark grey stone.

A stone a bit too perfect in form.

Darcy picked it up. It was smooth and almond shaped, weighing perhaps two or three ounces and easily fitting in the cradle of his palm. Of greatest interest, however, was the fact that it was not a stone at all, but a lump of molded lead.

Mr. Knightley pocketed his letter and rejoined them. "Have you found something?"

Darcy held out his open palm. "I believe this is a sling bullet."

He had not used a sling since boyhood, and then had nearly always thrown stones. One afternoon, however, whilst engaged in target practice with his cousins, the Fitzwilliams' gamekeeper had discovered the boys and provided a sack of sling bullets for them to try. Darcy had quickly come to appreciate their superior accuracy.

Mr. Knightley took the object and examined it. "It has a double notch on one surface—I expect from the mold." They surveyed the ground but found no additional missiles. "Mrs. Darcy, did you hear any sounds before the lamp shattered?"

"Only the raven and the horses. The bird agitated the team considerably, so they were snorting and rattling their harnesses."

"No indication of anything striking the coach?"

She shook her head.

"It appears, then, that at least one of the thieves is a highly proficient slinger."

Darcy had drawn the same conclusion. Not only had the ruffian used a molded bullet instead of an ordinary stone, but he had disabled the light with a single shot.

Elizabeth held out her hand for the bullet. "May I?" She weighed it in her palm and turned it over to examine both sides. "Why not simply use a stone? It would have been far easier and less expensive to obtain."

"Bullets cast from the same mold provide consistent weight, shape, and balance—and therefore improved accuracy for a slinger who uses them regularly," Darcy explained. "Our thief did not want to risk missed shots that would have drawn attention to himself or squandered the cover afforded by the raven's behavior."

"I did not realize slings were in such common use," Elizabeth said.

"Though primitive, they can be an effective hunting weapon. My brother and I took many a hare that way as boys," Mr. Knightley replied. "Because slings are more portable and less expensive than bows and firearms, especially if one throws stones instead of bullets, there are men who prefer to use a sling—particularly individuals who want a small, lightweight weapon with free ammunition that can be replenished as they roam."

Elizabeth returned the bullet to the magistrate. "Such as gypsies?"

Mr. Cole emerged from the elms. "Miss Jones's trail disappears into the woods, just like the others."

Mr. Knightley shared their discovery, then pocketed the bullet. "Try the Richmond road," he told the constable. "Look for signs of recent encampment. It may be that our gypsy friends have come back to Highbury."

Upon their return to Donwell Abbey, Darcy and the others found Mrs. Knightley in the morning parlor. Having just come from visiting her father at a neighboring estate, she was seated near the fireplace, about to start on some needlework. She happily set aside her thimble and turned to her husband with a hopeful expression. "Did you discover anything of use?"

"Possibly," Mr. Knightley replied. "We hope, however, that you might also provide some assistance."

"I certainly shall if I can." She invited them to join her near the fire and rang for tea. An autumn chill had settled in Surrey, and their morning errands had left them all in want of warm refreshment.

A servant entered with the tea accoutrements and arranged them on a round mahogany table circled by four shieldback chairs. After she left to retrieve the hot water, Mr. Knightley turned to his wife.

"The peddler who has been in the village this fortnight—Mr. Deal—do you know where he might be found?"

Mrs. Knightley frowned. "Surely you do not think Mr. Deal is involved with the robbery? I daresay he is the most honest peddler I have ever met, and Mrs. Weston will concur."

"I merely wish to ask him a few questions and secure his cooperation should the thieves approach him with the stolen items."

Mr. Knightley's reply seemed to satisfy his wife. "I believe that he generally calls upon people at their homes, but you might try Broadway Lane. That is where I last saw him."

"When was that?"

"Two days ago. I did not speak to him at the time, however, as Frank and Edgar Churchill occupied his attention."

"Indeed? What were they doing?"

"Frank purchased a snuff box. At least, I assume he bought a snuff box, as he was looking at a pair of them before his uncle and I became engaged in conversation."

The maid returned with the silver tea urn, and they all moved to the table. Mrs. Knightley prepared the tea, using a silver scoop to measure leaves out of a wooden caddy inlaid with ivory. She spooned the tea into a Wedgwood pot, then poured boiling water from the urn.

"How did Edgar Churchill appear?" Mr. Knightley continued.

"Out of sorts, though not nearly so out of them as when he arrived here for dinner. He seemed melancholy, and I supposed Frank's wedding had reminded him of his late wife. I tried to improve his mood but—" She glanced at the Darcys self-consciously. "I am afraid I made a blunder of it. I had half a mind to ask Mr. Deal afterwards whether one of his gypsy remedies could cure a broken heart."

"Gypsy remedies?" Darcy could not help but interrupt.

Mr. Knightley regarded his wife with equal surprise. "Mr. Deal sells gypsy wares?"

"Various physics and ointments," she said. "He had a chest of them when I first met him at Mrs. Weston's house—cures for everything from rheumatism to warts. They are quite popular with the villagers." The tea having steeped sufficiently, Mrs. Knightley turned to Elizabeth. "Do you take milk or sugar?"

"Let me be sure I understand you," Mr. Knightley said slowly as his wife poured tea. "Mr. Deal regularly consorts with gypsies?"

"Well, I do not know that he *consorts* with them. But even if he did, that is not a violation of the law, is it?"

"Not long ago, merely being found in their company would have put him at risk of hanging. Those laws have been repealed, but as you know from Harriet Smith's experience, gypsies remain uncivilized, lawless vagrants given to all manner of criminal behavior, and Mr. Deal would do well to avoid association with them. His own itinerant habits render him suspect enough."

"He is a peddler! How is he to practice his trade without traveling?"

"In a proper shop, as Mr. Ford does."

"I patronize Ford's as often as anybody else in Highbury. I have yet to see some of the goods there that Mr. Deal offers. The shawl Miss Bates wore last night came from him, as did the lace on the handkerchief Jane Churchill carried on her wedding day. The village is enamored with him and his merchandise. So long as he obtains his goods legally, what is it to us where or from whom he acquires them? Indeed, by engaging in business with the gypsies, he does us all a service—he deals with those people so that we need not."

"Did he mention when he had acquired the remedies?" Darcy ventured to ask. "Might the gypsies presently be in this area?"

"He did not say—I assumed he had brought them from elsewhere." Mrs. Knightley turned to her husband. "If he had indicated that gypsies were again in the neighborhood, I certainly would have told you."

"Did Edgar Churchill purchase anything from Mr. Deal?" Mr. Knightley asked.

"Not that I witnessed." She sipped her tea. "I suppose he might have before I came upon them, but judging from his demeanor, I doubt it. He seemed impatient for Frank to finish his transaction, so he likely did not engage in one of his own."

"Did Frank Churchill buy one of these elixirs?"

"Frank? No. Whatever would Frank Churchill need a remedy for? He is in excellent health. He could not even benefit from a potion that promises luck—he just wed a woman he adores, and stands to inherit a fine estate. Were it not for his uncle's death, his life would be perfect."

"Yes," Mr. Knightley said. "Perfect."

She set down her teacup. "Mr. Knightley, need I remind you that Frank Churchill is the stepson of my dearest friend?"

"Not at all. I am fully aware of that fact."

Mrs. Knightley glanced at Elizabeth and Darcy. All felt the awkwardness of the little moment of marital discord.

"Mr. Darcy," Mr. Knightley said, "I have an errand in the village. Would you care to accompany me? I could show you Highbury, which is a charming little village when one is not being robbed by highwaymen, and the walk would provide an opportunity for us to have that discussion about Stuart's theories."

Darcy wanted to talk about gypsies, not husbandry. Nor, having just returned from tramping about the London road searching for evidence, and having scarcely finished his tea, did he particularly relish the notion of immediately reentering the chill November air. Perhaps, however, they could visit Broadway Lane and find the peddler. "I would be pleased to accompany you."

"Mrs. Darcy, you are welcome to come with us," Mr. Knightley offered.

Elizabeth looked as if she had much rather not. "It is most kind of you—"

Mrs. Knightley intervened. "Mrs. Darcy, do not feel obliged to subject yourself to discourse on crop rotation and livestock breeding merely because my husband invited you. Most people tire of those subjects long before he does. Let us take our own walk and become better acquainted."

Ten

Though her nephew had had no particular reason to hasten back on her account, she had not lived above six-and-thirty hours after his return. A sudden seizure of a different nature from any thing foreboded by her general state, had carried her off after a short struggle.

—Emma

$\mathcal{D}$arcy and Mr. Knightley were not thirty yards from the house when Mr. Knightley dropped all guise of initiating an agricultural discussion.

"Mr. Darcy, I hope you will forgive me. While I do need to call upon someone—and would enjoy discussing Stuart's theories with you at some point—I have a more pressing issue upon which I wish to consult you."

The confession intrigued Darcy. "Go on."

Though reassured by this encouragement, Mr. Knightley yet seemed not altogether at ease. "I am hardly in the habit of imposing upon strangers, nor of confiding in gentlemen with whom I have so newly become acquainted. But finding myself in a complex and delicate situation, I am in need of disinterested aid, and after our conversation last night, I believed you might be the very man to help me. When I learned that we share a mutual friend, I wrote to Lord Chatfield and enquired whether my instincts were correct." A cold gust of wind rustled the dry leaves of the apple trees they passed. The faint scent of apples yet hung about the orchard.

"The letter I received while we searched for evidence on the London road this morning was his lordship's reply," Mr. Knightley continued. "Chatfield not only attested to your character and reliability, but also encouraged me, given the circumstances, to indeed solicit your assistance." He stopped to withdraw from his pocket a small sealed note, which he handed to Darcy. "The earl enclosed this for you."

Darcy,

Did I not urge you to stay in town long enough to cross swords with me at Angelo's before hastening off to Sussex? This is what comes of forgoing the pleasure of a fencing match. Now you are at the mercy of my friend Knightley. Despite the incident that brought you to his attention, however, fortune follows you, for you could not have found yourself in better company during a crisis. George Knightley is one of the most capable gentlemen I have the privilege of knowing— second only to you, of course. Had the two of you ever been in town at the same time, you would certainly have met in my drawing room. Depend upon it, he will do all he can to resolve your present difficulties, if you and your clever wife have not already settled the affair yourselves.

Meanwhile, I understand Knightley has a matter of his own which could benefit from your experience. Perhaps the fortune is all on his side, for you are the very man I would have recommended had you not presented yourself to him before I had the opportunity. I am still in your debt for the service you rendered me last year. Pray, aid Knightley if you can. Afterwards, you both must come to town and regale me with the tale of your success.

If I can be of assistance to either of you, know that you need only ask. I am—

Yours most sincerely,
Chatfield

The letter was classic Chatfield, full of good humor that to someone less well acquainted with the earl might disguise the keen intellect that lay beneath it.

Mr. Knightley watched him pocket the note. "In his letter to me,

Chatfield alluded to a sensitive matter involving his wife's brother. He did not disclose the particulars, but he credits you and Mrs. Darcy with resolving it with intelligence and discretion, qualities also essential in the matter on which I seek your assistance. It concerns Edgar Churchill."

Darcy had suspected as much. The death had obviously been much on Mr. Knightley's mind, and the magistrate had not been as reserved about discussing the subject in Darcy and Elizabeth's presence as Darcy would have expected among casual acquaintances. "I shall hold in confidence any information you choose to divulge."

"Thank you." He and Darcy resumed walking along a path that wound through Donwell Park towards the main road. "As you know, Edgar Churchill's death occurred under circumstances curious enough to warrant probing. His behavior before he took ill and the rapidity of his decline in themselves merit attention. But what most raises my concern is the timing of his death as it benefits one individual."

"His heir?"

"Yes, Frank Churchill. Frank is the golden child of Highbury. He left the village as a toddler to be raised by his aunt and uncle after his mother's death, and for two decades all Highbury—fueled by periodic reports by his father, Mr. Weston, on his advancement—eagerly awaited his return. When he finally came last winter, he was like a lost prince come home to claim his throne. This village adores him, and his recent marriage to another beloved resident, Jane Fairfax, secures him in the affections of everybody."

"Everybody but yourself."

He nodded. "I never thought Frank Churchill an inherently evil person, simply a self-absorbed gentleman lacking maturity, propriety, and a sense of duty. But now—where shall I begin? A year ago, he was an idle young man secretly engaged to a respectable but portionless young lady of whom his tyrannical aunt would have never approved. The sudden death of his aunt in June cleared the way for him to marry. And now, less than a se'nnight wed, the sudden death of his uncle awards him a substantial estate free and clear. The confluence of events strikes me as rather suspicious."

From the few particulars with which Knightley had acquainted him, Darcy agreed. "How did the aunt die?"

Mr. Knightley chuckled without mirth. "Agnes Churchill suffered various complaints for decades—generally, whenever she wanted a change of scenery or Frank at her disposal. Frank would make plans to visit his father, and just before his departure she would suddenly be stricken by some malady or nervous disorder that inspired her removal to whichever of their houses they did not occupy at the time, and required Frank to attend her there. Few in Highbury ever believed she was truly indisposed until she actually died."

"In hindsight, however, it sounds as though she suffered poor health the whole while," Darcy said. "It can hardly be suspicious that she would eventually succumb to an illness that plagued her for years."

"But she did not. When Frank Churchill wrote to his father and stepmother informing them of his aunt's demise, he reported that Mrs. Churchill had been taken by a seizure of a different sort than any of the earlier ones. Further, this unexplained fit occurred hard upon Frank's arrival at their Richmond house following a quarrel with Jane in which she told him she was calling off their betrothal because he would not openly acknowledge their engagement."

"And so you believe Frank killed his aunt rather than reveal the engagement to her and risk being disinherited?"

"I did not question her death at the time—only considered it extraordinarily lucky for Frank. But now, having seen Edgar Churchill also die of an unexpected ailment, I cannot help but wonder about the nature of the aunt's."

"Has Mr. Perry reached any conclusions about the cause of Edgar's death?"

Mr. Knightley stopped, his countenance grim. "He suspects Edgar Churchill was poisoned."

They had reached the road. Not too far distant, Darcy could see several buildings huddled at the village's edge.

"I find myself confronted with two suspicious deaths," Mr. Knightley said, "one of which occurred in my own home. And the chief suspect is a man against whom I have long harbored prejudice. I fear I am not capable of the objectivity required to properly investigate the matter."

Darcy respected the magistrate's self-knowledge, but also wondered why Mr. Knightley felt the responsibility fell entirely upon himself. "Ought not Mr. Perry, as coroner, conduct the enquiry?"

"Mr. Perry is a good apothecary and an excellent man, but he is no investigator. He will offer his medical expertise and hold his inquest, but unless someone actually witnessed Frank Churchill administering the poison, he will likely declare Edgar's death a case of accidental ingestion."

"Mr. Cole, then?"

"Mr. Cole is a reluctant constable. It is a position no one in this parish particularly wants, so it rotates annually. Cole does what is expected of him, but no more, and has not the drive to pursue an unpopular investigation against a very popular member of this community. I am afraid no one in Highbury does." He paused. "This case requires a disinterested party who can gather and evaluate evidence without the influence of prior connexions or fear of negative consequences to his own reputation within the village. After receiving Lord Chatfield's endorsement this morning, I am rather hoping that you, Mr. Darcy, will do me the great favor of guiding the investigation."

Darcy was surprised at being asked to take such a prominent role. His countenance must have registered his astonishment.

"You need not answer me this moment," Mr. Knightley said. They headed into the village, where Darcy hoped to catch sight of the peddler's cart. "I realize I ask a great deal—much more than our brief acquaintance supports. Pray, forgive my presumption. I ask not out of my own interest, but the interest of justice."

Darcy was not by nature disposed to insert himself into affairs which did not concern him. "I do not know whether I am the proper person to assist you so directly. I have no official standing—no legal or moral authority that would compel anyone to cooperate with my efforts."

"It is precisely your lack of formal status that I hope will enable you to undertake this enquiry in a subtle manner that does not alert the entire village to the fact that Frank Churchill is under suspicion of murder. Should a more official role become necessary, I can appoint you one. Pray, consider my proposal a while longer before refusing it out of hand."

They had reached the village centre. A signpost indicated that they stood in Broadway Lane, but to Darcy's disappointment, no peddler's cart greeted them.

Mr. Knightley noted Darcy's expression. "It would have been convenient to find Hiram Deal waiting here for us, but I suppose only Frank Churchill enjoys that sort of serendipity. We shall enquire after the peddler." He stopped before a respectable-looking house with a shop front on the lower level. A sign bearing a mortar and pestle hung above the door. "First, however, let us call upon Mr. Perry."

They entered the shop, a compact but orderly space designed to accommodate the apparatus of the apothecary's art. Two wooden cabinets with numerous small drawers held all manner of ingredients for medicines, salves, and other remedies, while shelves displayed the measuring tools, mixing equipment, and scales used to prepare them. In the far corner stood a bookcase, its neat rows punctuated by gaps from the removal of several volumes that lay open on the worktable. A portmanteau rested on the floor against one of the table legs.

The room was empty of people save for Mr. Perry himself, though scampering footsteps above revealed the presence of either several children or a scurry of squirrels. The sound put Darcy in mind of Lily-Anne, who could crawl across the floor of Pemberley's nursery with considerable velocity. It would not be long before she took her own first independent steps. He hoped the matter of the robbery would be resolved and their family united in short order.

Mr. Perry greeted them with an expression of concern. "Mr. Knightley, I did not expect to see you again until I returned from London. Has something else occurred?"

"Nothing of a sinister nature. I merely hoped that you might impart to Mr. Darcy the suspicions you shared with me this morning. Mr. Darcy has some experience probing unusual deaths, and I have solicited his assistance with the Churchill matter."

Darcy experienced a moment's apprehension that the coroner would resent the intrusion of a stranger into his enquiry, but Mr. Perry's countenance instead reflected relief.

"Indeed? Mr. Darcy, I welcome any wisdom you can shed on the matter. I have completed my examination of Edgar Churchill; he presently lies in the next room. Do you wish to see his remains?"

Darcy had no wish to see anything of the sort if he could help it. Though he had witnessed the results of violent death before, it was hardly a pleasant experience, and he still was not entirely certain he wanted to involve himself in this affair.

"I am not a medical man, so perhaps you could simply report your findings. Mr. Knightley said you found evidence of poison?"

"I found nothing definitive in respect to his remains. My suspicions, therefore, derive from the symptoms I and others observed in Edgar Churchill while he was yet alive. I believe them consistent with the consumption of belladonna."

Darcy had heard of the plant, but knew little of it. "Belladonna is also called 'deadly nightshade,' is it not?" The question comprised nearly his entire store of knowledge on the subject.

"Yes, and with good reason. It is highly toxic. People, particularly children, are sometimes tempted by its sweet purple berries, with tragic consequences. In fact, a colleague of mine in London treated three children this past summer who had eaten only a few berries each. Two of the children died."

"Are other parts of the plant poisonous?"

"All of it, in varying degrees—the root most of all. In controlled amounts belladonna possesses medicinal properties, but the leaves and roots can prove as fatal as the berries."

"What symptoms did Mr. Churchill exhibit?"

"It seems to have begun with fever and dry mouth," Mr. Perry said. "Mr. Knightley and others report that from the time Edgar Churchill arrived at the party, he was flushed and complained of being too warm."

"He also suffered thirst. Frank could not fill his wineglass fast enough," Mr. Knightley added. "He then became agitated and belligerent, raving incoherently and even suffering a hallucination. I confess, we merely thought him drunk. Mr. Perry, however, says that such behavior is also symptomatic of belladonna poisoning."

"As were the later signs I observed firsthand—dilated pupils, vomiting, extraordinarily loud and rapid heartbeat," Mr. Perry said. "The utter loss of voice and repetitive finger movements are particularly indicative." He winced and looked away, his gaze passing over the various tools of his profession. "In hindsight, of course. If only I had realized at the time what was happening, I might have been able to save him."

"Perry, you take too much responsibility upon yourself. None of us had any reason to suppose he had been poisoned, let alone with belladonna." Mr. Knightley gestured toward the book-strewn table. "As it was, you spent half the night perusing your references to identify the probable agent. Edgar Churchill cannot benefit from our self-recrimination. Our time and energy are best spent determining whether the poisoning was accidental or intentional."

"Where might Mr. Churchill or a poisoner have acquired the belladonna?" Darcy asked. "Does it grow in this area?"

"Though it is cultivated for its medicinal value, I do not grow it myself—I would not want the berries to entice my children or anybody else's. The small amount of dried root that I keep on hand, I obtain from a London chemist and keep hidden. I checked my store of it this morning, and it has not been pilfered. Belladonna could, however, thrive somewhere in the neighborhood without my knowledge, or even that of the landowner. Though more common on the Continent, the plant can be found growing wild here and there in England."

Mr. Perry withdrew his watch from the fob pocket of his waistcoat. "I should leave now, to ensure that I reach London before dark." He looked at Darcy apologetically. "Forgive me for cutting short our conversation, but I am going to consult my colleague to see if he agrees with my conclusion of belladonna poisoning. If he does, I shall be grateful for your aid in sorting out the rest of the matter."

Darcy glanced at Mr. Knightley. "If his colleague does concur, perhaps Mr. Perry should call upon Edgar Churchill's solicitor whilst in town and enquire into the particulars of his will. Frank mentioned the gentleman's name this morning—Ian MacAllister. While I understand that Frank is Edgar Churchill's primary heir, we need to determine whether other individuals have a financial interest in his death."

Mr. Perry agreed. "I will also stop in Richmond, to speak with the Churchills' physician about Mr. Churchill's general health."

"Frank Churchill said that his aunt and uncle were in the care of a Mr. Flint," Mr. Knightley told him. "While talking with him, pray also enquire more closely into the particulars of the seizure that claimed Mrs. Churchill."

Mr. Knightley and Darcy exited the shop, and Mr. Perry went to collect his horse.

"Despite my apprehensions regarding Frank Churchill, I cannot envision him tramping about the country harvesting wild nightshade," Mr. Knightley said.

"No—but a more knowledgeable person might."

"An herbalist?"

"Particularly one lacking a fixed location in which to cultivate his or her own plants."

"A gypsy herbalist."

"It would seem, Mr. Knightley, that our interests might be more allied than we realized. Both investigations could involve, directly or indirectly, gypsies." Darcy gazed down the street. He now wanted more than ever to speak with Hiram Deal, but there was still no sign of his cart in Broadway Lane. "We need to find that peddler and determine the extent of his relationship with the gypsies whose wares he vends, and ascertain to whom in the neighborhood he sold their so-called remedies."

" 'We'? You agree to assist me, then?"

Darcy was uncertain how Elizabeth would feel about his entering into such a commitment. She would not oppose it on principle; it was her nature to render aid when she could. However, taking on responsibility for a murder investigation would likely mean not only postponing their visit to Colonel and Anne Fitzwilliam at Brierwood, but also leaving Lily-Anne back in London with Georgiana a while longer. If an assassin indeed roamed Highbury, he wanted his daughter nowhere near.

Yet, as he had just told Mr. Knightley, it appeared that in lending his assistance to the Churchill matter, he might also forward his own interests, or at least ensure that the robbery investigation did not become altogether forgotten as the local authorities concentrated on the more serious Churchill affair. Too, he had to admit, if only to himself, that the Churchill matter intrigued him.

He extended his hand. "I suppose I do."

Mr. Knightley accepted it and shook firmly. "Excellent. For there is another individual whose association with the gypsies warrants questioning."

Darcy looked past Mr. Knightley's shoulder to a person who had just entered Broadway Lane.

Frank Churchill.

Eleven

The only literary pursuit which engaged Harriet at present, the only mental provision she was making for the evening of life, was the collecting and transcribing all the riddles of every sort that she could meet with.

—Emma

*L*eaving Donwell Abbey, Elizabeth and Mrs. Knightley set out in the opposite direction from the gentlemen. Though Mrs. Knightley affected to let chance choose their course, Elizabeth sensed that her hostess had a destination in mind. She walked with purpose, and carried on her arm a basket with several small jars inside.

Their strides eventually brought them to a stream spanned by a small wooden footbridge. On the far bank, a path ran alongside the water toward a mill.

"This is a pretty walk," Elizabeth said. "Do you take it often?"

"No. Mr. Knightley and I actually live at Hartfield, my father's estate. Papa is in declining health and dependent upon my companionship. When we married, we thought it best to defer my permanent removal from the house until . . . until my father no longer needs me. We are presently at Donwell only because of last night's party."

"Mr. Knightley sacrificed his independence to reside in your father's home?" Elizabeth could not imagine Darcy even temporarily relinquishing life at Pemberley to live with her parents at Longbourn.

"Mr. Knightley has known my father even longer than I have, and is as dutiful a son as Papa could wish for."

They crossed the stream and followed the path until they reached a farmhouse. It was a small but sweet cottage, well cared for and cheerful despite the gloomy clouds that obscured the sun. They had approached it from the side; Mrs. Knightley led them to the front, which faced a narrow lane.

"This is Abbey Mill Farm," Mrs. Knightley said. "We are here to visit Mrs. Harriet Martin, the young lady Frank Churchill rescued from the gypsies last May. If they have returned to the neighborhood, perhaps she can recall something that might aid us in apprehending your thieves."

Their knock was answered by a pretty woman with an artless manner and ready smile. "Mrs. Knightley! I did not anticipate the pleasure— Oh, do forgive me! I have not yet waited upon you since your wedding-trip, but I had heard how occupied you were with the Churchill party. Was it a lovely affair? With you hosting it, I am certain it was! Do come in. Robert is out—he has taken his mother and sisters into the village. They will be sorry to have missed you."

"I am sorry for it, too, but my object in calling was to see you. Here," she said, reaching into her basket, "I have brought you some apple butter from Donwell Abbey."

Mrs. Knightley made introductions, identifying Elizabeth as a visiting friend. Harriet offered a smile and invited them into her sitting room, a neat but busy space with an abundance of frilly curtains, pillows embroidered with flowery platitudes, and mediocre watercolors. A portrait of Harriet hung above the fireplace. It was a good likeness, painted by a more skilled artist than the other pictures, though in Elizabeth's opinion it rendered its subject too tall.

Harriet ushered them into seats and attempted several times to take one herself. She leaped out of it at random intervals, however, as new ways to accommodate her guests entered her mind. She must make them tea. No? Would they like a bit of cake? The fire screen must be adjusted. Were they quite sure they did not want cake? Perhaps toast spread with the Donwell apple butter? There was a note she had written for Mrs. Knightley that now she could hand-deliver.

"It is a charade, actually." Harriet seemed almost shy as she handed it to Mrs. Knightley. "I showed Robert the book of charades and other riddles I compiled last year. Do you remember what pleasure we had in collecting them? Why, even Mr. Elton contributed an original one. Robert asked whether I had written any of them myself, and when I said I had not, he encouraged me to try my hand at one."

Mrs. Knightley unfolded the paper and read the lines to herself. After a moment, she smiled.

"What do you think, Miss Woodhouse—I mean, Mrs. Knightley? Have you solved it already? Oh, I can see that you have! You are always so clever at working out puzzles."

"It is an excellent first attempt, Harriet. The meter in the last line wants refinement, but otherwise it is at least as good as some of the others in your book. Have you shown it to your husband?"

"Not yet. I wanted your opinion of it first."

"I am sure it will please him very much. Shall we share it with Mrs. Darcy and see whether she can solve it?"

Harriet looked at Elizabeth hopefully. "If you are interested?"

"Indeed, yes." Elizabeth accepted the page from Mrs. Knightley.

A place of worship, and a home
A place where wind or water turns
A place where crops and livestock grow
A place for which my heart yearns.

Elizabeth read it through twice. The third line came easily. From there, once she recalled the name of the Martins' home, it was a facile effort to solve the charade. "Abbey Mill Farm?"

"You guessed! Is it too simple?"

"Not at all. Had Mrs. Knightley not told me the name of your home just as we approached, I would have been altogether at a loss." Elizabeth handed the note back to Mrs. Knightley.

"The charade will be a worthy addition to your collection, Harriet." Mrs. Knightley set it on a small table beside her. "It is interesting that you should be thinking of days past, for I wish to ask you about something that occurred last spring—the day you and Miss Bickerton encountered the gypsies on the Richmond road."

"Oh." Harriet sank into her seat and at last appeared likely to remain still for two minutes together. "Why ever do you want to talk about that? I thought they were long gone."

"Mr. Knightley wishes to ensure that they remain so."

"Oh! Well, it is as I told you. We—Miss Bickerton and I—were walking along, never imagining such persons were about. When we reached that very shady stretch—you know, past the bend—we slowed our pace. The morning was warm, so the shade felt refreshing, and we were happily conversing when we noticed the gypsy camp just ahead, on the greensward. They must have noticed us at the same time, for within moments a girl came running towards us and begged for a shilling."

"How old was the girl?"

"Eight or nine. She had long, dark hair all tumbled about her."

Elizabeth heard this with disappointment. The gypsy girl could not possibly be Miss Jones.

"Remind me what happened next," Mrs. Knightley said.

"Miss Bickerton screamed and ran up an embankment to escape. I tried to follow her but a cramp in my leg stopped me. At least half a dozen more gypsy children rushed forward and surrounded me, all of them demanding money. And then a woman and a large boy appeared. I hoped they would tell the children to leave me in peace but instead they spoke gypsy-talk to them and the children begged all the more insistently. I have never been so frightened in my life. Look at me—I tremble even now to speak of it."

"How very alarming," Elizabeth said. "The woman—how old was she?"

"Oh, who can tell with such people? Fifty or sixty? Her hair was covered in a kerchief and her dress was wildly colored. Her eyes were even darker than the children's—so dark I thought she could stare right through me." Harriet shuddered. "She carried a basket of plants and had a charm around her neck, like some sort of witch-woman. I was terrified that she would give me the Evil Eye and throw a curse upon me, or worse! They say that is what gypsies do, you know. I offered them a shilling, and still they would not go away."

"And this is when Frank Churchill happened along?" Mrs. Knightley asked.

"Yes, thank heaven! I do not know what would have become of me had he not been traveling to Richmond that day. I was in such terror that I did not even see him approach. Nor did the gypsies, for they were quite surprised when he suddenly appeared."

Elizabeth recalled Mr. Knightley's having said that Frank arrived at the scene on foot. "How did Mr. Churchill rescue you from the gypsies? What, precisely, did he do?"

"He gave a shout to draw their attention, then ordered them to leave me be."

"And they immediately ceased harassing you?"

"Yes. He said he was going to summon the authorities and have them all arrested. I believe he quite frightened them. Even the woman looked at him in astonishment and hurried away."

"They disbanded the camp quickly," Mrs. Knightley added. "The entire party was gone by the time I told Mr. Knightley of the incident."

"Did you see any English among the gypsies?" Elizabeth asked. "Female or male?"

"Oh, believe me, Mrs. Darcy, I wish I had! I would have begged their aid."

A knock sounded on the door. It was not an unwelcome noise— Elizabeth hoped the arrival of a new visitor would enable her and Mrs. Knightley to exit gracefully. While she appreciated the opportunity to hear Harriet's account firsthand, Elizabeth by this point despaired of obtaining any useful information. Harriet Martin was a sweet girl, but not exceedingly clever.

"Oh, my! I am spoiled for company today." Harriet rose to answer the knock but continued talking over her shoulder. "No, the only English face I saw was Frank Churchill's, and I was grateful for the sight of him. When he interceded, the beggars all scattered. Even the bird flew away."

Elizabeth suddenly wished the new visitors away.

"Bird?"

Frank Churchill had just emerged from Ford's mercantile when Darcy caught sight of him.

"Apparently, Frank Churchill's grief does not run so deep as to prevent his spending the afternoon shopping," Mr. Knightley muttered as he raised his hand to hail him. "Though meeting him here is fortuitous, as we can question him alone. Had we been obliged to call upon him at Randalls, it might have been an awkward business to separate him from his new wife or the Westons for a private conversation."

Frank Churchill crossed the lane and greeted the gentlemen. Unfortunately, Darcy and Mr. Knightley were not the only persons who had seen him exit the shop, nor did they alone seek his conversation. Several villagers approached him to express their condolences on the loss of his uncle, and some minutes elapsed before he managed to disengage himself.

"Mr. Churchill, I wonder whether you might be able to assist us," Mr. Knightley said when they at last had Frank's attention.

"I shall if I can," he replied. "Does this concern my uncle?"

"Another matter entirely. My friend Mr. Darcy had an unpleasant encounter with some highwaymen recently, and we are hoping the incident does not herald the return of the gypsies from whom you rescued Harriet Smith last May. You were in such a hurry to reach London that day that I never had an opportunity to receive a firsthand account from you, but we would like to hear the particulars now."

"I shall tell you all I can remember. I was walking along the road toward Richmond. As I approached a bend, I heard voices ahead. Children's voices, primarily, but two women's voices, as well. One of them, of course, was Harriet Smith's, though hysteria raised her pitch so high that I did not recognize it before I laid eyes on her. The other voice belonged to an older woman who spoke in a language I could not comprehend."

Frank paused, momentarily distracted by activity down the lane. The mail coach had arrived at the Crown, and passengers hurried inside to obtain a quick meal in the brief time allowed whilst the horses were changed. Fortunately, Frank did not appear to have noticed Mr. Perry leaving on horseback from the inn's livery with his portmanteau—else he might have wondered where the apothecary was traveling whilst Edgar Churchill's corpse remained in his custody.

"When you heard the voices, what did you do?" Darcy asked.

The question diverted Frank's attention from the inn. "That stretch of road is heavily shaded when the trees are in full foliage, so I hid myself in the shadows as I approached. When I saw Miss Smith surrounded by gypsy beggars, I immediately stepped forward and bade them be gone. They took themselves off, and I assisted Miss Smith to Hartfield and the Woodhouses' care."

"Were they merely begging," Mr. Knightley asked, "or did any of them physically threaten Miss Smith?"

"Their verbal assault and proximity frightened her quite enough."

"Did any of them speak to you?"

"The children ran away directly, and an older boy also lumbered off. The woman stared at me hard—she seemed quite surprised—no doubt my sudden appearance startled her. She muttered a few words in her own tongue, then went back to the camp."

"It sounds as if the young lady was most fortunate that you happened along when you did," Darcy said.

"Indeed. Had my intended departure not been postponed by an errand to Miss Bates's house, I would have been halfway to Richmond by the time Miss Smith had need of me. As it was, I had to hurry off the moment I saw her safely settled at Hartfield, for my aunt impatiently awaited my arrival."

"And this encounter, I am sure, caused significant additional delay. Richmond is what—ten miles from here?"

"Nine."

"That is a long distance to travel by foot," Darcy said, "particularly if pressed for time."

"I planned to walk only part of the way," he replied. "It was a fine morning, so I sent my servant ahead with my horse by a different path. We were to meet where that road crosses the Richmond road, another mile or two past where the gypsies were camped."

Darcy found Mr. Churchill's account curious. That a man traveling such a distance, departing later than intended, would not only squander time completing part of the journey on foot, but also send his servant and horse ahead by another road entirely, rendering them inaccessible to him should he wish to hasten his pace—had the morning truly been *that* fine, to inspire such a decision? Moreover, for him to then arrive at the very stretch of road where the gypsies camped, at the exact moment he was needed . . . Frank Churchill's life truly did seem to be ruled by coincidence.

Darcy did not believe in coincidence.

As they talked to Frank, Mr. Cole had entered the lane on horseback. He now dismounted, looking as if he wanted to speak to Mr. Knightley. The magistrate walked forward to confer with the constable in private whilst Darcy continued his interview with Mr. Churchill.

"I appreciate your speaking with me about this incident on a day when I am sure your thoughts are elsewhere," Darcy said. "If my wife and I are to recover our stolen possessions, time is of the essence. As it is, I was just going into Ford's to replace some necessities. I heard there has also been a peddler in the village of late. Have you, by chance, seen him?"

"Not today. He stopped at Randalls the day we arrived from London—I saw him talking to Mrs. Weston, and later to my uncle. He was here in Broadway Lane the day before yesterday. I bought a very nice snuff box from him."

"Did you purchase anything else? Or did your uncle? I am hoping he has a broad selection of merchandise."

"I bought only the snuff box. My uncle bought nothing at all—at least, not when we saw him here in the village. In fact, he barely spoke to Mr. Deal."

"I understand his wares include gypsy-made remedies for various complaints. Did he show you any of those? The robbery greatly upset my wife, and she now suffers a headache that has defied traditional cures."

"I am sorry to hear it. I know nothing of any medicines. I suggest you consult Mr. Perry, the village apothecary."

"I shall, thank you."

Mr. Knightley finished his business with Mr. Cole and rejoined them, apologizing for the interruption.

"If Mr. Darcy has no more questions regarding the gypsy incident, I am expected back at Randalls," Frank said.

His account had raised a considerable number of additional questions in Darcy's mind, but none he wished to pose at present. "I believe we have done for now."

After Mr. Churchill left them, Mr. Knightley revealed the subject of his conversation with the constable. "Cole found evidence of a recent encampment, this time on the Portsmouth road. The gypsies, however, have fled. He will recruit some men and follow their trail."

"Let us hope he finds them. Meanwhile, Frank Churchill claims he has not seen Hiram Deal today." He gazed down the lane in the direction Mr. Cole had taken.

When he received no reply, Darcy turned. Mr. Knightley stared up the lane in the opposite direction, his attention commanded by a vehicle just entering the village.

A peddler's cart.

Twelve

Emma was not required, by any subsequent discovery, to retract her ill opinion of Mrs. Elton . . . —self-important, presuming, familiar, ignorant, and ill-bred. She had a little beauty and a little accomplishment, but so little judgment that she thought herself coming with superior knowledge of the world, to enliven and improve a country neighbourhood.

—Emma

*D*id I not mention the bird?"

Emma stifled an exasperated huff. "No, Harriet, you did not." And now the imminent entrance of a visitor threatened to curtail discussion of the one point of information that might prove useful to Mrs. Darcy.

"It was a great black thing—a crow or a raven or something like that. It swooped in just as the children swarmed around me, then circled above. Heavens, its caw was worse than their begging."

"Were they not frightened by it?" Mrs. Darcy asked.

"They paid it no mind at all, just kept pestering me." Harriet opened the door. "Oh, Mrs. Elton! Mr. Elton! I hardly expected—what an honor, for you to call! Why, I believe this is the first time I have had the pleasure of a visit from you."

Emma stiffened. The Eltons took advantage of every opportunity to snub Harriet. Depend upon it, this social call had an ulterior purpose, and Emma had little doubt as to its nature. They were come to gossip.

About her.

More specifically, about her deadly dinner party. It had truly been too much to hope that word of it had not spread throughout the village like wildfire. And of course the Eltons could be counted upon to fan the flames. If they were calling at Abbey Mill Farm, doubtless they had already circulated the news among those few of Highbury's better families that had not been personally present to witness the debacle.

Emma glanced at Mrs. Darcy, who studied her with interest. Emma realized that her countenance had momentarily betrayed her dislike of the new arrivals. "Mr. Elton is our parish vicar," she said simply. Mrs. Darcy impressed Emma as an astute woman. A few minutes in the Eltons' company would reveal every essential about the couple.

"It is indeed our first visit to you as Mrs. Robert Martin," Mrs. Elton said. "I just realized this morning that we had not yet acknowledged your new situation—our parish duties keep us so occupied that I declare I do not know where the time goes! But I told Mr. E. that we must correct the oversight immediately, and so here we are."

She shouldered her way past Harriet and into the sitting room, where she was surprised to discover Emma. "Mrs. Knightley! I daresay you are the last person I expected to find paying social calls today. I should think the events of last night would continue to absorb your attention."

Emma could not imagine why, when they were absorbing enough of Mrs. Elton's for them both. "There is little more to be done for Mr. Churchill, beyond treating his passing with respect."

Harriet, who had closed the door and now stood behind the Eltons, regarded them all with wide eyes. " 'Mr. Churchill's passing'? Has something happened to Frank Churchill?"

"To his uncle," Emma said before either of the Eltons could leap in with their version of events. "Edgar Churchill took ill and died last night. It is all very sad for Frank, certainly, but we can rejoice in the fact that Mr. Churchill lived long enough to celebrate his nephew's marriage." She hoped that would put an end to the subject.

Mrs. Elton pushed aside a pair of pillows to seat herself on the sofa. A pat on the space beside her commanded her husband to sit. Only the width of the small table now separated Emma from the couple, a proximity she found unpleasantly intimate.

"It was shocking to witness his violent death throes right in the middle of dinner," Mrs. Elton said. "Has Perry yet determined what made him so ill?"

Emma had no intention of offering information to feed Mrs. Elton's appetite for scandal. She left the question unanswered and instead introduced the couple to Mrs. Darcy.

"Mr. Knightley and Mr. Darcy are acquainted through the Earl of Chatfield," she added. Let Mrs. Elton, with her Maple Grove and its barouche-landau, ruminate on that.

Mr. Elton appeared impressed. "Did you attend the Donwell dinner party?" he asked Mrs. Darcy. "I do not recall having seen you last night."

"My husband and I arrived late to Donwell Abbey."

"That is too bad," Mrs. Elton said. "It was a nice little affair while it lasted. Almost equal to the soirees I have attended at Maple Grove. Everybody in Highbury is talking about it."

Of that, Emma had no doubt.

Mrs. Elton looked about the room with a critical eye. "What a charming little house you have. Exceedingly cozy." Her gaze fell upon the paper Emma had left on the table. "What is this?"

"A charade." Harriet moved forward to rescue it.

"Oh—do such games still amuse you? Since my own marriage, I have not time for such trifles." She took up the page before Harriet reached it. "Mr. E., no doubt you can solve this, for it begins, 'A place of worship . . .'" She read the remaining lines aloud. "Well, that is just delightful, Harriet. I suppose it must have occupied Mrs. Knightley and Mrs. Darcy for some time."

"Actually, Mrs. Knightley guessed it immediately," said Harriet, "and Mrs. Darcy soon after."

"Indeed? And what is the solution? I would work it out myself, but I do not want to miss a moment's conversation while I study it."

"My dear, it is Abbey Mill Farm," Mr. Elton said.

"Oh— Well, I suppose it is. How clever. Clever in its simplicity." She cast the paper aside. Harriet stared at it a minute, looking very much as if she wanted to snatch it up from the table and spare it from any further notice by Mrs. Elton. But Mrs. Elton appearing to have done with it, Harriet simply found a seat and perched on its edge.

"I am so glad, Harriet, that you are able to intersperse diversions with your new duties as a wife. Of course, my own obligations as the vicar's helpmeet consume so many of my hours.— Not that I am complaining, mind you. It is work I do quite willingly. As, I am sure, do you. You must be very happy in your new establishment."

Harriet began to reply, but Mrs. Elton's interest in her happiness did not extend so far as wanting to hear any assurance of it. Before Harriet had uttered two words, Mrs. Elton brought the discussion back to her favorite subject—herself.

"On our way here, we called upon the Bates ladies." She cast a pointed glance at Emma. "It was kind of you to provide Miss Bates with a new gown. I believe it was almost as becoming as the one I helped her make for the wedding. I refer to Frank and Jane's wedding, of course, but who knows? Perhaps she will participate in another wedding before long."

Emma refused to pose the question Mrs. Elton sought to provoke. Harriet, however, could not resist.

"Has someone in the village announced an engagement?"

"No—not yet. But I have hopes that Miss Bates herself will find such happiness as we four married ladies enjoy."

"Miss Bates! Imagine that! With whom?"

"Why, Harr—no, I ought not say a word! But I suspect Miss Bates has lately been on the mind of a certain eligible man in the village."

"Harry Simon?" Emma's tone revealed what she thought of Mrs. Elton's choice.

Mrs. Elton appeared startled by Emma's penetration. "Mr. Simon? Why ever would you think I refer to him?"

"Were you not about to say the name 'Harry'?"

"Harry? Heavens, no! I began to say 'Harriet.'"

Yes, Emma thought. And the Prince of Wales was engaged to dine at the vicarage on Wednesday.

"Harriet . . . of course," Emma said. "Well, I am relieved you did not mean Mr. Simon. Miss Bates can do better."

Mrs. Elton's lips curved into a forced smile inconsonant with the haughty glare of her eyes. "I know you cannot mean one of the gentlemen you put in her way last night. None of them have come calling today."

Nor would they, Emma ruefully acknowledged to herself. They were all fled. Fellow diners dropping dead hardly encouraged the forming of romantic attachments. Edgar Churchill's death had utterly undone Emma's plan.

"I would say that left to her own resources, or anybody else's, Miss Bates's chances of marrying are rather hopeless," Mrs. Elton continued. "Anybody's resources but mine, that is."

Emma froze as a dreadful thought entered her mind. Mrs. Elton had pointedly observed that none of Emma's potential suitors had visited Miss Bates this morning. Had Harry Simon? Was he in the cramped sitting room on Broadway Lane wooing the spinster even now? She must call upon Miss Bates immediately to discourage whatever machinations Mrs. Elton had initiated.

"Well, we shall see whether aught comes of your efforts." She picked up her basket and began to take leave of Harriet.

The moment she escaped, Emma strode away from the farmhouse at a pace that would have left most other companions struggling to keep up with her. Mrs. Darcy, however, matched her gait with no difficulty, a feat that might have raised her still further in Emma's regard had Emma's mind not been altogether employed by apprehension over what evils could even then be occurring in a certain brick house in Highbury.

"I take it we have another errand to perform?" Mrs. Darcy asked.

"We must call upon Miss Bates directly. I hope to find her unengaged—in all senses of the word."

"Is your objection to Mr. Simon, or to Mrs. Elton's presumption?"

Despite her ire, Emma noted with approval Mrs. Darcy's discernment. Her new acquaintance had more quickness about her than did any of Emma's other female associates, even her beloved Mrs. Weston.

"Mr. Simon is, sadly, not altogether right in the mind. And Miss Bates is a spinster who already has an elderly, deaf mother to care for—she does not need the additional burden of caring for him. Further, while Mr. Simon seems a gentle man, he is not a *gentleman*—he is a common farmer. Miss Bates deserves a more genteel husband. Meanwhile, Mrs. Elton—" She paused. Prudence cautioned her to censor her speech to such a recent acquaintance, but vexation spurred her forward. "Mrs. Elton is a vain, selfish creature whose motives for arranging a match between them have nothing to do with the happiness of the principals. I am determined to find a more appropriate suitor for Miss Bates."

"Have you someone particular in mind?"

"There were several candidates at last night's party, but they have left the village along with the other guests." She silently cursed once again the ill fortune that had brought Edgar Churchill's death to their door. Why could he not have expired a se'nnight hence, in Yorkshire?

"Is there no one local?"

Emma considered whether there might be someone in Highbury whom she had overlooked, but could think of no one. Everybody knew Miss Bates; everybody would agree that she was a kind, good-natured woman. However, everybody in the village had also spent decades enduring her tedious chatter. "I believe Miss Bates's chances are better with someone who has not known her all her life. I am sure an eligible candidate will present himself." They had reached the village. Emma glanced down the lane and released a sigh. "Somewhere."

They headed straight for the Bates house. As it came into view, two people were just entering it: Jane Churchill and Thomas Dixon.

The single Thomas Dixon.

Emma's gaze followed him through the door, but her mind was already upstairs with Miss Bates. Thomas Dixon might not possess a large fortune, but he had enough money to pay his tailor bills. And he had been amiable last night, which was more than she could say about Mr. Nodd, the major, or Mr. Wynnken.

Thomas Dixon possessed wit and taste, pleasant looks, cultivated manners, and an extraordinary wardrobe. Why had she not considered him before?

Thirteen

"I planned the match from that hour."

—*Emma Woodhouse*, Emma

*E*lizabeth followed Mrs. Knightley up the narrow staircase. They were admitted to a small apartment, wherein a middle-aged woman was receiving the two visitors who had just arrived.

". . . have been thinking about you all morning, Jane. Poor Frank! What a dreadful turn of events. He must be beside himself. So good of you to accompany Jane here, Mr. Dixon. And look! Now here is Mrs. Knightley and . . ."—she bestowed upon Elizabeth an uncertain but welcoming smile—"and . . ."

"This is Mrs. Darcy," Mrs. Knightley said. "Her husband is a friend of Mr. Knightley, and they are visiting from Derbyshire. Mrs. Darcy, I present Miss Bates—" Their hostess's smile brightened as Elizabeth acknowledged the introduction with a nod. Mrs. Knightley gestured toward an elderly woman knitting beside the fire. "—her mother, Mrs. Bates, and her niece, the former Jane Fairfax, now Mrs. Frank Churchill. Finally, Mr. Thomas Dixon."

Elizabeth recognized the Bates ladies as two of the guests who had been departing upon her own arrival at Donwell. Jane Churchill was a comely young woman of perhaps two-and-twenty, with dark hair and

125

grey eyes; not a classic beauty, but striking nonetheless. Mr. Dixon was considerably older, his temples touched with grey, yet still quite handsome. He was dressed impeccably in a cut-away green frock coat over a striped waistcoat, cream nankeen breeches, and highly polished Hessian boots. A monocle hung from a chain round his neck.

"Friends of Mr. Knightley? Well, you are certainly welcome here!" Miss Bates exclaimed. "Did you hear that, Mother? This is Mrs. Darcy." She raised her voice. "*Darcy.* Oh! Do sit down, Mrs. Darcy—yes, right there. Mrs. Knightley, take my seat. No, no—it is no trouble at all. We have a spare chair in the bedroom. Patty, bring in the spare chair for me. There, now—we shall all be quite comfortable."

Despite the effusive welcome, Elizabeth feared her presence as a stranger was an intrusion on the family so soon following Edgar Churchill's death. "Allow me to wish you joy upon your marriage," she said to Mrs. Churchill, who was seated beside Mr. Dixon on a worn sofa. "I believe I met your husband earlier today. I was sorry to hear about the loss of his uncle."

"It is all most distressing," said Miss Bates. "To be so happy at the start of a day, and end it so sadly. I am sure I never imagined Edgar Churchill would take ill—he seemed in perfect health when I saw him the day before. And Jane was just saying that he appeared fine at breakfast yesterday—were you not just saying that, Jane?"

"He was quieter than usual, but otherwise seemed well." She turned to Mr. Dixon. "You took a walk with him in the afternoon. Had you any suspicion?"

"None. I—" He shrugged. "Mr. Churchill was as robust a walking companion as ever I had. A fine gentleman all around, gone far too soon."

"Indeed. I am still not over the shock of it." Tears formed in Jane Churchill's eyes. "I am grateful he died among friends."

Mr. Dixon patted Mrs. Churchill's hand. The gesture struck Elizabeth as rather familiar, and she wondered what level of intimacy existed between the families.

Mrs. Knightley appeared to be studying him, as well. "Mr. Dixon, it is so good of you to stay on, along with your cousins, to console Mrs. Churchill and her husband."

"I would wish to be nowhere else, even were I not at my cousin's disposal."

"Where are Mr. and Mrs. Patrick Dixon at present?"

"We left them at Randalls."

Miss Bates turned to Elizabeth. "Jane said she longed for the company of her aunt and grandmama this afternoon. Frank being already out, Mr. Dixon kindly attended her."

"How could I neglect an opportunity to spend more time in your charming company, ma'am? When Jane revealed her destination, I insisted on escorting her."

The compliment delighted Miss Bates. "You are always welcome to visit our humble parlor, Mr. Dixon."

"Humble? Not at all. It is . . . unpretentious. Why, I believe it wants only new wallpaper to complete it—lend it final polish, one might say."

"New paper?" Miss Bates looked round, and Elizabeth could not help raising her own gaze to the walls and corners. It would take more than new paper to awaken the room from its tired state, but covering the present faded pattern would indeed improve it. "Oh, I see. Yes! There are a few worn patches, are there not? And it begins to peel up there, along the molding. Perhaps we ought to consider it."

"Ought? You must. And I know the very pattern: a paisley stripe. I have it in my own bedchamber. It will give this happy little room just the subtle touch of elegance for which it cries."

"Do you truly think so?"

"Oh, indeed! My friend Ridley, who just purchased a townhouse in Mayfair, utterly transformed his drawing room simply by changing the wallpaper—left all the furnishings just as they were. You need not alter another thing. Though if you were of a mind, new coverings might refresh the chairs."

The chairs were indeed in want of refreshment—at a minimum. The bottom of Elizabeth's own seat was so worn that she hoped it would hold her, and the sofa arms were as threadbare as the Bates ladies' attire. Indeed, the only object in the cramped room that appeared possessed of fewer years than old Mrs. Bates was a pianoforte wedged into a corner.

Although Mr. Dixon's assessment and proposed solutions were valid, Elizabeth doubted that the household could afford the changes he advocated. Surely, however, he would not have suggested them did he not believe the family had means—to do so would demonstrate a profound lack of feeling. Perhaps his recommendations had been meant as a hint for Miss Bates's niece, now that Jane had married well and Edgar Churchill's death had left her still more secure.

Elizabeth studied the new Mrs. Frank Churchill. Her expression was inscrutable. She was possessed of such strong self-command that Elizabeth could not upon this initial meeting penetrate it.

Mrs. Knightley, however, seemed undisturbed by the course of the conversation, and in fact smiled with approval. "Mr. Dixon, that is a splendid suggestion," she said. "Perhaps you might counsel Miss Bates on suitable fabric."

"I should be honored. Why, I know the very shop in London to help us. Extraordinary selection! My dear Miss Bates, if you will permit me, I would be delighted to undertake the commission on your behalf. There is nothing so satisfying as finding just the proper materials for fitting out a room—except, perhaps, the planning of a new waistcoat. Yes, you must allow me to assist you. I shall set off at first light tomorrow."

Mr. Dixon appeared quite pleased with himself, and Emma even more so, at this proposal. Miss Bates, however, became flustered.

"Oh! Your offer is so kind, Mr. Dixon—so very kind. Is it not, Mother? Imagine that! Fabric all the way from London adorning our plain chairs here in Highbury. But it is too good—you are too good—the present chairs will suffice. No need for new upholstery—"

"Heavens, I quite agree!" Mr. Dixon said. "Some simple coverings fitted over the seats were what I had in view. . . . Though now that you mention it, new upholstery might be the very thing." He was by now quite animated. "Yes! Why did I not suggest it at the outset? New upholstery—and draperies! Of course if we renew the wallpaper and upholstery, we simply must change out the draperies. And the carpet—there is no sense in refreshing everything else only to neglect what is underfoot. Harding and Howell, in Piccadilly—they will have everything we need!"

Emma appeared so delighted by the suggestion that one would think it was her sitting room about to be transformed. Miss Bates, however, paled.

"Draperies? Yes, they . . . I suppose these have served quite some time. But I beg you not to trouble yourself. These will do us nicely a while longer. The carpet, too. No need to change everything at once—"

"But there is every need, my dear lady! An utter transformation! What could be more pleasant?"

A tooth extraction, from the expression on Miss Bates's countenance.

"But the—" Miss Bates's expression beseeched her niece to put an end to the discussion. "The expense—we simply cannot . . ."

Jane glanced at Mr. Dixon, then reached over and took her aunt's hand. "Perhaps we can."

Fourteen

"One never does form a just idea of any body beforehand."
—Miss Bates, *Emma*

ood afternoon, sir. What do you seek today?"

Darcy hesitated. His natural impulse was to state his purpose and question the trader directly about his transactions with the Churchills and the gypsy remedies he had been selling. However, even a gentleman might dissemble when cornered, and Hiram Deal—a common peddler known to conduct business with gypsies, persons of disreputable character—was not by birth, circumstances, or association a gentleman. Neither his cooperation nor truthfulness could be assumed.

Though Mr. Knightley had never personally dealt with the peddler, he and Darcy agreed that Mr. Deal had been in the neighborhood long enough that he likely knew the magistrate's identity. An honest man might hear the local authorities named in ordinary conversation as he went about his business; a dishonest one would make it his business to determine, upon arrival in any new village, those persons whose notice he should avoid.

And so Mr. Knightley stood some yards away, engaged in conversation with a tenant who had happened along at an opportune moment, while Darcy approached Mr. Deal. He would learn what he could through informal means before Mr. Knightley joined them, if necessary, for official questioning. Darcy wished Elizabeth were with him. He disdained idle chatter; she was much his superior in this sort of thing.

"An acquaintance of mine owns a very nice snuff box, and tells me he purchased it from you," Darcy said. "His name is Frank Churchill. Do you recall selling it to him?"

"Indeed, yes! Mr. Churchill spent a considerable amount of time selecting it. I had two, and he liked them both so well that he could not quite make up his mind. I still have the other. Let me see—"

As Mr. Deal rummaged through his wares, Darcy noticed with surprise that the peddler had but one hand. In all the discussions pertaining to Mr. Deal, no one had ever mentioned the fact.

"Yes, here is the other snuff box," Mr. Deal said. "I warrant you will not find a finer one outside London, and perhaps within."

Darcy accepted the case and made a show of examining it, though his true object was examining the peddler. Mr. Deal's countenance was open and his manner warm, yet as Darcy handled the snuff case, Deal's gaze repeatedly darted past him to the street beyond. Darcy wondered whether he had spotted Mr. Knightley or merely canvassed the village for more potential customers.

"It is a very fine snuff case, though I prefer Mr. Churchill's. It is a pity he discovered it first. When did you sell it to him?"

"The day before yesterday."

"So recently? When next I see him, I shall have to commend him on his timing as well as his taste. Did he purchase anything else?"

"No, only the snuff box."

Frank Churchill had been telling the truth about not having purchased any of the gypsy remedies. But had Edgar bought a fatal physic? Darcy did not want to appear too interested in the family's affairs.

"My wife's birthday rapidly approaches, and I have not yet settled upon a gift for her. I hope to find something unusual. Have you any jewelry—something out of the ordinary?"

"I have a few items. How much do you want to spend?"

"That depends upon what you have to offer."

He began to open a small wooden box. "I have several necklaces that she might appreciate."

"I had hoped to find a ring."

Mr. Deal's gaze took in the quality of Darcy's attire beneath his open greatcoat, the gold fob chain dangling from his waistcoat pocket, his bearing. "I believe I can accommodate you. I recently acquired a gold ring. It is set with five small diamonds."

Darcy's hopes, briefly elevated, sank. "My wife is averse to diamonds."

Mr. Deal's lips curved in amusement. "A lady who would not welcome diamonds? I did not know such a creature existed."

A twelvemonth previous, Darcy and Elizabeth had seen all they wanted of diamonds for a lifetime. "You do not know my wife."

"Perhaps I could interest you in something else? Have a look about."

Darcy had been hoping for just such an invitation, and seized upon it readily. Mr. Deal traveled with an eclectic inventory of tinware, trinkets, tools, and textiles. Though according to Mrs. Knightley he had been peddling in the neighborhood for a fortnight, he had no shortage of wares. "I have heard such tell of you in the neighborhood that I should have thought your stock nearly depleted, but your cart seems a veritable emporium."

"I acquire new goods regularly. Customers offer me things in trade, or I buy them from local artisans in the villages through which I pass. I also visit London and other cities in the course of my travels."

"Do you ever obtain goods from less conventional sources?"

Mr. Deal regarded Darcy warily. He walked around to the opposite side of his cart and adjusted several items. "If you refer to smuggling, no. The profits might be high, but so are the gallows."

"I did not mean to suggest any such thing. My mind ran more toward gypsies." Darcy had intended by indirections to find direction out, but paltering did not come smoothly or comfortably to him. Indeed, thus far he felt himself the deceiver in this interview, and the sensation did not sit well. He would engage in a more direct manner of questioning.

"Gypsies?" Deal picked up a copper teakettle and hung it for display. It caught a shaft of low afternoon sunlight penetrating the clouds and glowed as warmly as if it boiled on a hearth. The flash lasted but moments, however, before the clouds obscured the sun once more, shadowing the peddler's countenance as well.

"The villagers say you sell gypsy wares."

"From time to time, I meet gypsies in my journeys—it is inevitable that someone who travels as much as I do will cross paths with other wanderers. Gypsies are renowned tinkers and woodworkers, and so, yes, I engage in business with them when the opportunity arises."

"I hear you sell remedies that rival anything the village apothecary can provide, and that you tout them as having been prepared by a gypsy."

"Gypsies have traveled for centuries; their healers possess knowledge gained in the many lands their forebears passed through. I would trust a gypsy remedy above anything concocted by an English chemist."

"Insofar as any gypsy can be trusted?"

Deal made no reply as he hung two pie tins next to the teakettle.

"When did you obtain the cures you have been selling in Highbury?" Darcy pressed.

"I met with a gypsy party not long before arriving in the village."

"So near? Are they still about?"

"I believe they have moved on."

"Do you know in which direction? My wife and I will be traveling, and we would not want to encounter such a group."

"I cannot say, for the Roma are as predictable as the wind. But should you happen upon them, you have nothing to fear. It was a band I have done business with before, and they will not trouble you if you do not trouble them. Indeed, if one of them offers to tell your fortune, the meeting might bring you luck."

Darcy had little interest in that sort of nonsense. "Are gypsy predictions more or less reliable than their remedies?"

"It depends upon the fortune-teller. There is one among that band who is both a seer and a healer, who earned my respect years ago.

Indeed, I cannot say with certainty that I would be standing here now were it not for her. It was she from whom I acquired the remedies."

"Have you any remaining?"

"A few. Do you need something in particular?"

"I should like to see what you have."

Mr. Deal moved to the opposite side of the cart, where several wooden cases of different sizes rested in a corner. As he rearranged them to gain access to the one he wanted, Darcy marveled at the smoothness with which he handled the task, not in the least slowed or hampered by the lack of one hand. He had learned to compensate well for the missing appendage—a necessity, no doubt, for a man whose profession required constant travel and brought him into contact with individuals from all walks of life, including ruffians only too eager to take advantage of any perceived weakness.

Mr. Deal also had much to gain from such individuals, were he a man of few scruples.

"Do you ever acquire items from gypsies that they did not produce themselves?" Darcy asked.

"Whenever a person, be he English or otherwise, offers me something of interest, I accept it if I believe it worth the price."

"With no questions?"

"On the contrary. An object's history adds to its value. If an item has a story, I ask to hear it." He lifted a medium-sized wooden chest and rested it atop another, then opened it to reveal two vials and a packet. "These are all the remedies I have remaining. You do not happen to suffer from dropsy or gout?"

Darcy enjoyed perfect health, but he wanted Mr. Perry to have a look at the preparations. "I will take them all."

"The third is for female complaints."

Darcy cleared his throat, declining to enquire into the particular complaints the concoction purported to cure. "My wife may find it of use. I shall purchase it while I have the opportunity."

"Very good, sir." Mr. Deal smiled. "Though I suspect it is hardly the birthday gift you had in mind." He gestured toward the cart. "Have you spotted anything else that might delight her? Is she musical? I have the most unusual wooden flute—"

Darcy shook his head and scanned the cart once more. Nowhere amid the coffers and cases lay the chest he had hoped to discover. If his stolen possessions were amongst the peddler's wares, they were well hidden.

A small doll, however, caught his notice. It reminded him of Lily-Anne, and the hope that he would see her again before much more time passed. Though Darcy had no intention of purchasing the doll, Mr. Deal noticed that it had momentarily captured his gaze.

"Ah—are there little ones at home? I have some colorful glass beads that children adore. Where did I put that sack?" He moved to another side of the wagon in search of it.

Darcy spied a cloth bag with rounded bulges protruding from its sides. "Is this it?" He untied the drawstring.

"No, no. I remember stowing it over here. Those are—"

Sling bullets. Darcy kept his countenance neutral as he glanced at the peddler.

". . . not what you are looking for." Mr. Deal smiled, but the expression appeared forced. "Those would hardly delight a little girl now, would they? Just set those down—what you want is over here."

Darcy did not set them aside. Instead, he removed one of the bullets from the sack. The missile appeared to be the same shape and weight as the one found at the robbery scene that morning. Mr. Knightley, however, had retained that bullet, and presently remained some yards distant engaged in conversation with his tenant.

"Yes, here are the beads." Mr. Deal came back to Darcy's side of the cart with a sack tucked under his left arm and several beads in the palm of his single hand. "Little girls love to play with them, and governesses use them to teach counting and simple arithmetic."

"I will take them. And these as well." Darcy pulled the drawstring shut and lifted the sack. The one sling bullet, however, he retained in his palm, not wanting to let it leave his grasp.

"Oh, I see—you must also have a son. Of course you cannot remember one child without remembering them all, if you want to keep peace. But hardly anybody uses slings—perhaps your boy would be more interested in something else. How old is he? Does he practice archery? I have some arrows with colorful fletching."

"No, the bullets will suffice. Do *they* have a story?"

The peddler looked ruefully at the bag and shrugged. "Not a very interesting one. I obtain them from a man in Richmond."

Darcy noted Mr. Deal's use of the present tense. "These were not a one-time acquisition—he supplies you regularly?"

"When I have need."

"As you said, slings are not a weapon in common use. I wager there are few people who possess the throwing skill to make purchasing molded ammunition worthwhile. Have you regular customers for the bullets?"

"They are yours if you want them—you will not leave me short."

That was not what Darcy had asked. "Have you slings for sale, as well?"

"No, only the bullets."

Darcy nodded. "Well, then, I believe I have done for today. How much do I owe you for the merchandise?"

Mr. Deal stated the total. Darcy took money from his purse and handed it to the peddler. Then he withdrew an additional coin.

"Do you accept commissions?"

Mr. Deal's gaze rested for several seconds on the silver, then rose to meet Darcy's. His eyes reflected interest—but also caution. "What do you seek?"

"Two things: a small chest, and information. The chest contains a set of christening clothes and a woman's signet ring with the initials *A.F.* Should anyone approach you with these items for sale or trade, I would make it worth your trouble to see that they reach me." Darcy studied Mr. Deal's countenance as he said this, but the peddler betrayed no indication that he was already familiar with the stolen articles. "I am also willing to pay for intelligence regarding the identities or whereabouts of the persons from whom you acquired them."

Mr. Deal studied Darcy in silence for a minute, but Darcy sensed the peddler had been taking his measure all the while he had been assessing Deal.

"And should I come across these goods in the course of business," Mr. Deal finally said, "where might I find you?"

"I am presently a guest of Mr. and Mrs. Knightley at Donwell Abbey, though I am uncertain how long I shall stay. If I have departed by the time you call, simply leave word with them that you wish to contact Mr. Fitzwilliam Darcy. They will know where I can be found."

Darcy placed the coin in the peddler's palm.

Fifteen

"As you make no secret of your love of match-making, it is fair to
suppose that views, and plans, and projects you have."
—Mr. Knightley, *Emma*

*E*mma was well pleased with the campaign under way for refur-
bishing Miss Bates's sitting room. Not only was the space in dire
want of attention, but it was her hope that the project might prove
the means by which an attachment between Miss Bates and Thomas
Dixon formed. That Mr. Dixon had taken such particular notice of
Miss Bates's circumstances, and rather than responding with disdain
or aversion had not only immediately initiated action to improve
them, but also wished to be so directly involved in the affair himself,
boded well. If romantic inclinations did not already kindle his interest, surely with proper management he would, by the time the last
drapery was hung, desire an even more dramatic transformation: installing Miss Bates as Mrs. Dixon in his own abode. He would, that is,
if Emma had her way about it.

Indeed, upon conceiving the notion, Emma had extended their
call longer than intended to subtly advance the match. She conceded
to herself that it was, on its surface, not the most likely of alliances,
but more improbable attachments had been known to occur.

She and Mrs. Darcy left the small apartment only when Mr. Dixon himself departed to engage one of the Crown's horses for the morrow so that he might complete posthaste his promised errands in London. "It must bring you pleasure to know how much happiness your endeavors will create for such a deserving lady," Emma said to him as they reached the base of the stairs.

He held the door open for them. "Yes. Mrs. Churchill certainly deserves a return to happiness after the events of last night. At least she will be able to settle in Yorkshire confident that her aunt and grandmother are comfortable here."

Mr. Dixon had mistaken Emma's meaning. Why ever would he think she referred to Jane? "I was speaking of Miss Bates."

"Oh, yes! Her happiness goes without saying. Who could fail to find joy in new wallpaper?"

Though she had hoped for a few additional minutes' conversation with him to advance her plan, Mr. Dixon split off as soon as they entered the street. She could only fancy that his passion for Miss Bates was already too great for words.

Emma and Mrs. Darcy proceeded toward Donwell Lane. Near the corner stood Mr. Deal's cart, where the peddler was showing Mr. Wallis a pair of pie tins. Emma wondered that the person who had operated the village bakery for some five-and-twenty years could be in want of more pie tins, but Mr. Wallis was easily persuadable these days. The unfortunate man had not been the same since he lost his wife last summer. For that matter, neither had his pies.

Just as they arrived at the cart, Miss Bates's voice reached her ears. "Mrs. Knightley! Mrs. Knightley—oh, do stop!"

Emma and Mrs. Darcy both turned round. Miss Bates hurried to them, quite out of breath. Emma's basket hung from one hand. In her rush to quit the apartment at the same time as Mr. Dixon, Emma had entirely forgotten it.

"Dear Miss Bates!" Emma took the basket from her hand. "Thank you—how good of you to bring it to me."

"Well, it was so kind of you to bring us the apple butter. There is nothing we like more than apples this time of year—apple butter, apple cider, apple dumplings . . ."

"And baked apples, I trust," said Mr. Wallis. He had a gentle, quiet manner well suited to a man who had spent every morning of his life working in the predawn stillness setting dough to rise. "I planned to bring yours over as soon as I finished with Mr. Deal." He offered Miss Bates a smile, the first Emma had seen from him since his wife's passing.

"Baked apples are our favorite! Oh, I am delighted that they are ready! Jane is in our sitting room at this very moment, and you know how she loves baked apples. Nothing so wholesome—why, even Mr. Woodhouse approves them. Yes, do send your boy over with the apples as soon as you can."

"I shall do better and bring them myself."

Mr. Wallis smiled again. Emma, her mind predisposed to interpret any man's attention toward Miss Bates as an opportunity to thwart Mrs. Elton's scheme, contemplated whether the widower would make a suitable alternate in the event her hopes for Mr. Dixon went unrealized. Though not a gentleman, he made a comfortable living, and as Mrs. Elton had so haughtily noted, the spinster was long past the point of being too particular. Plus, Miss Bates could serve Jane baked apples whenever she wished.

"Oh, Mr. Wallis, you are kindness itself! That you would take such trouble to personally deliver our apples. Jane will be so touched. Perhaps an apple will help cheer her after this wretched occurrence with Edgar Churchill."

"Yes, I heard he died suddenly. Please give my condolences to your niece and nephew." Mr. Wallis handed the pie tins back to Mr. Deal. He neglected, however, to look at the peddler as he did so—his gaze focused on Miss Bates—and he absently thrust them toward Deal's left side. Before Mr. Deal could grab them with his sole hand, they clattered to the ground.

"Oh, dear!" Miss Bates rushed forward to help Mr. Deal retrieve the tins from the road.

Mr. Wallis stepped back, embarrassed at having directed the tins toward a hand that did not exist. "How clumsy of me! I am so sorry."

"It is nothing." Mr. Deal tucked one tin under his arm, and reached for the second. He grasped it just as Miss Bates also took hold of it, and the two of them rose, the tin clutched between them.

"Oh!" Flustered, Miss Bates released the tin to him. "I suppose you did not need my help.—No, certainly did not.—Quite capable, of course."

"On the contrary, I thank you for coming to my rescue." He made an exaggerated bow, then proffered the tin. "Please—accept this as a token of my appreciation."

Miss Bates laughed self-consciously, unaccustomed to gallantry— real or playful—from anybody. "That is most kind of you, but unnecessary—truly—happy to help wherever I can—would have done the same for anyone—you have been so generous already—the combs—"

"Did you wear them to the party?"

"I did! I never felt so elegant!"

"And your mother—did she enjoy herself?"

"Oh, yes—thank you for enquiring. We both did, until the evening took such an unfortunate turn . . ."

Mrs. Darcy stepped closer to Emma. "Mrs. Elton just entered the street," she said quietly. "Is the person with her Mr. Simon?"

Emma followed Mrs. Darcy's gaze. To her chagrin, the vicar's wife indeed walked with Harry Simon, and the pair progressed toward them. It appeared, however, that Mrs. Elton had not yet taken notice of the persons assembled at the peddler's cart.

"Miss Bates," Emma interjected, "perhaps this would be a good time for Mr. Wallis to deliver your apples. If you accompanied him to the bakery, he could then walk with you back to your house." Emma hoped the errand would also enable Miss Bates to elicit another shy smile from the baker.

Mr. Wallis, still looking uncomfortable following his blunder, seized upon the chance to escape. "I can fetch them now, if you like."

"I—" Miss Bates glanced back to Mr. Deal as if she had something more to say but had forgotten what it was. As she was seldom in want of words, her expression held some confusion as she addressed Mr. Wallis. "Certainly—of course I shall go with you this minute. I must return to Jane, and to arrive with baked apples will surprise her indeed. Yes, let us go directly."

"Miss Bates—"

Emma wanted to stamp her foot in frustration. Why *must* the peddler persist in prolonging his exchange with Miss Bates? If only he knew what was at stake.

"—you have forgotten something." Mr. Deal once more offered the pie tin.

Emma took the tin from Hiram Deal, handed it to Miss Bates, and nudged her toward Mr. Wallis. "Mr. Dixon's errand at the Crown surely will not take long, and then he will escort Mrs. Churchill back to Randalls. It would be a shame if you returned with the apples only to discover that they departed in your absence."

"Oh! I had not considered that! Dear me! We cannot risk Jane's leaving before I return. Mr. Wallis, let us go at once. Thank you, Mr. Deal, for the tin. So generous! Indeed, I hardly know what to say. . . ."

If the peddler responded, Emma missed his reply, so concentrated was her attention on Mrs. Elton.

"Pray, excuse me for a moment," she said to Mrs. Darcy.

Sixteen

The Overton Scotchman has been kind enough to rid me of some
of my money, in exchange for six shifts and four pair of stockings.
                    —Jane Austen, letter to her sister, Cassandra

*L*eft alone with Mr. Deal, Elizabeth scanned the contents of his
cart. She most wanted information, but doubted she would
find intelligence regarding Miss Jones and her own stolen goods on
display amid the housewares and muslins. She had already determined, during the peddler's exchange with Miss Bates, that her chest
was not amongst the closed boxes and trunks visible in the back of
the cart. Some of them, however, were of a size that could easily accommodate the christening clothes and ring. She gestured towards
the cases. "You appear to have already begun putting away your wares
for the day."

"On the contrary, I am still setting up."

"So late in the afternoon?" It could hardly be worth the trader's
while to arrange all his merchandise so close to the arrival of dusk.
Almost as soon as he had everything in place, he would have to put it
away again.

"I had other business to attend to this morning. If you do not see
what you desire, simply name it, for I might indeed have it amongst
my stock."

"I find when dealing with peddlers that it is best not to come with a particular item in mind, for one never knows what treasure might be discovered quite by accident."

"Then, madam, you are a customer after my own heart. May I therefore take the liberty of selecting a few items to show you?"

"I am a discriminating buyer. I should like to begin with the newest merchandise you have, rather than articles that have already been passed over by countless others."

She hoped by this statement that he would produce her belongings if they had come into his possession. But such ease of recovery was not to be. Deal showed her many useful items and decorative objects, but neither the signet ring nor the christening set appeared. She endeavored to disguise her disappointment; after all, a woman who claimed to be seeking nothing specific could not very well appear dismayed at failing to find it.

Mr. Deal himself, she determined to be an amiable fellow—genial, considerate, warm. And he was handsome, though not so handsome as Darcy. Though it would have been a relief to recover her stolen possessions by discovering them amongst his wares, she found herself somehow glad of their absence, for she did not want to think him an accessory to robbery—or worse, himself one of the thieves. He was by turns amusing and instructive, and she quite enjoyed their conversation as he showcased his wide range of wares.

She selected a pair of patterned silk stockings, which she did not need—at least not for their usual purpose. Still hoping to obtain whatever information she could from the peddler, she sought to buy his goodwill along with the stockings.

She handed him her coins. "I had heard from one of your customers that I might obtain nearly anything imaginable from you, and I am begun to believe that is true."

Mr. Deal removed a pouch from an inner pocket of his coat, set it on a shelf built into the side of the cart, and loosened the drawstring. "And whom might I thank for the praise?"

The source had been Mrs. Knightley, and Elizabeth nearly named her. But on impulse she said, "Miss Jones."

It was a gamble, her attempt to lead him into revealing a relationship that might not in fact exist. Miss Jones had not, of course, said anything whatsoever about Hiram Deal. But if, as Elizabeth and Darcy speculated, she and her accomplices had approached the peddler to sell their stolen goods, he might inadvertently reveal their association.

"Indeed?" Deal counted out her change. "I do not believe I have met a Miss Jones since arriving in Highbury."

"She is a young woman, perhaps sixteen. Petite. Blond hair, blue eyes?"

He smiled as he dropped three shillings into her palm. "You have just described half the girls in Britain. I am afraid I have no recollection of this particular one."

"Are you certain? She was quite pretty."

"Every English village boasts pretty young maids. And a few old maids. I am more likely to recall the latter, for too often, the former are all the same."

Further conversation was disrupted by the reappearance of Mrs. Knightley, who returned with a self-satisfied expression on her face and Harry Simon in tow. Mrs. Elton looked on from a distance, and Elizabeth needed no closer proximity to feel the displeasure radiating from the vicar's wife.

"Mr. Simon has business with my husband," Mrs. Knightley said. "As there is no time like the present, I have suggested that he accompany us back to Donwell to speak with Mr. Knightley."

Harry Simon was being whisked off to Donwell and away from Miss Bates. No wonder Mrs. Knightley was so pleased, and Mrs. Elton so vexed.

Mr. Simon glanced at the peddler's inventory with eyes as wide as a child's, his gaze lighting first on one item, then another. "I do not believe I have ever seen so—so—so many—what is that?"

Mr. Deal smiled. "A wooden flute." He picked up the intricately carved instrument and offered it to Mr. Simon. "Would you like to try it?"

Mr. Simon looked as if he would like to try it very much indeed. However, Mrs. Knightley, with a glance in Mrs. Elton's direction, gently drew Mr. Simon away.

"We have not time, Mr. Simon, if you want to speak with Mr. Knightley. You can peruse the peddler's wares tomorrow."

Before Mrs. Elton could waylay them with a manufactured excuse to retain Mr. Simon for her own purposes, they took leave of Mr. Deal and set forth for Donwell. As the shadows were grown long and the temperature falling, Elizabeth was grateful to be turning their steps towards the warmth of her temporary abode. She was also eager to see Darcy again, and hear whether he and Mr. Knightley had learned anything of use this afternoon.

"Mrs. Knightley, do you—do you think the peddler sells hair ribbons?"

"He does." She regarded him curiously. "Why do you ask?"

"I want to buy one for Doris."

"Doris?"

"Doris Cooper."

"Mrs. Cooper's eldest? Is she a friend?"

"She comes each day to cook and such. Been coming since she was twelve. The same year we bought our cow. She's calved one, two— three times." He paused. "The cow, not Doris."

Both ladies smiled. "So I presumed," Mrs. Knightley said.

"Lost her hair ribbon a few days ago. Doris, not the cow. I found it later all shredded by one of the chickens. I want to get her a new one. I saw a girl this morning about Doris's age with a pretty pink ribbon in her hair. She was talking to the peddler, so I thought maybe she got it from him. Was going to ask him, but then we had to leave."

"I think it is lovely that you want to replace her ribbon. If Mr. Deal does not have any more, you can certainly find one at Ford's."

They arrived at Donwell. Though invigorated by their walk, Elizabeth was happy to retreat from the brisk air and gathering dusk. Her nose and cheeks tingled with cold, and she longed for the warmth of a glowing hearth. Parting from Mrs. Knightley and Mr. Simon, she went to her chamber in hopes of finding an established fire and Darcy.

She discovered that she would have to settle for one out of two. Her husband was absent, but a cheerful blaze greeted her. So did her maid, Lucy, who advised her that Darcy had been closeted with

Mr. Knightley in the study since their own return three-quarters of an hour earlier.

Elizabeth set her new stockings on the dressing table and went to the fireplace. When sufficient warmth had seeped into her bones, her maid helped her dress for dinner. Lucy had just finished arranging Elizabeth's hair when Darcy entered the room.

He appeared pensive, and perhaps weary. It had been a long, busy day for them both. He carried two small sacks, which he deposited on a table beside the door. Their contents clacked against each other and the table's wooden surface, engaging her curiosity.

Lucy smoothed one last lock of Elizabeth's hair and departed. When the door had closed, Darcy approached.

"How was your outing with Mrs. Knightley?" he asked.

"Illuminating. How was your excursion with Mr. Knightley?"

"Intriguing."

He tucked her wayward lock of hair, which had come loose the moment Lucy quit the room, behind her ear. As he regarded her reflection in the glass, he noticed the stockings on the dressing table. "Are those new?"

"I bought them from Mr. Deal today."

He picked them up, holding them by their tops so that the silk unfurled to full length. "Did you need new stockings?"

"We need the peddler's cooperation. I considered them an investment." She turned away from the mirror and reclaimed them. "I did not realize you took such interest in ladies' stockings."

"Only yours, Mrs. Darcy."

She rose to put them away, deliberately brushing him as she passed. "Next time I shall buy two pair."

He laughed and stole a kiss. "It seems the peddler did quite well by us today, for you are not the only one who encountered him."

"Indeed? And what did you purchase?"

He nodded toward the sacks. "See for yourself."

Requiring no further encouragement, she crossed to the table, took up one of the bags, and opened it. The sack held colored glass beads of varying sizes. She withdrew a handful.

"And you questioned the stockings. What are we to do with these?"

"They are for Lily-Anne."

"Lily-Anne?" Whatever was her husband thinking, buying scores of beads no larger than acorns for a nine-month-old child? "I hope you do not intend them for her until she is older. If you give them to her now, she will put them straight into her mouth."

"Then I suppose you will consider the other bag even less appropriate for her."

She had assumed the sacks shared the same contents. She returned the beads to the first and lifted the second. It was much heavier. With a questioning glance at Darcy, she loosed the drawstring and looked inside.

Her gaze immediately returned to him. "Mr. Deal sells sling bullets?"

"He not only sells sling bullets, he sells sling bullets identical to the one we discovered this morning. Distinctive markings identify them as having almost certainly come from the same mold."

"And to whom does he sell them?"

"That, Mr. Knightley and I have yet to determine."

"Mr. Knightley is the magistrate. Cannot he compel Mr. Deal to name his customers?"

"As you well know, simply asking someone a question does not guarantee a truthful reply, particularly if it could incriminate the respondent. We have been discussing whether to arrest Mr. Deal outright. The sling bullet connects him to the robbery, and so provides sufficient cause. At present, however, we believe he will prove more useful to us if he remains at liberty. Mr. Knightley has assigned a man to monitor him."

"The two of you think he was directly involved in the robbery?"

"Even if Mr. Deal knows nothing about the crime, it is highly probable that the thieves obtained their bullets from him."

"Unless they obtained them from the same source as the peddler. In fact, he could have acquired the bullets *from* them in trade for something else."

"Mr. Deal claims that he obtains the bullets from a man in Richmond. Granted, that same man could supply other merchants, could have sold the bullets directly to the robbers, or could even have committed the crime himself. However, our thieves were here in Highbury last night, and Mr. Deal has been in the neighborhood for a fortnight, so the bullets used in our robbery likely came from him."

"Merely selling ammunition does not make him an accessory to robbery." She paused. "Does it?"

"No, but it is possible that he sold—or even gave—the thieves the bullets in full knowledge of their intended purpose."

"For a share of the stolen goods?"

"Our robbers were practiced criminals, and Mr. Deal is in a perfect position to profit from their crimes. Whatever they steal in one town, he can sell in the next. He could even be one of the thieves himself."

"He has but one hand."

"Mr. Deal, I am sure you observed, is extraordinarily adept. And a cord-sling can be wielded by a one-handed man. Were it not for the fact that we found two sets of footprints, I would say that he and Miss Jones could have comprised the entire conspiracy."

Elizabeth considered the man she had met only a couple hours earlier, and tried to reconcile the person who had treated a spinster and a simpleton with kindness, with the image of him as a conspirator in a robbery ring. He had seemed so agreeable. But then, experience had taught her that outward appearances could not be trusted. She had known—or thought she knew—other individuals whose amiable veneer had hidden a less-than-honorable heart. A man persuasive enough to sell a sack full of colored beads to Darcy could sell anything—including himself.

"There was at least one other conspirator besides the slinger and Miss Jones," she said, "for we saw him with our own eyes."

"Whom?"

"The raven."

"Its appearance was indeed timely, but I doubt the bird plotted robbery."

"No, but perhaps its trainer did."

Darcy looked at her in surprise. "A trained bird—I had not considered that possibility."

"The raven startles and distracts potential victims, then its master presses the advantage."

"I have to concede, it is a good stratagem. What led you to think of it?"

"I met Mrs. Martin today—the young woman Frank Churchill rescued from the gypsies last spring. When she described the incident, she said that a large black bird had swooped around while the beggars harried her. How many such birds can there be in Highbury, appearing so conveniently?"

"So, our thieves are indeed gypsies, almost certainly the same ones Frank Churchill encountered. Did Mrs. Martin spy Miss Jones or Hiram Deal among the band?"

"She said she saw no English. It sounds, however, as if she was too much terrorized to notice anything beyond her immediate situation. We shall have to ask Mr. Churchill whether he saw Miss Jones or the peddler that day."

"Frank Churchill might not be forthcoming on that point."

"Why not?"

"It is increasingly possible that his appearance on the scene was even less coincidental than that of the bird. Mr. Knightley and I suspect he might have deliberately sought out the gypsies. Mr. Deal says there is an herbalist among them who makes up the physics he sells, and Frank might have gone to her for a specially prepared one."

"Whatever for?"

"To poison his aunt."

She stared at him. "I discerned from Mr. Knightley's earlier manner that he harbored doubt towards Frank in the matter of his uncle's death. But in the aunt's as well?"

"Mr. Perry has determined that Edgar Churchill most likely died of belladonna poisoning. Agnes Churchill died of a suspicious seizure within a month of Frank's allegedly chance meeting with the gypsies." Darcy explained how old Mrs. Churchill's death had enabled Frank's marriage to Jane, and how the uncle's death now secured Frank's independence.

"Good heavens," she said when he finished. "That is quite the cold-blooded scheme, if these suspicions about Frank Churchill prove accurate. I wonder, however, that Mr. Knightley shared them with you, a near-stranger. He impressed me as a more discreet gentleman, particularly regarding a matter yet under investigation."

Darcy cleared his throat. "The investigation is the reason he took me into his confidence. Frank Churchill's status within the village, coupled with Mr. Knightley's admitted bias against him, render it necessary to have a more objective individual probe the affair. Upon Lord Chatfield's recommendation, Mr. Knightley solicited my assistance." He paused. "And upon Chatfield's request, I agreed."

At the mention of the earl, Darcy's willingness to involve himself became more understandable. Elizabeth could not, however, help feeling her spirits sink at the realization that Darcy's participation in a murder enquiry would necessitate an extension of their unplanned stop in Highbury. She wanted to reach Brierwood. And she missed her daughter. "Should we send for Lily-Anne?"

"It is my hope that we will not be here overlong. Mr. Perry has gone to London to consult a colleague more knowledgeable about belladonna, and travels home by way of Richmond to learn more about Agnes Churchill's seizure from her physician. We also await information from the Churchills' solicitor. If all goes well, this matter should be resolved within days. If you wish, however, I can take you to the townhouse and return here. Your continuance in Highbury is not required merely because I am committed."

"Indeed? So you do not want to hear what I know of the gypsy herbalist?"

That commanded his attention. "How came you by information regarding the herbalist?"

"From Mrs. Martin. She said one of the gypsies who accosted her was an older woman—a 'witch-woman,' Mrs. Martin called her—gathering plants. I would wager that she is your healer."

"Did she appear to know Frank Churchill?"

"She appeared startled by his appearance and fled with the rest of them, so whether she knew him or not is a subject for further speculation. I suppose it certainly would have been surprising to be chased off in such a manner by a gentleman to whom one just sold poison, if that was Frank Churchill's true purpose for being there. Do you and Mr. Knightley believe, then, that Frank obtained from this same gypsy the belladonna that killed his uncle?"

"Directly or indirectly. He possibly acquired it through Mr. Deal."

"Surely the peddler would not trade poison so openly?"

"The poison could be passed off as one of the remedies he sells. Or belladonna could be a component of some of the physics, added intentionally or in error. Mr. Perry says that in small amounts it has legitimate medicinal value, and that the berries are sometimes mistaken for edible ones. I suspect, however, that if this gypsy herbalist incorporated deadly nightshade into one of her concoctions, she knew precisely what she was doing."

"If she were accidentally poisoning people, Mr. Knightley would have heard by now of other customers who had suffered ill effects."

"Even so, I purchased Mr. Deal's remaining gypsy remedies, ostensibly for personal use, but I have given them to Mr. Knightley so that the apothecary can have a look at them."

"What do they purport to cure?"

"Gout, dropsy, and—" He coughed. "Female complaints."

She regarded him archly. "What sort of female complaints?"

"I hoped you would know, for I have not the faintest notion."

Elizabeth found it both amusing and charming that, after nearly two years of marriage and the birth of their child, such a subject could discompose him. "So now Mr. Deal believes I suffer from a peculiarly feminine malady. I thank you for that—it should make my next encounter with him all the more delightful. Is there anything else I ought to know about the reputation I am forming in Highbury?"

"No." He paused. "Well . . ."

She raised a brow.

"Should Mr. Churchill enquire, you were all but debilitated by a headache today."

"Indeed? It seems I am on the verge of becoming a professional invalid. Are the gout and dropsy my ailments as well?"

"No, only the headache and the . . . other."

"Thank heavens. I would not want my deteriorating state to burden anybody. Incidentally, I understand that Mrs. Knightley's father suffers ill health, and that the Knightleys reside with him when not hosting lethal routs. As we returned this afternoon, Mrs. Knightley expressed a wish for us all to quit Donwell for Hartfield, as she is needed there. Her sister and family, who have been staying with Mr. Woodhouse, must go home to London tomorrow, and now that all the other guests save Thomas Dixon have departed, there is no reason for us remaining few to continue at Donwell."

"When is the removal to occur?"

"On the morrow, as early as is reasonable. From the sound of it, you and Mr. Knightley intend to spend the day capturing criminals, and therefore will scarcely notice the transition."

"Will you?"

"Not as much as our servants." She opened the armoire, where her maid and his valet had just hung all the clothes from their trunks, which would have to be repacked. "Now, you had better dress for dinner, or we shall be late."

"The Knightleys keep country hours, then?"

"Yes, and I am glad of it, for after the events of last night and to-day, I would like to retire earlier tonight."

Darcy raised a roguish brow. "How early?"

She smiled and moved towards him, holding his gaze all the while. When she reached him, she placed a hand on his chest, which he covered with his own as she stood on tiptoe to whisper in his ear.

"I am afraid tonight is inconvenient, dear. . . . Apparently, I have a headache."

Seventeen

"I do not look upon myself as either prosperous or indulged. I am thwarted in every thing material."

—*Frank Churchill,* Emma

The room Mr. Knightley had made into his study at Hartfield was smaller than that of Donwell, but reflected the character of its new resident nonetheless. Oak-paneled walls, paintings of country scenes, and burgundy draperies tied back with braided gold cords surrounded sturdy yet graceful mahogany furniture. Two Sheraton armchairs encouraged conversation over tobacco or the Madeira wine that stood ready on a side table between the east windows. A third chair—the one which saw the most use—waited behind the inlaid satinwood writing table; a matching glass-fronted library case dominated the north wall and held the magistrate's most oft-referenced books. It was a gentleman's room, suited to the serious purpose that occupied the three gentlemen gathered there.

Mr. Perry called directly after he returned from London. Though his mission had required little more than four-and-twenty hours to complete, it had yielded intelligence of significance. Barely had he taken a seat in the armchair opposite Darcy than he commenced his report. "My colleague confirms my suspicions," he said. "Edgar Churchill almost certainly died of belladonna poisoning."

The news came as no surprise to Darcy. The more he had heard about Frank Churchill's encounter with the gypsies and the fact that the band apparently included an herb-woman, the less he believed Edgar Churchill's death had occurred by natural means.

"What did his physician say?" Mr. Knightley brought a third chair from the writing table so that they might have a more intimate discussion. "Had he been taking any medicines that might have contained belladonna?"

"None at all. Mr. Flint reported that other than experiencing occasional fits of gout, Edgar Churchill was in good health and seldom had need of his services. It was Mrs. Churchill who kept him and the local apothecary employed. She suffered from nervous complaints and took several physics regularly. I spoke with the apothecary. They were standard remedies, nothing unusual about their composition."

"The peddler who has lately been in Highbury sells a cure for gout," Darcy said. "I purchased one for you to examine."

"I will have a look. Did you learn whether Mr. Churchill might have bought one? He did not have anything of that sort on his person when he died."

"We found no such items among his possessions," said Mr. Knightley. "What of Mrs. Churchill's final illness? Were her symptoms similar to Edgar's?"

"No. To all appearances, she died of apoplexy."

"The physician is quite sure?" Darcy asked.

"Mr. Flint was with her at the end, but she was too far gone for his ministrations to have any effect. He is insistent, however, that Mrs. Churchill died of natural causes." He paused. "Mr. Flint is a physician of no small renown. He did not appreciate my questioning his professional judgment."

Darcy had never met Mr. Flint, but he had met his ilk: medical men so full of their own self-importance that their patients were an afterthought. He had probably taken great umbrage to the suggestion that he could have failed to recognize a murder occurring before his eyes, particularly as it had been voiced by a mere apothecary. "Mr. Flint sounds unlikely to reconsider his diagnosis. We should therefore focus our efforts on resolving Edgar Churchill's death, which we know more about. What that investigation brings to light might then illuminate Mrs. Churchill's."

Mr. Knightley agreed. "Perry, what did you learn from Edgar Churchill's solicitor?"

"Mr. MacAllister set down the particulars for your reference." Mr. Perry produced a sealed packet and handed it to Mr. Knightley. "As is generally known in Highbury, when Frank Weston reached his majority three years ago, in exchange for legally adopting the name 'Churchill,' Edgar designated him his heir."

"Is anyone else named in the will?" Darcy asked.

"Edgar inherited Enscombe unentailed, so it was his to leave to whomever he chose," Mr. Perry said as Mr. Knightley broke the seal and scanned the pages. "Upon his marriage, Edgar wrote a will granting Agnes a life interest in the estate should he predecease her, with the property then passing to Edgar's issue upon her death. As they had no children by the time Frank attained his majority, and Mrs. Churchill was past childbearing age, they formally adopted Frank."

"Even so," Mr. Knightley said, still reading, "the codicil adding Frank to the will leaves the estate to him only if Edgar Churchill died without issue." He looked up from the page. "Under these terms, if Edgar had remarried and produced a child, Frank would have been left with nothing."

"Was Edgar Churchill likely to remarry?" Darcy asked.

"Neither Perry nor I knew him well enough to answer that," said Mr. Knightley. "This visit to Highbury was his first. To all appearances, he was still grieving, but that is not to say that remarriage would never have entered his mind. He did, however, seem to truly bear affection for Frank and regard him as a son, so I cannot imagine him deliberately cutting off Frank altogether."

"Might Frank have killed him to prevent the possibility of remarriage ever occurring, thus insuring his inheritance?"

"That would seem an extreme, premature act," Mr. Knightley replied, "given that there was no actual marriage on the horizon."

"Premature to you or me, yes," Darcy said. "But to an impatient young man who spent his life subject to the caprice of a controlling benefactor, ever conscious that should he cross his aunt he could be disinherited? With the estate unentailed, Edgar was free to change his will at any time, and by all accounts Agnes had tremendous influence over her husband. Though Edgar's affection was steadier than Agnes's, and Frank's future therefore more assured after she died, Frank's status as heir to Enscombe could never be entirely secure until the moment of Edgar's death."

Darcy paused, another thought occurring to him. "Too, you have stated that you were not well acquainted with Edgar Churchill, had never seen him outside of this single visit to Highbury. Though re-marriage might not have yet entered *his* mind, it could already occupy the thoughts of some enterprising lady—or her mother—among their larger circle. Many a young woman has wed an old man, willing to in-vest a few years in a short marriage that leaves her a financially inde-pendent widow. Mrs. Churchill has been dead nearly five months, during which time her widower likely received countless expressions of sympathy and solicitude. If Frank suspected a particular lady of scheming to become the second Mrs. Edgar Churchill, now would be the ideal time to act—before an impending marriage made his motive more apparent, and before his uncle had an opportunity to change his will for any other reason."

"Indeed, Edgar Churchill might already have intended to change his will," Mr. Perry said. "Mr. MacAllister told me that on the day of Mr. Churchill's death, he received a letter from Edgar requesting a meeting."

"On what business?"

"Mr. Churchill did not specify."

"He could have wanted to discuss any number of matters," Mr. Knightley said. "We cannot assume that he wished to discuss his will."

"The search of his chamber at Randalls turned up no physics or other evidence of belladonna, but were any papers found?" Darcy asked. "Perhaps he retained a draft of his letter to Mr. MacAllister, or received correspondence from somebody else that might have prompted the need to consult his solicitor."

"If he did, those documents were gone by the time anybody thought to look," Mr. Knightley answered. "With no such proof of his intent, I am afraid there is but one person who might have been privy to Edgar's thoughts: Frank Churchill."

Eighteen

"A piece of paper was found on the table this morning—(dropt, we suppose, by a fairy)—containing a very pretty charade."
—Emma to Mr. Woodhouse, Emma

The reestablishment of the Donwell party at Hartfield much soothed Mr. Woodhouse. He had not been easy while his beloved daughter and Mr. Knightley resided, however temporarily, at Donwell; indeed, his imagination conjured more horrors to be endured in an old abbey than any gothic novelist could invent. Let readers of Mrs. Radcliffe and Mr. Lewis shudder over skeletons and clanking chains; to Mr. Woodhouse, these terrors were nothing to the potential threat of drafts, damp, or food prepared by any cook but Hartfield's own Serle.

So comforted was he to see his younger child safe once more under Hartfield's roof, that relief overrode the anxiety occasioned by the influx of strangers along with her. Mr. Thomas Dixon's tenancy he accepted on the basis of the gentleman's vague connection to Jane Fairfax Churchill, whom Mr. Woodhouse had always esteemed. Too, it helped that although the prodigious number of wardrobe trunks with which Mr. Dixon traveled arrived along with the Darcys' luggage, the man himself would not appear until late in the day, after carrying out his promised errand in Piccadilly.

To the Darcys, Mr. Woodhouse was cordial, if wary. Their unanticipated arrival in Highbury coinciding so closely with Edgar Churchill's permanent departure fixed them in his mind as being somehow associated with it—not in the sense of having contributed to Mr. Churchill's demise, but in their being the sort of individuals who possess a regrettable tendency to attract misfortune. Indeed, so convinced was he of their ill luck that Emma was forced to embroider the truth by suggesting that Mr. Darcy's purpose in coming to Highbury was to assist Mr. Knightley in apprehending the poultry thieves terrorizing the neighborhood. This intelligence raised Mr. Darcy considerably in Mr. Woodhouse's regard, for in his opinion one could not be overaggressive regarding such persons.

It was Mrs. Darcy, however, who in the end most completely earned Mr. Woodhouse's solicitude. In this coup she received unwitting assistance from Frank Churchill, who called to determine whether his uncle's body could yet be released. Upon being told that Mr. Knightley was presently occupied with Mr. Perry and Mr. Darcy, he sat with the ladies and Mr. Woodhouse to pass the time until Mr. Knightley was at liberty to see him. Emma ordered tea, and as they waited for it, Mr. Churchill enquired after Mrs. Darcy's headache.

As Emma had not known her guest suffered any discomfort, she wondered how Frank had heard of it. Mrs. Darcy, however, smiled.

"It is much improved, thank you."

"Have you the headache, Mrs. Darcy?" exclaimed Mr. Woodhouse, his thin face and slight frame becoming animated by the subject. He gripped the arms of his chair as he leaned forward. "Why did you not speak of it sooner? I would have sent for Mr. Perry posthaste."

"It troubled me yesterday; I feel quite better."

Her recuperation did little to placate his apprehension. There was no one more generously the object of Mr. Woodhouse's sympathy than a fellow invalid, and he would not be denied the pleasure of commiseration. His watery eyes lit with interest. "Does it pain you still?"

"Not at all," she assured him as tea was brought in. "Indeed, I am altogether recovered."

Emma poured tea. Serle had also sent up a warm plum cake, which Emma sliced to serve to her guests, and dry toast for Mr. Woodhouse.

"Even so, you ought not indulge overmuch, or it could return," Mr. Woodhouse said. "Plum cake is far too rich for a recovering constitution. Do not jeopardize your hard-won health, Mrs. Darcy. Emma, tell Serle to send up dry toast for her."

Emma, hoping to spare her new friend from this little peculiarity of her father's—of serving food to guests but then insisting they not eat it—handed a serving of cake to Mrs. Darcy. "I think plum cake will not adversely affect Mrs. Darcy's head, Papa."

"One cannot be too cautious. In fact, my dear, we should summon Perry from the study immediately. Surely Mr. Knightley has done with him by now."

After some little debate between father and daughter, the apothecary was allowed to remain undisturbed, but dry toast was brought up for Mrs. Darcy. Elizabeth politely nibbled upon it between surreptitious tastes of cake.

Before long, Thomas Dixon entered. "Fresh from Piccadilly," he announced, "my mission fully executed. I come bearing fabric and wallpaper samples. The upholstery, however, I reconsidered. Though I would never utter this in the presence of Miss Bates, her furnishings are so worn that she needs must replace the pieces altogether. I have selected new furniture—my friend Ridley helped me decide. He has a marvelous eye for such things. The furniture maker awaits only my confirmation to execute the order."

"On whose authority were these items purchased?" Frank Churchill asked.

"Your wife's."

"Indeed?" Frank began to say more, but instead lapsed into silent contemplation.

Emma handed Frank a cup of tea. Apparently, Jane had not broached the subject with her new husband, an oversight Emma hardly found astonishing. Even the faultless Jane Fairfax Churchill must be hard-pressed to introduce a discussion of redecorating her aunt's tired old rooms, into conversations dominated by funeral preparations. Seeking to avert any conjugal disharmony that might result from the omission—and the danger of Frank's subsequently rejecting the entire enterprise—Emma thought it prudent to voice a few words in its favor. The project, after all, advanced not only Miss Bates's domestic happiness, but also his own: if new furniture could help bring about a match for Jane's spinster aunt, the young Churchills would be relieved of responsibility for her care and comfort . . . not to mention spared the possibility of her taking up residence with them. Though Frank could not, of course, be directly told of Emma's matchmaking scheme and its benefit to himself, he must not unknowingly thwart it.

"When viewed in light of the more weighty matters commanding your attention in recent days, changing out draperies is so trivial a subject that doubtless your bride either wished to spare you the trouble of contemplating it, or herself forgot it in the course of other conversations," Emma suggested. "But during previous visits to your new aunt and grandmother, a gentleman of your discernment could not help but observe that they might be made more comfortable by the improvement of a few aesthetic details in their apartment."

Frank rewarded her with a smile reminiscent of their former rapport. "Perhaps a few."

She returned to the tea table and sliced a piece of cake for him. "And having already proved yourself possessed of a generous spirit—who but you would have arranged for a pianoforte to grace their sitting room?—surely you wish to do more for them, now that you have the means. Under other circumstances, you no doubt would have initiated the project yourself. I am certain you wish to assure their continued independence."

"New wallpaper and furniture will preserve their independence?"

"And draperies!" Mr. Dixon added. "Do not forget the draperies!"

"And draperies." Frank turned to Emma. "Freedom can be purchased with brocade?"

"Yes." Emma smiled. Then she crossed to Frank, handed him the cake, and said in a tone so soft only he could hear, "At least, yours can."

His eyes narrowed as he tried to puzzle out her meaning. She resumed her seat beside Mrs. Darcy.

"As you are in mourning," Emma continued, loudly enough for all to hear, "with more serious arrangements occupying your notice, Mr. Dixon has been so kind as to assume the management of this comparatively trifling matter."

"Indeed, I am pleased to be of use," said Mr. Dixon.

"Did you make certain that the draperies are of a heavy fabric?" Mr. Woodhouse asked. "Take care that they are strong enough to withstand drafts." It was difficult to determine whom he eyed with greater fretfulness—Mr. Dixon, who had been entrusted with so critical a selection, or Frank, who had started to eat the plum cake and seemed quite in danger of enjoying it.

He appeared to settle on Mr. Dixon. In truth, Emma mused, in this instance her father's perpetual fear of drafts was not unfounded. In winter months, the Bates's sitting room inspired a new definition of "airiness," and there was a reason the chair nearest the fireplace was permanently reserved for old Mrs. Bates. But then Mr. Woodhouse's gaze happened to stray toward Mrs. Darcy, who had been so reckless as to finish her cake.

"Oh, dear, Mrs. Darcy! Are you still feeling well?"

Emma sought a subject to distract him. "Shall I see what today's post brought? Perhaps there is a letter for you." She hoped the day's mail would include a note from her sister confirming their arrival in London. Whilst Emma had no reason to doubt a successful journey, Isabella's departures always left Mr. Woodhouse nervous until he knew she and her family were as safe in Brunswick Square as anybody could be who breathed London air.

A servant brought in the mail, which included the much-anticipated letter from Isabella. As he read the note aloud to the assembled company—for surely they all, too, waited anxiously upon the news—Emma broke the plain seal of another letter addressed solely to her.

She quickly discovered that it was not a letter at all, but a message of an entirely different sort.

My first rhymes with an object made of hemp
Howe'er, no object this, instead a ray.
My second, used with ciphers on a slate,
Will undo sums, and reduce some, I'd say.

Conjoined, a single word, a single lass
A single appellation for your cause.
You see, not all the scheming in the world
Can undo human nature or its laws.

The verse was unsigned. Frowning, Emma read the lines to herself once more.

"What have you there, Emma? It is not bad news, I hope?"

Reluctantly—for she had not yet puzzled out the solution to the charade, let alone the identity of its author—Emma lifted her gaze from the paper and donned a bright smile for her father.

"No bad news at all, Papa. An entertainment, in fact—a charade. Remember what amusement we had last autumn with Harriet Martin, collecting charades?"

"Ah, yes—poor Miss Smith that was." Mr. Woodhouse grieved change of any kind, but most particularly that which affected his own domestic circle, to which Harriet had been a more frequent visitor before her marriage. Emma wondered how much time would pass before her father could bring himself to call Harriet "Mrs. Martin." Emma's former governess, Mrs. Weston, though enjoying perfect felicity for over a twelvemonth in her own marriage, would forever remain "poor Miss Taylor" in Mr. Woodhouse's heart. And she had yet to hear him refer to herself as "Mrs. Knightley."

"If that charade was meant for Miss Smith's book, it has arrived quite late," her father said.

Emma scanned the lines again. Whatever *had* prompted its authorship and delivery? Save for her conversation with Harriet the day before yesterday, such a diversion had not come before her in months. "I imagine Mrs. Martin herself sent it. We were just recalling her book, and she revealed that she had recently tried her hand at writing a riddle. This must be her latest attempt."

In point of fact, Emma imagined nothing of the sort. The language was more elevated than anything she would expect of Harriet, and the solution, being not obvious, more clever than she would credit her with devising. She had deciphered the first half, but not the second, though she was confident that she wanted only a minute's uninterrupted study to work out the charade entire.

"Oh, how charming!" Mr. Dixon said. "I adore word games—I find them the most diverting challenges. Ridley once presented me with a series of riddles on various themes—plants, birds, monarchs, cravat styles. There was even one on an Oriental theme. Do read it aloud."

She recited the first two lines, sure that at least some of the company would solve them as quickly as she had. Frank had proven himself adept at word games on previous occasions, and at Abbey Mill Farm, Mrs. Darcy had scarcely blinked before stating the solution to Harriet's riddle.

"'My first rhymes with an object made of hemp . . .'" She continued through the reference to ciphers and slates. When she reached the fourth line, however, her tongue stumbled over the words as she suddenly realized their meaning. She finished reading the line aloud, then broke off and skimmed the second stanza in silence. She had unraveled the charade—and was not amused by its solution.

Her father penetrated her thoughts. "That seems terribly short. Is that the full charade, my dear?"

"Yes, Papa," she answered absently, a suspicion forming in her mind of the puzzle's author. Closer attention to the handwriting confirmed it. Spiteful, vain creature! Emma endeavored to mask her vexation as she folded the paper and tucked it away. She glanced at Mrs. Darcy, who alone sat in sufficient proximity to have observed that additional lines filled the paper. Their gazes met; Emma could read in Mrs. Darcy's expression that she had been caught in the falsehood. However, her new friend betrayed nothing to the others and merely regarded her with curiosity.

"We had longer riddles in my day," said Mr. Woodhouse. "There was one in particular that I can never quite remember in full. 'Kitty, a fair but frozen maid'—"

"Yes, Papa. We entered it in Harriet's book, remember?" So oft during their enterprise had Mr. Woodhouse repeated the riddle, or at least the opening stanza of it, that Emma had heard enough of Kitty for a decade. "Garrick wrote that one; this riddle's author must be less clever." Far less clever, Emma declared to herself, if her deduction proved accurate.

"An object made of hemp would be a rope, I suppose," offered Mr. Dixon. "And a ray that rhymes with 'rope' . . ."

"Hope," Frank finished.

"So it is!" said Mr. Woodhouse.

Frank gave her a knowing look. "But surely Mrs. Knightley had already figured that out."

Emma, despite her irritation over the puzzle itself, could not help but admit that she had. "It was not a difficult clue."

"Nevertheless," her father said, "I am amazed at how quickly you struck upon it, my dear. Though I should not be." He turned to Mrs. Darcy. "Emma's mother had the same quickness for these sorts of puzzles. They take me much longer, though I was faster in my youth. I suppose you, also, had guessed 'hope'?"

"I thought perhaps that might be the answer." She smiled. "I am sure you would have realized it, too, in another moment."

"I am not so certain, but nor am I wont to reject the flattery of a lady. Emma, read the remainder again and let us see whether our guests can solve the whole."

Emma would much rather have quit the exercise altogether, but could contrive no graceful means by which to discontinue it. Wishing to keep the charade's incriminating second stanza out of sight, lest anybody in addition to Mrs. Darcy become aware of its existence, she did not reopen the note but instead relied upon her memory. "I believe it was, 'My second used with ciphers on a slate, will undo sums, and reduce some, I'd say.'"

Mr. Dixon pondered the clue with brows drawn together. Frank, in contrast, exhibited the open countenance of one who has either determined the answer or was content to let somebody else discover it. He shot her a conspiratorial glance that seemed to say, "Let us see how long this takes the others," and then set about finishing his cake.

"'Ciphers on a slate . . . '" Mr. Woodhouse muttered. "I never cared for arithmetic as a boy. 'Ten plus fifty,' 'sixty less ten.' I had not the patience for it."

"But you have given us the answer, sir," said Mrs. Darcy.

Mr. Woodhouse was all disbelief. "Have I?"

"The word is 'less'—subtraction undoes sums." Mrs. Darcy smiled. "And if one begins with 'some' quantity and reduces it, there is less."

"Indeed! Imagine that—I struck upon it without my even realizing. Emma, had you worked it out? Oh, of course you had. Well, no matter. So the second half is 'less.' That gives us—" His cheerfulness diminished. "Why, that makes the full solution 'hopeless.' What sort of melancholy riddle is that?"

A mean-spirited one, writ by a person of small mind and smaller intellect, Emma wanted to say. But instead she fixed a bright smile upon her countenance. "No one ever said a charade must be cheerful, Papa."

"But who would compose such a sad verse?"

All save Emma looked at Frank, who of anyone in Highbury had the greatest cause for doleful thoughts. Having just raised his teacup to his lips, he drained it and returned it to its saucer.

"I have not the least idea," he said.

"Nor I," Emma said quickly, wanting more than anything to move the discourse along to some other subject. Fortunately, a servant entered to remove the tea things and deliver the message that Mr. Knightley now awaited Mr. Churchill in the study.

It was not without some little trepidation on Frank's behalf that she watched him go. She knew Mr. Knightley harbored suspicion toward Frank Churchill, and doubted that the length of time her husband had been shut up with Mr. Perry and Mr. Darcy since the apothecary's return from London presaged an amiable meeting for Frank.

His departure produced the welcome effect of breaking up the rest of their party. Mr. Dixon excused himself with the stated intention of writing a letter, and Mr. Woodhouse retired to his own chamber for a nap before dinner. Emma soon found herself alone with Mrs. Darcy, who looked as if she wanted to enquire about the charade but hesitated to ask.

Emma spared her further awkwardness and handed her the paper. "Go ahead—open it." She desired Mrs. Darcy's opinion on it anyway. Though confident of the solution, she sought confirmation.

Mrs. Darcy scanned the remaining stanza. "A hopeless lass, a hopeless cause . . ." She raised her gaze to meet Emma's.

"Can that refer to anyone save Miss Bates?" Emma asked.

"Not knowing your entire acquaintance, I cannot say for certain, but from what I have observed, I suppose this could apply to Miss Bates."

"I am sure of it, and its author."

"Mrs. Elton?"

"Who else but she would be spiteful enough to write such a message, ill-bred enough to send it, and cowardly enough to do so anonymously?"

"Despite having met her only briefly, I have little doubt of Mrs. Elton's spite, breeding, or nerve. I do, however, wonder that she possesses the cleverness."

"She never would have thought to compose a charade were we not just discussing them with Harriet. But after that conversation, and my later circumventing her machinations with Mr. Simon, she no doubt resolved to prove herself superior. In the writing itself, she might have had help from her husband. He wrote a charade for Harriet's book that was not half bad." The solution to that riddle, written when Mr. Elton was a bachelor, had been "courtship," and Emma had realized too late that it had been an attempt to woo her. The clergyman yet harbored resentment toward Emma for having rejected him. "His pride and disdain toward me matches his wife's, and creating a puzzle meant to mock me would gratify his vanity. Whether he knows that she sent it is another matter."

"Do you intend to respond?"

"Not directly. However certain I may be that this came from Mrs. Elton, I cannot prove my suspicions, nor will I give her the satisfaction of knowing how it vexes me. But that petty, disagreeable little upstart will eventually receive a response."

"In what form?"

"The most satisfying of all. In sending this, she has thrown down a challenge. A challenge I shall win."

Nineteen

"Do you think you perfectly understand the degree of acquaintance between the gentleman and lady we have been speaking of?"
—Mr. Knightley to Emma Woodhouse, Emma

*D*arcy rose from his seat and moved to an unobtrusive position near one of the study windows, hoping to diminish the effect of his presence on the imminent interview. Were he in Frank Churchill's position, he would be reluctant to discuss family matters in the company of a stranger. Not all gentlemen, however, conducted themselves as guardedly as did Darcy, and his previous, albeit limited, intercourse with Mr. Churchill engendered hope that the young man would prove to be among those less circumspect than himself.

Upon entering, Mr. Churchill returned Mr. Knightley's greeting in a genial manner, and extended the same to Mr. Perry and Darcy.

"So this is where the gentlemen are hiding." Mr. Churchill took the chair Darcy had vacated and settled against its back. "I almost feel as if we should invite Mr. Dixon to join us—I abandoned the poor fellow trammeled in talk of draperies and charades. He did seem rather loquacious himself on the subjects, though, so perhaps he is happier left with the ladies."

"Better he than I," Mr. Knightley said.

Frank grinned. "The conversation was most enlightening, actually.

I learned that my bride already conspires to spend my money on new furnishings. Perhaps you had rather be in the drawing room after all, to ensure yours does not do the same."

"Mrs. Churchill decided to reappoint Enscombe without first seeing the extant furnishings for herself?"

"Oh, no—it is not our home she refurbishes. Her generosity is on behalf of her aunt and grandmother, which of course puts it entirely out of my power to object to the scheme. So she and Thomas Dixon will have their way about it."

"Mr. Dixon?" Mr. Knightley asked. "What has he to do with the matter?"

Frank shrugged. "As I said, he is quite keen on the enterprise, to the point of having designated himself the executor of it. And as you said, better he than I."

His buoyancy diminished as he turned toward Mr. Perry. "I came on a more serious errand. Have you done with my uncle's remains? You must understand my desire to proceed with funeral arrangements."

"Indeed, I have," the apothecary said. "The undertaker may collect the body at his first opportunity."

"Thank you. I shall so advise him."

"I hope," Mr. Knightley said, "that, having died so suddenly, Mr. Churchill can rest easy and not be troubled by unfinished business. No gentleman wants to depart this earth without his affairs in order."

"My uncle had no concerns on that count. He was ever attentive to matters of business."

"Even in the months following your aunt's death? Sometimes men lose interest in such details while mourning."

"Fortunately, my uncle did not have many pressing issues these several months past; those few that arose were handled quite capably by Mr. MacAllister."

"Was he in frequent communication with his solicitor?"

"As often as was necessary."

"I understand he recently requested a meeting with Mr. MacAllister, but died before it could take place. Have you any idea what he wished to discuss?"

"I have no knowledge of any such request, let alone what might have inspired it." Frank's mood darkened. "I might ask, Mr. Knightley, how *you* came to learn of it."

"It was I who told Mr. Knightley," Mr. Perry said. "Mr. MacAllister mentioned it when I officially notified him of his client's death."

"I expect my uncle simply wanted to take advantage of the opportunity to confer with his solicitor a final time in person before retiring to Enscombe for the winter." Frank leaned back once more, but one hand yet firmly held the chair arm. "I told you, he was a man who kept his affairs in order." Though the words were delivered smoothly, his tone held a defensive edge.

Darcy, who had to this point refrained from inserting himself into the conversation, now stepped closer to the window and gazed at the darkening landscape. "I imagine he looked forward to returning to the quiet of Yorkshire. Were I grieving, I would find more solace in the peace of Pemberley than in the bustle of London." He turned toward Frank. "Though I suppose he had many friends in both places to console him."

"He had not been keeping much company since my aunt's death, only his most intimate circle. He did, however, happily anticipate the companionship of his longtime neighbors at Enscombe."

"Old friends are a blessing at such times. I have seen widowers so fear loneliness that they rush into poorly considered second marriages to avoid the silence."

"I would never speak ill of the dead, but I will venture to say that after decades spent with my aunt, my uncle was not altogether averse to experiencing silence for a while."

Darcy studied Frank Churchill as closely as he dared, trying to make him out. Had the nephew, for self-serving purposes, ultimately fulfilled the uncle's wish?

There was, after all, no silence like a grave.

Dinner at Hartfield this evening would be limited to Emma and Mr. Knightley, her father, and the Darcys. Thomas Dixon had received an invitation to dine with the Eltons.

Emma was vexed.

Her displeasure derived not from dissatisfaction with the Darcys' society, but from her own having been snubbed. Mrs. Elton's hospitality toward Thomas Dixon had been extended as part of an impromptu dinner party, ostensibly a "small, quiet affair" held to console the newlywed Churchills in their time of unexpected sorrow. The guest list comprised the Randalls set—Frank and Jane, the Dixons, the Westons—as well as several of Highbury's better families. The Knightleys were conspicuously excluded.

Any number of excuses had indirectly found their way to Emma's ears: the Eltons' table could accommodate only so many; a larger party would appear unseemly in light of the Churchills' state of mourning; the Eltons did not want to intrude on the Knightleys' time with the Darcys. None of these justifications, however, diminished Emma's conviction of their—most particularly, herself—having been deliberately and publically slighted.

Mr. Knightley found her vexation bemusing. "I should think you would feel relief at having been spared the ordeal of an evening spent at the Eltons' mercy," he said as he led her down to Hartfield's dining room. "Or did Mrs. Elton injure your vanity by depriving you of the opportunity to decline her invitation?"

Under other conditions, her husband's suggestion might have struck too close to the mark, but tonight more than her vanity was in jeopardy. Since receiving the spiteful charade, Emma feared that Mrs. Elton had somehow divined Emma's ambitions of a match between Thomas Dixon and Miss Bates, and that the vicar's wife had contrived tonight's dinner party entirely to sabotage the scheme. It had not escaped Emma's notice that the Bates ladies were also uninvited. She loathed to contemplate what mischief that vulgar little woman attempted even now, with the unsuspecting Thomas Dixon under her roof, and Emma unable to intervene.

"Nonsense," she said, avoiding his gaze. "The Eltons' guest list holds no interest for me."

The Eltons' dinner party, however, held great interest for Mr. Woodhouse, who could not seem to stop talking about it throughout their own meal. Every lull in conversation, he filled with speculation over whether poor Miss Fairfax or poor Miss Taylor that were, presently suffered the same menu of roast pork that had been inflicted upon him the one time he had supped at Mrs. Elton's table. His apprehensions continued after their own party finished their dinner and withdrew to the drawing room. Though of the opinion that merely dining at the vicarage was disagreeable to one's digestion, Emma forbore voicing it. Instead, she reminded her father that Mrs. Weston—capable, sensible Mrs. Weston—was among the company, and would doubtless act to preserve her new daughter's well-being if necessary.

"Mr. Thomas Dixon, too," Mrs. Darcy ventured. "He seems a most attentive friend to Mrs. Churchill."

"Yes, Papa—Mr. Dixon is quite solicitous regarding Mrs. Churchill. He . . ."

Her words trailed off as a jumble of unpleasant thoughts entered her mind. Thomas Dixon was clearly on familiar terms with Jane Churchill, an intimacy that a twelvemonth ago might have inspired speculation on Emma's part. After all, before Emma ever met the Dixons, she *had* formed suspicions of an improper attachment between Jane and the younger Mr. Dixon, now Miss Campbell's husband. Had she indeed stumbled upon something—but presumed the wrong Mr. Dixon?

Emma blushed to recall her previous error, now compounded by the inclusion of Thomas Dixon in her wild conjecture. The gentleman was old enough to be Jane's uncle.

Just as Mr. Knightley was old enough to be hers.

No! Surely there had never been anything but platonic regard between Jane Fairfax and Thomas Dixon. And if there had been something more, it had ended with Jane's marriage. Emma would not demean her own intellect with such ignoble speculation again.

"He what, my dear?" Her father's voice drew her back to the conversation. "You were speaking of Mr. Dixon."

"He is a good man," she declared. "No one ought ever think otherwise."

Mrs. Darcy looked at her oddly. "Of course he is. I did not mean to suggest—"

"Heavens, Papa—look at the hour! I have been neglectful. It is well past your customary time to retire."

"So it is. But I have not yet had my basin of gruel. Mrs. Darcy, perhaps you will join me? Nothing is so wholesome as gruel for keeping the headache away, and no one prepares it better than Serle—very thin. Emma, order up a basin for Mrs. Darcy."

Emma rescued her guest with the gentle suggestion that, the evening spent, perhaps her father would prefer to take his gruel in his chamber.

"You are perfectly right, Emma. I shall do just that. It is not healthy to sit up until all hours. Promise me you will retire soon yourself. You, as well, Mrs. Darcy—nothing brings on the headache more quickly than staying up too late."

As Mr. Knightley helped Emma escort her father upstairs, Mr. Woodhouse opined anew upon the evils of roast pork and the goodness of gruel, interspersing his culinary lecture with convictions of Hartfield's being the best possible place for Mrs. Darcy to recover her health. If, somewhere between the staircase and his chamber, he finally found another subject of discourse, Emma could not have said. She but half attended, her concentration given over to a subject of greater import.

Arranging Thomas Dixon's future happiness with Miss Bates.

Left with her husband while their hosts saw Mr. Woodhouse settled, Elizabeth pondered how her words about Mr. Dixon could have been construed by Mrs. Knightley as anything but complimentary. She had said nothing derogatory, only praised his attentiveness to Jane Churchill.

"You are pensive this evening."

Elizabeth glanced at Darcy, who sat in a nearby chair, and realized he had been studying her. She shook off her abstraction. "I was thinking about another man."

"That is exceedingly unfortunate. I had hoped to avoid calling anybody out during this trip."

"You might forbear yet. Though the gentleman in question has proven himself most solicitous, he has provided no cause demanding a contest of honor on my account."

"Then Mr. Woodhouse must be the object of your reverie, for nobody has been more solicitous towards you than he. Confess—you regret having declined his offer of gruel."

"Indeed, I was wishing I had encouraged him to order a basin for you."

"Then allow me to lift that burden from your conscience. I do not feel deprived, I assure you."

"Are you quite certain? At Mr. Woodhouse's order, his indispensible Serle could prepare it extra thin for you."

An appalled look was his only reply.

Elizabeth laughed. Gruel was fine nourishment for infants and invalids, but elsewise her enthusiasm for it ran closer to Darcy's than to Mr. Woodhouse's.

A set of children's alphabets on the table beside her caught her gaze. She had first noticed it this afternoon; Emma had explained that the Knightleys' nephews and nieces often played with the box of letters while staying at Hartfield, and it had not yet been put away following their recent visit. She now removed a handful of tiles from the box. *D, M, N, R.* The letters had been drawn by a fine hand. She placed them one by one on the table.

"Actually, it was Thomas Dixon who preoccupied me." She wished she could arrange her thoughts as easily as one could sort alphabet tiles into words. But they, too, defied order: there was not a vowel among the random few she had chosen.

"Mr. Dixon has been particularly attentive towards you?"

She did not need to look at her husband to know he frowned. She could hear the displeasure in his voice. "No, towards Jane Churchill."

"Towards Mrs. Frank Churchill?"

Now she did look up. Darcy appeared to be pondering something. "Inappropriately attentive?" he asked.

"No." She withdrew another tile from the box. "Well . . ." Elizabeth considered anew the conversations she had witnessed, the degree of accord between the married Mrs. Churchill and the bachelor Mr. Dixon: the pat on Jane's hand in Miss Bates's apartment; the freedom with which Thomas Dixon spent Jane's money—Frank's money, in point of fact, and he only having just come into it himself.

"It is difficult for me to say, based on such limited acquaintance with either of them," she finally stated, "but I do think he is on unusually familiar terms with her."

"How does she conduct herself with him?"

"Jane Churchill possesses a reserved nature. Her manner towards everybody, including Thomas Dixon, is restrained. She does not, however, appear averse to the liberties he takes." She looked at the tile in her hand. *X*. That would be of no help.

Darcy was silent a moment. "Earlier today, Frank mentioned that his wife was already spending his inheritance, and that Thomas Dixon was helping her do it. Apparently, they have purchased new furnishings for her aunt and grandmother's apartment?"

Elizabeth nodded. "Mr. Dixon insisted that the Bates ladies need to completely refurbish their rooms. In truth, they do, but even the most casual visitor can see that the pair lacks the means to institute even minor changes. So Jane Churchill authorized the expenditure. The news came as quite a surprise to Frank, especially since he heard it not from his wife, but from Thomas Dixon."

Darcy's frown deepened. "Mr. Knightley and I learned today that Frank Churchill is his uncle's sole heir." He recounted their meeting with Mr. Perry, including his colleague's confirmation of the poisoning diagnosis, and the solicitor's revelation that Edgar Churchill had requested a meeting before he died.

"All of this intelligence increased my suspicions about Frank's role in the deaths of both Edgar and Agnes Churchill," Darcy finished. "Frank, however, declares himself ignorant of his uncle's desire for a meeting, and of other questionable circumstances surrounding their demises. Your information about Jane Churchill and Mr. Dixon leads me to wonder whether we have not considered broadly enough who else benefits from the two deaths."

"I hardly think fresh draperies and wallpaper constitute sufficient motive for a double murder. At a minimum, new plate and silver ought to be included in the bargain." She set the *X* upon the table and took up two more letters. Vowels at last: *O* and *I*. "Besides, neither Thomas Dixon nor Jane Churchill ultimately benefits from the purchases."

"Do you yet discuss Mr. Dixon?" Mrs. Knightley and her husband reentered the drawing room. "Surely there must be more interesting subjects of discourse than his shopping on behalf of the Bates ladies."

"What interests me is who financed it," Darcy replied.

"Frank Churchill can well afford it now," Mrs. Knightley said, "and I consider it an admirable gift to his bride, seeing to the comfort of her only family."

"What of the Campbells?" Elizabeth set the two vowels upon the table with the consonants she had already spread out, but took no more letters from the box. "Are they not also her family, in a manner of speaking?"

"They might have raised her, but they are not blood relations. One cannot feel the same depth of affection as that between parent and child—or in the case of Mrs. Bates and Jane Churchill, between grandmother and grandchild." Mrs. Knightley moved towards an empty chair, but paused as she passed the table with the alphabets. Disapproval clouded her features, and she scooped up the strewn tiles. "Has this silly children's amusement not been put away yet?" She deposited the letters into the box and shut the lid. "I shall have to speak to the housemaid."

The conversation turned to other subjects. By now, Elizabeth and Darcy had established a rapport with the Knightleys which, while still new, had achieved a degree of relative ease, and Elizabeth found it refreshing to talk about something besides robbery and suspected murder. Darcy seemed to particularly enjoy Mr. Knightley's society. Just as tea was brought in, Thomas Dixon appeared.

"You return earlier than I anticipated," Mrs. Knightley said. "How was Mrs. Elton's party?"

"It began unexceptionally enough, until Frank Churchill's disagreeable behavior put a damper on the evening."

Mrs. Knightley poured tea and handed a cup to Mr. Dixon. "Indeed? Frank Churchill is usually so charming."

"Not this evening. He could barely hold still while we waited to go in to dinner, and was hard-pressed to follow the conversation." He sipped his tea, then gestured towards Mrs. Knightley with the cup.

"Thank you. I had no tea at Mrs. Elton's following dinner. The situation with Frank Churchill was so awkward that everybody found excuses to disperse before any was served."

Concern overtook Mrs. Knightley's features. "Do you think he was upset about something?"

"From the flush of his countenance, I think he was foxed. His father thought so too, I wager, for as dinner was concluding, Mr. Weston asked Mr. Churchill to leave the dining room with him on some pretext. When Frank Churchill stood up, he swayed and complained of dizziness. I pity Mr. Weston—he must rue the day he turned his son over to the Churchills." He heaved a great sigh. "I hope for Jane Churchill's sake that her husband learned something from his uncle's death. I would hate to see him come to the same end. At least Frank Churchill held his liquor, which is more than Edgar Churchill proved able to do."

Foreboding took hold of Elizabeth. There were similarities indeed between the accounts of Frank's and Edgar's recent dinner party behavior. But Edgar Churchill had not been drunk.

She looked toward Darcy and Mr. Knightley to see whether they shared her thoughts. The magistrate was already standing.

"Where is Frank Churchill now?"

Twenty

*"I am persuaded that you can be as insincere as your neighbours,
when it is necessary."*
　　　　　　　　　—*Emma Woodhouse to Frank Churchill,* Emma

*F*rank Churchill's status as the favorite of fortune endured: unlike his uncle, he survived belladonna poisoning.

He owed to his stepmother his continuance as an inhabitant of this world. Mrs. Weston, though as embarrassed as her husband by Frank's behavior, possessed that intuition peculiar to mothers that prompts them to seek medical counsel under circumstances in which others underrate the severity of signs. Such was the case on this occasion, and upon their hasty departure from the vicarage, she had insisted not merely that Mr. Perry be consulted, but consulted before they returned to Randalls.

By luck or by grace, they had found the apothecary at home. Mr. Perry had immediately recognized Frank Churchill's danger and administered a mustard emetic, followed by a purgative to eliminate as much of the poison as possible from his system. Since Frank's symptoms were fewer and less pronounced than Edgar's had been, Mr. Perry was of the opinion that he had taken in a smaller amount of belladonna than had his uncle. The treatment was successful; Mr. Perry predicted a full recovery.

How Frank came to ingest the toxin was a subject that occupied the Knightleys and Darcys long after the victim himself had improved. After hearing the apothecary's report, Mr. Knightley and Mr. Darcy spent the following afternoon interviewing those who had been present at the Eltons' dinner. The Westons and Jane, Mr. Perry had spoken to the night before while treating Frank; the Patrick Dixons he questioned when he transferred his patient to Randalls after breakfast. In the interest of expediency, Mr. Knightley and Mr. Darcy divided the remaining calls and agreed to meet Mr. Perry later at Randalls, where the apothecary monitored his patient. Together they would quiz Frank Churchill more thoroughly than Mr. Perry had been able to while his patient suffered agitation and confusion.

The interviews yielded nothing valuable. No one had observed anything irregular regarding Frank Churchill during dinner, save symptoms they had ascribed to intoxication. The Eltons' discourse on the subject was all self-interest; Frank's brush with death was nothing to the insult they believed themselves to have suffered by his behavior. To protect their ability to investigate effectively, Mr. Darcy and Mr. Knightley did not contradict anyone's assumption that drink had been the sole cause of Frank's indisposition.

"I pray we learn something useful from Frank Churchill himself," Mr. Knightley said as he and Emma walked to Randalls with the Darcys. Emma wanted to check on Frank Churchill as much as the gentlemen wanted to interrogate him, and Mrs. Darcy had said she would welcome the exercise. Emma feared that Mrs. Darcy also sought respite from her father's concern for her health. Though Mrs. Darcy appeared to find Mr. Woodhouse's crotchets more amusing than vexing, she had already submitted to one basin of gruel that day and ought not be subjected to another, however kindly intended.

"With our chief suspect now a victim, we need to learn something soon," Mr. Darcy replied, "before the poisoner eliminates all of the Churchills."

"I am glad the pair of you have finally realized that the idea of Frank Churchill's having killed his uncle is ludicrous," Emma said, "though I am sorry it required his own life becoming endangered. Do you believe Jane Churchill is also at risk?"

The path through the shrubbery became uneven, and Mr. Knightley offered Emma his arm. "That depends upon the murderer's motive," he said. "If he is driven by revenge, the perceived wrong might or might not encompass her, as she but very recently joined the family. If the killer seeks more worldly gain, however, I expect she may indeed be threatened. We need to learn who stands to benefit from Frank Churchill's death."

"Beginning with Jane Churchill," Mr. Darcy said.

Emma gasped. "You cannot be serious! Jane Fairfax Churchill, a murderess? If you knew her as we do, you would realize how absurd a notion that is. Mr. Knightley, assure Mr. Darcy that Jane Churchill cannot possibly have committed such sordid acts."

Mr. Knightley, however, had halted his strides and regarded Mr. Darcy in startlement. "Jane Churchill. I had not considered her."

"Oh, come, now!" Emma exclaimed. "Mr. Knightley!"

But Mr. Knightley was all rapid deduction, new hypotheses developing in his mind. "I agree that Jane Churchill's involvement is highly improbable. Yet it is not impossible. Consider, Emma, that six months ago she was a portionless orphan on the verge of hiring herself out as a governess to support herself—a fate so abhorrent to her that she likened it to the slave trade. Now she is mistress of a large estate, and last night almost became a wealthy widow. Do I think her guilty? No. I have admired her character too long—even defending it to you—to believe her capable of premeditated murder. As her friend, I am convinced of her innocence. But as the parish magistrate, I cannot eliminate her entirely from the list of suspects, however far down on it she might appear. Not at present, with so few other candidates and motives."

"But she has no cause to kill Frank Churchill. His aunt and uncle, perhaps—as far-fetched as that seems—but not her husband. As Frank's wife, she already has the Churchill fortune at her disposal. And she loves him."

"Does she?" Mrs. Darcy asked. "You would know better than we.

The couple is barely one week wed, yet I have seen her only in the company of Thomas Dixon—never with her husband."

"The Churchills are very much in love," Emma insisted. The observation about Mr. Dixon, she did not address. Jane Churchill's friendship with Thomas Dixon forwarded Emma's own plan for the gentleman, by advancing his intimacy with Miss Bates. She shook her head emphatically. "Depend upon it," she said to them all, "Jane Churchill is not the person you seek."

Mrs. Weston rejoiced at the arrival of her friend and, after allowing Mrs. Knightley ample time to ascertain for herself the state of Frank's health, invited Emma to accompany her to another room to see a muffler she was knitting for Mr. Woodhouse. She included Elizabeth in the invitation, but Elizabeth, noting the lines in Mrs. Weston's countenance that evidenced the anxiety of a long night just past, supposed the muffler merely a pretext for a much-needed tête-à-tête between old friends. She declined to intrude, and instead remained with Darcy, Mr. Knightley, Mr. Perry, and the Churchills.

Frank Churchill's own account of the evening offered little more information than had the others. It differed, however, in his insistence that he had not come to the vicarage drunk; in fact, he had not consumed any wine or liquor all day. When Darcy suggested that perhaps something he had eaten disagreed with him, he repeated what he had told Mr. Perry: at dinner, he had eaten only what everyone else had. And nobody else had become ill.

"What about before dinner—before you went to the Eltons'?" Mr. Knightley asked. "What did you consume earlier in the day?"

"I breakfasted at Randalls. In the afternoon, I had cake at Hartfield while waiting to speak with you. And tea. A cup—no, two cups of tea."

Elizabeth did not recall anyone's having enjoyed a second cup of tea before the arrival of Mrs. Elton's antagonistic charade, probably because such an indulgence would have sent Mr. Woodhouse into paroxysms. Mrs. Knightley must have somehow poured it for him when nobody else was looking.

"Are you certain, Frank?" Jane Churchill, sitting beside him, covered his hand with hers. Apparently, at least fondness existed between them. "When you went into the village, you did not stop at the Crown?" She turned to Darcy and Mr. Knightley. "After calling on you at Hartfield, he met us at the vicarage rather than return to Randalls."

Frank Churchill withdrew his hand from hers. "I was not drunk at dinner. Will my own wife not believe me?"

Jane stiffened. The fleeting moment of affection was gone, replaced by what Elizabeth sensed was not the newlywed couple's first experience of discord.

"Of course I believe you. It is only that Thomas Dixon mentioned that he saw you near the inn—"

"Did he? And is that Irishman my keeper now? Or does he merely consider himself the keeper of my accounts? He certainly feels at liberty to spend them."

"That is unfair, Frank. Thomas Dixon has been nothing but kind, and is only trying to help—"

"Help himself to my fortune, since he does not have one of his own."

Her face reddened. She swallowed whatever she had been about to say next, and instead drew a deep breath. With a pointed glance in Darcy and Mr. Knightley's direction, she said in a calmer tone, "You are still not yourself after last night."

Frank said nothing.

"Mr. Perry," she continued, "you held Mr. Churchill's remains for some time before releasing them for burial. Did the same illness that killed him cause Frank's infirmity last night?"

Mr. Perry paused before replying. Elizabeth knew that he, Mr. Knightley, and Darcy had debated how much to reveal to Frank and Jane Churchill about the belladonna. Frank was still a suspect in Edgar's death; full disclosure would compromise the investigation irreparably. But last night's incident demonstrated that Frank was himself in danger, and any man so exposed deserved to be warned. Too, Mr. Perry would soon hold the formal inquest for Edgar, and once it took place, all Highbury would know that at least one Churchill had been poisoned.

"I believe it did. But it was not an ordinary illness. It was poison."

So much color drained from Jane's face that she looked as if she herself had been poisoned. "Good heavens! Someone tried to kill Frank? And—oh!—someone *did* kill his uncle? Poor Mr. Churchill!"

Her shock and dismay seemed genuine. Yet Elizabeth could not help but reflect that if Jane Churchill were indeed involved in the poisonings, she had had plenty of time to rehearse her reaction.

Frank Churchill appeared dumbfounded. "I was poisoned?" He stared at Mr. Perry as if he could not possibly have heard him correctly. "What kind of poison?"

"Belladonna. It is sometimes mistaken for other plants, so it is possible that you and your uncle ingested it accidentally. Since you were both guests here when the poisonings occurred, I will speak with the cook and have a look about the kitchen to make sure it has not inadvertently entered the house. But given that deadly nightshade is not common in this neighborhood and that no one else has experienced symptoms, until we ascertain the source we should for caution's sake act under the assumption that the poisonings were deliberate."

Jane Churchill released a soft cry that was half sob, half whimper. "Why would anybody want to kill Frank? Or his uncle?"

"That is what we are trying to determine." Mr. Knightley gestured towards Darcy. "My friend Mr. Darcy, who has experience in such matters, has consented to assist us. I trust you will extend to him the same cooperation you would show me and Mr. Perry."

"Of course." If Mrs. Churchill thought it unusual that an outsider was being entrusted with an important role in the investigation, she did not show it—her countenance was full of too many other emotions.

Darcy, who had quietly observed the Churchills' reactions while Mr. Perry and Mr. Knightley guided the conversation, now took command of it. He leaned forward, his manner direct but not confrontational. "Mr. Churchill, do you have any enemies? Did your uncle? Anybody who might wish you or your family harm?"

Frank shrugged. "None that I can think of."

"Servants or former associates who might hold a grudge? An

acquaintance who came out on the losing end of a wager placed at cards?"

Without even a pause to search his memory more thoroughly, Frank shook his head.

"I understand that your late aunt was not the most amiable person. Might she have earned someone's animosity?"

"She had a strong will, a difficult temperament, and unrestrained pride. She therefore had few real friends. But I can think of no one who would consider himself so injured by her that he would avenge himself months later by killing her husband and nephew."

"What about individuals who might benefit financially from your uncle's death and yours? Do you have any business partners?"

"Until last week I had no fortune with which to do business."

Elizabeth could see Darcy's frustration mounting. Though Frank Churchill answered the queries willingly—or at least, gave the appearance of doing so—his replies provided no leads to follow. Why was he not more forthcoming, with his own safety at stake?

Darcy released an exasperated breath. "Mr. Churchill, it is very likely that someone murdered your uncle, and has attempted to murder you. Are you telling me that you have not the faintest idea why, or who that individual might be?"

"Believe me, sir, I wish I did."

Darcy sat back and studied Frank, who shifted self-consciously under Darcy's silent brooding. Then Darcy looked at Elizabeth, glanced at Jane Churchill, and met Elizabeth's gaze once more. Without his having said a word, she understood.

Perhaps Frank Churchill knew quite well why someone might want to kill him. And perhaps it involved something, or someone, he would rather his new wife not know about.

"Mrs. Churchill," Elizabeth said, "I have need of Mrs. Knightley—she is somewhere in the house with Mrs. Weston. Might I impose upon you to help me locate them?"

Though comfortable and well appointed, Randalls was not a very large house. Elizabeth estimated that she had five minutes—ten if she were very lucky—in which to both invent a reason for seeking Mrs. Knightley *and* elicit as much information as she could from Jane Churchill before their discovery of the other two ladies' whereabouts put an end to this spontaneous interview.

"Mr. Darcy and I found ourselves ensnared in a murder plot within a fortnight of our wedding," Elizabeth said as soon as they had quit the drawing room and entered the hall. It was not an elegant or subtle opening, but it had the desired effect: Jane Churchill regarded her in amazement—and lost some of the defensiveness from her posture. "So I sympathize with your current circumstances," she continued. "This might not be the most auspicious manner in which to begin a marriage, but we are proof that one can endure it."

Jane turned her head away, focusing her gaze on the central staircase that dominated the entry hall through which they passed. "Was the murderer caught?"

"Yes, by Mr. Darcy—and me. We were relieved when the matter was finally resolved, and we could at last retreat to Mr. Darcy's home in Derbyshire. Just as I imagine you are anxious to reach Enscombe."

"Indeed, yes. I wish we were there now." Jane led her past the staircase and down a corridor. Paintings lined the walls—a few landscapes, including one depicting Randalls, and portraits of the Westons and Frank.

"Will your friends, the Dixons, travel there with you?"

"No, they return to Ireland on Friday next."

"So soon? Mr. Thomas Dixon will no doubt be disappointed to leave Highbury before the transformation of your aunt's apartment is complete."

At the mention of Thomas Dixon, Jane stiffened. "Perhaps he can visit some other time."

"He seems a kind gentleman—generous with his time and attention. One wonders why he has never wed."

Mrs. Churchill directed her gaze towards the portrait of Frank as they passed it. "He was a younger son, and remains dependent upon his relations."

"But surely a man as handsome and affable as he could charm an heiress," Elizabeth said. "Is that not how most men in his situation secure their independence?"

Her companion stopped short. "Perhaps he has not the inclination."

They had arrived at an open doorway that led into a bright parlor. Female voices carried from within. "I believe we have found Mrs. Knightley," said Mrs. Churchill.

"So we have," Elizabeth replied.

Both of their smiles were forced.

"So, what did you ask Frank Churchill about, once his wife and I left the room?"

Darcy reached for his cravat. They had returned late from Randalls and had little time to dress for dinner, a process hindered by the fact that he had dismissed his valet so that he and Elizabeth could talk freely. "Can you not guess?"

"Disappointed debutantes? Rejected lovers? Discarded mistresses?" Elizabeth adjusted the short sleeves of her gown to give the white sprigged silk more puff, then left the glass to Darcy.

"All of the above. He claims to have none. Also no natural children."

"Any previous wives or legitimate children?"

"Not this time."

She sat down on the chaise longue to don her slippers. The set of rooms they had been given at Hartfield—a bedchamber and dressing room—was smaller than what they had enjoyed at Donwell, but more comfortably appointed. Elizabeth preferred the relatively slender furniture to some of the older, heavier pieces that had dominated their chamber at the abbey.

"Not even a scandalous ancestor lurking in the family tree? What about the uncle?"

"To hear Frank tell it, both he and Edgar are the dullest victims we have ever investigated." He lifted his chin to tie the neckcloth.

"We can only hope that the poisoner has a more interesting past, though I presently favor Jane Churchill, whom everybody else seems to consider beyond reproach. It is always the quiet ones, you know."

Darcy looked at her askance. "In our experience, it has never been the quiet ones."

She contemplated that for a moment. "I suppose you are right. Oh, well—then it is time for a quiet one. And poison is a quiet weapon."

"That does not mean Jane Churchill is the one who used it. I confess myself very nearly persuaded by the Knightleys regarding her. They know her character better than we do."

"I thought you were asked to aid this investigation precisely because you do not harbor preconceptions about the principals' characters."

"So I was. Regardless, Mrs. Knightley makes a good point about Jane's not needing to kill Frank. As the new Mrs. Churchill, she already has everything she wants."

"You assume that she wants to remain married to her husband."

Darcy muttered something indistinguishable under his breath. He had pulled one end of the neckcloth too far and had to begin the entire process anew.

"Why would she not?" he said. "Frank Churchill seems a decent, amiable fellow, her own age, with a comfortable home and generous income. Were I choosing a husband for my sister, I would prefer a more serious gentleman, but many young ladies marry worse."

She rose and went to the dressing table, where Lucy had laid out her long kid gloves. She slid them on until they reached past her elbows. For once, she had completed her preparations before Darcy.

"Perhaps Jane Churchill is in love with somebody else."

"Thomas Dixon?" Both Darcy's tone and expression reflected his disdain for the gentleman. Mr. Dixon was too frivolous to ever earn Darcy's esteem.

"They seem to be on unusually familiar terms, and you witnessed how the mere mention of his name provoked Frank Churchill. When

I tried to coax her into speaking about Mr. Dixon while we were alone, she hedged."

"Why would any woman of sense—which Jane Churchill appears to be—choose Thomas Dixon over Frank Churchill? He may be charming, but he has not a guinea to call his own."

"If she were a wealthy widow, he would not need a shilling." At his dubious look, she continued. "Imagine, Darcy: They meet at Weymouth—a watering hole devoted to pleasure. Patrick Dixon is courting Miss Campbell, Jane's dearest friend and near-sister. She and Thomas Dixon, constantly in company together, fall in love but cannot marry because neither has the means. Then along comes Frank Churchill with an offer of marriage and the promise of a fortune. All Jane need do is marry Frank, ensure his aunt and uncle predecease him, then wear widow's weeds for a twelvemonth."

"And murder her husband. You omitted that part." He adjusted the cravat a final time and reached for his coat.

Elizabeth helped him into it, smoothing the black wool across his shoulders. "Well, yes—that, too. I never said it was an admirable plan. But murder plots seldom are."

"This one is so coldly calculating that I can scarcely believe I just heard you utter it. And if Jane Churchill likened service as a governess to slavery, consider what profession your hypothesis suggests."

They left their room to go down to dinner. In the corridor they met Thomas Dixon—resplendent in an embroidered satin waistcoat, frilled shirt, and cutaway maroon frock coat with a high velvet collar and brass buttons. Whatever secrets his heart might conceal, the gentleman certainly knew how to dress.

"I understand you are just returned from Randalls," Mr. Dixon said. "How is Frank Churchill today?"

"Much improved," Elizabeth replied.

"I am glad to hear it. What a fright for poor Jane! I hope he learned from this experience. If not"—his eyes twinkled—"we shall have to bring him to Ireland and teach him how to drink." He seemed to be in a more pleasant mood than he had been the night before; Elizabeth wondered how he had spent his day.

"Frank claims he was not intoxicated," Darcy said, "—in fact, that he did not have a drink all day. But I understand that he was seen near the Crown shortly before the Eltons' party."

"Was he?" Mr. Dixon began to remove his left glove, gently tugging on each finger. "I wonder what he was doing there."

"He claims he was on his way to the vicarage."

"I am sure that is all there is to it, then."

"The reports we have heard of his conduct at the Eltons' sound similar to what we heard of his uncle's final night," Darcy continued. "Did you not take a walk with Edgar Churchill earlier on the day of the Donwell party?"

"Yes." He removed the other glove and held the pair in one hand as he tucked two fingers into his fob pocket.

"Did he already seem to be feeling poorly when you were together?"

Mr. Dixon fumbled with his fob chain, trying to retrieve his watch from its pocket. "He appeared fine."

"Perhaps the exercise strained him. Did you walk far?"

He at last succeeded in withdrawing the watch. "We went nowhere in particular." He sprung open the lid. "So late already! I must go dress for dinner." He snapped the lid shut and hurried off.

Elizabeth followed him with her gaze until he was well out of hearing. "I thought he *was* dressed for dinner."

"For all your speculation about Thomas Dixon's relationship with Jane Churchill, I think the most significant connexion in his life is his tailor." Darcy took her arm and led her towards the staircase.

"All the more reason to plot marriage to a wealthy widow—he could afford a fleet of tailors. He is definitely hiding something."

"His quizzing glass?"

"Jane said it was Thomas Dixon who saw Frank near the Crown before the party. And it was Thomas Dixon who took a walk with Edgar Churchill shortly before the Knightleys' party—information also revealed by Jane. Thomas Dixon was the last person to see either poisoning victim in good health, before any symptoms appeared. And he seems quite reluctant to talk about it."

"You take this as evidence that he conspires with Jane Churchill? If she were indeed plotting to kill her husband so that she could become Mrs. Thomas Dixon, why would she volunteer any information that betrays his involvement?"

"I do not yet relinquish the possibility of collusion between them," Elizabeth said, "but there is an alternative theory we have not yet considered. Perhaps Jane does not know about the plot. Perhaps it is all Mr. Dixon's."

Twenty-one

"Mr. Frank Churchill writes one of the best gentlemen's hands I ever saw."

"I do not admire it," said Mr. Knightley. "It is too small—wants strength. It is like a woman's writing."

—Emma Woodhouse and Mr. Knightley, *Emma*

The second riddle arrived as had the first: in the post, anonymously.

This one was not a charade, however, but a much shorter puzzle. And it came addressed not solely to Emma, but to both the Knightleys.

It was Mr. Knightley, alone in the study, who opened it as he sorted through the letters that had arrived while he and the others spent the day interviewing the Eltons and their dinner guests. His first response, upon breaking the seal and seeing that the note contained but a single sentence, was annoyance that he had paid good coin to receive such a short message—particularly one postmarked in Highbury.

His next response, upon reading the enigmatic line, was to immediately seek his wife to ask whether she had any better notion than he why the mysterious missive had appeared.

He found her in the drawing room with her father, Thomas Dixon, and the Darcys, who had gathered there in anticipation of dinner and waited only on him to go into the dining room. His thoughts full of the Churchill matter, he had not realized the hour. He apologized to the company for having kept them from their meal, and drew Emma aside as the others started into the dining room.

"We received a rather unusual message with today's post."

Emma took the paper from him. With a glance at her father, who talked to Mr. Dixon as he made his slow way to the table, she unfolded the note.

PERHAPS AN UNKIND INDIVIDUAL WITNESSED THE GATHERING OF BRAGGARTS OF AN ELEVATED RELIGIOUS HOUSE.

It was penned, unlike the last riddle, in block letters to disguise the hand. Emma, however, needed no additional evidence of its authorship. She rolled her eyes ceilingward. "It is only Mrs. Elton again."

"Mrs. Elton?"

"She sent me the most spiteful charade yesterday. Apparently, she has not done venting her spleen."

"What did it say?"

"Nothing significant." Emma knew her husband's opinions on the subject of matchmaking, and did not care to hear them again at present. He might just side with Mrs. Elton. "Come look at this, Mrs. Darcy." She hoped that a third party in the conversation would quell any lectures on matrimonial manipulation that her husband might feel inspired to deliver. "We have received another attempt at cleverness from the vicarage."

Mrs. Darcy came to her, curiosity writ on her countenance. Mr. Darcy crossed the room with her. She frowned as she scanned the note, which Mr. Darcy also read. "That is rather an odd message," she said. "I cannot grasp quite how it relates to the content of the first. Are you certain it is from Mrs. Elton?"

"Who but the Eltons would consider Highbury's vicarage 'an elevated religious house'? Their self-consequence never fails to astonish me." At Mrs. Darcy's expression of confusion, Emma continued. "This refers to their dinner party. Mrs. Elton must take one final opportunity to remind me that I was not invited."

"I do not believe that is her meaning at all, if this note is indeed from her," said Mr. Knightley. "She is unlikely to call her own guests 'braggarts.' "

"Yes, it is a term better applied to the hosts." Emma read the message again: *braggarts of an elevated religious house*. She drew a sharp breath as she realized its meaning. "That woman is altogether insufferable! Gathering of braggarts, indeed! Well, she need not ever concern herself about associating with such company again."

Her three companions all regarded her in puzzlement.

Emma turned to her husband. "Do you not see? Donwell Abbey is the religious house. She refers to *our* dinner party. More specifically, to you and me—she says 'braggarts *of*'—not *at*—an elevated religious house. Donwell is *our* home—nobody is 'of' Donwell but we."

"The reference could be to Donwell parish, which is home to half the guests who attended."

"Why do you defend her?"

"I do not—I am simply trying to comprehend the message. You have not yet convinced me that it is from Mrs. Elton. What has she to gain by sending such a note?"

"The satisfaction of vexing me."

"Then do not give her that satisfaction," Mr. Knightley said. "Let us consider this more objectively. The message arrived addressed to both of us, on the day following an attempt on Frank Churchill's life. The first note, you say, arrived yesterday?"

"Yes."

"So, two days after Edgar died. And it was addressed solely to you?"

Emma nodded.

"What did it say?"

"It was a charade. The solution was 'hopeless.' "

"Unfortunately, that could just as easily refer to our investigation. What made you believe the note was from Mrs. Elton?"

"The penmanship appeared to be hers. And she and I are . . . having a bit of a disagreement."

Mr. Knightley regarded her suspiciously. "On what matter?"

She hesitated. "Mrs. Elton is quite put out by my recent attention to Miss Bates."

"I see. So put out that she was inspired to write verse on the subject?"

To avoid his gaze—and her increasing self-doubt—Emma once more studied the sentence. This time she took particular note of the penmanship. Though she did not have yesterday's charade at hand for comparison, it appeared to her that these block letters were larger, scribed in bolder strokes than Mrs. Elton's feminine script. "Perhaps someone else did write it," she conceded.

"The letter bears a local postmark, and Highbury is a small village," Mr. Darcy said. "Would not the postmaster recall who brought it to the post office?"

Emma laughed. "We can ask him, but I doubt he will be able to enlighten us. Mr. Fletcher is a man of rather advanced years, as deaf as Mrs. Bates and even more prone to nodding off in his chair. People leave letters on the counter all the time rather than disturb his naps. Jane Fairfax managed to conduct a secret correspondence with Frank Churchill all last winter and spring without anybody in the village being the wiser."

"I am afraid my wife is correct in her description of the postmaster," Mr. Knightley said. "I will visit him tomorrow, but we are more likely to determine this note's author through our own deduction."

"Might the author be the 'unkind individual'?" Emma offered.

"Unkind persons generally do not recognize that failing in themselves," Mrs. Darcy said. "If this was written by someone in attendance at either party, it most likely refers to one of the other guests."

"The writer went to this much trouble to advise us that someone unkind was among the company? One need look no further than Mrs. Elton to know that."

"Your dislike of the vicar's wife is blinding you, Emma," said Mr. Knightley. "I believe Mrs. Elton is neither the composer of this message, nor the person the author wishes to bring to our attention."

"You spoke with every guest following both parties," Emma said, "and most of them are people you have known for years. Of all the individuals present, who is more unkind than Mrs. Elton?"

"The person bent on killing the Churchills."

Emma was silent. Despite the mounting evidence that Edgar

Churchill's death was no accident, and Frank's indisposition no coincidence, she did not want to believe that a murderer roamed Highbury. She cast about for some better explanation, one that would not involve such appalling suspicions about so many persons of her acquaintance.

"I think our anonymous correspondent wants us to know that the unkind individual was one of the guests," Mr. Knightley said more gently. "The poisoner was at the party."

Twenty-two

Mr. Elton had retreated . . . looking (Emma trusted) very foolish.
She did not think he was quite so hardened as his wife, though
growing very like her.

—Emma

*T*he following day saw an excursion to the vicarage, contender
for the title Elevated Religious House.

Elizabeth found it neither elevated nor particularly religious. It
sat in a low spot at the end of Vicarage Lane, rising only by virtue of
its being the only two-story domicile on the road, and the one in best
repair. It must be approached by passing several lesser dwellings
exhibiting various degrees of deterioration and equally assorted
shabbily clothed children spilling out of them in search of more entertaining occupation than could be had by assisting their mothers
within. At present, these fair innocents found diversion in watching
three crows compete for the choicest parts of an unfortunate creature
that looked to have once been a squirrel.

Elizabeth and Mrs. Knightley left the children—and the crows—
to their amusement and continued towards the vicarage. They were
on a scavenging errand of their own.

Mrs. Knightley was determined to prove Mrs. Elton the author of
the two enigmatic messages, her motive malice, and their meaning

mundane. Elizabeth hoped to induce the vicar's wife to betray more knowledge of the poisonings than Darcy and Mr. Knightley had been able to draw out of her, and that perhaps she herself did not realize she possessed.

"Let us hope she is at home." Mrs. Knightley lifted the knocker, a heavy, ornate piece of ironwork more suited to a mansion than a clergyman's abode. "I would just as soon not have to return."

Seen up close, the vicarage boasted more age than beauty; its architecture was uninspired, and it sat so near to the road that the windowed front parlor might have staged theatricals for passers-by. Within, for all of Mrs. Elton's obvious effort, the house lacked the charm of even Harriet Martin's smaller cottage. While the sitting room of Abbey Mill Farm was crowded with objects meant to welcome and comfort, the vicarage parlor, where the housekeeper left them to await Mrs. Elton, was crowded by objects meant to impress. In their abundance, the impression they made was one of overweening pride, that most deadly sin of all.

Mrs. Elton greeted their arrival with no small amount of surprise. Elizabeth gathered that Mrs. Knightley was not a frequent visitor.

"Mrs. Knightley. Mrs. Darcy. I was just departing to call at Randalls."

"Then we shall not keep you long," Mrs. Knightley said.

"I want to assure Jane that I do not hold her to account for her husband's recent comportment, howsoever it might have embarrassed me," Mrs. Elton continued. "I understand now that Frank Churchill was feeling indisposed. Poor man! And yet he *would* come to my little gathering, with no concern for his own discomfort, so as not to incommode me after all the trouble I took to arrange the evening. Not that I would have minded, of course. What would have been the inconvenience to me, when one is suffering a loss such as his? A trifle. I shall insist that he and Jane think no more upon it."

"I rather imagine they will not," Mrs. Knightley replied.

"I am sure they appreciate all you have done on their behalf," Elizabeth added. "Indeed, I wish I enjoyed such attention from our own vicar's wife back in Derbyshire. She is a fine woman, but you,

Mrs. Elton, have proven yourself so very attentive in the short time I have known you, that I confess myself envious of those who have the good fortune to live in this parish."

Mrs. Elton curled her lips into a self-satisfied smile and straightened her posture. "I only do my duty."

"But you perform it so charitably."

"Mr. E. said that very thing to me this morning! 'My dear Augusta,' he said, 'you are charity itself.' As the vicar's wife, you know, I must set a proper example for those who look up to me." At this, she tilted her chin so high that anybody who did happen to look up at the vicar's wife would experience a view of her nostrils that was not altogether desirable. "I do not suppose, Mrs. Darcy, that you are acquainted with my brother-in-law, Mr. Suckling, of Maple Grove?"

"I have not the pleasure."

"But you *have* been to Bath?"

"Indeed, yes."

"Then you understand the standards for which I strive when entertaining. Although our village is small, those of us with connexions and resources can bring touches of elegance to the neighborhood."

Mrs. Elton had provided the very opening Elizabeth sought. "I am sure your recent soiree was an affair no one will soon forget," she said. "You must have spent hours simply drawing up the menu. Did your housekeeper prepare the entire dinner herself?"

"Heavens, no. For a party that size, Wright brought in two girls to help her."

"Of course. Does she do that often—bring in additional help?"

"Mr. E. and I receive so many invitations that we dine out more often than not. But when we entertain, we do so in the proper style."

"Well-trained servants must be difficult to find in such a small village. Were they local girls?"

"I assume so. I am too busy to attend to those sorts of matters. Wright hired them, and she knows what she is about."

But did Wright know what the girls had been about on that night? If they had not themselves slipped Frank Churchill the poison, perhaps they had observed something that could lead Darcy and Mr. Knightley to the person who had.

"Mrs. Knightley, does Hartfield ever want additional help?" Elizabeth asked. "Perhaps you might ask the housekeeper—with your approval, of course, Mrs. Elton—for these girls' names and characters in case you ever have need."

The expression of Mrs. Knightley's eyes, visible only to Elizabeth from the angles at which the three of them were seated, said that she would rather go to work as a kitchen maid herself than solicit references from Mrs. Elton or anybody in her employ. Mrs. Knightley, however, kept her features in check as she turned to Mrs. Elton. "I would welcome any such recommendations you are willing to extend."

The housekeeper was summoned, the names given, and Mrs. Elton's vanity satisfied. To have been placed in the position of offering domestic guidance to Mrs. Knightley was a coup beyond any she could have anticipated at the start of the call. She radiated triumph as Mrs. Knightley conveyed her gratitude.

"I must thank you also for the word puzzles you recently sent to me," Mrs. Knightley added.

Mrs. Elton carefully held her expression, but the exultant light in her eyes dimmed. "Puzzles?"

"Yes—the charade that arrived the day we returned to Hartfield. And the enigma last night."

Mrs. Elton rearranged her skirts, smoothing a nonexistent wrinkle from them. "I am afraid I have not the slightest idea what you refer to."

"Indeed?" Mrs. Knightley affected perplexity. "We had just been talking of such entertainments at Abbey Mill Farm, you recall. So when these puzzles arrived, the lines were so clever I thought they certainly must have been penned by you."

A fleeting look of gratification flickered across Mrs. Elton's countenance. "I—well—perhaps I *might* have been inspired to exercise my intellectual resources. But—"

They were interrupted by the entrance of Mr. Elton, who seemed as surprised to discover Mrs. Knightley in his home as his wife had been. "Forgive my intrusion," he said. "I did not realize you had visitors, Augusta."

"We were just come to thank Mrs. Elton for the puzzles she sent to Hartfield," Mrs. Knightley said. "We found them most diverting, particularly the charade."

"But I never said I—"

"You sent our charade to Hartfield?" Mr. Elton turned his head towards Mrs. Knightley, but his incredulous gaze remained on his wife. "It was an innocent little ditty—meaningless—composed as a private amusement." At last, he looked at Mrs. Knightley. "I entreat you to destroy it and forget it ever found its way into your hands."

Though Mrs. Knightley affected indifference, Elizabeth knew she must feel vindicated. "Shall I destroy the second puzzle as well?"

"Second puzzle?" He turned back to his wife. "You wrote another?" Though restrained, his tone held an icy edge.

"No! Indeed, my *caro sposo,* I certainly did not! You know I do not profess to be a wit. I do not know what she is talking about."

Both Mr. Elton and Mrs. Knightley appeared in doubt as to the truth of this statement. Elizabeth, too, was inclined to skepticism. But there was in Mrs. Elton's tone and manner a note of desperation, a need to be believed by her husband, that rang more genuine than the falsetto performance she had given to Elizabeth and Mrs. Knightley earlier. In any event, it was clear that Mr. Elton, at least, had been entirely ignorant of the second puzzle until Mrs. Knightley mentioned it.

The overstuffed parlor contracted with tension, but Mr. Elton was too conscious of himself and his audience to say more to his wife. "The other puzzle must have come from Mrs. Martin, then," he said to Mrs. Knightley. "She is the only person besides ourselves who was there discussing charades."

"Yes!" Mrs. Elton exclaimed. "The enigma *must* have been written by Harriet. It is she, after all, who finds such diversion in these silly little word games."

The visit soon concluded, and yielded no more. Mrs. Knightley came away still convinced that Mrs. Elton had authored both messages. "She did not even ask what the second one said," she offered as evidence to Elizabeth. "Who, after sending the first puzzle, would not express even the slightest curiosity about the one that followed? Someone who already knew its content."

Elizabeth remained less certain, though she considered Mrs. Elton a far likelier author than Harriet Martin. She was more satisfied with the results of her own enquiry, and intended to seek directly the two village girls whose names Mrs. Wright had supplied.

The ladies walked down Vicarage Lane again, passing the same children still occupied by the same diversion. The crows, though nearly done with their feast, yet vied for the remaining morsels. Apparently, one had seized upon a particularly coveted tidbit, provoking the jealousy of its fellow diners. They cawed their outrage, flapping their wings and snapping their beaks in an attempt to steal the delicacy. The offender flew off into a nearby tree, where it continued to loudly boast its triumph—in the process, dropping its prize.

"Apparently, this part of the village attracts all manner of braggarts," Elizabeth said. "Though I cannot say who is more obnoxious— the Eltons, or the crows."

"Are they not one and the same? Mrs. Elton crows at every opportunity."

"You truly dislike her."

"I have no patience for her conceit and presumption. She believes herself superior, but in truth she is no better—in fact, altogether more vulgar—than many of those whom she purports to eclipse. She is like the bird that flew into the tree just now, so busy proclaiming her superiority that she fails to realize how ridiculous she appears when she proves herself merely one of the flock."

They followed the lane to Broadway. Mrs. Wright had said one of the girls lived just past the Crown, and it was to her house that they headed. However, as they passed the inn, a different girl caught Elizabeth's attention.

The last person in England who she expected to see casually strolling the streets of Highbury.

Miss Jones.

Twenty-three

"A very pretty trick you have been playing me, upon my word!"
—Emma Woodhouse, *Emma*

*E*lizabeth was all astonishment.

So was Miss Jones.

Elizabeth recovered herself first. She took a step toward the Crown Inn, whence the girl had just emerged. The movement, however, penetrated Miss Jones's own shock, and she instantly fled down the lane.

"Stop, thief!"

Elizabeth's cry drew the attention of several passers-by, including Hiram Deal, whose cart Miss Jones was running past. He intercepted her flight and turned her around to face Elizabeth.

"I believe the lady wishes to speak with you," he said.

Miss Jones cast him a scathing look. By the time she turned back to her accuser, however, she wore an entirely different expression.

"Oh! Ma'am! I recognize you now. Mrs. Darcy, is it not? The very person I hoped to meet."

"Indeed?" Elizabeth was amazed by her brazenness. "Whatever for?"

"Why, to beg your forgiveness, of course! For the incident the other evening—I cannot think upon it without regret."

"Nor can I." Elizabeth cast a sidelong glance at Mrs. Knightley. "This is the young woman Mr. Darcy and I encountered on the London road." She nodded towards Miss Jones's foot. "Apparently, your ankle has healed."

"Oh, Mrs. Darcy! If you would but listen—" She wrenched against Mr. Deal's grasp. He released her, but remained near. "I did not want to deceive you! Truly, I did not! They forced me to."

"Who?"

"The gypsies!"

This declaration raised echoes in the gathered onlookers.

"Gypsies!"

"The gypsies have returned?"

"Someone send word to Mr. Knightley!"

A sturdy young boy dashed off toward Hartfield to report the news, unaware that the magistrate had been in possession of this intelligence for days. Meanwhile, the crowd's exclamations drew still more villagers. Among the new arrivals was Mr. Elton, who must have left the vicarage almost the moment Elizabeth and Mrs. Knightley had. He strode toward them with an air of self-importance.

Elizabeth had little desire to cause a scene. But she also would not allow Miss Jones to disappear a second time. "I saw no gypsies the other night," she said to her. "Only you, imposing most shamefully on my husband and me."

Mr. Elton reached them. "What is transpiring here?"

Though Elizabeth addressed the clergyman, she kept her gaze fixed on Miss Jones. "This woman stopped our carriage and robbed Mr. Darcy and me on the London road four nights ago."

"That is not true!" Miss Jones turned to Mr. Elton with wide, tearful eyes. "Indeed, sir, she misunderstands. I would never do such a thing—not willingly!"

"I do not see how this young woman could act as you describe. Stop a carriage and overcome the driver and Mr. Darcy? That is improbable for any female, let alone one of such petite stature."

"She had accomplices. They stole our belongings while she diverted our attention."

"I did not!"

"Perhaps you have mistaken her for someone else?" Mr. Elton suggested. "What is your name, miss?"

"Loretta. Loretta . . ." The woman hesitated, staring at Elizabeth. "Jones," she said finally. "Loretta Jones."

"I would know 'Miss Jones' anywhere," Elizabeth said. "Her voice is unmistakable." The caterwaul yet resonated in her memory. "And she is wearing the same dress."

With little else over it. The girl had acquired a lightweight shawl since Elizabeth had last seen her, but it held more colors than warmth, and on this blustery November day she must be freezing. She still wore no hat; her flight had caused several locks of hair to come loose from its ribbon. Miss Jones rubbed her arms and shivered, eliciting sympathetic looks from more than one observer. A man offered her the use of his coat, which she accepted with abundant expressions of gratitude for his kindness to a "poor, lost stranger."

She lavished similar praise on Mr. Elton. How providential that a man of God should happen along just at her moment of need, while she was trying to explain to Mrs. Darcy the most unfortunate incidents that had led her to this state.

"How did you come to be lost?" Mr. Elton's manner was not that of a clergyman ministering to a member of his flock, but rather that of a man whose sense had been banished by the flutter of eyelashes. Mrs. Knightley released a sound of disgust perceptible only to Elizabeth.

"I was kidnapped by the gypsies," Miss Jones announced.

Gasps and small cries rippled through the assembly. Even the women regarded Miss Jones with sympathy.

"I was out walking one day—on my way to . . . church . . . with caps and mittens I had made to give to some poor families in our village. I try so hard to be mindful of others less fortunate than myself, you see. Well, a band of gypsies appeared from nowhere. I thought they wanted to steal the woollens, and I said welcome to them, but they seized me, too. I tried to run away but they said I must cooperate or they would go to my house and steal my sister instead—she only six years old! Of course I could not put her in such danger. So I consented, and they have been dragging me across England with them ever since."

"Where are these gypsies now?" Elizabeth asked.

"We were camped nearby, and they decided to move on. When they broke camp, I made my escape. I do not know where they have gone, and I do not care. I am only grateful to finally be free of them."

"Are you no longer anxious for the safety of your sister?"

"She lives in Northumberland, far enough away that I hope they will not return for her."

And far enough away—the farthest north one could travel and still remain on English soil—that verifying Miss Jones's story would prove difficult and time-consuming.

"That is a long journey," Elizabeth said. "When did they abduct you?"

"Months ago. In spring."

"You were bringing mittens to the poor in spring?"

"It is cold in Northumberland." She jerked her chin toward Hiram Deal. "You, peddler—have you traveled there?"

Mr. Deal regarded Miss Jones steadily. "Aye," he said. "The cold there can last well into spring."

"If you have been missing since spring, your parents must be sick with worry," said Mr. Elton.

Miss Jones turned to the clergyman with a piteous expression. "I am an orphan—my parents died just before the gypsies stole me. I am alone in the world."

"Not entirely alone," said Mr. Elton.

"You are too kind, sir."

Mr. Elton regarded her with a look of perplexity. "Your sister—"

"Oh, yes—my sister." Her eyes scanned the crowd until her gaze fell upon a girl of five or six, to whom she offered a wobbly smile. "The child I spoke of is in fact the daughter of a family who took me in when my parents died. She is like a sister to me, but not a blood relation."

The mother of the little girl Miss Jones had singled out was a plump middle-aged woman dressed in half-mourning. Her hands were work-roughened and strong, her face weathered but gentle. She stepped forward and put an arm around Miss Jones's shoulders. "Poor lonely creature! Hardly a friend in the world."

Miss Jones sagged against the woman. "Indeed, I have come to feel so." She wiped her eyes.

Elizabeth had seen no tears. Otherwise, it was a performance worthy of the Theatre Royal.

"What about the cousins you mentioned the other night?" Elizabeth asked. "The ones named Jones who live on a nearby farm?"

Miss Jones dropped her gaze. "I have no cousins. I—I invented them so that you would believe I had others to depend upon." She looked up—not at Elizabeth, but at Mr. Elton and Mrs. Todd. "I did not want to impose upon such a fine lady and gentleman, or create in them a sense of obligation to help me."

"Well, you have friends now," the woman declared. "And you can count Mrs. Todd and her daughter Alice among them."

"Thank you, Mrs. Todd." Miss Jones—Loretta—whatever her name might be—knelt and threw her arms around the child. "Alice reminds me of my sweet foster-sister." She looked up at Mrs. Todd. "And you, of my own dear mother."

Alice, bewildered by the sudden affection from a stranger, submitted to the embrace but soon wiggled out of it to cling to her mother's side. Loretta straightened and gazed at the assembly. "With such friends as I have found here already, I feel safe for the first time since being torn from my home. At last, I am free of my captors."

Mr. Elton stood a little straighter and puffed his chest. "We will see them brought to justice."

"Oh! Do not pursue them, I beg you! I do not want them to know where I am. They might steal me again—or worse."

"But surely you wish them to be arrested for what they have done?"

"I would rather they go unpunished than myself live in fear of retribution for bringing them to the law."

"Their continued freedom threatens the safety of others," Elizabeth said. "They might steal another young lady. You must at least report their presence in the area to the authorities."

"Why, I—I was about to do just that. I was at the Crown to enquire whom I ought to inform and where he might be found. But when I went inside, the smell of food—since fleeing, I have been in hiding, and have not eaten in days—the scent of cooking weakened me, so I came out before I fainted away."

If Mrs. Todd's sympathies had not been fully engaged before, they were now. "Poor creature! Come with me to my house, and I will cook you a proper meal."

"That will take too long—the girl is famished." Mr. Elton gestured toward the inn. "Let us get her something to eat without delay."

"Oh, but I haven't any money—"

"Do not concern yourself about that for now."

The minister led Miss Jones back to the Crown. Mrs. Todd, hovering maternally, followed with her daughter, as did a few others. Hiram Deal looked as if he might join the party, but then glanced at his unattended cart and started towards it instead.

"Thank you for stopping Miss Jones," Elizabeth called to him.

He turned and shrugged. "I cannot disregard a lady in distress."

Elizabeth had thought the peddler a better judge of human character than to have fallen for Loretta's story. Her disappointment must have shown in her face.

"I referred to you," he clarified.

She nodded towards the inn. Loretta and her entourage had disappeared inside. "What do you think of her?"

"Miss Jones?" He stared at the inn for a moment, as if he could see its occupants through the building's façade. Finally, he shook his head and looked at Elizabeth. "I confess, I do not know what to make of her. I am glad, however, that she has left the gypsies, and I hope she finds her way home." Mr. Deal returned to his cart.

Elizabeth turned to Mrs. Knightley. "I do not believe one word of that woman's account."

"Mr. Knightley will draw the truth from her, when he comes."

"In the meantime, I do not want to let the girl out of my sight. She has already proved herself skilled at disappearing."

They went into the Crown. It was a large inn, with assembly rooms as well as sleeping accommodations and a common dining area. Spots of dirt on the wallpaper and scratches in the heavy old wooden tables of the common area suggested that the room had long been in service and saw considerable use, and Elizabeth imagined it became quite busy when mail coaches and post-chaises stopped in the village. It was not a bad inn, but she was nevertheless glad the Knightleys had offered their hospitality and spared her and Darcy from lodging in such a bustling environment.

Only half full, the common room was not bustling at the moment. It did, however, hold an atmosphere of anticipation. Miss Jones held court among her new passel of admirers at one of the two long tables that dominated the room's center. Smaller tables dotted the perimeter, their occupants also taking interest in the proceedings. Though the vicar did his best to exert an authoritative presence, this was clearly Loretta's show.

Elizabeth and Mrs. Knightley quietly took seats on the bench at the table's far end. Miss Jones noted their arrival but was too much occupied in regaling her audience with tales of her captivity among the gypsies to acknowledge the two ladies with more than a glance—a glance which, to Elizabeth's perception, seemed rather smug.

The serving girl brought out a steaming bowl and a hunk of bread, which she placed before Miss Jones, along with a pint of stout. As Loretta started on the stew, the server glanced pointedly round the table and asked what she could bring the rest of them. Elizabeth wanted nothing, but feeling compelled to order, requested tea.

Miss Jones's tales slowed as she ate. Whatever lies she might be weaving—and Elizabeth was sure they numbered many—her hunger was real. She had already emptied her bowl when Elizabeth's tea arrived.

"What do you intend to do now that you are free of the gypsies?" Mr. Elton asked.

"I—I don't know. I do not even know where I shall sleep tonight."

"Poor lamb! You must stay with me!" said Mrs. Todd.

"I could not trouble you."

"Oh, it's no trouble at all! I've taken in boarders since Mr. Todd died, and I've a room that has been vacant since old Mrs. Fisher passed on at Michaelmas. We would love for you to stay with us—wouldn't we, Alice?"

"But I have no means to pay rent."

"We can discuss the rent later. Where else have you to go, child? We are a quiet pair, now that my two older boys have joined the militia. Come keep a poor widow and her daughter company."

"I shall, then—but only until I earn enough money to return to Northumberland."

"Have you skills to earn a living?" Mr. Elton asked.

Miss Jones certainly had the ability to support herself, Elizabeth mused, though it was a matter of debate whether "earn" was the proper term for how the girl went about it. Her dramatic talents, which so recently won her the Darcys' possessions, had just procured her free bed and board.

"I learned many things from the gypsies—from weaving to singing. In fact"—a gleam lit her eyes—"I even learned how to tell fortunes."

"Truly?" Mrs. Todd exclaimed.

"Indeed, yes—shall I tell yours?"

Mrs. Todd looked as if she very much wanted to have her fortune told. But she shook her head. "Dear me, no—I don't hold with such nonsense. Telling fortunes! Mr. Todd would roll in his grave to hear it."

"Oh, it is not nonsense! The old gypsy woman I learned from was a talented seer—it was astonishing the things she could tell about a person. Do allow me. You have been so kind—it is the least I can do."

"I . . . I suppose. Go on, then. But I can't say as I'll believe anything I hear. What do I need to do?"

"Simply give me your hand."

Mrs. Todd extended her arm. Loretta took the woman's hand in hers and lightly stroked the palm. "You will remember all your years what I tell you this day."

Mrs. Todd laughed self-consciously. "That, I shall!"

Loretta studied the lines of Mrs. Todd's palm, tracing. "I see a long life for you. There is much happiness. Sadness too, but in smaller amounts. You lost your husband recently?"

"My goodness, yes! Not quite a year ago."

"Your grief has begun to heal. Oh! What is this? A stranger will cross your path."

"Well, that must be you."

"No, I think the stranger will be a man—a new husband, perhaps."

"Ha! Indeed? Mr. Todd surely must be spinning in his grave now."

Loretta next read Alice's palm, declaring that the child was bright, and artistic, and would live to see the next century. She then turned to Mr. Elton.

"Reverend, do you care to have your palm read?"

Mr. Elton looked startled by the suggestion—and, fleetingly, not entirely opposed to it. But then he shrouded his countenance in inflated dignity. "I do not think it would be seemly for a minister to engage in such an activity."

"Even as a harmless diversion?"

"I am afraid not."

Loretta's gaze continued round the table until it landed on Elizabeth. "Mrs. Darcy?"

Elizabeth suspected that if she extended even an empty hand toward Loretta, the beguiler would somehow manage to take something from her. "I thank you for my share of the favor, but no."

Loretta nodded toward Elizabeth's cup. "Allow me to read your tea leaves, then?"

The girl was a charlatan, likely hard-pressed to read a primer, let alone portents. But, curious about what sort of flummery she would concoct, Elizabeth consented to the leaf-reading.

"Have you finished your tea?" Loretta asked.

"Not quite."

"Drink all but the tiniest amount. And if you want a particular question answered, concentrate upon it while you drink."

Though Elizabeth had one very simple question—whether she would ever see her belongings again—she did not dwell upon it as she sipped the last of her tea. She would allow destiny—or, rather, Loretta—to determine what the leaves would reveal.

"Now," Loretta said, "take the handle and swirl the remainder around—yes, just that way. Then overturn the cup onto the saucer."

Elizabeth inverted the cup. When the small amount of remaining liquid had drained out, Loretta instructed her to right the cup. Dark brown leaves and stems were randomly scattered and clumped against the pale china. Most of the clusters were on the bottom; a few clung to the sides, along with a fine trail of tea dust. One grouping was almost at the rim. Elizabeth saw nothing prophetic in the arrangement—save a vision of the serving girl washing out the cup when they had done with this game.

Loretta took the cup from her and studied the leaves. "A bouquet—that is always a good sign. It means a happy marriage. The lines reflect that you are on a journey, one that will eventually bring you back home." She offered Elizabeth a smile, but Elizabeth did not return it. So far Loretta had divined nothing, only stated information she could easily have observed or guessed from their encounter on the highway.

The would-be seer rotated the cup a quarter-turn. "A letter will arrive soon, from someone named 'D.'"

Again, not a startling proclamation. Their surname was Darcy; it was no great hazard to suppose that some family member might contact them. In fact, they anticipated letters from Darcy's sister, who wrote them daily with news of Lily-Anne.

Loretta seemed put out that Elizabeth was not issuing exclamations of amazement as Mrs. Todd had done. She rotated the cup another quarter-turn, so that the handle was now at the top. "There is a cat near the rim . . ."

"And what does that portend?"

"Difficulties." Loretta set the cup down.

Aha. Elizabeth would not play her assigned role in this performance, and so her fortune was becoming more dire. The prediction did not intimidate her; she had already experienced trouble aplenty on this journey. "What sort of difficulties?"

"How am I to know?"

"I thought you were a fortune-teller," Elizabeth said.

Alice squirmed. "Mama—"

Loretta pushed away the cup. "I have seen all I can."

"Mama, I don't think that is a cat. It looks like a wolf. Do you not think it looks like a wolf?"

"It is not a wolf," Loretta snapped.

"It *is* a wolf," the child persisted. "Next to a big hammer."

Loretta smiled at Alice, but it was a tight smile that did not reach her eyes. "That is not a hammer, sweeting."

"What is it then?" the child asked.

Loretta looked at Elizabeth sharply. "A snake."

She offered no further explanation, evidently waiting for Elizabeth to ask. Loath to indulge her but out of patience, Elizabeth submitted.

"And what does a snake signify?"

Loretta reached for her stout, raised the glass to her lips, and drained it.

"Snakes are always bad omens."

Twenty-four

Disingenuousness and double-dealing seemed to meet him at every turn.

—Emma

*D*arcy assessed Miss Jones in the dim light of the Crown. "If you wanted to escape the gypsies, why did you not ask us for assistance while you had the opportunity to speak to us alone on the road that night?"

Miss Jones glanced at Mr. Elton, one of her few supporters who remained. Mrs. Todd now sat at a nearby table, diverting her daughter as she waited to see whether Loretta would be enjoying her hospitality or that of the county gaol tonight. Mr. Knightley had dismissed Loretta's other hangers-on from the inn, and the absence of an appreciative audience had diminished her dramatics significantly. So, too, had Mr. Knightley's advisement that the Darcys' stolen goods were of sufficient value to warrant deportation or hanging. At this news, Miss Jones had paled.

Mr. Elton apparently knew better than to interfere with the magistrate's business. He offered Miss Jones a sympathetic look, but no more. Miss Jones turned back to Darcy, who towered over her. Though Miss Jones remained seated where they had found her, Darcy had not sat down at the table. He was reluctant to so relax his guard.

215

"I did not think you would believe me. And I was afraid of what they would do to me if I was unsuccessful."

Mr. Knightley crossed his arms in front of his chest. He, too, remained standing, and regarded Miss Jones with the stern expression of a parent admonishing a wayward child. "So instead of soliciting the Darcys' aid, you helped your captors rob them."

"I robbed no one. While the gypsies stole their belongings, I stole away—into the woods, where I prayed they would not come looking for me when I did not meet them back at the camp as I had been instructed. It was my hope that having robbed a gentleman's carriage so near the village, they would not dare linger in the neighborhood to collect me." She addressed Darcy and Elizabeth. "I am sorry that your things were taken. But they are things. This was my chance to escape, and I took it. You may criticize the manner in which I went about it, but you have not lived my life these several months."

On the surface, Darcy conceded, her explanation held credence. He doubted that every word of it was true, but there were parts that might be, or close to it. However, having once been deceived by this girl, he would not be twice duped. "Did you never attempt escape before?"

"I never had the opportunity."

"In all those months?"

"They kept a close watch on me. It was only because they thought I had at last accepted their ways that they trusted me to participate in their scheme."

Elizabeth shifted in her seat. She was relenting; Darcy could read it in her countenance.

"Miss Jones, if you but return the gown to us, we will drop this matter," Elizabeth offered.

"What gown?"

The contents of the missing chest had not been mentioned to Miss Jones before now. Darcy wondered whether Elizabeth's direct reference to the christening set had been a test.

"There was a gown among our stolen possessions that I am particularly impatient to have restored to me," Elizabeth said.

"I know nothing about your belongings, for I never saw them. I did not meet the gypsies after the robbery—I was moving as fast and far as I could in the opposite direction."

"Do you know where the band was next journeying?" Mr. Knightley asked.

"My captors were not in the habit of discussing their plans with me."

"What were their habits, then?"

Mr. Knightley enquired into the particulars of how the gypsies lived, how they worked, how they traveled—how they might dispatch stolen goods. Unfortunately, Miss Jones's replies offered little intelligence to aid their present purpose.

"I understand gypsy parties often include women skilled in herbalism," Mr. Knightley continued. "Was there any such practitioner among your band?"

"Pray, do not call it 'my' band, for I want no part of it and never did," Miss Jones said. "But yes, there was an old woman who provided most of their healing. Madam Zsófia. She was also what in the North Country we would call a 'spaewife'—a seer." She looked at Elizabeth. "It was she who taught me to read tea leaves, though there were others in the caravan who also practiced the art."

"Did any English ever consult her?" Mr. Knightley asked.

"For healing or fortune-telling?"

"Either."

"From time to time when we passed through a town, several of the women would earn coin by studying palms or turning cards . . . or reading leaves. 'Dukkering,' they called it. Sometimes Madam Zsófia would dukker, but more often than not she left it to the younger women. She did not like to interact with English. She rarely practiced her healing skills on them directly. She believed most English dishonorable."

Darcy scoffed. "A gypsy thinks the *English* dishonorable?"

"She said that a people who could treat their own so heartlessly was capable of treachery toward anyone, and they were not to be trusted."

"Yet she trained you."

Miss Jones shrugged. "Madam Zsófia is a woman of contradictions. I cannot attempt to explain her."

"Have you been in this neighborhood before?" Mr. Knightley asked.

"Once. We did not stay long."

"How long have you been here this time?"

"A se'nnight, perhaps a day or two more."

The gypsies had been in Highbury, then, since before either of the Churchill gentlemen were poisoned—long enough for the murderer, whomever he was, to have obtained his belladonna from the herb-woman. "Did any English visit the gypsy camp during that se'nnight?" Darcy asked. "Perhaps in want of a remedy from Madam Zsófia?"

"I know of none who came with such a purpose."

Mr. Knightley studied her. His own countenance was inscrutable; Darcy could not tell how much of the girl's story the magistrate believed.

"Miss Jones, does the name Churchill mean anything to you?" Mr. Knightley finally asked.

"Should it?"

"You tell me."

"The only 'church hill' I know is the one I passed coming into the village, with the church and cemetery upon it."

After a few additional questions, Darcy and Mr. Knightley had done with Loretta Jones. Mr. Knightley, who knew Mrs. Todd, dismissed the young woman into the widow's care, with a request—phrased and delivered so as to leave no doubt of its in fact being a command—that Miss Jones not leave the village.

As they all entered the street, Alice spied Mr. Deal's cart and dashed toward it, ignoring her mother's call. Mrs. Todd huffed her frustration. "That child . . ."

"I will retrieve her," Miss Jones offered. Without waiting for a reply, she followed Alice. Mrs. Todd started toward the cart as well, but Mr. Knightley stayed her.

"A word, Mrs. Todd."

She stopped immediately. "Of course, sir."

"It is generous of you to take Miss Jones into your home, but I caution you to beware. Though the gypsies have left, they could return."

Mrs. Todd went to collect her daughter and Miss Jones, who was talking with the peddler while Alice played with a trinket. The conversation appeared to take a heated turn. Mr. Deal regarded the young woman sternly; Miss Jones shook her head and took a step toward him. The peddler glanced at Darcy and the others, then turned back to Loretta and said something that made her take the trinket from Alice, thrust it at his chest, and stride away with the child.

"I wonder what that was about?" Mr. Knightley said.

"It was Mr. Deal who stopped Miss Jones from fleeing when she saw Mrs. Darcy today," Mrs. Knightley replied. "I expect she was expressing her opinion of his interference."

The reappearance of gypsies in the neighborhood, and Loretta Jones's escape from them, was discussed at every table in Highbury by day's end. At tea in the Bates ladies' sitting room, over supper at Abbey Mill Farm, during whist club at the Crown, the story was told and embellished until the village had reached such a general state of alarm that Mr. Knightley was obliged to offer assurance that the wanderers had indeed wandered out of the vicinity, and that the village was safe. This he did with caution, wanting to subdue panic yet urge residents to vigilance. If the gypsies did return, hundreds of eyes stood a better chance of spotting them than did the few pairs belonging to parish officials.

While Mr. Knightley held a special parish meeting that night to calm the masses, the Darcys remained at Hartfield to help calm Mr. Woodhouse.

Darcy believed that Mr. Knightley got the better part of that bargain.

Though until today Mrs. Knightley had managed to keep news of the gypsies' return from her father, this afternoon he had overheard the boy sent to inform the magistrate, and from that moment forward could think of little else. Mrs. Knightley did her best to soothe his apprehension for the safety of his family—and the poultry—but the event of Mr. Knightley's leaving the house that evening created in the old gentleman such uneasiness that only Darcy's offer to stay behind mitigated his agitation. Mr. Woodhouse was then in fear for Mr. Knightley's safety, and that of James the coachman, and all his neighbors venturing out after dark to the meeting, and it was all the three of them—Mrs. Knightley, Darcy, and Elizabeth—could do to divert him.

Elizabeth even joined him in another basin of gruel.

This last finally assuaged his anxiety enough that Mrs. Knightley persuaded him to retire for the evening. With solemn promises to inform him of any developments, including her husband's safe return to Hartfield, Mrs. Knightley accompanied her father to see him comfortably settled in his chamber.

Left in the drawing room—and to themselves for the first time all day—Darcy and Elizabeth could at last freely discuss the day's events.

"Do you believe our chances of recovering our belongings have improved or diminished now that we have located Miss Jones?" Elizabeth asked.

He hesitated to share his honest opinion, for it was not optimistic. "I should be very surprised if we ever see the christening set again. The ring, I have entirely given up as lost."

She nodded in resignation. "I, too."

"Do you believe that she was held by the gypsies against her will?"

Elizabeth pondered his query for a longer time than he had required for hers. "That is a difficult question," she finally said. "As a victim of her ruse, I am disposed to doubt every word she utters. Yet as a woman, I do not want to disserve her if her story is indeed true."

"You said that Miss Jones was less cooperative before Mr. Knightley and I arrived. Did she reveal anything to you that I do not already know?"

"Only that I should avoid serpents." She offered no further explanation, only an enigmatic smile.

He toyed with the idea of affecting disinterest; with anyone else he would resist on principle alone such deliberate baiting. But Elizabeth was not anybody else. Nor was he wont to resist her. "Does Highbury suffer some sort of snake problem?"

"Miss Jones read my tea leaves and claimed that a cluster of them formed a snake, apparently a potent sign of ill luck."

"We are now resorting to prognostication to guide our enquiry?"

"It was not my idea, but hers."

"Then it is most fortuitous that you happened upon Miss Jones just in time for her to warn us of impending doom. And what did *you* make of the serpent?"

"I saw a clump of wet tea leaves and a fortune-teller who is herself our bad luck."

Darcy went to a decanter on the side table and poured two glasses of wine. He handed one to Elizabeth. "Was your call at the vicarage any more successful?"

"Potentially. It seems the housekeeper hired two local girls to help in the kitchen on the night of the Eltons' dinner party. Mrs. Knightley and I were on our way to speak to them when we encountered Miss Jones, and I must confess that I forgot our errand entirely once I saw her."

"We can seek them out tomorrow. My visit with Mr. Knightley to the post office proved as futile as predicted. We had to rouse Mr. Fletcher from a sound sleep when we entered, and he has no memory of either letter's being left there. Is Mrs. Knightley yet convinced that Mrs. Elton authored the riddles?"

"More than ever. Mrs. Elton admitted to sending the first, though I believe Mr. Elton wrote most of it. As to the second, however, she claimed ignorance. I must confess that after today, I understand Mrs. Knightley's inclination to attribute any unpleasantness to the vicar's wife. Mrs. Elton is more boastful and vulturous than the bunch of crows we observed fighting over carrion as we departed."

Her choice of words amused him. "*Bunch* of crows?"

"You would criticize me for linguistic imprecision after I just endured gruel?" She paused. "Very well—flock of crows. Though three seems rather small to constitute a flock. And doubtless there is some more colorful word than 'flock' to describe crows. Something akin to a 'gaggle' of geese, or a 'parliament' of fowls."

"I believe that there is, but I cannot recall the term."

"The way they were cawing and vaunting their triumph, I might use our mysterious riddler's 'gathering of braggarts.' The village children found them quite a spectacle."

Darcy sipped his wine, his thoughts idly skipping upon other names for groups of birds, terms he used when shooting. A nide of pheasants, a bevy of quail, a covey of partridges. He had never hunted crows, though anyone who had ever heard the wretched cries of the trouble-some creatures might be tempted to cut them short. A group of crows in great agitation sounded like they were screaming bloody—

Murder.

Twenty-five

A murder of crows."

Elizabeth, who had been about to sip her wine, lowered her glass. "I beg your pardon?"

"A gathering of crows is called a 'murder,'" Darcy said.

"Indeed? Well, now—that is a rather ominous term." She took a drink from her glass after all.

"It is an old word. I cannot now recall where I read it."

"I think I prefer 'gathering of braggarts.'"

He was silent a moment, brows drawn together. "If a braggart is one who crows—"

She set aside her wineglass. "'Perhaps an unkind individual witnessed the *murder* of an elevated religious house'? Oh! But should that not read 'at'—the murder *at* Donwell Abbey? The abbey was not murdered; Edgar Churchill was."

"Maybe it is not the abbey."

She recalled Miss Jones's flippant dismissal of his question regarding the Churchills. "The village church, then? It sits on a hill."

Darcy was silent, his countenance drawn into the expression that

223

always overcame it when he was deep in contemplation. His gaze seemed to light on various objects in the room, but Elizabeth knew he saw none of them.

"Suppose Churchill himself is the elevated religious house?"

Her eyes widened. "His name! Of course—a church on a hill. 'Perhaps an unkind individual witnessed the murder of Churchill.' Now we are progressing!" She was so delighted by the breakthrough that she repeated the sentence. "Oh!—but who is the individual? It all keeps coming back to that, does it not? Somebody saw more than he—or she—has revealed. But is it *that* fact—the withholding of information—which makes the individual unkind? Or is he an unkind person in general?"

The return of Mr. Knightley from the parish meeting temporarily suspended their discussion. Upon entering the room, he sensed their excitement. "What occurred in my absence?"

"We believe we have solved part of the riddle," Darcy said.

"Does it shed light on the Churchill matter?"

They shared their partial solution. Mr. Knightley was at once galvanized. "A murder of crows. . . . I never could have provided the word myself, but now that you say it, I remember having heard the term before."

"Perhaps now that we have worked out part of the riddle, you might supply the identity of the unkind individual, since you know the villagers better than we," Elizabeth suggested.

"The more I think upon it, the less I believe the first portion of the message simply refers to a disagreeable resident of Highbury," Darcy said. "As the message's second and third parts required deeper penetration to divine 'murder' and 'Churchill,' doubtless the first part holds hidden import as well. Perhaps someone more knowledgeable about words and language—a professor or philologist—could make better sense of it."

"Are you acquainted with any such persons?" Mr. Knightley asked.

"Not directly. But I would wager we all know someone who is."

"I trust it is an individual who understands the need for discretion?"

"Without question," Darcy said, and Elizabeth knew precisely whom he had in mind. "Lord Chatfield."

Though of ordinary English origins, Miss Loretta Jones was the most exotic creature in the village's collective memory to take up residence in Highbury. The young woman and her tale offered a combination of beauty, tragedy, and mystique that trumped even Hiram Deal's charm. When word spread that the former gypsy captive had set herself up as a fortune-teller to earn her way back home, men, women, and children flocked to have their palms or tea leaves read—and to have a look at Miss Jones.

To her own happy fortune, having taken up residence with Mrs. Todd lent Miss Jones a degree of respectability. The honest widow held a solid reputation within the village, and many took it as a sign of endorsement that Loretta now enjoyed her hospitality. Mrs. Todd, everyone agreed, would not allow just anybody into her home. Though in their minds, some harbored dark doubts about the extent of misuse a pretty, unprotected young woman might have suffered at the gypsies' hands, no one dared ask her about it directly. They accepted her outward show of wide-eyed innocence as hope that she had somehow maintained it in truth, and her entrepreneurial efforts as proof that her innate quickness had not left her entirely defenseless.

In short, the good folk of Highbury saw in Loretta Jones the same thing Loretta saw in their palms and teacups—precisely what they wanted to see.

"A ring! That means a wedding." Miss Jones looked up from the teacup into which she had been peering. The young woman seated at the table with her blushed but could not suppress a smile.

"When?"

"Before too long, I should think. Within a twelvemonth."

"A whole year?" The woman cast a disappointed glance across the common room of the Crown Inn, where Loretta conducted her augury. The soothsaying trade had proved too brisk for Mrs. Todd's cottage to accommodate it, so she had commandeered a corner of the public house as her workplace. As her prophecy-seeking clients consumed not only tea, but considerable quantities of other food and drink while awaiting their few minutes of forecasting, it was an arrangement that proved as beneficial to the proprietors of the Crown as to Miss Jones.

Elizabeth followed the woman's gaze. A group of farmhands, one of them quite handsome, occupied a table in the opposite corner. The fellow stole a surreptitious glance at Loretta's client, but self-consciously shifted when he realized he was himself an object of observation.

Loretta noticed the young man, too.

"I said *within* a twelvemonth," the seer added quickly. "It could happen sooner." She studied the leaves again. "In fact, the ring lies so close to the rim of your cup that I daresay it will happen much sooner."

The woman's shy smile returned.

Darcy, his back to the table of young men, listened to Loretta's divination with obvious disdain. "I fail to comprehend how anyone can place credence in such patent balderdash." He spoke in a low voice that reached Elizabeth's ears alone.

"You doubt Miss Jones's prediction?"

"Should it come to pass, the event will have been entirely coincidental. Meanwhile, she has given herself a year in which to get herself gone before anyone can accuse her of false prophecy."

Elizabeth watched the undeclared lovers again not quite make eye contact as the girl gathered her shawl and rose to leave. "Miss Jones might possess more insight than you credit her with."

"Surely you do not think she possesses the ability to read signs of future events?" Darcy asked.

"Oh, I believe she is quite adept at reading signs. Just not necessarily in teacups."

Darcy shook his head and took a draught of the beer he had been nursing since they took their seats. It was spruce beer, something she had never seen him drink before they came to Highbury. She nodded toward the tankard.

"How is it?"

"Not as good as Mr. Knightley's." He consulted his pocket watch.

"I wonder what delays his wife. Were not she and Mr. Dixon to meet us here five minutes ago?"

Elizabeth smiled. Mrs. Knightley and Thomas Dixon were calling upon Miss Bates. Was that not explanation enough for their tardiness? "I expect they are too engaged in conversation to break away."

The opening of the door caught her attention. The new arrivals were not Mrs. Knightley and Mr. Dixon, however, but the Eltons. The couple acknowledged the Darcys with a nod before going to Miss Jones, over whom they made a great show of solicitude.

Miss Jones assured them of her health, her comfort in the accommodations at Mrs. Todd's house, and her contentment as Highbury's newest, if temporary, resident.

"You poor creature—my heart weeps for you," Mrs. Elton said. "From the moment Mr. E. shared your story with me, I have been able to think of nothing else. I told him this morning that I simply cannot rest until I have done something to improve your situation. Of what use are all my resources, I asked, if I do not employ them in this unfortunate girl's aid?"

"You are kindness itself, Mrs. Elton," Miss Jones said. "What did you have in mind?"

"In mind?" Mrs. Elton blinked several times. "Why, I—I have numerous ideas. I simply have not settled on one yet."

"I shall be grateful for any attention from so fine a lady." She gestured toward the empty seat across from her. "Perhaps in exchange I could read your fortune."

"Oh, gracious! I could not possibly—the vicar's wife—whatever would people say? I would be the talk of the village."

"There is no harm in it. And not only would you honor me by the privilege, but also do me a great favor, for as the vicar's wife surely you set the example of fashion in Highbury. Once it was known that you allowed me to read your tea leaves—purely for entertainment, of course—there would be those as would come every morning to have me look into their cups to see what the day might bring."

"Well, I—it is true that people look to me as a model of taste and propriety. Is that not true, my *caro sposo*?" Her husband directly affirmed her status as the arbiter of style in Highbury.

She glanced at the empty teacup still on the table beside Loretta. Mrs. Elton's face revealed longing that had nothing to do with thirst.

"I am thinking, Mr. E., that if I submitted—only this once—strictly for amusement, of course—that no one could find fault with me. It would be merely an innocent diversion. And my patronage would benefit poor Miss Jones and her efforts to return home."

"Oh, do allow her, Mr. Elton," Loretta said.

Mr. Elton gave his consent, Mrs. Elton sat down, and tea was ordered.

As it arrived, Mrs. Knightley and Mr. Dixon entered. The room seemed to brighten immediately, though whether from Thomas Dixon's warm greeting to the Eltons or the high polish of his top hat, leather boots, and silver-handled walking stick, Elizabeth could not decide.

Mrs. Knightley's greeting to the Eltons was cooler but gracious. She gestured towards the tea. "Are you having your fortune read?"

"Why, yes! Mr. E. and Miss Jones simply insisted. It is all in sport, of course. Perhaps when we have done, you would like a turn?"

"Not today."

"I should think you would enjoy the entertainment. It would be a change of pace from the word games that have lately occupied you." Mrs. Elton forced a smile. "Have you identified the author of that other puzzle you said arrived in the post?"

"No, not yet."

"How very frustrating. Does not the handwriting offer some clue?"

"It was penned in block letters, which are not very revealing."

"Well, I should think that Mr. Knightley could determine their writer, if he turned his mind to it."

Mrs. Knightley managed a polite smile. "Mr. Knightley's mind has been occupied with weightier matters."

"Ah, yes—Mr. Churchill's death. It must indeed weigh upon you both that he died at your house. He was such a good man! Generosity itself towards Frank, and Frank not even Edgar Churchill's blood son." She shook her head and sighed. "I grieve for the whole family."

"I am sure we all do," Mrs. Knightley said.

"With tragedy such as that surrounding you, I understand why you do not wish to have your fortune told, even for amusement. I would dread to hear that more ill luck awaited me." She turned to Miss Jones. "Or do you tell only happy fortunes?"

Miss Jones had grown quiet during the exchange between Mrs. Knightley and Mrs. Elton. Elizabeth was hardly surprised. Though their words were perfectly civil, the undercurrent was strong and deep, and no one of sense would have intentionally ventured into those waters unprepared.

"I speak the truth as I see it," Loretta said.

Mrs. Elton appeared flustered for a moment, but then adopted a bright smile. "What about you, Mr. Dixon? You *must* have your fortune read!"

Thomas Dixon, who had seemed to be concentrating more intensely on the shabby state of the room's wallpaper than on the conversation taking place before him, gave a start at Mrs. Elton's suggestion. His gaze shifted from the Eltons, to Mrs. Knightley, to the Darcys. He barely glanced at Miss Jones. "Thank you, no."

Elizabeth had expected a gentleman whose life was so wholly given over to idleness and pleasure to have seized the opportunity for a novel form of entertainment.

"Why not, sir?" Loretta challenged him with a bold gaze. "Do you fear what I might reveal?"

Mr. Dixon adjusted the cuffs of his coat and picked an imaginary piece of lint off his left sleeve. "Not at all."

"Then what is the harm?" Her tone turned teasing. "Perhaps we might learn the name of your true love."

The very notion seemed to appall him. With a stiff bow, he encouraged the others to enjoy their diversion and told Mrs. Knightley that she would find him waiting outside whenever it pleased her to return to Hartfield.

Elizabeth watched with disappointment as he quit the inn. She had wanted very much to learn that name.

As much as Mr. Dixon apparently wanted to keep it secret.

Twenty-six

"She will never lead any one really wrong; she will make no lasting blunder; where Emma errs once, she is in the right a hundred times."

—Mrs. Weston to Mr. Knightley, Emma

*E*mma was beginning to dread the arrival of the post.

Each day brought something more vexing. First the charade. Then the riddle. Now a word puzzle of yet another sort.

GRAL IRNIE DNOMHC

VEIHTTS HTSASE LYE DEVI

EWDEH LL MADE GNO

What vexed her most was not the challenges presented by the puzzles. It was the fact that their continued accumulation rendered it increasingly unlikely that Mrs. Elton had authored all of them.

When the third note arrived, addressed solely to Mr. Knightley, Emma had at first ascribed it to Mrs. Elton along with the others. The infuriating woman had, after all, brought up the subject of the puzzles only the day before, as Miss Jones prepared to tell her fortune. Like the first two, this latest bore a local postmark. But each puzzle had become successively more difficult to decipher; Mr. Knightley and Mr. Darcy still awaited a response regarding the second one from the friend they thought might be of assistance. They were not even entirely certain as to the nature of the third.

"I believe it is a cipher puzzle." Mr. Darcy cast it back onto the writing table in Mr. Knightley's study. "Though I cannot begin to guess how we are to determine the key."

"There may be no method to it at all," Elizabeth said. "The arrangement could be random—a simple anagram."

"Not so simple when one is trying to work out the solution." Mr. Knightley picked up the note and scanned it once more. "If it is indeed an anagram, one cannot form 'Churchill' or 'murder'—there is no *U*."

"That is why I favor the cipher," Darcy replied.

Cipher or anagram, Emma grudgingly conceded to herself that Mrs. Elton could not possibly have created all three word puzzles. The woman was simply not that clever. Which meant that Emma had been wrong.

Emma despised being wrong. Particularly when in the process, her husband was proved right. Emma loved Mr. Knightley beyond expression, felt blessed indeed to be the recipient of not only his affection, but also his wisdom and experience. But she could not help wishing that events would prove *her* correct on occasion.

As the Darcys deliberated solution tactics, Mr. Knightley noticed Emma's state of glum contemplation.

"I daresay Mrs. Knightley has more experience with word puzzles than any of us. Last year she and a friend compiled a book of riddles, conundrums, and so forth. Emma, what strategy would you recommend for solving this?"

The question drew her from her brooding. "The original letters could have been systematically rearranged, such as moving the first letter of each word to its end," she said. "Or they might have been substituted one for one—*A* becomes *B*, *B* becomes *C*, and so on. I propose that we each copy out the lines and work independently on different methods. Perhaps the gentlemen could attempt to determine a substitution alphabet, while Mrs. Darcy and I experiment with rearranging the existing letters."

It was agreed. Three copies of the message were made and, equipped with pencils and large sheets of foolscap, all four of them settled down to apply themselves.

Elizabeth, wanting no distractions, retired to the library to work.

As she had in Mr. Knightley's study, she stared at the message again. This time, however, she thought not of the letters on the page, but of the unknown person who had arranged them.

This was not a conundrum in a book, written to amuse and entertain. It was a communiqué, written to deliver information. The puzzle's author wanted the message to be deciphered, or he would not have sent it. If his goal was to challenge, not to thwart, the solution might not prove as difficult as they anticipated.

The most sensible way to begin, she decided, was to simply write out the puzzle backwards. There must, after all, be some method to the placement of the letters and "words" as arranged—mustn't there? She need not put herself through mental contortions if the author had not.

Reversing the first line, however, revealed only that the solution would require more effort. "Chmond einri larg" made even less sense than elevated religious houses and gatherings of braggarts. Nevertheless, she reversed the rest of the puzzle to see whether any patterns emerged.

CHMOND EINRI LARG
IVED EYL ESASTH STTHIEV
ONG EDAM LL HEDWE

When finished, she allowed her gaze to drift over the letters, giving the words an opportunity to reveal themselves. "CHMOND" drew her attention, for it composed most of the word "Richmond," the city where the Churchills had been living when Mrs. Churchill died. In fact, the "RI" needed to complete the name was on the same line— preceded by "IN."

Something in Richmond. The remaining letters on that line spelled LARGE.

Large in Richmond. Whatever could be the sense of that? But the phrase was formed by rearranging the reversed letter groupings—not the individual letters—and then merely adjusting the word spaces: LARG EINRI CHMOND . . . LARGE IN RICHMOND.

Excited, she tore slips of paper and wrote a grouping on each so she could rearrange them more easily. She had been right: the solution was not as difficult as she had first imagined.

HEDWE LL EDAM ONG STTHIEV ESASTH EYL IVED LARG EINRI CHMOND

But now . . . what did it mean?

Emma set down her pencil and rubbed her temples. She, too, had left Mr. Knightley's study to better concentrate, and had chosen the drawing room. Now sheets of paper covered in cross-outs and false starts lay strewn on the card table, and pencil lead darkened her fingertips.

She had nearly given up, had even risen to rejoin the others in the study and admit defeat. But then her gaze had landed upon her nephews' box of alphabets, still not returned to the nursery.

She had removed the letters she needed, supplementing the tiles with small pieces of torn paper to create necessary duplicates. Three *D*'s. Eight *E*'s. Then she had spread them out upon the table, arranging and rearranging letters in seemingly endless combinations until something of sense began to form.

Now the solution stared back at her.

She counted the letters once more, again checking them against the original message to ensure she had used each one the proper number of times.

Then she reached for a fresh sheet of paper, dipped her quill in the inkpot, and wrote out the message to share with the others.

"'He dwelled amongst thieves as they lived large in Richmond.'" Darcy handed the paper to Mr. Knightley and regarded Elizabeth with admiration. "Well done."

"Indeed, very well done," Mr. Knightley echoed. "Mr. Darcy and I were having a miserable time attempting to work out a substitution scheme. I must go find Mrs. Knightley. She will be pleased that you discovered the solution."

Elizabeth appreciated their praise, but felt it only half earned. "Discovering the solution is one thing," she said. "Interpreting it is quite another."

"Given that the previous riddle holds a clue to the murder of Churchill, 'they' almost certainly refers to the Churchills here," Mr. Knightley said as he moved towards the door.

"But who is the 'he'?" Darcy asked. "Frank, who had been our primary suspect, lived in Richmond *with* his aunt and uncle."

"And our other suspect, Thomas Dixon, has spent his life dwelling with wealthy relations," Elizabeth added.

"Yes, hardly criminals—Oh! Here you are, Emma. I was just coming for you. Mrs. Darcy has solved the cipher."

"Indeed?" Mrs. Knightley turned to Elizabeth in amazement. She held up a slip of paper. "So have I."

"That is hardly surprising, given your talent for word puzzles," Elizabeth said. "After all, the message was simply written backwards, with the word spaces altered randomly and the groupings rearranged."

Mrs. Knightley looked at Elizabeth oddly as she accepted the piece of paper Mr. Knightley offered her. "The spellings were not backwards. Nor were the word spaces at all random. They were the key to sorting out the letters—which were entirely rearranged." She glanced down at the paper she had just received. "He dwelled amongst thieves'?"

Now Elizabeth was all confusion. "Well—yes. Did you not work out that part?"

Mrs. Knightley glanced at her husband, then crossed to Elizabeth. Her face was troubled as she handed over the writing she had brought with her to the study. "I worked out an altogether different solution."

CLEVER LYING GIRL. DEAL HAD HIDDEN MOTIVES. NOT WHAT HE SEEMS.

Twenty-seven

To guess what all this meant, was impossible even for Emma.

—Emma

*M*inutes elapsed before all overcame their astonishment. That a single group of letters could yield two complete messages, both with disturbing implications, was extraordinary. Though Elizabeth had worked out one of them herself, she now regarded both in wonder.

Darcy was the first to recover. "If the puzzle's two solutions are to be taken as a single message, our peddler does not merely trade with the gypsies—he is a member of their band."

"Or was," Elizabeth countered. "The message says 'dwelled,' and he remains here in Highbury despite the rest of the caravan's having moved on."

"Even so, it implies more than a business relationship between Mr. Deal and the gypsies—and between Mr. Deal and Miss Jones, whom I presume is the girl referenced. If his contact with the gypsies was sporadic and minimal, as he would have us believe, they could have kept her hidden from him during her period of alleged captivity. In fact, they likely would have gone to considerable trouble to keep an Englishwoman out of his sight. But if he lived amongst them, he surely knows her; moreover, he did nothing to help her escape the caravan. Which means that either Miss Jones is lying about having been held against her will, or Mr. Deal's allegiance to the gypsies surpasses his loyalty to his own people."

Elizabeth preferred believing Miss Jones a liar to discovering the amiable peddler capable of dishonor towards a distressed young woman of any race. If they in fact had been living together amongst the gypsies, she found it curious that Mr. Deal had been the person who prevented Miss Jones from fleeing when Elizabeth had first sighted her in Highbury. Had he wanted to help Elizabeth, win her trust and favor? See Miss Jones brought to justice for theft? Return Miss Jones to the gypsies for some reward, only to have been thwarted by the intercession of Mr. Elton and Mrs. Todd? Hidden motives, indeed.

"Whatever Mr. Deal's actions—or lack thereof—by Miss Jones, the author has drawn our attention to him in some connection to Richmond," Mr. Knightley said. "We know that Mr. Deal does business there, for Richmond is where he obtains his sling bullets. We need to determine whether he was there at the same time as the Churchills, and what, if any, contact he had with them."

"Mrs. Weston's housekeeper has a sister in Richmond," Mrs. Knightley said. "She wrote of doing business with Hiram Deal this past summer."

"Did not Mrs. Churchill die during the summer?" Darcy asked.

"Yes," Mr. Knightley said. "On the twenty-sixth of June."

"Perhaps Mr. Deal is the unkind individual who witnessed the murder of Churchill—*Agnes* Churchill." Darcy paused. "Or perhaps he committed it."

"I thought her physician determined that she died of an apoplectic seizure," Mrs. Knightley said.

"It is in his professional interest for that to be the case. It might not be in the interest of justice for us to accept the diagnosis without question," Mr. Knightley replied.

"Let us begin by ascertaining whether Mr. Deal's time in Richmond coincides with that of the Churchills," Darcy said. "We should speak to the Churchills' servants and learn whether he ever called at their house. If we are fortunate, the attendants who accompanied Frank and Edgar Churchill to Randalls will be able to help us."

Mr. Knightley nodded. "If not, we shall have to track down the staff who served them while they leased the house."

"Should a journey to Richmond prove necessary, I can depart as soon as a horse is readied," Darcy offered.

"I hope it is not needed," Mr. Knightley said. "The afternoon is already half gone, and I want to confront Mr. Deal himself by day's end."

Thanks to the recollective powers of a footman who had served the Churchill family for twoscore years, Darcy was spared a hasty ride to Richmond. He instead spent the evening with Mr. Knightley and Hiram Deal. It had been Mr. Knightley's idea to host the intimate little gathering in his small study at Hartfield, which afforded more privacy than the Crown, his usual venue for magisterial business.

It had not been Mr. Deal's idea to attend it.

The peddler arrived in the escort of Mr. Cole. Though Mr. Deal labored to maintain his customary affability, there was wariness in his manner as he greeted Mr. Knightley and Darcy.

At Mr. Knightley's nod, Mr. Cole left the study. The constable would wait in the drawing room with the ladies and Mr. Woodhouse, near at hand should he be wanted. As far as Mr. Woodhouse knew, Mr. Cole—and his waiting carriage—were at Hartfield to visit Mr. Woodhouse. Mrs. Knightley's father need not know that a suspected murderer was presently under his roof.

With brusque civility, Mr. Knightley invited Mr. Deal to take a seat opposite himself, the large writing table between them. Mr. Deal sat on the edge of the chair, leaning slightly forward like a man ready to engage in conversation—or poised to flee. Darcy remained standing off to one side.

The magistrate did not waste time on pleasantries. "Mr. Deal, have you any notion why I asked you to come here this evening?"

"None, sir. Though I suspect you do not wish to see my inventory of brandy."

The attempt at levity failed to elicit a smile from Mr. Knightley. "Tell us about your business with the Churchills."

"The Churchills?" The peddler, clearly perplexed, glanced from Mr. Knightley to Darcy and back. "I thought I had—when we spoke some days ago, Mr. Darcy—but certainly, I can repeat it for you. I sold the younger Mr. Churchill a snuff box."

"We mean your previous business with the family," Darcy said. "In Richmond."

The peddler blinked. "Richmond? I never met either of the misters Churchill in Richmond."

"But you did visit their house. On June twenty-sixth."

"I visited many homes in Richmond last June. Usually I deal with the servants or the lady of the house. Rarely gentlemen. As to whether I stopped at the home of a family named Churchill specifically on the twenty-sixth, I cannot say. Surely you do not expect me to remember with such clarity the calls I made five months ago?"

Darcy stepped closer, forcing the peddler to tilt his head up to look at him. "You recall the history of every item you hawk from your cart. I indeed presume you capable of recollecting a meeting on the twenty-sixth of June that resulted in a heated argument with the lady of the house. The servant I spoke to today certainly remembers it."

Mr. Deal shifted, turning his body so that he no longer faced Darcy, but Mr. Knightley. He did not, however, look at the magistrate. He stared at the clawed feet of the writing table as he brought up his maimed arm and absently rubbed the stump with his hand. His countenance bore an expression of defeat. And shades of fear.

Mr. Knightley rested his own arms on the table and formed a temple with his fingertips. "Mr. Deal, the servant's testimony provides sufficient cause to arrest you tonight. If you wish to offer your own explanation of events, or have anything to say on your behalf, now would be the time to do so."

Mr. Deal opened his mouth to speak, but no words issued forth.

"You had a row with Mrs. Churchill, after which she suddenly died. I doubt you fought over the price of lace," Darcy said. "The servant told me that he had seen you loitering near the house for a se'nnight previous."

Mr. Deal's jaw tightened.

"What business brought you to the house?" Mr. Knightley asked. "How did you know Agnes Churchill?"

Mr. Deal raised his head. The look he gave Mr. Knightley was direct and unapologetic.

"She was my mother."

Volume the Third

IN WHICH HIGHBURY BECOMES ACQUAINTED
WITH A MURDERER

Seldom, very seldom, does complete truth belong to any human disclosure.

—*Emma*

Twenty-eight

"Oh, Mrs. Churchill . . . What a blessing, that she never had any children! Poor little creatures, how unhappy she would have made them!"

—Isabella Knightley, Emma

We are to believe that in her youth, Agnes Churchill secretly bore a child that she kept hidden for decades?" Though Mr. Knightley voiced the question, Darcy was equally incredulous.

"My birth was not a secret, only my life—even to her."

"Mr. Deal, kindly explain yourself."

As Mr. Knightley spoke, movement at the door caught Darcy's attention. Elizabeth silently entered. Her expression indicated that she had something to tell him, but a brief exchange of unspoken communication indicated that it was not exigent. As he did not want to interrupt Mr. Deal or miss what he was about to say, Darcy motioned her to wait quietly. Mr. Deal's back was to her; he had not seen her enter. Elizabeth's attendance would not inhibit his admissions. Mr. Knightley gave no sign of disapproval and did not betray her presence.

"I have had, in truth, three mothers," Mr. Deal said. "Only two, however, deserve the name. Though Agnes Churchill gave me life, she would have stolen it from me just as quickly had the nurse who attended my birth followed her orders. Thankfully, the nurse instead took me far away and gave me to her childless cousin."

Since entering Highbury, Darcy had not heard one favorable word about Agnes Churchill. Still, he found it difficult to comprehend any mother's being capable of what Mr. Deal alleged. Or any father. "Were you born out of wedlock?"

"Indeed, no. Edgar Churchill was my father, and my arrival, a little more than a year into their marriage, was entirely legitimate. But I learned this only recently. Growing up, I knew merely that I had been born in London to parents either unable or unwilling to keep a maimed child. I always imagined they were a kind but fortuneless couple with so many other mouths to feed that they could not afford to raise a son whose deformity would forever be a burden."

"And the woman who did raise you?" Mr. Knightley asked.

"My adoptive parents were hardly wealthy themselves. They owned a modest shop in a village not unlike this one, and it was there that I learned my sums and began to develop the skills of a salesman. They also taught me my letters and manners, for they knew the life of a cripple would not be easy, and they wanted to prepare me as best they could to make my way in the world."

"How, then, did you come to consort with gypsies?"

Mr. Deal leaned back, settling into both his chair and his story. His manner, however, did not have quite the ease with which he spun his trader's patter. This time, instead of selling his wares, the peddler had to sell himself, and Darcy and Mr. Knightley were determined not to be taken in.

"When I was nine, scarlet fever claimed both of my parents, along with most of the village. Before she died, my mother told me that my birth name was Churchill, but cautioned me against trying to find my true parents. I would be safer and happier in the village, she said, running the shop with the guidance of a friend she asked to look out for me until I could manage independently. But her friend died, too. The outbreak left the village decimated; parish relief was exhausted, and nobody wanted the trouble of caring for a child not theirs, not whole, and of unknown origins. I sold everything I could not carry, packed my haversack, and left the village determined to somehow find my way to London.

"I had not journeyed a mile when I encountered a *kumpania*—a caravan—of gypsies moving through the area. They had heard of the contagion that claimed our village and, afraid I carried the fever, warned me to keep my distance. But they had among them a *drabarni*. In the Romany tongue, that word can mean a seer or a healer; Rawnie Zsófia was both. There are many pretenders to both arts among the gypsies, but if there is one who truly possesses the gifts of prophecy and medicine, it is Rawnie Zsófia. She told her fellow gypsies that they had nothing to fear, that I must join them. She was a young woman then, not yet thirty and unmarried, but already they respected her as if she were an elder.

"She asked me where I traveled. Her black eyes at once fascinated and frightened me—I was certain she could see straight into my mind and heart. I stammered out that I was seeking my mother. 'You need look no farther,' she replied. 'I foresaw that you would come to me. From today, you are my chosen son.'" His voice grew thick as he recalled the meeting and repeated her words.

"And so I became a gypsy, with a gypsy life and a gypsy name. Among the Roma, Rawnie Zsófia's protection was better than royal patronage, and they accepted me without question. My deformity was nothing to a people who had themselves endured centuries of persecution, and they taught me such skills as were within my power to make others overlook my missing hand. It was in this *familia* that I learned the art of storytelling. And a few other talents."

What these other talents were, Mr. Deal did not specify. Darcy suspected that a number of them were of questionable legality.

"In turn," the peddler continued, "I became the caravan's middleman with the *gorgios*. My English features and respectable speech enabled me to move freely wherever we traveled, and I soon earned my keep by selling the gypsies' wares in towns we camped near. As I grew older, the path of my journeys often divided from that of the caravan, sometimes for prolonged periods. But always I returned to my gypsy mother, the woman known to others as Rawnie Zsófia, but to me alone as *dai*."

Darcy stirred impatiently. The peddler had an interesting history, but none of it explained his recent dealings with the Churchills and the events of June twenty-sixth. "When and why did you seek out the Churchills?"

"Though I was content with my gypsy *familia,* I often wondered about my birth parents. Whenever Rawnie Zsófia told my fortune, she would not reveal anything she saw about the Churchills, and a sorrowful expression would overcome her face if I asked whether I would ever meet them. 'In time, my *chavo,*' she would say. 'In time.'

"Last spring, the caravan camped just outside of Highbury. I was not with them, but there was an incident involving a young woman who became frightened when some of the children begged her for a coin. A gentleman intervened—Mr. Churchill, the woman called him. Though he bears a resemblance to my own appearance fifteen years ago, Rawnie Zsófia needed no physical cues to know him immediately for my kin. She had already seen him in visions. When I was next with her, I sensed that something had changed. I asked why she was so heavyhearted. 'The time is come,' she said.

"I traced Frank to the Churchills' house in Richmond, then over the next month ascertained that the senior Churchills were indeed the couple who had abandoned me. Though I trusted the truth of Rawnie Zsófia's visions, I needed more objective proof before attempting to meet them. And that is *all* I wanted—simply to meet them. I did not intend to reveal my identity."

Mr. Knightley, who had been taking occasional notes as Mr. Deal spoke, stopped his pen midstroke. "After spending years among a race infamous for thievery, you discovered that your parents were quite wealthy, yet you had no ambitions of claiming some of that wealth as your own?"

A wry smile formed on Mr. Deal's lips. "My life with the gypsies indeed influenced me, but not in the manner you assume. The Roma are, in fact, not an avaricious people; their language does not even include a word for 'possession.' They take and use only what they need, and cannot comprehend the compulsion of 'civilized' men to acquire more." His expression grew serious again. "When I say I did not aspire to the Churchills' riches, I speak the truth, and after seeing the creature my birth mother became under the malignant influence of money, I am even more decided. I want no part of the Churchill fortune; my cousin Frank is welcome to it."

"And is this what you told Agnes Churchill?"

"Our conversation never progressed that far. Even if it had, her own enslavement to power and wealth so distorted her thinking that I doubt she would have believed me."

Mr. Deal cleared his throat several times. It was dry in the room, and he had been speaking some time with little interruption. Mr. Knightley rose and went to a small side table that held a decanter and glasses. As he poured a glass of wine and handed it to Mr. Deal, Darcy went to Elizabeth.

"What brings you?" he whispered.

"Mr. Cole was called away," she whispered back, "but says he will return directly." She nodded towards Mr. Deal. "This is quite a tale." She appeared reluctant to leave.

Indeed, he would not mind hearing her assessment of the story when Mr. Deal had done telling it. "Stay if you wish. Though be discreet."

He returned to his position near the table with the wine. Mr. Knightley had just topped off Mr. Deal's glass.

"Pray, describe exactly what transpired during your meeting with Mrs. Churchill," Mr. Knightley said.

Mr. Deal swallowed more wine before continuing. "I thought it would be best to meet only my mother first, so I waited for a time when Frank and Edgar Churchill were out—that is why the servant saw me loitering in the neighborhood. When the opportunity arose, I called at the house as a peddler and was granted an audience with Mrs. Churchill."

Darcy having declined Mr. Knightley's silent offer of wine for himself, the magistrate returned to his writing table and once more took up his pen.

"It was not a joyous reunion," Mr. Deal continued. "Though I took care to hide my maimed arm from view, it caught her notice. She started, and peered into my face, where she found enough Churchill in my features to confirm her suspicion—which I did not deny.

"She paled and stepped back, arms thrust defensively in front of her, as if she beheld a ghost. I suppose in a sense, she did, for she had presumed me dead all these years. But she quickly recovered herself. Before I could offer even a word of explanation for having sought her out, or tell her how long I had imagined that moment, she accused me of coming to blackmail her, to steal her fortune, to threaten her position in society. How dare I appear after all these years to take what she had spent a lifetime protecting? How dare I presume to even breathe?"

He took a fortifying draught. "The full story of my nativity tumbled out. Her travail was long and difficult, surpassed in dreadfulness only by the horror of her first sight of me. The trauma she experienced was somehow my fault—I, an infant but minutes old. She refused to present a crippled son to her husband, or to acknowledge the deformed child as her own for all of society to judge her. What little blame that remained unassigned to me was laid on the head of the expensive London physician who had delivered me. Though the physician asserted that my deformity had manifested long before her lying-in and had nothing to do with the instruments he had employed as she labored, she threatened to destroy his reputation if he did not help her get rid of the child by telling Mr. Churchill that it had been stillborn. The attending nurse was paid to dispose of 'the monstrosity.' Mrs. Churchill did not care what happened to me, so long as she was never reminded of *her* terrible ordeal again."

Darcy glanced at Elizabeth. Her countenance was full of pity and sadness. He, too, felt sympathy, yet—he hoped—maintained enough detachment to respond to Mr. Deal's revelations objectively. As all Highbury had already witnessed, the peddler was a consummate storyteller.

Mr. Deal drained his wineglass. "You can imagine my pain upon hearing myself so described, my very existence thought of only in terms of its affront to her. But more was to come: When Mrs. Churchill had done spewing out the details of my first rejection, she cast me off a second time. After all these years, my father still believed I had been stillborn. She threatened my life if I revealed myself to Edgar Churchill or exposed them to society. Should I speak of this matter to another soul, no one would miss a lying vagabond peddler, she said, or question his disappearance.

"Her cruelty and selfishness stunned me. I told her, quite honestly, that neither she nor her husband need fear further contact from me. I had done with them both."

Darcy refilled Mr. Deal's wineglass. "She worked herself into this terrible temper entirely by herself? With no provocation from you?"

Mr. Deal stared at the glass thoughtfully. "Though her words were strong, I could see fear in her eyes at the threat my existence posed to her power and position in society, and within her marriage. I think that in the hidden recesses of her heart, where she dared not ever look, she had been waiting her whole life to be called to account for what she had done—a criminal living in perpetual dread of being caught. I think the knowledge of her sin preyed upon her nerves for nine-and-thirty years, growing sharper as she aged and came ever closer to facing her Creator. And when I appeared, the greed and guilt that had been feasting upon her soul came rushing forth in a torrent."

He looked up at Darcy. "You said she died following our meeting— I heard that a seizure took her." He set his wineglass on the candle pedestal beside his chair and turned to Mr. Knightley. "I swear to you, I did nothing to antagonize Mrs. Churchill or provoke her anger. Nor did the seizure begin while I was with her, though she was in such a state of agitation that I can well imagine it coming upon her. When I quit the house, however, she was alive and in full possession of her faculties. My only crime was that I was, too."

Though Agnes Churchill had provided her son with ample motive for murder, Mr. Deal's account of events was supported by the reports they had already received from her Richmond physician and household servants indicating that she died of an apoplectic fit. It seemed that if anybody was to blame for her death, it was Mrs. Churchill herself.

Edgar Churchill's death, however, remained suspicious.

"You claim that you told Agnes Churchill you would attempt no contact with your father," Darcy said, "yet you were seen with him here in Highbury at least twice—once in conversation at Randalls, and again in Broadway Lane whilst Frank purchased his snuff box."

Mr. Deal nodded. "When I said that to Mrs. Churchill, I was so wounded by her treatment of me that I assumed I would receive a similar reception from her husband. But after my initial shock subsided and I had time to consider the matter, I realized that I was not the sole victim of her pride and deceit. In discarding me, she had denied Edgar Churchill his only son. I thought what my own feelings would be if I learned that an infant I believed I had buried more than half a lifetime ago was found to have lived. To the Roma, family is everything; to the English . . . not always. I had little reason to hope that Edgar Churchill was any different than his wife. He had married her, after all, and lived with her some forty years. But the fact that she had been so desperate to maintain his ignorance of me made me wonder what sort of man he was, and whether he might want to choose for himself to accept or reject me.

"My gypsy mother discouraged my wish to meet him. The omens were unclear, and she did not want to see my heart rent twice. I was persistent, however, and when the Churchills came to Highbury after Frank's wedding, so did our caravan.

"As I had with Mrs. Churchill, I presented myself to my father first as merely a peddler, so that I might judge his character. I found him so very different from his wife that I could scarcely imagine them together. His manner encouraged my hopes and, with great caution, I revealed myself to him. He was understandably shocked, and grieved by my account of such deceit and cruelty on the part of his late wife. Yet he saw in me a glimpse of his younger self, and remembered irregularities in long-ago conversations with his wife, that made my story plausible."

"He simply accepted you as his long-lost son upon the spot?" Mr. Knightley asked.

"Heavens, no. He was no gull. He intended to verify my history as best he could, and said he would write to his solicitor immediately. The physician who attended the birth was long dead, but the nurse might yet be found, and some of the servants present in the house that night were still with the family."

"Money seemed to be foremost on Agnes Churchill's mind," Darcy said. "Did either you or he make any mention of your inheritance?"

"I assured him I did not want anything from him, save the pleasure of knowing him at last."

"And how did he respond?"

"He promised that if I were indeed his son, I would finally know my father's affection and acknowledgment." He picked up his wine once more but did not drink, only stared at the glass in his hand. "That was the first and last conversation I had with him. We did not speak while Frank was purchasing his snuff box. It was too awkward, our acquaintance too new—more fragile than this glass."

"Did he tell Frank Churchill about your conversation?" Darcy asked.

"If he did, my cousin has superior bluffing skills to even the gypsies, for he has betrayed no hint that he knows me as anything but a peddler."

"You must have suffered quite a shock when your father died," Mr. Knightley said.

"Indeed, yes." He emptied the wineglass again, but declined Mr. Knightley's offer of a third. "I grieved at the news. I grieve still."

Mr. Deal rose and returned his wineglass to the side table from which Mr. Knightley had taken it. Elizabeth slipped out of the room. As she did so, Darcy caught sight of Mr. Cole in the hall.

"It sounds as if you learned a considerable amount about Edgar Churchill in a short period of time." Mr. Knightley left his seat and approached him. "As you have no doubt heard, the coroner's inquest ruled his death a case of poisoning, though whether accidental or deliberate remains undetermined. Can you think of anybody who might have wished him harm?"

The table rested beside a window, and Mr. Deal gazed into the gathering darkness. "I certainly did not. For me, his death could not have come at a worse time." Bitterness tinged his voice. "I no sooner found my father than lost him."

He turned to face Darcy and Mr. Knightley. "I have given you a full accounting of my dealings with the Churchills," he said to the magistrate. "Am I free to leave?"

Mr. Knightley and Darcy exchanged glances. Mr. Knightley stepped forward.

"I am afraid not."

Twenty-nine

"There is something so shocking in a child's being taken away from his parents and natural home!"

—Isabella Knightley, *Emma*

*P*ending verification of his story and further enquiry into his gypsy associations, Hiram Deal was committed to the county gaol. Mr. Knightley could not risk such an experienced itinerant fleeing. After thirty years of wandering with a gypsy caravan, the peddler surely knew every cove and corner of England, and Mr. Knightley and Darcy had no doubt of Mr. Deal's success should he take it into his mind to disappear.

As the Darcys crossed Broadway Lane toward their waiting carriage the following morning, Elizabeth recalled her first meeting with the peddler. Though she presumed he possessed a colorful history, she had never imagined it so extraordinary. God forgive her, she was almost glad Mrs. Churchill had met her demise. It was fitting retribution, unjust only in that she died of natural causes while her guiltless husband had been poisoned.

"Are you quite certain you wish to accompany me to Guildford?" Darcy asked. "I should think you could find any number of more pleasant ways to occupy the day."

The street was busy, Highbury already abuzz with word of Hiram

Deal's arrest. Elizabeth would just as soon escape the small village for a time.

"None superior to enjoying your companionship en route; we have had precious little time to ourselves since arriving here. Too, as much as I esteem the Knightleys, I do not mind absenting myself from Hartfield for a considerable portion of the day." She smiled. "If Mr. Woodhouse orders me one more basin of gruel, I fear I shall choke on it." The old gentleman meant well; she had come to realize that his gruel-mongering was a sign of regard. The two of them had developed an odd but congenial rapport. "But explain to me why you need to see Hiram Deal straightaway this morning, when he was just taken to gaol last night."

It had required no small effort to persuade Darcy to allow her to ride with him to Guildford. Gaols were filthy places, breeding chambers for typhus, lice, and all manner of other plague and pestilence. By agreement, she would remain in the carriage while he met with Mr. Deal.

"Mr. Knightley and I did not complete our interrogation. By the time Mr. Deal explained his connexion to the Churchills and Mr. Cole returned, dusk was approaching, and Mr. Knightley wanted Mr. Deal on his way to Guildford before the hour grew late in case any of his gypsy *familia* lurked along the road with notions of liberating him."

Darcy's tone held a shade of derision as he pronounced the gypsy word. Though Elizabeth had been fascinated by Mr. Deal's experience among the Roma and his friendship with Rawnie Zsófia, Darcy was more cynical.

"What else do you wish to ask him?"

When Darcy did not reply, she followed his gaze. Miss Jones had just emerged from Mrs. Todd's house, apparently headed for the Crown Inn to ply her fortune-telling trade. She saw the Darcys, paused, and glanced towards her destination. They stood directly in her path to the Crown; there was no way to avoid them.

Miss Jones straightened her shoulders and continued towards them. "Good day to you," she said in passing.

"Miss Jones—a word, if you please," Darcy said. It was not a request.

Miss Jones stopped. She considered Darcy in silence for a moment. "And if I do not please?"

"I am confident that is not the case."

"Then pray, be quick, for I have business this morning. There are those who will not begin their day until I have looked into their teacups."

"I, too, have business this morning," Darcy said, "with a man who I believe is a mutual acquaintance. How well do you know Hiram Deal?"

"The peddler? Perhaps hardly at all." She tilted her head to one side and regarded Darcy brazenly. "Perhaps very well. Why do you wish to know?"

"I understand he travels with the same gypsy caravan that you claim kidnapped you. I wonder if he might tell a different tale of your experience than the one that you related."

"Hiram came and went. He was not with the caravan when I was taken—we met later."

"And what was your relationship then?"

"Our friendship is . . . an unconventional one. We were the only two English living amongst the gypsies. Infer what you will."

Until that moment, Elizabeth had contemplated only a business relationship between the two—Mr. Deal selling what Miss Jones and the other gypsies stole. Had there been a romantic liaison? Mr. Deal was easily old enough to be Loretta's father, but more disparate unions occurred in all classes of society. The handsome peddler had attracted the interest of many a maid in Highbury.

"Mrs. Darcy! Good morning!"

Elizabeth turned at the familiar voice behind her. Miss Bates approached, carrying a basket covered by a checkered cloth.

"I see you have your carriage. It is a fine day for a drive, is it not? Though a bit cold—I am glad to see you have a blanket with you. We have not had rain for several days, so the roads are plenty dry—that makes such a difference when traveling—dry roads. Mr. Deal and I were just discussing that fact on Sunday, and he would know, traveling as much as he does.—But the most shocking rumor is circulating the village this morning. Our dear Mr. Deal has been taken to gaol!"

"Gaol?" Miss Jones appeared genuinely stricken. The defiance left her countenance. She looked to Darcy. "Is it true? Has Hiram been arrested?"

"He—"

"I learned it straight from Nellie Hopkins, who works in the kitchen at Randalls," Miss Bates said. "I met her early this morning at the bakery. She was sent to fetch baked apples for Jane.—Dear Mrs. Weston! She has been sending her apples to Mr. Wallis for baking ever since I mentioned Jane was partial to them—he does them just right. But what was I saying? Oh, yes! Nellie told me about Mr. Deal. She had it from one of the Randalls housemaids—Hannah—her father is the coachman at Hartfield. An excellent driver, James— whenever Mr. Woodhouse invites my mother and me to Hartfield, James always collects us and brings us home. It was he who drove Mr. Deal to Guildford with Mr. Knightley and Mr. Cole. Nellie was half beside herself. I think she is sweet on Mr. Deal—calf love, you know—eyes big as moons whenever she sees him. She is such a pretty little thing, and says he is so charming towards her."

"Indeed?" Miss Jones's face bore an expression of annoyance. Even Elizabeth, who had more patience for Miss Bates's chatter, wished the spinster could keep to her narrative without so much digression.

"Oh, he is charming towards everybody—even me," Miss Bates continued. "He is such a nice man. I do not know what he was arrested for. If James knows, he did not tell Hannah—as he should not—a good servant keeps his master's business to himself. He only said Hannah should not use a gypsy elixir Mr. Deal had given her. Nellie had one, too, that she bought from him—a love philtre, she said it was. Imagine, believing in such a thing! Oh, to be that young again. Nellie said she did not believe one word against Mr. Deal. Nor do I. This whole business must be a mistake. Yes, I am certain— simply some dreadful, unfortunate mistake that will be rectified as rapidly as possible. Surely Mr. Knightley is taking care of the matter even now. I saw him pass through town very early this morning, looking so businesslike. Doubtless, that was his errand. . . ."

In truth, Mr. Knightley was gone to London in search of the nurse who had attended Hiram Deal's birth. As nearly forty years had passed, he harbored little hope of determining her name, let alone finding her alive, but he needed to at least attempt to locate her. He planned to call upon the Churchills' solicitor as a starting point, and engage the aid of his own brother, a lawyer, as well. Elizabeth wished he and Darcy had traded errands—she would have preferred to accompany Darcy to London, where she could spend time with Lily-Anne while Darcy did his detecting—but Mr. Knightley's status as a magistrate lent him more authority to loosen unwilling tongues.

". . . all most shocking. Why, mere hours before Mr. Cole took him, Mr. Deal was in our parlor—he has visited my mother and me three days this se'nnight. Had a spot of tea with us on Wednesday, and brought us each a rose. Roses in November! They were dried roses, of course, but still so fragrant! I was quite speechless. . . ."

Elizabeth was amazed that anyone could render Miss Bates speechless. She met Darcy's gaze; he looked eager to conclude their interview with Miss Jones and be on their way.

Miss Jones did not appear amused, either. Vexation continued to dominate her features as Miss Bates rattled on.

". . . such an interesting man! I could listen to his tales for hours. He has started to call me 'Bella' when he relates them—it is a little joke between us, you see—instead of 'Bates,' he says 'Bella'—It is Italian for 'beautiful,' he tells me.—'Miss Bella, I have another story for you today.'—I expect he would call my mother 'Mrs. Bella' but she would not quite hear him and it would only confuse her. Oh! Here is Mrs. Elton coming up the lane. I heard you told her fortune, Miss Jones. What an extraordinary hobby! My mother and I only knit. I do not know that I believe one can see the future in a teacup, but there seems no harm in trying."

"A teacup can indeed hold one's fate." Miss Jones regarded Miss Bates appraisingly. "I would be happy to look into yours this morning."

"Would you? Gracious! I cannot imagine you would see anything interesting."

"You might be surprised."

"Well, I—perhaps another morning? I do need to speak with Mrs. Elton. Who is that with her? Oh! I believe it is Mr. Simon.—Indeed, it *is* Mr. Simon. Poor fellow—there is something not altogether right with him, I think. Good day to you, Mrs. Elton! Look—she motions for me to come to her. Oh, I nearly forgot! This basket is for Mr. Deal—bread and a pork pie and a cheese. I simply could not stop thinking about the poor man, cold and hungry in that dreadful gaol. Can you give it to Mr. Knightley, to see that Mr. Deal receives it?"

"I will make sure that it reaches Mr. Deal," Darcy said. Elizabeth, who stood closer, accepted the basket from her.

"Thank you, Mr. Darcy! So kind of you. Do tell him I pray that his health does not suffer while he is there. I understand that gaols are such ill places. Poor man!—Look, Mrs. Elton motions me again. I must go."

"I will walk with you," Miss Jones said.

"That would be lovely. Oh—there is Nellie, going into the Crown. What a list of errands she must have this morning! You can ask her more about Mr. Deal. Good day to you, Mrs. Darcy! Mr. Darcy!"

Miss Jones thus made her escape, and Darcy did not prevent her. They had a fourteen-mile drive to Guildford, and needed to be on their way. Darcy handed Elizabeth into the carriage and soon they were in motion.

Elizabeth set Miss Bates's basket on the seat beside her, along with the blanket they had just purchased at Ford's. "I expect Mr. Deal will appreciate Miss Bates's thoughtfulness."

"He will, indeed."

Elizabeth heard the odd inflection in his tone. Darcy knew too well the conditions Mr. Deal presently suffered. A year ago he had been gaoled for two days on a false accusation. It was an experience he still avoided discussing. But the fact that it had been his idea to bring the blanket for a man who might have been complicit in robbing them, spoke volumes.

She was not sure, however, that even Darcy would do the same for a man he thought was a murderer. "Do you believe Mr. Deal's story about the Churchills?"

He frowned. "I was just asking myself that very question."

"And what was your self's reply?"

"You interrupted at the very moment I was about to find out. Now we shall never know."

The carriage increased its speed as it left the village. Darcy tilted his head back against the seat and let his gaze wander along the roof. "In the matter of his true parentage, all of the principals who could have corroborated his tale are dead, with the possible exception of the nurse—a circumstance rather convenient to Mr. Deal's cause if he is lying."

"Let us assume for the moment that he is indeed their son—that *that* much of his tale is true—the scarlet fever, the gypsy caravan—everything up to his confrontation with Mrs. Churchill. Do you think he is our poisoner? We have only his word that Edgar responded favorably to his revelation. Even if Mr. Deal truly had no interest in the Churchill fortune, people kill for reasons other than money. If Edgar Churchill rejected him, Mr. Deal might have killed him—and tried to kill Frank—out of revenge, or despair. And with an herbalist as his gypsy mother, he is the likeliest of anybody to have access to belladonna."

"That last would be true no matter what his motive."

"Perhaps Mr. Deal *did* do it for the money—and then also tried to kill Frank, the Churchills' heir. Oh! But that makes no sense. Frank's will likely leaves the estate to Jane, so Mr. Deal would have no claim upon it. For Mr. Deal to benefit from Edgar's death, he would have had to wait until he had been written into Edgar's will. The murder took place too early. So if we solely consider money, we are back to Jane Churchill and Mr. Dixon as our chief suspects, and of the two of them, I favor Mr. Dixon. He was not pleased when Miss Jones offered to divine the name of his true love. I think he carries a torch for Jane. Perhaps he intends to fuel it with the Churchill fortune, after she becomes a widow."

Darcy shook his head. "You are mistaken. Frank is not Edgar Churchill's heir."

"Whatever do you mean? The Knightleys said that the Churchills had formally adopted him."

"According to Edgar's solicitor, the will names Frank as his heir only in the absence of a child of Edgar's body. If Mr. Deal is truly Edgar's son—"

"Then when Edgar died, Mr. Deal became the owner of Enscombe." Elizabeth tried to sort out the implications of this unexpected fact. "But does Mr. Deal know that? And is Frank aware of Mr. Deal's identity? It all comes down to how much each suspect knows, and when he learned it. Edgar requested a meeting with his solicitor just before he died. Did he want to write Mr. Deal into the will more formally? Eliminate him from it altogether? Perhaps the meeting was not specifically to discuss the will at all, but to initiate an investigation to confirm Mr. Deal's parentage."

"Regardless of the meeting's purpose, it was in Mr. Deal's financial interest for Edgar Churchill to die before it took place," Darcy said. "He was already the heir; there was nothing more to be gained by the meeting and much to lose if Edgar in fact wanted to write him out. If Mr. Deal knew the terms of the will, he had motive to kill Edgar before those terms could be changed. Though he claims not to want the money, it is now his by default if he can prove his identity."

"And the motive behind Frank's poisoning, if Mr. Deal is guilty of Edgar's?"

"Kill off the pretender for good measure." Darcy frowned in concentration. "Let us skip over Frank as a suspect for the moment and move on to Jane Churchill and Thomas Dixon, or Thomas Dixon acting alone. They are the least likely to know about the 'heir of the body' provision. If we assume their ignorance, they believe their interest lies in first eliminating Edgar, then Frank."

"They are in for a rude surprise when they learn that Mr. Deal's existence has undone all of their careful scheming, if indeed either of them is the poisoner."

"Now to Frank Churchill. Of all the suspects, he is the most likely to know that the will contains the provision, but does Frank know that Mr. Deal is Edgar's son? If so, Frank has no motive for killing Edgar—he is better off trying to persuade his uncle to change the terms of the will to do right by his adopted heir. But if he does *not* know Mr. Deal is Edgar's son—and Mr. Deal says Frank does not—then Frank believes he benefits immediately from Edgar's death. And if he knows about Mr. Deal but does not know about the provision, he believes he benefits by killing Edgar before his uncle can write Mr. Deal *into* the will."

"But in any case, if Frank poisoned Edgar, who poisoned Frank?"

"Perhaps Frank himself? His poisoning was less severe than Edgar's. He could have taken a smaller dose, or pretended the symptoms, to give the appearance that he, too, was a victim. He maintained a secret engagement for months—this would not be the first instance of Frank's acting in deceit to throw suspicion off himself in pursuit of greater gain."

Elizabeth sighed and looked out the window at the passing autumn landscape. "This was simpler when Mr. Deal was merely a friendly traveling peddler."

Darcy handed Mr. Deal the basket and blanket, and endeavored not to touch any surface in the cell or breathe too deeply of its air. Mr. Knightley said there had been no recent cases of gaol-fever in Surrey, but one never knew.

Mr. Deal accepted the gifts with surprise, glancing inside the basket to quickly ascertain its contents. "Thank you, sir. I fair near froze last night, and the food is not fit for swine."

"The basket is not from me, but from Miss Bates."

Mr. Deal's face brightened a little—as much as anything could appear bright in such dismal surroundings. "Indeed?"

"She also sends many wishes for your continued health and a swift resolution to what she is certain must be an extraordinary misunderstanding."

He smiled. "Miss Bates is a lady with a heart full of affection and generosity. It is a shame she has only her mother on whom to expend it. You, too, sir, are most compassionate. The blanket—"

"Yes, well . . ." Darcy coughed, uncomfortable being thanked by a man he had helped incarcerate, and still more disturbed by their present surroundings: an all-too-concrete reminder of the ordeal that had motivated the gift. "I am not come here on a social call. Now that you have admitted the extent of your gypsy associations, I have questions for you regarding our robbery and your acquaintance with Miss Jones."

"I swear to you, sir, I do not have your belongings."

"But you know who does. The thieves were part of your caravan."

"The caravan departed immediately after the robbery."

"Where has it gone?"

"I do not know. I have not been in contact with them."

"Surely you have some notion. How else would you know where to meet the caravan when you wish to rejoin it?"

"Perhaps I do not intend to rejoin it."

"Because you plan to live on Edgar Churchill's fortune?"

"What? No!" He swept his hand as if sweeping away the suggestion. "I told you, I have no interest in his money. I simply grow tired of tramping."

Mr. Deal's earnest expression and manner inclined Darcy to believe him. But Darcy knew that in any conversation with Deal, he could not allow himself to forget that he spoke with a salesman.

"Would you not miss your gypsy mother?"

"I would find a way to see her. Or she would find me."

Though a high, barred window revealed a patch of sky, the cell was dim. The gathering clouds reflected Darcy's mood. If the peddler would not, or could not, offer any information regarding the gypsies' present whereabouts, Darcy would never see the christening garments, or his mother's ring again. The thieves knew they were being hunted. Doubtless, the caravan was far from here.

Though Elizabeth had promised to wait *in* the carriage, it was not long before cramped muscles led her to amend her agreement to *beside* the carriage. Darcy was inside the gaol; he need never know that she had quit their coach for a time to circle the vehicle and breathe fresh air.

Their coachman eyed her askance. "Now, Mrs. Darcy, I am going to be in a world of trouble with your husband if—"

"Nonsense, Jeffrey. I am not going anywhere."

The gaol stood some thirty yards away. Two gaolers guarded its entrance. They appeared ignorant, unclean fellows, distinguished from the prisoners within only by their liberty to leave at the end of their shift. They lounged on tipply wooden stools and occasionally passed between them a flask that Elizabeth doubted contained water.

She gathered her cloak more tightly about her. Though the morning had begun promisingly enough, dark clouds now hung heavy in the sky, threatening rain. As eager as she had been to leave Highbury, she now wished Darcy would hasten his business so they could return.

A woman wandered into view. She was tall, and wore a brightly colored dress that swirled about her legs as she walked. Long, thick black hair streaked with grey hung down her back, tumbling over her dark purple shawl and bound only by the kerchief tied round her head. She carried a basket trimmed in red, gold, and purple, similar to one Elizabeth had seen on Mr. Deal's cart. She walked with purpose towards the gaolers.

Elizabeth could not hear what she said to them, only the mocking laughs they issued in reply.

"He's busy—got a gen'leman with 'im now," said the stouter of the two guards. "But even if he didn't, I'd 'ardly let in the likes of you."

The woman spoke again, gesturing towards her basket.

Elizabeth moved several yards closer. Her footman was beside her in an instant. "Ma'am . . ."

If Darcy questioned her, she was still *near* the carriage. "Hush, Ben. I only want to hear."

The gaoler stood up, knocking over his rickety stool. "Prisoners ain't allowed stuff from outside." He lied—Darcy had walked in carrying both the blanket and Miss Bates's basket without eliciting so much as a second glance. "Whatcha got hidd'n in there—knives'n such?"

His hand darted towards her. The woman quickly stepped back, but not before the gaoler managed to snatch something from the basket. "An apple? Surely y'got somethin' better in there." He took a bite and spat it out at her feet.

"Aw, Joe, can't you see she was saving that for 'im?" The smaller fellow, emboldened by his comrade's bottle-fed bravado, now rose. "What else are you savin' for 'im? Are you his gypsy whore?" He yanked off the woman's kerchief, revealing a greater proportion of grey.

Elizabeth had witnessed enough.

She started towards the entrance. Her footman matched her strides. Behind, she could hear Jeffrey trotting after them.

"Ma'am, surely you are not contemplating—"

"Indeed, I am not contemplating. I am quite decided."

The stout guard barked out a laugh. "She's old for a whore."

"There's no accountin' for some men's taste." The woman tried to grab her kerchief, but the gaoler crumpled it in his grimy fist. "What will you gimme for it?"

"*Sheka.*"

"Gypsy dog!" The guard with the apple threw it at her. It struck hard enough to make the woman stumble. The taunts escalated, slurs so cruel and coarse that Elizabeth's ears burned to hear them.

So engrossed were the gaolers in tormenting the woman that Elizabeth was upon them before they noticed her.

"Is this how Englishmen in service to the king treat a woman?"

The gaolers said nothing in response, but ceased their abuse. The stout guard spat in defiance.

Elizabeth held out her hand, palm up, towards the other gaoler, and fixed him with what she hoped was a commanding stare. Apparently, it was forceful enough, for he surrendered the kerchief. She turned to the woman to give it back to her, and met eyes as black as night.

"*Nais tuke.*"

"You are welcome." Elizabeth gestured towards her coach. "Come with me. We can speak in my carriage."

They started back towards the vehicle, her servants following. The coachman cleared his throat. "Mrs. Darcy, if I may speak freely?"

She paused. "What is it, Jeffrey?"

He cast a wary glance past her shoulder at the gypsy woman. "Are you certain it is wise to invite a . . . a person you do not know . . . into the coach?"

"I appreciate your concern," she said, "but I know perfectly well who this woman is."

Rawnie Zsófia.

Thirty

*"This is a circumstance which I must think of at least half a day,
before I can at all comprehend it."*
                                        —Emma Woodhouse, Emma

*B*racelets clinked and jangled as Rawnie Zsófia stepped into
the carriage. She sat down opposite Elizabeth and assessed
her with an unwavering gaze. Perfume, barely noticeable when they
had been outside, now added to the air a foreign scent Elizabeth
could not identify. Though the coach was Elizabeth's domain, it was
difficult to say which woman occupied the small space with greater
presence.

"So." The gypsy woman set her basket on the floor and adjusted
her skirts. "You are Rawnie Darcy."

"Rawnie?" Elizabeth regarded her in puzzlement. She had thought
"Rawnie" was Zsófia's Christian name. If indeed gypsies were Chris-
tians.

"*Rawnie*—'lady.' Lady Darcy. Or madam, if you prefer." She brought
a hand to her own chest. "The *gorgios* sometimes call me Madam
Zsófia."

"It is simply Mrs. Darcy. I have no title."

"You are more a lady than many who boast the title, Rawnie
Darcy."

Elizabeth wondered how Rawnie Zsófia had known her surname, and asked whether she had divined it.

The old gypsy smiled enigmatically. "If I told you that your name formed in the mist of my crystal ball, would you believe me?"

Elizabeth hesitated.

"Do not answer. I heard your servant address you."

Rawnie Zsófia shook out her kerchief, determined that it was none the worse for having been clutched by a cretin for several minutes, and retied it round her head. Though according to Mr. Deal's tale she must be sixty, she was yet a striking woman. While threescore years and a lifetime of traveling had etched lines in her dark skin, her angular face reflected wisdom as well as age, and her eyes appeared to hold secrets as numerous as Mr. Deal's wares. She gingerly touched her side where the apple had struck.

"Did they injure you?" Elizabeth asked.

"They did nothing I have not endured many times before. But you did not invite me here to talk about Zsófia. You want to talk about my son. What is it you wish to know?" She had a low, mellisonant voice, one that charmed and disarmed its listeners.

"Whether he poisoned Edgar Churchill."

Rawnie Zsófia laughed. The sound blended with her clattering bangles to form its own music. "You are direct. I admire that. So few *gorgios* are. I shall answer you with equal frankness. No, he did not."

"How can you be certain?"

"I know Hram."

"Hram?"

"That is his *nav romano*—his gypsy name. Hram Deal. It was I who gave it to him. It is not a name from the modern Romany tongue, but one formed of older words from the mountains of Romania, whence my mother's people came. It means 'church hill.' The name connected Hram to his past, which I scryed in my ball, and to his future trade, which I read in his hand. He alters it to 'Hiram' when dealing with the *gorgios,* but among us he remains Hram. And Hram, despite having formed in the womb of a cold-blooded *gorgie,* has the heart of a Rom, and could never betray or harm a member of his *familia*— Romano or English."

"He considers himself a gypsy, then?"

"*Nai*. He has learned our ways, and he sells our goods. He sings and dances with us, has celebrated and sorrowed with us. But he is not fully a Rom. Yet he is no longer purely English, either. *Hai shala*—do you understand? From nine to nine-and-thirty, he has divided himself between two worlds, existing in both but belonging to neither. I suspect that is why he has never taken a wife—though I sense, too, that he fears passing to a child the deformity that has so troubled his own life. Hram has a good heart and would make a fine husband to any woman. I know he would never stray, for he does not even accept what some would freely give."

Rawnie Zsófia's last statement brought to Elizabeth's mind the morning's conversation with Miss Jones. "There is a young Englishwoman whom I believe has been traveling with your caravan."

"*Hai*. Loretta. She left the *kumpania* several days ago, I hope to return to her family." Rawnie Zsófia sighed heavily and shook her head. "Her signs are very difficult to read. She is clever but not wise. Passion rules her instead of reason."

"Was she kidnapped, as she claims?"

"*Nai*. She fell in love with a handsome young Rom of our *kumpania* and ran away from her family to be with him. Unfortunately, he did not return her love. She stayed with the caravan, hoping to win him, but he did not want a *gorgie* wife, especially one so headstrong and foolish. Two months ago he married a Romani."

"And yet she continued to travel with the caravan?"

"I counseled her to go back to her own kind. So, too, did Hram. He had been away when she first joined the *kumpania,* but he returned shortly after the young man rejected her. She spent much time with Hram, following him like new pup, and he pitied her. I hoped that since he is English, like her, she would listen to him, but *nai*."

"Did they—were they ever—" Elizabeth faltered, unsure how to delicately phrase her question. They were, after all, discussing Rawnie Zsófia's son.

"Were they lovers? *Nai*. Hram has long been a man, and Loretta, though she has a woman's body, is still very much a child. Perhaps she offered herself—sons, especially grown ones, do not tell their mothers everything, and even the most gifted *drabarni* cannot discern all. But he has no interest in her, save that of offering guidance to a fellow *gorgio*. He helped her understand the ways of the gypsies, but he did not teach her the ways of men and women."

"Did her education in gypsy ways include the art of fortune-telling?"

"She is dukkering for the *gorgios,* is she?" Rawnie Zsófia released a low chuckle. "*Hai,* she asked me to teach her, and I saw that she has the intelligence to learn. But she had not the patience. Learning to read leaves or the cards or a palm takes time. One must know what to look for, and then how to interpret what is seen, and this knowledge comes only through practice. But Loretta, she wanted this understanding instantly. By the gods, she wanted to begin her training with the crystal! She sulked when I said we would start with tea. It was the same when she asked to learn the healer's art. We were not an hour gathering plants when she complained of boredom and went off to watch her young Rom train ravens."

Trained ravens. Elizabeth had suspected that the bird which appeared so conveniently at the time of their robbery had been a party to the conspiracy. She now had confirmation.

Rawnie Zsófia continued. "I do not think Loretta wanted to gain the skill of a *drabarni,* so much as the mystique of one. She is not alone in this. There are many Romani who learn only enough to persuade *gorgios* to part with their money. Loretta found such a one in our *kumpania* to teach her, and was starting to earn a fair number of coins. But it will be luck, not prophecy, if any of her foretellings actually come to pass. When she told Edgar Churchill's fortune, she made such a jumble of it that another *drabarni* had to help her."

"She met Edgar Churchill? When?"

"He came to our camp one afternoon, the day after Hram revealed himself to his father. Another gentleman was with him. I do not know his name."

"How did you know he was Mr. Churchill?"

"My son had told me about his meeting with Churchill the day before, and my tea leaves that morning had told me to expect a visitor named 'C.' But even without that sign, I would have known him for Hram's father."

That Edgar Churchill had visited the gypsy encampment was certainly an interesting turn of events. "Why did Mr. Churchill come?"

"They were not seeking our camp, but when they came upon it, Loretta and a Romani girl persuaded the other gentleman to have his fortune told. Churchill looked uneasy, but also curious. He kept glancing about—maybe he hoped to see Hram, who was away in the village, or maybe he simply feared someone else would pass by and see him talking with gypsies. The girl and Loretta took them aside, and I busied myself nearby so I could observe the man my son had so long yearned to meet.

"Loretta made tea while her friend read the gentleman's palm. After telling that fortune, the girl invited Churchill to give her his palm, but he refused. Loretta encouraged him to drink his tea, and talked very prettily to him, and by the time he finished the tea she had persuaded him to let her read the leaves." Rawnie Zsófia rolled her eyes skyward and shook her head. "Of course, she had no idea what she was looking for. She uttered such nonsense that her friend took the cup from her and added her own forecast, so Churchill would feel that he got something for his coin. But even she seemed unsure. As Churchill and the other gentleman rose to go, one of the ravens flew over to them. It landed beside Churchill and let out a cry that sounded almost like a laugh. The other gentleman was amused, but the bird made Churchill even more uneasy, and they hurried away. I cannot blame him."

"Why?"

"Ravens are bad omens. They nearly always mean trouble. And they often mean death."

A chill passed through Elizabeth, and she burrowed more deeply into her cloak. "Did you warn Mr. Churchill?"

She shook her head. "The true meanings of omens take time to reveal themselves. The raven could be seen as a portent for Hram, that Churchill meant to harm him as his wife had threatened. Until I was sure, I had my son to protect."

Rawnie Zsófia's shawl had slipped. She returned it to her shoulders and started to rise. "The clouds grow thicker, and I have a long walk back to the *kumpania*. I must go."

Elizabeth offered to drive her, but Rawnie Zsófia declined. She allowed the footman to assist her out of the coach, then extended her basket toward Elizabeth.

"I brought my son food, and medicines to keep him well in that unhealthy *staripen*. Will your husband give this to Hram?"

Elizabeth accepted the basket. She could predict Darcy and Mr. Knightley's response. Heaven only knew what the "medicines" might contain, and who they were really intended for. "Only with the magistrate's approval. I will be truthful with you—I doubt Mr. Deal will be allowed to have the medicines. He is suspected of poisoning someone, after all."

"My son is suspected of many things he has not done." She nodded towards the basket. "Look you inside, Rawnie Darcy. You will see." She closed the coach door.

Elizabeth leaned against the seat. The air inside the coach still held the scent of perfume, and her mind whirled with all she had just heard. A few minutes passed before she returned altogether to the present, still more time would be required to absorb what she had learned.

She pulled the basket onto her lap and drew back the cloth that covered its contents. Apples and other foodstuffs filled it, along with several stoppered phials. She removed the food and medicines, setting them on the seat beside her. Another cloth lined the bottom, apparently bunched to form a cushion. She lifted out the cloth and discovered that the fabric did not itself form the cushion, but covered something else.

In the bottom of the basket, carefully folded, lay the Fitzwilliam family christening garments. And on top of them, Lady Anne's signet ring.

Thirty-one

"How animated, how suspicious, how busy their imaginations all are!"

—*Emma Woodhouse,* Emma

id we not agree that you would stay in the carriage?"

The set of Darcy's jaw told Elizabeth that he was not furious. But he was not happy. An unkind thought regarding their servants passed through her mind as the coach lurched into motion. She could not believe they had betrayed her, however good their intentions. "Jeffrey told you?"

"Jeffrey? No. The gaolers saw fit to inform me. They are fine fellows—the very sort from whom one wants to hear reports about one's wife."

"I *was* in the carriage—" He gave her a hard look. "Well, *in view* of the carriage."

"That is hardly the same thing."

"You will be glad I took the liberty, when I tell you what occurred."

The journey back to Highbury passed swiftly as Elizabeth recounted her conversation with Rawnie Zsófia. Thankfully, Darcy's mood improved with each detail.

"So," he said when she had done, "Edgar Churchill visited the gypsy camp on the day he died. I wager the other gentleman was

Thomas Dixon. He was evasive when we asked him where he and Mr. Churchill walked that afternoon."

"But why the secrecy? Does Mr. Dixon simply not want to bear the stigma of a person who associates with gypsies? Does he think he would appear foolish if it were known that he consulted a fortune-teller?" She paused, attempting to imagine the impeccably dressed Thomas Dixon in the midst of a roisterous gypsy camp. "Or did he lead Mr. Churchill there for some reason? Did they truly just happen upon the camp, or did one or both of them deliberately seek the caravan?"

"If either of them went there intentionally, I should think it would have been Edgar Churchill, seeking Mr. Deal."

"Unless Mr. Dixon had intentions of his own. Rawnie Zsófia said that he was entirely willing to have his fortune told that day, yet he refused to let Loretta read his tea leaves two days ago at the Crown. Perhaps he was afraid that the second reading would reveal something about him that he does not want known."

"Or he realized that the only revelation Miss Jones made at the camp was that she is an utter charlatan, and he was wise enough not to be taken in twice. Too, bear in mind that we have only Rawnie Zsófia's account of what occurred in the camp, and she is not to be trusted."

"Because she is a gypsy?"

"That alone is reason enough. But she is also Mr. Deal's mother, and admitted that she protected her son at the expense of Edgar Churchill's safety."

"When did she say that?"

"In regards to the raven's warning."

Though it was dim inside the coach, Elizabeth beheld him with astonishment. "And when did Fitzwilliam Darcy start believing in omens?"

"I do not. But if Rawnie Zsófia does, then declining to act upon what she perceived as a warning bespeaks a less than honorable character. And if this renowned fortune-teller does not believe in portents, she is a greater fraud than Miss Jones. Either way, she is guilty of deceit and could be guilty of more. Indeed, she herself could very well be the poisoner. Of all the suspects, she alone possesses expert knowledge of herbs, and now we know she had the opportunity to administer the poison hours before Edgar Churchill died."

"But she had no direct interaction with Mr. Churchill while he was at the camp."

"So she claims. As I said, we have no reason to trust her."

Though Elizabeth followed Darcy's logic, she could not deny her own instincts. Darcy had not met Rawnie Zsófia; he had only cold reason and secondhand accounts to guide his interpretation of her. While Elizabeth remained cautious, she was not unwilling to believe that Zsófia's words contained at least some truth. She considered the return of the baptismal clothes and signet ring an act of good faith— a development she had not yet shared with Darcy.

"We started discussing Edgar Churchill's visit to the gypsy camp before I reached the most surprising part of my conversation with Rawnie Zsófia."

"Did she tell *your* fortune?"

"No, she left this basket." It remained beside her on the seat. Elizabeth had repacked it with the most interesting article on top, protected by the cloth cover.

"I just delivered Miss Bates's. Are we starting a collection?"

"This one was also intended for Mr. Deal, but it contains something for us, as well."

"Indeed?" He said no more, but the tone of his voice conveyed in that single word the full measure of his skepticism.

"See for yourself."

Darcy grasped the basket by its handle and brought it beside him. Casting Elizabeth a dubious look, he lifted the cover.

And suddenly looked up at her again. "The christening set?"

"And your mother's ring." She removed her glove. "I put it on my finger for safekeeping."

He leaned forward, took her hand, and examined the ring as best he could in the dismal light. "It appears undamaged." Though done with his inspection, he retained her hand. His knees brushed against hers as the coach jostled. "What explanation did she give?"

"None. She was gone before I found them in the bottom of the basket. She said only that Mr. Deal was suspected of many things of which he is not guilty."

"His mother had our stolen belongings in her possession. I would say that connects him rather strongly with the theft."

"Unless she obtained them herself from the thieves in order to return them to us."

"Why would she do that?"

"Perhaps to win our goodwill toward her son? To demonstrate that gypsies—some, at least—are acquainted with honor?"

"Or to distract us from the more heinous crime of Edgar Churchill's murder."

"Or that," she conceded. "Whatever her motive, we have recovered our possessions, which means that as soon as Edgar Churchill's poisoner is identified, we can collect our daughter and Georgiana, and finally join Anne and Colonel Fitzwilliam at Brierwood."

"You could go now. Jeffrey can drive you to London tomorrow to retrieve Lily-Anne and my sister, then take all of you to Brierwood whenever you wish. I will meet you there when this Churchill matter is resolved."

She was tempted, but shook her head. Her place was with Darcy.

"Mrs. Knightley would never forgive me," she said. "I would return in a month to find the case still unsolved, and you and Mr. Knightley discussing husbandry over spruce beer."

"Thank goodness you have returned."

Had Mrs. Knightley not said a word upon their arrival at Hartfield, Darcy would have seen in her face that something had changed. He and Elizabeth hastily removed their cloaks and followed her to the drawing room. She shut the doors.

"Mr. Perry was here earlier," she said. "He came directly from Randalls, where one of the maids is ill. He suspects belladonna."

"Will she recover?" Elizabeth asked.

"Mr. Perry is confident. He treated her as he did Frank Churchill, and she is already improved. Like Frank, she is young and of stronger constitution than Edgar Churchill was."

"Who is she?" Darcy asked.

"One of the kitchen girls—Nellie."

The maid Mrs. Bates had been talking about that morning. "Does Mr. Perry have any notion how she might have ingested the poison?"

"He says she imbibed a philtre she had obtained from Mr. Deal."

Darcy could scarcely comprehend anybody's being so foolish. "Why would she do that, knowing he had been arrested?"

"Young girls do unwise things," Elizabeth said.

"Apparently, she meant to prove to some of the other servants that Mr. Deal is innocent of any wrongdoing," Mrs. Knightley explained. "While in the village earlier today, she asked Miss Jones for a tea leaf reading, and when that failed to produce the 'evidence' she hoped for, she went back to Randalls and drank the whole phial."

"Good heavens!" Elizabeth looked down at the signet ring on her finger. "I had wanted to believe him guiltless."

So had Darcy. "Mr. Deal might not be the poisoner. It could be his mother. She shares at least some of the guilt—by Mr. Deal's own admission, she was the one who prepared the remedies he sold."

"I cannot believe that of her." Elizabeth glanced at Mrs. Knightley. "I met Rawnie Zsófia, Mr. Deal's gypsy mother, today, while Mr. Darcy was in conference with Mr. Deal." At Mrs. Knightley's expression of astonishment, she continued. "I will tell you more about our interview later, but she did not impress me as a capricious person." Elizabeth turned back to Darcy. "Why would she poison people randomly? Edgar Churchill, I can understand, if she thought she was somehow protecting her son. Frank Churchill, I can understand—he grew up in the privilege that was by right Mr. Deal's. But a naïve kitchen maid infatuated with a handsome peddler? I fail to comprehend why either Mr. Deal or his mother would harm her, or sell tainted physics to the village at large."

"Perhaps the philtre was meant for someone else and accidentally found its way into her hands," Darcy said. "Or it was unknowingly contaminated with belladonna while the poison was being prepared for the Churchills. Regardless, it implicates Mr. Deal, which means I will be making another trip to Guildford to question him. And this time I will travel alone." He did not want to chance Elizabeth's having another private encounter with Rawnie Zsófia. She might not survive it.

"Mr. Knightley might go with you," Mrs. Knightley said. "As soon as Mr. Perry suspected that Nellie had been poisoned, we sent an express to London. If I know my husband, he will lose no time returning here to attend to this latest incident himself."

Darcy would prefer Mr. Knightley's companionship. In truth, he would prefer to not immediately climb back into the carriage for another journey to Guildford. He consulted his watch. "I do not want to delay too long. Among other questions, we need to ask Mr. Deal how many remedies he sold in Highbury and to whom. If Mr. Knightley has not returned in two hours, I shall go without him. Meanwhile, Mr. Perry should advise the villagers against trusting any preparations purchased from Mr. Deal, if they have not already used them."

"We can stop at the apothecary shop to see him on our way to speak with Miss Jones," Elizabeth said.

"He is not there," Mrs. Knightley replied. "He has gone back to Randalls to check on his patient. However, he promised to stop here again with a report. I will convey your recommendation about warning the villagers."

"We also need to talk to Thomas Dixon. Is he here?"

"No, he is gone to London to see about Miss Bates's new furniture."

Was nobody in Highbury today? "When he returns, try to keep him here until we have an opportunity to question him. It seems he knows more about Edgar Churchill's final hours than he has admitted."

As Darcy and Elizabeth waited for their cloaks, Mrs. Knightley suddenly recalled another matter for Darcy's attention. "In all the business about Nellie, I nearly forgot—a letter arrived for you. Actually, it was addressed to both you and Mr. Knightley." She went to retrieve it and returned directly.

Darcy knew the hand at once.

Gentlemen,

I am delighted to be of service in your investigation, particularly in regards to this most intriguing clue. I assure you of my discretion, as well as that of the young philologist to whom I referred your query. Mr. Atwell has a keen interest in lexicography; indeed, I believe he means to be the next Samuel Johnson. I enclose herewith his reply. You will see that although he offers several possible meanings for "unkind individual," he decidedly favors one. Mr. Atwell believes the writer's employment of the collective noun for crows to denote "murder" suggests the use of the same strategy in the earlier portion of the message. For my part, although I find it fascinating to learn that a group of ravens is called an "unkindness"—an altogether fitting term for the gloomy creatures—I fail to see how that information can possibly aid your quest. Shall I present the message to another connoisseur of language? I know a professor at Oxford who might be consulted. Consider me at your disposal. I am—

Yours sincerely,
Chatfield

Thirty-two

*It was the very event to engage those who talk most, the young and
the low; and all the youth and the servants in the place were soon
in the happiness of frightful news.*

—Emma

*P*erhaps a raven witnessed the murder of Churchill."
The fully revealed message sent a shiver through Elizabeth
as she spoke it aloud. "If the riddle is true, the raven did not merely
portend Edgar Churchill's death—the poisoning occurred at the
camp."

"I do not understand," said Mrs. Knightley. "Do you speak of the
bird that appeared during your robbery?"

"Yes, or one kept by the same individuals—Rawnie Zsófia said that
the gypsies train them," Elizabeth replied. "Regardless, Edgar Churchill
and Thomas Dixon visited the gypsy camp several hours before your
party, and while they were there, a raven took particular notice of
Mr. Churchill."

"Madam Zsófia must have found an opportunity to administer the
poison to Edgar Churchill while he was there," Darcy said. "Perhaps
through one of her physics."

"But Miss Jones said that while the gypsies camped outside of
Highbury, no English came to Rawnie Zsófia for healing."

"Since when have we considered Miss Jones a trustworthy source of information? Moreover, I believe she said that none had come to the camp for that purpose—which does not mean that no one came for a different purpose, and received treatment while there."

The servant appeared with their cloaks. As Elizabeth donned hers, she pondered a point that had been troubling her. "We have neglected to consider the second poisoning—Frank's, which occurred several days after the gypsies quit Highbury. Perhaps the poison was not given directly while Edgar Churchill was at the camp, but sent home with him and taken afterwards."

"Self-administered?" Darcy asked.

"Or administered by Thomas Dixon."

"I cannot believe that of him," said Mrs. Knightley. "If Mr. Dixon is guilty of any crime, it is idleness. Or perhaps too great an attention to fashion."

"Well, someone is guilty of murder," Darcy said. "And someone else knows more than he or she has said, because the raven did not write that riddle. It is now even more critical that we talk to Miss Jones and Thomas Dixon about what occurred at the gypsy camp. Perhaps with three versions of events, we can begin to piece together what actually happened."

The Darcys were very nearly deterred from interviewing Miss Jones by the sight of Miss Bates approaching Mrs. Todd's house at the same time as they.

Darcy emitted a low groan. "If that lady takes hold of the conversation, we shall never get it back."

Elizabeth feared the same thing. She had come to believe that Miss Bates could talk for an hour without pausing for breath. They did not have an hour to waste.

"I shall take care of Miss Bates."

She deemed it best to seize the initiative. "Good afternoon to you, Miss Bates! How delightful to meet you again. Is your business with Mrs. Todd, I hope? For we were hoping for a private consultation with Miss Jones."

"Oh! Mr. and Mrs. Darcy! You are returned from Guildford! I

was—" She glanced at the door on which she had been about to knock, then back at them apologetically. "I came to see Miss Jones myself. I thought perhaps she could tell me about Mr. Deal— whether the terrible things I hear are true. Why, people are saying he poisoned poor Nellie, and probably Frank and Mr. Churchill. Oh, Mrs. Darcy! He cannot have poisoned Frank—or anybody—can he? I will not believe it of him. Not our Mr. Deal! I thought perhaps Miss Jones could read it in the tea leaves, or something.—It is nonsense, I know—fortune-telling—but I simply have not been able to stop thinking about it all. I found a note from Mr. Deal today.—Nothing improper, mind you.—Gracious, it is years since a note to me from any man might excite speculation!—He must have left it before all the unpleasantness."

"May I ask what it said?" Darcy enquired.

"Oh, he thanked me and Mother for the tea we shared on Sunday. It should more properly have been addressed to my mother, or to us both, I suppose, but it was thoughtful nonetheless. He is all consideration, Mr. Deal—though he forgets it was Wednesday we had the tea, not Sunday. Men do not have the memory for such details that we women do—is that not true, Mrs. Darcy? Pray, forgive my saying so, sir. I only mean it in good nature. But you have seen Mr. Deal, yes? How does he get on?"

"As well as can be expected," Elizabeth said, "and he thanks you for the basket."

"Oh!" A smile spread across her face. "I am so glad! I—"

"In fact," Elizabeth continued, "if you care to send anything else by Mr. Darcy tomorrow, he would be happy to accept the commission."

Miss Bates looked to Mr. Darcy. "Would you? Oh! Perhaps I should—why, yes—I shall gather some more things together right now, and you can bring them whenever you next go there. Will you be long with Miss Jones?"

"We have several errands this afternoon," Elizabeth said. "I will call for the parcel in the morning."

Miss Bates departed in happy occupation—leaving them in happy solitude. Darcy looked at Elizabeth with admiration.

"That was well done."

Their luck held: Miss Jones was at home. Mrs. Todd invited the Darcys to wait in the small sitting room, then sent her daughter to summon Loretta. Alice returned a minute later to report that Miss Jones would be down to receive them directly. The child then hung about, staring at their visitors to the point where Mrs. Todd gave her a coin and dispatched her to the post office to see whether any letters had arrived from her brothers.

"She goes every day," Mrs. Todd explained when the child had scampered off. "Since my younger son followed his brother into the militia, posting my letters or calling for theirs has become her special responsibility." The landlady then busied herself in the kitchen, leaving the Darcys to themselves.

As they waited for Miss Jones to appear, Elizabeth wondered whether Mrs. Todd could possibly fit one more item of bric-à-brac into the tight space. Little figurines, small pieces of china, and trinkets littered every horizontal surface, each one seeming to call, chirp, or cry out for notice. She could not imagine Mr. Todd, whatever manner of man he had been, living in this cacophony of clutter. Darcy looked entirely out of place. She felt crowded herself.

Miss Jones took so long about appearing that Elizabeth was not without anxiety that the girl might have fled, but at last she found her way to them. She greeted them with a breezy "good day" and an insouciant smile, and sat down on the edge of the chair nearest the door.

"We are pleased to find you at leisure to see us," Elizabeth said. "We had feared you would be too busy peering into teacups at the Crown."

"I was on my way over there, in fact," she replied. "The present situation has the village at sixes and sevens, so many are seeking my insight."

"Present situation?" Darcy asked.

"Mr. Deal's arrest, and a poisoner about." She rose to rescue a soldier statuette standing at attention precariously close to the edge of a shelf. She slid it back several inches to keep watch beside a painted cat with a chipped ear. "First the Churchills, now a maid—my customers want to know if they will be next."

"If they fear being poisoned, Mr. Deal's arrest ought to reassure them."

"Only if he is indeed the poisoner."

"Do you believe him innocent?" Elizabeth asked. "You know him better than anybody, I suppose, having traveled in the caravan with him."

Miss Jones appeared gratified by this acknowledgment. "I do, indeed, and he is not a treacherous man. I blame the gypsies."

"I thought the gypsies have left the neighborhood?"

"They have, so far as I know." She adjusted a china creamer shaped like a dairy cow. "But they are a devious lot—one among them in particular. I told you, they have an old woman who claims to be a healer. Madam Zsófia knows everything about plants and poisons, and she is secretive and stingy with her knowledge. And Madam Zsófia dislikes the English. I would not be at all surprised if she gave Hiram poisoned physics to sell unknowingly to innocent villagers."

"Did she poison Edgar Churchill when he visited the gypsy camp?"

Loretta accidentally bumped the cow against another figurine, knocking a shepherd boy onto his back. She murmured an indistinguishable word and righted the shepherd. When she turned to face them, she wrapped her arms in front of her as if she were cold.

"I am afraid she might have. She was hovering around us—she probably slipped it to him when nobody realized."

" 'Us'—who else was there?"

"Mr. Dixon and another gypsy woman. There were more gypsies in the camp, but they left us to ourselves. All but Madam Zsófia."

"Why did you not mention Mr. Churchill's visit when we last asked you about him?" Elizabeth said.

"Because Madam Zsófia is a frightful old hag! I am afraid even now that she will somehow know what I told you and put a curse on me."

Elizabeth had hardly considered Rawnie Zsófia an old hag, though she imagined the master *drabarni* could indeed create a frightening presence if she wished. "She cannot hear us; I am sure you are safe."

"Even so . . . I would not cross her."

Darcy lifted a carved wooden cottage off the table beside him and turned it over in his hands. "Why did Edgar Churchill and Mr. Dixon come to the camp?"

"To have their fortunes told."

Darcy pretended to examine the carving; Elizabeth knew that knick-knacks held no attraction for him. "If Mr. Dixon was so interested in prognostication that he strolled out of the village to find the camp"— he traced his finger along the miniature roofline, then looked up at Miss Jones—"why, then, did he refuse to let you tell his fortune when he came upon you in such a convenient place as the Crown?"

"I can read tea leaves and palms, not a person's thoughts. You shall have to ask him. Perhaps he is afraid of what I might reveal."

"What was revealed at the gypsy camp?"

She shrugged. "That a death would bring him money."

Elizabeth tried to gauge Darcy's response to that interesting little prediction, but his attention remained on Miss Jones.

"And Mr. Churchill's tea leaves?"

"I could not make them out."

"Why not?"

"I do not know." She recrossed her arms. "Even Madam Zsófia cannot always read the signs."

"Did Madam Zsófia attempt to read theirs?"

"No."

Darcy set the wooden cottage back on the table. "When, then, was she in close enough proximity to slip Edgar Churchill the poison?"

Loretta stared at him a moment, blinking. "At one point, he seemed in some discomfort and said he was bothered by gout. Maybe she overheard and followed them afterwards to give him one of her concoctions."

Additional questions yielded little else, and they were conscious of time passing. They soon left to see whether Mr. Knightley had returned from London.

"To hear Miss Jones describe Mr. Deal's gypsy mother, Baba Yaga is come to England," Darcy said as they headed back to Hartfield. "I half expected her to tell us that Madam Zsófia rides through the night in a mortar and pestle, stealing children."

Elizabeth, too, thought Loretta's description greatly exaggerated.

"When I met Rawnie Zsófia, she did not look like an old Russian witch from legend."

Darcy glanced at the gloomy blanket of clouds above; Elizabeth hoped the rain would hold off until he had completed his second trip to Guildford.

"Perhaps not." Darcy's tone matched the weather. "But she is increasingly looking like a murderess."

Thirty-three

"A vast deal may be done by those who dare to act."
—*Mrs. Elton,* Emma

*M*r. Knightley returned to Hartfield just as Darcy was preparing to leave for Guildford. After a brief update from Mr. Perry on the maid's condition and a summary of Darcy's findings just detailed enough to convey the necessity of another gaol visit, Mr. Knightley traded Hartfield's coach for Darcy's, and both gentlemen began their second long journey of the day. The only thing that might be said in favor of the drive was that it provided an opportunity for Darcy to more fully recount the day's conversations with Mr. Deal, Madam Zsófia, and Miss Jones, and to share the letter from Lord Chatfield. Mr. Knightley had nothing to report of his investigation into Mr. Deal's birth; he had only just begun when Mr. Perry's message brought him home.

"In light of these new developments," Mr. Knightley said when Darcy had done, "you lean, then, towards Mr. Deal or Madam Zsófia as the poisoner?"

"I still want to talk to Mr. Dixon again, and I have not altogether eliminated Frank Churchill, but . . . yes. Mr. Deal's participation might prove unwitting, but his mother's involvement would be entirely deliberate."

Darcy paused. Elizabeth, perhaps beguiled by Madam Zsófia's gypsy charms, favored Thomas Dixon as the killer. He admitted as much to Mr. Knightley. "I cannot discount Mrs. Darcy's opinion," he added. "She is the only one who has met and spoken with Madam Zsófia, and my wife's instincts have served us well in the past."

Mr. Knightley nodded. "Mrs. Knightley also has her own views on the matter. She will not hear a word against Thomas Dixon, or Frank Churchill, and still harbors hope that her favorite peddler will be exonerated. I think she would very much like to see this crime laid at Madam Zsófia's feet."

"And you?"

Mr. Knightley gazed out the window at the dimming landscape. "I am trying to withhold judgment until we learn all we can."

By the time they reached Guildford, both men were weary, hungry, and thoroughly tired of the insides of coaches. They were also not inclined towards pleasantries when Mr. Deal was at last before them in the private but dreary room they were granted for the interrogation. Barely had the peddler's face registered surprise at seeing Darcy for the second time that day—with another basket, no less—than Mr. Knightley motioned him onto a splintery wooden chair beside the table, sat down on an equally suspect seat across from him, and commenced the interview.

"Mr. Deal, is your mother—your gypsy mother—familiar with belladonna?"

Mr. Deal regarded Mr. Knightley warily. He glanced up to Darcy, who remained impassive, then back at the magistrate.

"Of course she is. I would venture to say that Rawnie Zsófia knows every plant that grows in England, and many that do not."

"Did she share her knowledge with you?"

"She did not formally train me as a healer—she saw that my talents lay elsewhere. But she taught me some rudiments, that I might tend to myself if the need arose. And she taught me to identify many plants in regions through which we regularly passed."

"Was belladonna among them?"

"Aye. In fact, it was one of the first. Gypsy travelers often forage to feed themselves, and when I joined the *kumpania,* my mother taught me which plants were poisonous and which were not. She especially made sure I could identify belladonna—she did not want me or any other child in the caravan to be tempted by its sweet berries, or mistake them for something else."

Mr. Knightley regarded the peddler in consternation. "Are you telling me that from childhood, every member of the caravan can recognize belladonna?"

"I expect so."

The magistrate rubbed his temples. Darcy nearly did the same. Their pool of suspects had just expanded exponentially.

However, the number with clear motive remained finite. "We have been told that Edgar Churchill and Thomas Dixon visited the gypsy camp the day Mr. Churchill died," Darcy said. "Did Madam Zsófia speak of the event to you?"

If Mr. Deal feigned his look of astonishment, the peddler was a better player than many on stage. "No—I knew nothing about it. From whom did you hear this?"

"Madam Zsófia herself."

"You have spoken with my mother?"

Darcy handed him Madam Zsófia's basket, from which the medicines had been removed. "This is from her."

His face still all amazement, Mr. Deal accepted the basket but did not examine its contents.

"We would like to speak with Madam Zsófia further," Mr. Knightley said. "Where might she be found?"

"With the caravan, I assume."

"And where is the caravan?"

Mr. Deal turned to Darcy. "As I told you this morning, I do not know." He ran his hand through his hair. "By the gods, I would like to speak to her myself. I cannot believe my mother met with Edgar Churchill and did not tell me. Are you certain you understood her correctly?"

"Miss Jones has confirmed it."

"Loretta met him, too?" He stared at them, his expression transforming from surprise to dismay. "What—" His gaze drifted along the cell walls as if answers to the questions tumbling through his mind might be found etched in the cold stone. Then he closed his eyes and swallowed. "What occurred?"

"Allegedly, the two gentlemen had their fortunes told."

"By my mother?"

"By Miss Jones and another girl."

Mr. Deal's eyes opened, but he did not look at either gentleman. He stared instead at a large knothole at the edge of the table, though Darcy doubted Mr. Deal even saw it. "What was my mother's contact with Edgar Churchill?"

"We hoped you could tell us. Miss Jones claims he complained of the gout. What might Madam Zsófia have given him for it?"

Mr. Deal thought for a moment. "Tansy root." He looked at Mr. Knightley. "Preserved in honey. Gout is not a common ailment among members of our caravan, but I sell many preparations of tansy root to *gorgios*. I believe I sold one to you, Mr. Darcy. It is not a cure that works immediately, however—one must take the remedy daily for it to have effect."

Mr. Perry had said the gout remedy Darcy purchased was indeed tansy. "She could have given him anything and told him it was a cure for gout. Including belladonna."

"She would not do that!" Mr. Deal said.

"Are you certain?" Darcy countered. "Particularly if she thought she was protecting you?"

"From my father?"

"From his rejection. Or from want—perhaps she intended to secure your inheritance."

"I told you, the Roma do not think that way."

"Maybe one does," Mr. Knightley said. "One who has lived amongst them but is not truly a gypsy."

Mr. Deal turned his head sharply to stare at Mr. Knightley. "What do you mean?"

"If Madam Zsófia did not poison Edgar Churchill, perhaps you did. You just admitted that you sold many gout remedies—or something passing for gout remedies—to *gorgios*."

"Not to him." Mr. Deal slowly shook his head. "And none of the remedies I sold were anything but what I claimed."

"If you did not prepare them yourself, how can you be certain?"

Thirty-four

A mind like hers, once opening to suspicion, made rapid progress.
                                                           —Emma

*E*mma wished Mr Knightley had not needed to rush off to Guildford nearly the moment he returned from London. In the wake of his abrupt departure, it had taken some effort to convince Mr. Woodhouse that his son-in-law was quite safe and not out personally nabbing gypsies. If only she could assure herself of that fact.

There being only three remaining at Hartfield—Emma, her father, and Mrs. Darcy—dinner was a quiet event. After the meal, Emma anticipated a long evening spent diverting her father with games of backgammon or cards. But Mr. Woodhouse surprised her by announcing his intention to retire to his chamber for the night. She immediately became anxious for his health.

"No, my dear, I am fine. Only a little tired, is all. When Perry was here earlier, he asked me whether I had been sleeping well, and I said how could anybody, with all these gypsies about? He made me promise to retire early tonight. So I am off to bed."

Emma could not imagine anybody's being able to fall asleep this early and hoped her father, in his determination to follow Mr. Perry's advice, was not consigning himself to hours spent fretting in the dark about trampers stealing his poultry.

She saw him comfortably settled in his chamber, and after assuring herself that he would indeed drift off to sleep, went to the drawing room. Mrs. Darcy stood at one of the windows.

"Has the rain started?" Emma asked. She had not heard any drops falling, but it had threatened all day.

Mrs. Darcy started and turned round. "What? Oh—no, it has not. I beg your pardon—I did not hear you enter." She moved away from the window and sat down on a chair near the fire. "I was contemplating something Miss Bates said this afternoon, though it might be entirely insignificant."

"If Miss Bates said it, it probably was." Emma took the seat opposite her. "However, tell me anyway."

"She mentioned that she had just found a note from Mr. Deal, and assumed he had left it at her door sometime before his arrest. But were that so, would she not have discovered it earlier? We encountered her in Broadway Lane this morning, and she had already been to the bakery and back to pack a basket for Mr. Deal. Surely she would have seen the letter lying there?"

Emma found it rather curious that Miss Bates should be sending anything to the peddler, as she suffered such straitened circumstances herself. But Miss Bates had a kind heart, and even in her own want shared what she could with those less fortunate.

"Miss Bates lives for letters. I cannot imagine that a note from anybody would have repeatedly escaped her notice." The room was cold; Emma rose and stirred the fire. "Indeed, I am surprised she did not recite it verbatim when she spoke of it later. Or did she?"

"No, she said only that he thanked her for the tea he had shared with her and Mrs. Bates on Sunday."

"Mr. Deal has been taking tea with the Bateses?" Even more curious. Was he on such familiar terms with other customers?

Emma sank back into her seat as the most extraordinary thought took hold. Was Mr. Deal wooing Miss Bates? Impossible! But . . . taking tea at her house . . . small little gifts . . . writing to her—a practice decidedly improper unless a couple were engaged. . . .

Could it be? It would not be the first instance of a courtship having advanced right before her eyes without her realizing it. But—independent of his status as a murder suspect—he was entirely unsuitable! A peddler—an itinerant—raised by gypsies!

It was inconceivable that a respectable lady such as Miss Bates—a clergyman's daughter, no less—could consider such a disreputable character. Even if he were cleared of the murder, even if his claims upon the Churchill name proved true, he had no claim upon the Churchill fortune. It belonged to Frank. Was Miss Bates—Mrs. Hiram Deal—to tramp across England with him, living out of his cart? The notion was absurd.

Still more absurd, however, was Mr. Deal's interest in Miss Bates. With every scullery maid and farmer's daughter in the village making eyes at the man, what attraction did a windy spinster hold for him? He could not possibly have fallen violently in love with her.

Did he prey upon her sentiments for some ulterior purpose?

Emma realized that she yet held the fire poker. She rose and replaced it, but did not sit back down.

"Mrs. Darcy, I am suddenly quite interested in that letter myself. Would you care to take a drive with me?"

Thirty-five

*M*r. Knightley withdrew a notebook and pencil from his pocket. "I want a list of every person in Highbury to whom you sold any sort of remedy—a physic, tincture, ointment, infusion—anything purportedly medicinal."

Mr. Deal regarded him incredulously. "I do not know the name of every single customer."

"No, but you know some of them quite well—such as the maid Nellie, who spent half her wages buying philtres from you and who is now abed with belladonna poisoning."

"Nellie? Poisoned!" Mr. Deal looked genuinely horrified. "Will she recover?"

"We believe so."

"There are others to whom you have given particular attention," Darcy said. "What is your design on Miss Bates?"

"Miss Bates? Why, nothing at all unseemly. I meant only kindness."

"Nothing unseemly?" Mr. Knightley said. "Everything perfectly proper? Such as corresponding with her—an unmarried lady?"

"We are not corresponding."

"Miss Bates told me this morning that she had received a letter from you," Darcy said.

"What are you talking about? I wrote no letter to Miss Bates."

"You did not leave her a note thanking her for the tea you took together on Sunday?"

"No, though perhaps I ought to have. But it was only Wednesday—yesterday—that we had tea and"—he gestured at his surroundings—"I have been a little occupied."

Darcy noted Deal's memory for dates, which coincided with Miss Bates's account. The letter's author had erred; Mr. Deal had not. Who, then, had written the letter? And to what purpose? Why would anybody trouble himself to forge a thank-you note?

Unless it was not a thank-you note.

Someone in the village had sent three letters to Hartfield with hidden meanings. Though Mrs. Elton had admitted to writing the first, he could not credit her with the others. Had Miss Bates's note been authored by the writer of the latter two? Was it not a simple thank-you, but another word puzzle?

Darcy drew Mr. Knightley aside. In a low voice, he shared his conjecture. Mr. Deal watched them with open interest, making no attempt to pretend he was not trying to hear their conversation.

"We need to see that note," Darcy finished.

"We will call upon her tomorrow as early as possible."

"I think you should go now," Mr. Deal said.

The peddler's impertinence took Darcy aback. "I do not recall our having solicited your opinion."

"I give it to you freely." He leaned towards them on the rickety chair. "Gentlemen, someone has murdered my father, attempted to kill my cousin, and poisoned an innocent young girl. Now a fraudulent letter bearing my name has appeared at the home of one of the few people in Highbury who has extended friendship—honest, disinterested friendship—towards me. This letter concerns you enough that you suspended your interrogation of me to discuss it between yourselves. I have told you that I am not the criminal you seek, told you in so many ways that I do not think there is another manner of expressing it. Yet you waste your time here with me while Miss Bates might even now be in danger. I beg you—set off without delay for Broadway Lane to examine the note and ensure that good lady's safety. If you insist on continuing this interview, we can do so another time." He motioned towards the stone walls with a defeated shrug. "I am not going anywhere."

Mr. Knightley turned to Darcy and nodded. "He speaks sense. We can finish this tomorrow, after we have determined more about the letter and taken steps to protect Miss Bates, if necessary."

Much as Darcy hesitated to trust the peddler, any threat he posed was contained by prison bars—while if the poisoner yet roamed free, Miss Bates was not the only person at risk. "Let us go directly."

Mr. Knightley approached the door to signal the guard. Mr. Deal rose.

"Mr. Knightley—"

He turned back to the peddler. "Yes?"

"I do not suppose, sir, that you would contemplate taking me with you?"

At the magistrate's startled gasp, Mr. Deal held up his palm. "Pray, do not dismiss the idea yet. Only consider—I might be able to help. That letter allegedly came from me; it was almost certainly written by someone familiar with my movements. If I were to examine it, I might find something in it that you cannot."

Mr. Deal also might use the opportunity to lead their investigation further astray. Or to escape. Or worse. "We can bring the letter back with us if we believe his perspective would prove useful," Darcy said to Mr. Knightley.

"How many trips to Guildford do you want to make?" Mr. Deal responded. "At the expense of valuable time?"

"Is it not rather late to be calling upon the Bates ladies unanticipated?" Elizabeth asked as she and Mrs. Knightley negotiated the dark staircase that led to the apartment. She was anxious herself to see Mr. Deal's letter, cherishing faint hope that it might somehow illuminate larger questions about the peddler, but she did not want to incommode or intrude upon the older women.

"Trust me, they will be grateful for the company."

Mrs. Knightley knocked upon the door. Voices within indicated that at least one other visitor was with the ladies. She and Mrs. Knightley were not only intruding, Elizabeth thought ruefully, but also unlikely to obtain a glimpse of the letter depending upon who was present.

Miss Bates was delighted by their arrival. "Oh, do come in! Mother, look who has come! It is Mrs. Knightley and Mrs. Darcy. You remember Mrs. Darcy? *Darcy*. What an impromptu little party we are forming! Mrs. Darcy, can you guess who else is here?" She moved aside to allow them passage into the apartment.

At the tea table sat Miss Jones.

Elizabeth endeavored to disguise her chagrin. Loretta Jones was the last person before whom she wanted to broach the subject of Mr. Deal's letter. She still did not know quite what to make of the relationship between the young woman and the peddler. Though Rawnie Zsófia had refuted any romantic attraction on Mr. Deal's part, Loretta's words this morning suggested a rather proprietary interest in the man.

Miss Jones seemed equally discomposed by Elizabeth and Mrs. Knightley's appearance in the apartment. She forced a laugh. "How very unexpected, Mrs. Darcy, to see you again today."

"Indeed. I had no idea you were a friend of Miss Bates."

"My mother and I were just getting better acquainted with Miss Jones," Miss Bates said. "Do sit down."

The parlor looked much the same as it had upon Elizabeth's last visit, right down to old Mrs. Bates knitting in her customary place. Apparently, Thomas Dixon had not yet implemented any of his grand plans for the room. Elizabeth wondered whether the elderly lady was among the few furnishings he would allow Miss Bates to keep.

Miss Bates adjusted her mother's lap blanket. "Are you warm enough, Mother? To me it feels quite warm over here by the fire, but I know you are often cold. Do you need your shawl? Your *shawl*? No? Do but say the word if you change your mind." She drifted back towards the tea table, where a pair of cups, one overturned onto its saucer, rested near a small pot. "Miss Jones has come to tell my fortune. You have arrived just in time to hear it."

Elizabeth supposed the fortune-telling trade was not as lucrative as Miss Jones had hoped, if she was going door to door attempting to increase business. "I did not realize, Miss Jones, that fortune-tellers make house calls."

"For particular persons, I do." She smiled at her hostess. "As Miss Bates said, we are getting better acquainted."

"I am so glad you came by, Miss Jones! Indeed, at first I declined to have my fortune read, did I not? But afterwards, I said to myself, 'Now, Hetty, what is the harm?' I hoped perhaps Miss Jones could read Mr. Deal's fortune for me, that I might learn how long he will be consigned to that horrible gaol. But she says that is not the way such things work—he is not here to drink his own tea, which is required.— Do I have it right, Miss Jones?—I have been learning all about fortune-telling this evening! One must drink one's tea and then swirl the leaves to get a proper reading, she tells me. I cannot do it on Mr. Deal's behalf. Though, in a sense, it *would* be Mr. Deal's tea, as it came from him. Is that not sad, that his tea should be here but not him?"

"Whatever do you mean, Miss Bates?" asked Mrs. Knightley.

"Why, the tea was a gift from Mr. Deal! He took tea with my mother and me yesterday, and afterwards he left us a lovely note expressing his thanks, and a small parcel of tea. Oh! Now where did that note go? I showed it to Miss Jones, and now I cannot remember where I placed it. Do you recall, Miss Jones?"

Miss Jones glanced about, her brow furrowed. "I do not. But surely it will turn up."

"I regret you have misplaced it," Mrs. Knightley said. "I should like to see what sort of letter a peddler writes."

"Oh, Mr. Deal writes a fine letter! Do you not agree, Miss Jones?"

"Yes, very fine."

"When did you find the parcel?" Elizabeth asked.

"I went out around noon today, and there it was, just inside the door at the base of the stairs. Such a surprise! I do not know how I overlooked it earlier. And so thoughtful of Mr. Deal! I was going to save the tea for his next visit, but when I told Miss Jones of it, she encouraged me to use it tonight for the fortune-reading. She said if I used Mr. Deal's tea and concentrated on a question pertaining to him while I drank it, the leaves might reveal the answer."

"As there is much in question about Mr. Deal at present, I am sure you will have no trouble," Mrs. Knightley said. "Except, perhaps, limiting the experiment to a single query."

Elizabeth did not think Miss Bates ought to consume anything provided by Mr. Deal until the poisoning matter was resolved. "It seems a shame not to save the tea to enjoy with Mr. Deal. Maybe you should reconsider."

Miss Bates laughed. "Oh, it is too late to reconsider now! The tea is already made. Would either of you care for some? There is plenty. My mother does not drink tea this late when we are at home—she says it keeps her awake—and Miss Jones declined. I have already drunk mine and swirled the leaves. Miss Jones was about to read them when I heard your knock. Why do not both of you take some, too, and we can all have our fortunes read together?"

"Miss Jones has already read my fortune, several days ago." Alarm passed through Elizabeth at the news that Miss Bates had drunk the tea. She assessed Miss Bates for indications that the tea had been tainted. Unfortunately, Elizabeth realized that she had not the faintest idea what she ought to be looking for. To her untrained eye, Miss Bates appeared her usual self, if perhaps a little flushed from the excitement of visitors and fortune-telling.

Miss Bates reached for the pot. "What about you, Mrs. Knightley? Would you care for tea?"

"I think it has gone cold," Miss Jones said. She moved the pot to the other side of the table and reached for one of the teacups. "Let us read your fortune, Miss Bates, before your impression fades from the leaves. Afterwards, we can make a fresh pot if anybody cares for a cup. Where is your maid? The remaining tea from this pot should be dumped so that nothing interferes with the signs."

Elizabeth did not recall such interference having been a concern when Miss Jones told her fortune at the Crown; the would-be *drabarni* had embellished her patter with experience. Considering how unpracticed Loretta's "dukkering" had been when she arrived in the village, Elizabeth could only imagine how she must have sounded while affecting to read Edgar Churchill's leaves at the gypsy camp. The fortune that poor Nellie heard this morning had likely been far more intriguing and smoothly delivered than Edgar's, at a fraction of the price. She wondered how much Miss Bates was being charged for this performance.

"Oh! Well! We certainly do not want anything to fade or interfere. Patty, come take away this pot for us.—She will be but a moment, I am sure. Can we begin? What must I do?"

"Simply take a seat and keep still, so I may concentrate."

"Ah, I can do that." She sat down at the table, across from Miss Jones. "Right here—as I was before?"

"Yes, just so. Now, tell me the question you held in your mind as you drank the tea."

Miss Bates closed her eyes and rested one hand on the table. "When will poor Mr. Deal return to his friends in Highbury?"

Thirty-six

"Vanity working on a weak head, produces every sort of mischief."
—Mr. Knightley, Emma

ou may open your eyes, Miss Bates. Let us see what the leaves say." Miss Jones rotated the teacup. "Look—there is a *D*—and a trail of leaves—that means a journey." She looked up at her client. "I said you may open your eyes, Miss Bates."

The spinster blinked several times and brought her other hand to her head. "Forgive me—I feel a bit dizzy. It must be the excitement. Though it is exceedingly warm in here."

Elizabeth and Mrs. Knightley exchanged glances and went to her directly. Mrs. Knightley put a hand to the spinster's forehead. "She does feel quite warm."

"Maybe someone should open a window," Miss Jones suggested.

While Mrs. Knightley attended Miss Bates, Elizabeth approached not the window, but the teapot. Perhaps she could determine by smell whether the tea had been adulterated. Before she could reach it, however, Miss Jones seized the pot.

"Good idea," said Miss Jones. "We should get these things out of the way." She picked up Miss Bates's teacup with her other hand.

Elizabeth reached again toward the pot. "I was not—"

Miss Jones rose and spun away from her chair to take the tea things into the next room.

A folded sheet of paper fell from her skirts.

They both watched it slide to the floor. And then both scrambled to retrieve it. Though Miss Jones was closer, her hands were full, and Elizabeth snatched it up first.

It was Mr. Deal's note. He thanked Miss Bates for the tea he had enjoyed with the ladies on Sunday, and in return humbly offered a special China black he reserved for his best customers. He further urged her to try it before he next saw her, so that she might tell him whether she liked it.

Miss Jones disciplined her anxious expression into one of false brightness. "Look at that! It must have fallen aside after Miss Bates showed it to me. Thank heaven we found it.—Good news, Miss Bates—Mrs. Darcy has found your letter."

Miss Bates blinked. "The letter from Mr. Deal?" She rubbed her eyes and blinked again. "I am having trouble seeing it. Patty," she called out, "can you bring my spectacles? Everything is a blur."

Elizabeth fixed Miss Jones with her own gaze. She could see quite clearly.

Miss Jones had taken the letter. Just as she had seized the teapot. Or—more to the point—seized the tea inside it. The tea that had arrived with the letter. The tea that she did not want anybody else examining too closely.

Elizabeth no longer needed to whiff the tea to guess whether it had been poisoned. Or to guess how Edgar Churchill and Nellie had been poisoned. Like Miss Bates, both of them had drunk tea with Miss Jones shortly before falling ill. Elizabeth could not account for Frank Churchill's poisoning—yet—but the other three could not be coincidence.

Much as Elizabeth doubted, it remained possible that someone else had poisoned the tea—Mr. Deal or Rawnie Zsófia—but it was beyond doubt that Miss Jones had knowingly administered it. *Clever lying girl.*

Elizabeth looked again at the note. She would have to study it more thoroughly later, but the handwriting bore similarities to that of the anagram she and Mrs. Knightley had solved.

The maid entered with the spectacles. "I am sorry to be so long. I could not immediately find them."

Miss Jones thrust the teapot and cup toward the maid. "Patty, kindly take these and wash them. We will not need them any more tonight."

"No, Patty—do not wash them." Elizabeth looked at Miss Jones. "Mr. Knightley will want them."

Loretta's gaze darted from Elizabeth to the door and back. Then she let go of the china and sent it smashing to the hard oak floor.

As Darcy reached the top of the stairs, a loud crash within the apartment propelled him through the door without pausing to knock. He knew Elizabeth was inside—Hartfield's coachman, waiting in his own vehicle in front of the house, had told Mr. Knightley that their wives were on a social call. As social calls did not generally involve shattered porcelain, Mr. Knightley and Mr. Deal followed hard upon.

The spectacle that greeted them required a few moments to absorb. Elizabeth stood near Miss Jones and a maid, shards of china and clumps of brown matter scattered at their feet, dark liquid spattered on their hems and spreading across the wood floor to soak into the worn Oriental rug on the other side of the room. Mrs. Knightley and Miss Bates were nearby; Miss Bates was seated at a table, gripping it with one hand as she peered toward the sodden mess on the floor. A bewildered Mrs. Bates looked as if she had just risen from her chair beside the fire. The crash was probably the first sound she had heard in a decade.

Whether all were startled more by the crash or by the abrupt entrance of the gentlemen, Darcy could not tell. He crossed to Elizabeth and satisfied himself that she appeared unharmed.

Miss Bates, however, looked ill.

"We need Mr. Perry at once," Elizabeth said. "I believe Miss Bates has been poisoned—by the tea Mr. Deal enclosed with his letter."

Mr. Knightley was halfway to the stairs in an instant. "I will send James for Perry."

"Mr. Deal did not write the letter," Darcy told Elizabeth. "We are unsure who did."

At that news, Elizabeth looked hard at Miss Jones. "Perhaps the person who served the tea."

"What is happening? Oh! What is happening? Mrs. Darcy, what did you say about poison?" Miss Bates squinted toward the door. "What was that crash? Who is here?" She tried to rise but sank back into the chair and brought her hands to her temples. "Oh, my head! It spins. . . ."

Mr. Deal regarded Miss Bates in consternation. Then turned a disbelieving gaze upon Miss Jones.

"You?" His face held shock, betrayal, bewilderment.

Miss Jones stared at him dumbly.

"What have you done, Loretta?"

"I—" She swallowed and looked down at the shattered teapot. "I accidentally dropped—"

"What have you *done*?" He crossed to Miss Bates and gently lifted her chin so that he could examine her eyes. The pupils were so wide that Darcy could see them from where he stood.

"Mr. Deal?" Miss Bates squinted at him. "You are out of gaol! Oh, I am glad. But I feel so poorly—"

Mr. Deal strode towards Miss Jones. He scooped up a wad of wet leaves from the floor and thrust them towards her. "You put belladonna leaves in the tea?"

"And some of the root."

Her unapologetic admission shocked him as much as the act. "Did you poison my father, too? And Frank?"

"And that little scullery wench at Randalls."

"Oh, it is so warm in here," Miss Bates moaned. "And my head . . ."

With a look of anguish, Mr. Deal threw the clump of leaves at Loretta's feet. "Patty, fetch mustard powder and a tumbler of warm water as quick as you can."

Darcy wondered whether they ought to wait until Mr. Perry arrived rather than trust Mr. Deal to properly treat Miss Bates. But Mr. Deal seemed to know what he was about—Mr. Perry had treated Frank Churchill with mustard—and time was of the essence.

Patty brought the mustard and tumbler, along with a towel for Mr. Deal. As the peddler wiped the tea from his hand, Mr. Knightley returned.

"What is transpiring?" he asked Darcy.

"Miss Jones has admitted to poisoning all four victims—with belladonna, just as Mr. Perry thought. Mr. Deal had no idea. I believe he now intends to administer an emetic to Miss Bates."

"If one of you ladies would mix a spoonful of the powder with the water?" Mr. Deal asked. As Elizabeth took the jar from the maid and began to prepare the mixture, he glanced to Mr. Knightley. "Sir, Miss Bates might be more comfortable in the privacy of her bedchamber when the mustard-water takes effect. Will you help me move her?"

Mr. Knightley met Darcy's gaze, then looked pointedly at Miss Jones.

Darcy nodded.

Mr. Deal and Mr. Knightley assisted Miss Bates into the bedroom. The magnitude of her distress was evidenced by the dearth of her discourse. She went in comparative silence, issuing only occasional murmurs. Elizabeth followed them with the mustard-water, while the maid set about cleaning up the mess of tea and broken china.

Old Mrs. Bates, upset and confused, called out for her daughter. Mrs. Knightley went to her. She tried to explain what was occurring—which, indeed, they all were still trying to figure out—but as it seemed inappropriate to shout the details of Miss Bates's distress at the volume required for the elderly lady to comprehend them, Mrs. Knightley soon gave up. She instead settled Mrs. Bates into her chair, brought over one for herself, and sat beside her, holding her hand and soothing her as best she could.

Miss Jones, meanwhile, attempted to take advantage of everybody's divided notice to make an escape. Darcy put a swift end to that notion. She had moved a single step toward the door when he swung it shut and interposed himself.

He had but one question for her.

"Why?"

She laughed derisively and said nothing, turning her head away. But her insolent expression transformed to pained when she caught sight, through the bedroom doorway, of Mr. Deal dabbing Miss Bates's flushed face with a damp cloth.

Her countenance hardened. "He does not love her, you know. He *cannot* love her."

"Why not?"

"Because he loves me." There was an odd light in her eyes. "Or he will—once I explain it all to him."

Darcy could not fathom an explanation that would excuse her crimes, let alone win a man's affection. She would be lucky to escape hanging.

Mr. Perry arrived and went immediately to his patient. With Miss Bates now in the apothecary's care, Mr. Knightley, Elizabeth, and Mr. Deal came out of the bedroom and closed the door behind them.

"Mr. Perry praised Mr. Deal for acting so quickly," Mr. Knightley said. "Once she voids her stomach, she should be out of danger."

Mr. Deal's anxious gaze lingered on the bedroom door.

"Hiram?"

The peddler flinched at the sound of Miss Jones's voice.

"Hiram, when you understand why I—"

He whirled to face her. "Understand? What is there to understand, Loretta? What could possibly justify what you have done?"

"I did it for you."

"You poisoned Miss Bates—a gentle soul who could not harm a mouse—for me?" He looked as if he, too, were about to become ill.

"She cannot make you happy, Hiram. She is like that little slut Nellie and all the other women."

"What women?"

"Every village, every borough we passed through—all of them throwing themselves at you. But none of them know you as I do. At the end of the day you are still nothing but a peddler to them. Whereas I— I would follow you anywhere! I told you so—I offered you a woman's heart and a woman's body." Her voice grew hoarse. "But I was just a child in your eyes. You told me to go home, back to my parents."

"And you should have listened! But instead—instead of returning to your father, you murdered mine? Did you do *that* for me, too?"

"Edgar Churchill was never a father to you, any more than his wife was a mother."

A fresh expression of horror overtook his features. "Did you kill her, as well?"

She laughed. "I wish I could take credit. That hateful old lady deserved to die—when I overheard you tell Madam Zsófia what she had said to you, I was only sorry that God took her before I thought of it. But her death made me realize that all of the Churchills needed to be punished—and I knew that if I could be the one to bring them to justice, to make them pay for what they had done to you, to vindicate you—then—then you would see that I am not a child."

"What did Edgar and Frank Churchill do to me that merited poisoning them?"

"All of the Churchills treated you cruelly! While your parents lived in their fancy houses and wore fine clothes, while your cousin usurped your birthright, you lived amongst gypsy thieves."

He shook his head in disgust. "I have never regretted my life with the Roma."

Miss Jones's last statement brought to Darcy's mind the puzzle they had received. "Was it you who left the anagram? 'He dwelled amongst thieves'—"

"'—as they lived large in Richmond'?" Her mouth twisted into a self-satisfied smile. "I most certainly did. I could not be silent. Everyone mistook the Churchills for victims. Their hypocrisy needed to be known."

"But why did you implicate yourself and Mr. Deal with the second solution—the one about hidden motives?" Mrs. Knightley asked.

Miss Jones regarded her as if she were daft. "There was no second solution."

"Indeed, there was."

"If you found one, your own imagination created it, for I did not."

"But I—" Mrs. Knightley stared at her unbelievingly. "'Clever lying girl—Deal had hidden motives—Not what he seems'—You did not hide that second message in the puzzle?"

Now Miss Jones's expression was scornful. "Why on earth would I?"

"Perhaps," Mr. Deal said quietly, "the powers you mocked by engaging in false prophecy caused you to reveal more than you intended."

Loretta looked as if she were about to mock that suggestion as well, but then appeared to think better of it.

"Did you author the previous puzzle, too?" Elizabeth asked.

"The one Mrs. Elton spoke of? No. But hearing her talk about it at the Crown gave me the idea of writing my own message as a puzzle, and I sent it to the post office with Alice when she took Mrs. Todd's letters so that no one would know it came from me. I hoped you would assume the two puzzles were written by the same person— and I see that I was successful." She turned back to Mr. Deal. "Hiram, do you understand now how I planned for us? When the caravan moved on and you stayed behind, I remained as well—to help you avenge yourself on your father, and clear the way for you to claim your rightful inheritance."

Mr. Deal turned away, unable to look at her any longer. He crossed to the window and stared through the rain-spattered glass into the night. Darcy could only imagine his thoughts.

"When did you poison Frank Churchill?" Mr. Knightley asked Miss Jones.

"At the Crown. I had been lingering round the village since leaving the caravan, eavesdropping for news that Edgar Churchill had in fact died, and watching for an opportunity to punish Frank. I followed him to the inn. It was very busy—a stagecoach had just arrived, and the kitchen was in disorder trying to serve all the passengers quickly to get them back on the coach. When the serving girl left his tea unattended before bringing it to him, I added my own ingredient."

"Nobody noticed you?"

"I learned a few things from the gypsies." She took obvious pride in her acts.

"I suppose that is how you poisoned Nellie, too—tainting her tea when she had her fortune read at the Crown," Elizabeth said.

"That was a bit more difficult, but I managed. Edgar Churchill was the easiest of all, as I made his tea and served it myself."

Mr. Deal cast her a look of utter revulsion. "I am going to check on Miss Bates."

"Hiram—"

He did not look at her as he passed, but went straight to the bedroom and shut the door.

"Did not Thomas Dixon become suspicious, once Edgar Churchill had died?" Darcy asked.

"Thomas Dixon knows enough to leave other people's secrets alone, if he wants to keep his own."

"What secrets would those be?"

"Nothing that pertains to the Churchills or anybody else in Highbury. But my gypsy friend told me his palm was rather revealing, to one who knows how to read them. If you want to learn more, you shall have to ask him."

Footsteps on the staircase announced the arrival of another visitor. As nobody was expected, they all waited in some suspense as Mr. Knightley answered the knock.

Thomas Dixon appeared, his arms laden with parcels. "Where is Miss Bates? I come bearing new draperies! And her carpet will be delivered tomorrow."

He paused, taking in the scene around him—most particularly the great brown stain on the rug. He stepped aside to avoid soiling his shoes. "Well! It seems I am just in time!"

Thirty-seven

"Oh! If you knew how much I love every thing that is decided and open!"

—*Emma Woodhouse,* Emma

$\mathcal{M}$iss Jones took Hiram Deal's place in the Guildford gaol pending trial. Had she read her own tea leaves before embarking on her murderous plan, she might have foreseen where it would end. Then again, given her competence as a fortune-teller, perhaps not. As it was, she managed to attain at least tolerable conditions for herself by plying her dubious soothsaying talents (supplemented by considerable theatrics) among her fellow prisoners, earning enough coppers to secure small comforts while she awaited the spring assizes.

Thomas Dixon, when questioned, admitted to having authored the raven riddle. Following Edgar Churchill's death, he had thought perhaps the poison had been administered at the gypsy camp, but had not wanted to betray his own presence there for fear of implicating himself in the crime. The appearance of the first charade had inspired him with a means of aiding the investigation anonymously through a puzzle of his own, and it was an easy matter to leave the letter on the post office counter as the aged postmaster snored in his chair. As for the secret to which Miss Jones had alluded, no one ever asked him about it, and he never told.

Eventually, as his fortune had predicted, Mr. Dixon indeed came into money as a result of a death—just not that of a Churchill. Years after the Highbury intrigue was resolved, his friend Ridley passed out of this life while defending his honor in a duel. A lifelong bachelor estranged from his relations, the gentleman bequeathed his fortune and London townhouse to Thomas Dixon. Mr. Dixon assuaged his grief and memorialized his friend by immediately embarking on a comprehensive redecorating scheme. He was last seen engaged in a spirited debate with his favorite upholsterer over the virtues of paisleys versus stripes.

Hiram Deal was proved to indeed be the son of Edgar and Agnes Churchill. The discovery of the nurse who had attended his birth, combined with the testimony of a superannuated servant, corroborated his story, and the court officially recognized him as Edgar Churchill's legal heir. The events in Highbury having left him feeling his age and weary of wandering, Mr. Deal exchanged his itinerant lifestyle for a more settled existence. His years amongst the gypsies, however, forever influenced his perspective. He rejected the considerable estate of Enscombe and the responsibility—and values—it represented. He signed over his inheritance to his cousin, Frank, reserving for himself only enough money to open a respectable shop and live a comfortable existence with his new wife: a woman of maturity, of gentle, even temperament, of cheerful disposition, and of open heart.

Miss Henrietta Bates became Mrs. Hiram Deal in a simple ceremony performed by Mr. Elton in the village church. Mrs. Elton pronounced the wedding entirely devoid of elegance or fashion, citing in particular the insufficient quantities of lace and beadwork adorning the bride's dress. Her opinion of the new Mrs. Deal's exotic mother-in-law, who attended the nuptials in full *drabarni* regalia, she dared not utter for fear of attracting unfavorable attention from Madam Zsófia.

The rest of Highbury, however, rejoiced that the spinster whose prospects had so long appeared hopeless (particularly to the Eltons) made so happy a marriage, one of affection, esteem, and companionship. Mrs. Deal, at last sharing her life and home with someone who both heard and responded to her, was no longer dependent solely upon the sound of her own voice to fill the silence, and gradually came to better govern her own discourse. Mr. Deal, in turn, at last enjoyed the felicity and contentment of ending each day in comfortable conversation with an intimate audience before his own hearth. Both considered themselves to have come into wealth—true wealth—beyond any they expected to know in this life.

The newlyweds took up residence in a larger house, appointed in a discordant combination of plain English style and eclectic foreign embellishments that would have given Thomas Dixon seizures had he known. Frank and Jane Churchill were delighted to see both Bates ladies established in the new home, which included old Mrs. Bates's familiar chair by the fire and a room for her that no longer required the elderly lady to hazard a dark, narrow stair. What Mrs. Bates thought of her new son's history was anybody's guess, but she welcomed him into her family with warmth, and the expressions on her countenance as she attended the conversations between him and her daughter on winter evenings led one to believe that she actually heard them.

Emma, who had first introduced Mr. Deal to Miss Bates—as peddler to customer—took credit for the match. Or at least, consolation in the fact that Mrs. Elton's matchmaking efforts did not succeed. Once Mr. Deal's legitimacy was confirmed and it became known that he was a Churchill, she deemed the union suitable. She took greater pleasure in her new friendship with the Darcys, a pleasure shared by her husband, who at last had a peer with whom he could discuss agricultural issues to his heart's content. Upon parting, the two gentlemen made plans to meet again in London, and to include Lord Chatfield among the party.

Mr. Woodhouse bemoaned the departure of "poor Mrs. Darcy" from Hartfield. He exhorted her to dress very warmly for the journey to Brierwood, and made her promise never to eat bisque. He also hinted that when she arrived at the home of Colonel and Anne

Fitzwilliam, she should look inside her trunk for one final mysterious message.

Elizabeth smiled when she found it. Though penned in the less-than-steady hand of Mr. Woodhouse himself, it was easily deciphered.

Serle's recipe for gruel.

Epilogue

In general, it was a very well approved match. Some might think him, and others might think her, the most in luck.

—Emma

*D*arcy and Elizabeth enjoyed a happy Yuletide with their daughter and Georgiana at Brierwood, and continued on for several weeks afterward with Colonel and Anne Fitzwilliam. Yet their unanticipated adventure in Highbury made them anxious to return home to the serenity of Pemberley, and so, not long after Twelfth Night passed, they journeyed northward. As their coach entered Derbyshire, Elizabeth welcomed the familiar landscape.

"Will you be ready to travel south again in the spring?"

Darcy, she knew, had been quietly observing her—inasmuch as there was anything quiet about the inside of their carriage on this trip. Lily-Anne, just learning to walk, was impatient with the confinement of recent days.

She shifted Lily-Anne to her other knee, wrapped her arms around her, and rested her chin on her daughter's head. A smile spread across her face. "Indeed, yes." She had promised Anne to return for her lying-in. Georgiana would accompany her. On that visit, Elizabeth would bring with her another family heirloom that had once belonged to Darcy's mother.

"I was thinking that perhaps after Anne's confinement, you might join us, and we could all take a summer holiday," Elizabeth said. "Mrs. Knightley told me that she and her husband went to the seaside for their wedding-trip, and she highly recommended it. I have never been to the sea, but I would like very much to see it."

"Oh, can we?" Georgiana asked. Lily-Anne expressed her approval of the scheme by squirming vigorously.

Elizabeth sensed reluctance on Darcy's part, and understood its source. She knew he had little inclination for spas and watering-holes, and the shallow society they often attracted. "We do not have to choose the most fashionable town," she assured him. "Indeed, I had just as soon not."

He leaned towards her, lifted Lily-Anne, and settled their daughter on his own lap. The infant reclined against Darcy's chest and ceased her struggles. At just shy of a twelvemonth, Lily-Anne already knew better than to misbehave for her father.

"The seaside?" He raised one brow at his wife and heaved an exaggerated sigh.

Then he bestowed on Elizabeth her favorite of all his expressions— the one that said he loved her more than he could convey in words— and smiled.

"Perhaps I can be persuaded."